Quentin Smith is a medical doctor and practising anaesthetist with a background of writing magazine articles of topical or historical interest, usually with a discernible medical flavour. He served as the editor of a national anaesthesia publication for several years before devoting more free time to the enjoyment and pursuit of writing fiction. He lives in Durham with his wife and son. *16mm of Innocence* is his third novel.

www.quentinsmithbooks.com

By the same author:

The Secret Anatomy of Candles

Huber's Tattoo

16MM

OF

INNOCENCE

QUENTIN SMITH

Matador
9 Priory Business Park,
Wistow Road, Kibworth Beauchamp,
Leicestershire. LE8 0RX
Tel: (+44) 116 279 2299
Fax: (+44) 116 279 2277
Email: books@troubador.co.uk
Web: www.troubador.co.uk/matador

ISBN 9781784625498

British Library Cataloguing in Publication Data.
A catalogue record for this book is available from the British Library.

Printed and bound in the UK by TJ International, Padstow, Cornwall
Typeset in 11pt Minion Pro by Troubador Publishing Ltd, Leicester, UK

Matador is an imprint of Troubador Publishing Ltd

Dedicated to my siblings:
for naturally blood will be of kind

Children begin by loving their parents; after a time they judge them; rarely, if ever, do they forgive them.

Oscar Wilde

ONE

6 April 1985

"Mum's in trouble."

Dieter fumbled with the receiver and struggled onto one elbow. The phone call had interrupted that awful recurring dream that he had experienced over so many years and it had once again left him feeling disorientated, unsettled and even worse, guilty. It was always the same.

"Who is this?" Dieter asked sleepily, his eyes gritty as he rubbed them blindly in the dark.

"It's Otto..." Pause. "Your brother." Dieter exhaled. He couldn't remember when last they had spoken. "Jesus, Otto, do you know what time it is in Hong Kong?"

"I'm sorry, I know it's early, but this is really serious." Through the Venetian blinds Dieter could see a filleted image of dawn shimmering across the water of Repulse Bay, where he had lived since the late 1960s. He loved Hong Kong: city of enterprise, and for him personally, city of escape.

"What's wrong with Mum?" Dieter asked.

Otto sighed heavily. "Nothing wrong with Mum, per se."

"What then?" Dieter said irritably.

Otto paused, as though mustering courage. "They found a body in the garden of our old house, Dieter."

Dieter's skin felt clammy as a vision burst forth instantaneously from the vagueness of his dream, churning his stomach.

"A body?"

The sleeping figure under the duvet beside Dieter stirred, and in a low voice asked who it was. Dieter hastily covered the mouthpiece.

"Who's that?" Otto asked.

Dieter glared at his bed companion and pressed a finger against his lips.

"When did this happen?" Dieter asked.

"Mum's just phoned me."

"You're talking about a… a human body are you?"

"Yes, but I don't know the details. Mum's pretty shaken by it all… she didn't say much."

"But I don't understand… where was it found?" Dieter said.

"The big tree, remember it?"

"Uh–huh, the camelthorn."

"Mum said a storm blew it down, and the roots must have exposed… I don't know… bones."

Silence for a moment, just the sound of Dieter's breathing and a distant foghorn in the bay.

"Well, who is to say it has anything to do with Mum?" Dieter said emphatically. "I mean, it could have been there long before we arrived."

Otto rubbed his temples. He was sitting at his desk in Durham watching his children, Max and Karl, replenish the birdfeeders under the vigilant gaze of their mother, Sabine, as darkness enveloped the grounds of his riverside garden. The boys looked up and, seeing him through the window, waved animatedly.

Little Karl dropped the birdseed in his enthusiasm, spilling it all over the frosty grass.

"Mum and Dad built that house, Dieter, and planted the tree," Otto said.

"What are you saying? It's probably just a local Herero, been there for years before we even arrived."

"God, I don't know. It's all such a shock." Otto paused. "I'm really worried about Mum."

"Do they know who it is – the body, I mean?" Dieter asked.

"I don't think so, but Lüderitz isn't a big town, so…"

"Yeah, maybe. What happens next?"

"Well, the police are investigating. Mum thinks they may want to interview us as well."

"Us?"

"You, me and Ingrid."

"Why?"

"I think we should fly out to support Mum," Otto said.

"What, to Lüderitz? Christ, I haven't been there for years."

"Not since Dad's funeral, actually."

"That's a cheap shot, Otto. I am very busy here, you know that – with the business I've built up and everything. I'm in the middle of a massive merger. I don't have much idle time on my hands."

"You mean, unlike me?" Otto finished, bristling. Silence amplified the static waves of interference on the phone line. "You could at least call her, Dieter."

Dieter sighed. "Yes, of course I will. What time is it in Lüderitz now?"

"Early evening. How are things?" Otto asked, to avoid another pause.

"Fine, fine. What about Sabine and the kids?"

Otto never went into detail. There was little point in telling him that Max was excelling on the piano and Karl had just started at school, because from one rare contact to another Dieter could never remember which child was Karl and which one was Max. Birthdays came and went unnoticed and Otto sometimes had to make a point of reminding them who Uncle Dieter was.

"They're all well thank you. And… er… how about you?"

"Still single."

"Not found the right girl yet?" Otto said.

Dieter snorted. "Not likely to, either."

"I'll phone Ingrid and tell her, if you prefer," Otto said.

"Do what you like, Otto, but I won't be calling her."

"Have you two still not made peace?" Otto said, exasperated.

"Last time we spoke, years ago, she called me a parasite or something, living off the success of others." Dieter made a guttural sound of disapproval. "The nerve – how many sugar daddy alimony settlements has she pocketed up to now?"

Otto was not in the mood for idle conversation and neither, it appeared, was Dieter. With the phone call terminated Otto sat in silent contemplation. He had always felt that his older brother dismissed his work as a general practitioner. It seemed to him that Dieter believed that his fortune had been forged out of determined hard work, whereas Otto was merely a public servant living off the state.

Otto heard his family entering the house, taking refuge from the biting cold outside, stamping their feet and removing coats, hats and scarves – familiar sounds of family life that cast his mind back to his childhood home in Lüderitz, and fragmented images from so many years ago.

How on earth could a body have lain buried beneath their feet all that time? To think that he and Dieter used to climb

4

that very tree, the desert-loving camelthorn, dig holes all around it, playing with their lead soldiers and building makeshift dams in the sandy soil. He shivered. How close might they unwittingly have been to a truly macabre discovery?

Then an uncomfortable thought entered his mind. Had Mother known as she watched them playing outside? What if it was not pride and contentment that they had seen on her face as she watched through the kitchen window while they dug holes and played? What if it had been anxiety, apprehension? Could they have known the difference at their young age? And what about Father? Well, he was hardly at home often enough to have even seen them.

There surely must be a rational explanation for all of this. Dieter was probably right: Lüderitz had existed for at least sixty years before their arrival and the body could have been there all along. It was in all probability a local Herero.

"Daddy!" came the shrill call of an enthusiastic youngster bounding up the stairs.

Otto glanced at his watch. It was nearly 8pm, still early afternoon in New York: plenty of time yet to call Ingrid. For now he would play with Karl and try to banish the worries from his mind.

A beaming young blonde boy sprinted into the room with a flash of his red and yellow striped socks, flinging himself into Otto's arms.

"Did you feed the birds?" Otto asked.

"Yes. Mummy said they must be really hungry."

Otto smiled and kissed Karl's fair head. The warmth and love of his children constantly surprised him. It was not something he had been accustomed to in a family. He never understood why.

TWO

29 July 1945

Resembling a mythical sea serpent amidst the clinging fog, the rusting grey conning tower of U-977 broke through the mercurial waters off Lüderitz, followed soon after by the rounded bow. When the hatch opened it was as though a seal had been broken, allowing the salty sea air to rush into the malodorous metal tube, submerged for nearly sixty days since hastily leaving the North Sea.

Several bearded submariners wearing soiled blue denim Kriegsmarine jackets emerged onto the small deck of the conning tower and peered through the swirling fog. One of them began to send a coded message with a shuttered signal lamp. No–one spoke. Submariners were accustomed to maintaining prolonged silences, as if they had forsaken the art of idle conversation. The solitary sound of the bracing South Atlantic waters lapping against the grey hull, streaked with rust, remained unchallenged.

"There it is!" one of the men said, pointing to a flashing light dimly visible off the starboard bow.

"I see it. Did they use the password?"

"They did, Oberleutnant."

"Signal for them to approach immediately and call the doctor from his bunk."

"Yes, Oberleutnant."

The commander peered over the waters surrounding his vessel with narrowed eyes, fidgety body language betraying his discomfort as his dirty fingers twiddled his unkempt beard. The flashing signal light drew closer until a small rowing boat began to emerge from the shadowy protection of the fog. Now the sound of water lapping against the submarine hull was joined by the rhythmical splash of oars.

A man wearing a black leather jacket and carrying a brown canvas holdall appeared on the conning tower.

He took a deep breath as he contemplated the approaching rowing boat. Then his searching eyes settled on the commander's unwashed face as the two men squared up to each other. They shook hands firmly.

"Oberleutnant Schäffer, I am forever indebted to you."

"Please, the war is over now. Call me Heinz," Schäffer said.

The two men seemed oblivious to all around them.

"May God be with you in your new home, Doctor. Good luck."

"Thank you, Heinz." The doctor forced a little smile. "My friends call me Ernst."

The two men stared into each other's eyes as though letting go might signal the end of everything they knew in this world.

"I will admit Lüderitz looks a little foreboding at first appearances," Ernst said.

"They don't call it the Skeleton Coast for nothing," Schäffer replied with a little chuckle.

"When do you expect to reach Argentina?"

"We should be there by mid-August, if the engines don't fail again."

The two men nodded to each other, still gripping each other's hand, afraid to let go, to break with the familiarity of the past and embrace the uncertainty of the unknown. By this time the rowing boat had drawn up to U-977 and bumped against its hull on the ocean swell. Three men in civilian clothing were huddled together in the wooden vessel, one holding aloft a shaded lamp that scattered halos in the swirling fog. Ernst clambered down the steel rungs of the ladder, his boots scraping on the metal. Schäffer tossed his canvas holdall down to him and raised a hand to wave.

"Where are you headed?" one of the men in the rowing boat shouted up to Schäffer.

"I cannot tell you," Schäffer yelled back. Then, in a softer voice, "Better that you don't know. Look after Dr Adermann, he is a good man."

"I wish you all a safe journey. Goodbye Heinz," Ernst shouted as he settled into the rowing boat.
Schäffer rested his arms on the metal railing and watched Ernst, sitting with the canvas bag in his lap, looking up somewhat mournfully at the faces not only of his companions of the past two months, but of a life he was leaving behind, forever. The small rowing boat began to move away as the oars sliced into the water.

"Goodbye Ernst."

Ernst waved. He looked so insignificant in the rowing boat. How things change, Schäffer thought to himself.

THREE

Ingrid, holding several large Bloomingdale's shopping bags, stepped out of the yellow cab on the upper east side of Manhattan where she was comfortably settled into a privileged world of old money, even though she was a relative newcomer.

The doorman tipped his hat and held the polished glass door open for her. "Afternoon Mrs Forsythe."

Ingrid ignored him, flicking her bouncing ash blonde hair as she strode past. She kicked the door to her third floor apartment shut behind her and dropped the shopping bags onto the sofa. Her apartment was in Yorkhill near the corner of Lexington and 77th, not far from Central Park Zoo and her favourite department store. The heavily framed mirrors, cream high-backed sofas and brushed aluminium lamps revealed her taste for Bloomingdale's classic styles. She prised off her Ralph Lauren heels and flopped into an armchair still wearing her fur-lined coat. The phone rang.

"Oh God!" she mumbled.

She watched the phone with a disdainful look until the answer machine eventually clicked in.

"Hi Ingrid, it's Otto. I'm not sure if you've been getting my messages…"

"Shit!" Ingrid muttered as she heaved herself up and strode towards the phone. "Hi Otto."

"Ingrid?" Surprise in Otto's voice.

Ingrid glanced at her gold wristwatch. "It must be very late in England, little brother."

"Yes, it is… quite. I really need to speak to you."

Ingrid picked up the phone and dragged the lengthy cord with her to the sofa where she resumed her original pose.

"Sorry, Otto, it's been hell here."

"Did you get my messages?"

Ingrid hesitated, examining her nails. "Yeah. Look, Otto, I don't know what I can do. I haven't spoken to Mum since…" Ingrid lifted both feet onto a cream pouffe and crossed her ankles, wiggling her painted toes. "She never did approve of my… lifestyle."

Ingrid remembered the men she had brought to the house: successful, rich, usually divorced and universally disapproved of by both Mother and Father. In the end she married Frederick, who had taken her to New York. Ever since she considered that things had never been the same between her and the rest of the family again.

"How is Maurice?" Otto asked.

Ingrid pulled a face. "I divorced him six months ago."

"Oh, sorry. No-one tells me anything."

"Don't be sorry, Otto, I got his lovely apartment," Ingrid said with a smile as she glanced around the spacious living room.

"I thought you got Larry's apartment?" Otto said.

"I got his money, and so I should have for putting up with the bastard. No, it was Newman, my second husband's apartment that I got, but this one is better so I sold his. That really pissed him off." She snorted.

Otto sighed. "Can we get back to Mum and this business back home?"

"That is not my home any longer, Otto; hasn't been for a very long time. But I did get your message about finding a body or something. What the hell's that all about?"

"We don't know yet?"

"They identified the body?"

"No. It's been sent to forensic labs in... er... Windhoek, I imagine."

Ingrid raised her waxed eyebrows. "I can't help you with this, Otto, and Mum certainly hasn't called me about it," she said, sounding indifferent and cold. "As she pointed out to me after I married Larry – or was it Frederick? – we all have our crosses to bear."

Otto sighed irritably. "Ingrid, Mum has suffered a massive stroke."

Ingrid's feet dropped off the pouffe as she sat forward. "Stroke?"

"Yes. Quite a bad one, I'm afraid."

"Why? How?"

"The stress, I expect. The discovery of the body really affected her."

"Did she tell them anything?" Ingrid's voice was suddenly a semitone tauter.

"Like what?"

"I don't know," Ingrid said, trying to sound nonchalant.

"I'm flying out tomorrow to see Mum. I'm really worried about her. I think Dieter is coming too."

"Did Mum phone him?" There it was again: that insecure, bitter edge to her voice. She seldom referred to Dieter by his name, not since he had called her a gold–digger when she met Newman and divorced Larry. That was years ago, even before Father died.

"No, Ingrid, I did, the same day I left my first message for you."

"Is Mum really that bad?"

"Yes. She's in hospital in Swakopmund and she's not waking up."

Ingrid managed to cradle the phone against her ear and bury her face in the open palms of both hands, her eyes staring over her fingertips into her past.

"Will you come out and join us?" Otto asked.

Ingrid took several deep breaths, feeling her eyes twitching. In the background a distant NYPD siren filled the silence.

"I don't think I can go back there. Lüderitz is such a dump and that house is filled with too many—"

"Come on Ingrid, we haven't all been together for… I can't even remember when last it was," Otto pleaded.

Ingrid snorted. "Together? What's 'together' about our family, Otto?" she said sharply.

"Let's not get into this now. Mum needs us."

"I have nothing to say to Dieter, you know that."

Otto tactfully ignored the Dieter issue. "Let's not have a repeat of Dad's funeral. Come out this time, before it's too late."

Ingrid's chest rose and fell with bottled-up emotions. "You really think there might be a funeral?" she said eventually.

"It's a distinct possibility I'm afraid."

Ingrid rubbed her temples. "I don't know. What's the point? The past is in the past."

"Mum – your mother – may well die, Ingrid, that's the point. Perhaps you could see her one last time, even speak to her. Eventually you will be free from the past that you seem to so despise, and then you can get on with your New York lifestyle unhindered." Otto's voice rose, a sudden loss of composure.

"Don't lecture me, Otto, you of all people. You don't know the half of it," she replied venomously.

"Well then, after all these years of sniping and bitterness, come and explain it to me. I'll be there from tomorrow night."

"I'll think about it."

"You'll be pleased afterwards if you make the effort," Otto said, sounding much softer again. "It'll be good to see you."

Ingrid emitted a derisive nasal sound. "I wish I shared your optimism. Where the hell do you get it from, Otto?"

FOUR

12 April 1985

It was never clear how many people were carrying the rolled-up carpet – at least that's what it appeared to be. The carpet seemed strangely familiar too, perhaps the old green one out of his bedroom, though of course that was never pulled up so it couldn't have been. That was the carpet Mum and Dad said was so durable and tough it had put the company out of business; perhaps that and its hideous colour.

Dieter always imagined that Dad must have been one of the taller people carrying the carpet, but somehow he remained deeply unconvinced that his father was one of the shadowy figures shouldering the awkward bundle. So who were these people then, their faces always turned away slightly, obscured by the subversive shadows of a dreamscape? How many were there? Two, three, definitely no more, but was he one of them or was he watching? Had he witnessed this, or was he recalling an event he'd been told about?

The next oddity was where they were, because something deeply familiar seemed to suggest the back porch of their old house, yet he often got the impression that vine leaves were dangling down above them. This could not be because no vines would ever survive in Lüderitz's harsh desert climate, and they certainly did not have any at their old home. So perhaps they weren't at home, but if not, then where on earth were they?

The next bit was often where Dieter would wake up. Having relived the first half of the dream more or less consistently countless times over, the ending was frequently interrupted. What were they carrying, and where were they headed with this rolled-up carpet? Sometimes he saw a skip against the garage wall and this fitted in with a sweaty panic about someone finding the grim contents of the carpet in the skip. But they never had a skip at home, of that he was certain, so this part was surely imagined.

Did this mean that the rest was imagined too? Why would they be taking something that they should not have, whatever it was, something that would be discovered and traced back to them, out of the house in a rolled-up carpet? Who or what was in the carpet? Who put it there? Where were they going with it?

The strangest part of this experience was the incongruity of it all. Why on earth should such a mountain of guilt be manifesting itself in his subconscious mind? It all seemed so utterly out of place, so out of context and alien compared to his childhood memories. Yet he would awaken from it disturbed, frequently shaken and sometimes covered in a sheen of nervous perspiration. Why was he plagued by this?

Dieter believed that if he could sleep and dream just a little longer the mystery might be revealed. But this never transpired and he seriously considered that it was because there was no conclusion stored in his memory. This dream was the equivalent of a sandstone engraving weathered by the wind to the extent that most of it was no longer legible.

The phone was ringing.

"Yeah?" Dieter said, irritably and half-asleep.

Foghorns vibrated in the distance across Repulse Bay. Dieter reached across the bed in the streaky light cast by the blinds and realised the bed was cold and empty beside him. Then he remembered.

"It's Otto. Sorry to wake you."

Dieter rubbed his eyes in the dark without lifting his head off the pillow. "What is it now?"

"Mum died, Dieter."

Dieter stiffened. "Huh?"

"It was peaceful."

Dieter's eyes opened and he stared ahead, suddenly wide awake. "Where are you?"

"I'm in Lüderitz, at home."

"When…?"

"I arrived yesterday," Otto said.

"Did you see her?"

Otto hesitated. "I was too late." He sounded deeply remorseful.

"Shit, I'm sorry Otto, I know you were very close." Dieter empathised with his younger brother, who had just lost his last remaining parent without the opportunity to say goodbye.

"Yes, very close. I live in Durham and she lived in Lüderitz and I didn't see her often enough."

"Hey, hey, this is not your fault, Otto, don't beat yourself up about it," Dieter said. He had sat up in bed and placed his feet on the wooden floor.

"Are you coming out?"

Dieter nodded before he answered. "Yes. I'll get the next flight I can. It's not a good time with the business mind you, so much happening. Is there a fax machine at the house?"

"I'm sure Mum did not plan to be awkward, Dieter."

"What do you mean by that?"

"I recall you running around making phone calls and sending faxes throughout Dad's funeral," Otto said.

Dieter recollected groups of stuffy old men standing about quaffing schnapps and small pumpernickel Appetithäppchen over muted conversation, praising Ernst Adermann. Christ, he'd had to walk to the local library to send a fax. Dieter stood up, suddenly impatient to end the call.

"I've got to go, Otto, lots to organise before I leave. Is Ingrid coming this time?"

"I couldn't say. She knows, though."

"Mmmmh," Dieter said. "Bloody poor show at Dad's funeral."

"I agree."

"I'll pick up a nice bottle of scotch at duty free. What you drinking these days?" Dieter blurted, as though he was preparing for a party.

"Surprise me," Otto replied.

"Do you want anything from Hong Kong for the boys, for Max and er…"

"Karl," Otto said, accustomed to this. "Don't worry yourself."

"No, no, I am really shit at remembering their birthdays… and Christmas. I'm sorry."

"It's OK."

"Do you celebrate Christmas?" Dieter asked after a brief pause.

"Yes, why ever not?"

"Oh, I just wondered… I don't know why but I thought Sabine was Jewish – something Ingrid might have said once, long ago when we still… you know… spoke."

"I don't know what you're on about. Sabine is as German as you and I are. What did Ingrid say?" Otto's voice could not contain his evident irritation.

"I can't remember – I obviously got it wrong, I'm sorry. Look, I'll see you in a day or two; we'll have a scotch or three and catch up."

Otto looked out of the window across the lengthening evening shadows. A stiff breeze bowed the plastic crime scene tape stretched between four metal staves around the roots of the fallen camelthorn in the bleak, rocky, sand–strewn garden. There had been a forensic tent over the hole in the ground but it blew away on the night Mother passed away.

He knew Dieter would bring expensive scotch and share it generously, but also be completely absorbed in his own world, preoccupied with his business back in Hong Kong. And if Ingrid came too, it would be very interesting.

F I V E

15 April 1985

The South Atlantic Ocean, undulating like a restless sheet of liquid lapis lazuli, repelled the brightness of the high sun at its zenith. The heat scorched the arid earth and forced Otto to squeeze his eyelids together protectively. The broad crime scene tape cordoning off the disfigured hole beside the fallen camelthorn's roots felt surreal and yet indefatigably final between Otto's fingers. He stared at the broken sandy soil where he had played as a child, recalling the hazardous climbing expeditions into the tree's unwelcoming thorny bosom. It was difficult now to recreate the perspective in his mind, though, with the stricken tree lying as it was, prostrated on the ground.

"I don't recall this place being quite so desolate," Dieter said, stroking his Thomas Magnum moustache.

The Adermann family home, an imposing double storey Bavarian-styled colonial house, was built on a steep incline of harsh black rock near the corner of Bismarck and Bülow Streets. Most of Lüderitz was chiselled into this brutal terrain, softened only by the desert's relentless sandy incursions into every corner of the town – the roads, the sidewalks – heaped by the strong coastal winds against every vertical intruder, be that lamppost, wall or broken-down vehicle. The only clean and immovable boundary was the edge of the bitterly cold South Atlantic waters lapping the sandy shore.

"It's grim, isn't it?" Otto agreed, staring at the hole in the ground. "Yet Lüderitz still has a unique charm for me. I don't know what it is… a paradox perhaps. You just wouldn't expect to find humans settled in such a…" He searched for the word. "A foreboding place."

"I wonder why Mum and Dad chose to come here?" Dieter kicked at the stony ground. "To this remote, desolate corner of Africa?" He chuckled, waving his arm aimlessly. "I mean, there is nothing in any direction for hundreds of miles."

Otto was mesmerised by the roughly excavated hole in the ground where the sanctity of a human grave had been desecrated, first by nature and then by inquisitive police hands. Someone had been lying down there amongst the struggling roots of one of the few trees to successfully survive the Namib Desert's unforgiving climate. Just four feet up, in blissful childhood ignorance, he had played on top of it. A chill ran down his spine and he felt himself shiver.

"Do you remember how Mum used to watch us through the kitchen window when we played out here?" Otto said, glancing up to the rear wall of the house, through the large square kitchen window, imagining his mother standing at the kitchen sink, hands out of sight and busy as she watched them play.

"You mean, what was she thinking?"

Otto met his brother's eyes. "Possibly."

Dieter turned and looked around the large, white-walled garden imposed upon the steeply angled rocky slope. The relatively level soil around the camelthorn tree had provided one of the few child-friendly places for he and Otto to play.

The only greenery to punctuate the black rock and sandy brown hues were succulents of various shapes and sizes: aloes, Damara milk-bushes, and the incredibly rare Welwitschia with its odd-looking pinky-red flowers, fed by the dense Skeleton Coast fogs.

"I only have happy memories of this garden, apart from the later years… you know, the squabbles with Ingrid." He looked back at Otto. "We used to fight too, but we got on well mostly, didn't we, despite our age difference?"

"How old are you now?"

"Forty-seven," Dieter said. His long, neatly groomed sideburns and short fair hair made him look younger, Otto thought.

"You're right, I was much younger than you, but somehow you were quite a patient brother, as I recall. In fact you kind of did the things with me that Dad never did, sort of like a younger father sometimes, more than an older brother." Otto shrugged. "I don't know, that's what it felt like, when I was a boy."

"Yeah, Dad was pretty preoccupied with his work, wasn't he?" Dieter said. "It used to feel as if he lived in… where was it again?"

"He had a clinic in Keetmanshoop," Otto said.

"Yeah, that's it – well, he seemed to be there more than he was at home."

Otto turned away and rubbed his exposed arms. He was only wearing a white T-shirt with Queen printed on it, over blue denim jeans. "I can't look at this hole anymore. Let's go in. The air's getting cooler."

Lüderitz was blessed with a constant, mild climate, a compromise between the harsh dry heat of the Namib Desert

F/2330474

and the cold air blowing off the Benguela Current in the South Atlantic. The dramatic collision of the two produced dense coastal fogs that had sunk many a ship over the centuries. But despite a clear sky and a reasonable air temperature the coastal breeze was intensifying, and across the blue ocean Otto could see a fog, like a concrete wall, obliterating the horizon. He knew that soon the sky and the sea would both be grey and Lüderitz's harsh, inhospitable qualities would be softened in the ensuing murky haze.

At that moment a taxi stopped in the sandy road below them. A tall woman wearing high-heeled, knee-length black boots and a long sable fur coat with mink trimming emerged and stared up at the house. Her eyes met Otto's but she did not wave.

"My God, it's Ingrid, I think," Otto said.

Dieter looked surprised, or perhaps disappointed, and scuffed the sandy soil with his shoe. Otto watched Ingrid climbing the twenty-three steps from the roadway to the house. He would never forget the number of steps because they had formed the backdrop for many a childhood game with his brother. There was bouncing the ball from the top to the bottom, seeing how many steps one could land the ball on. They would take turns waiting at the bottom to retrieve the tennis ball and throw it back up to the top. Otto had always struggled with throwing it back; it had seemed such a long way. Yet Dieter, older and stronger, had managed the high trajectory so easily.

They even tried sliding down the steps once on a flattened cardboard box, but it snagged on something, sending Dieter flying. Mum had flown out of the house in a swirl of anger and concern. That was how Dieter came by the chip on his front

tooth, and it was still there, Otto noticed, despite the access to expensive Hong Kong dentistry.

"Hello brother," Ingrid said as she reached the top step, eyes fixed on Otto. Plum lipstick, coiffured hair, French manicure, Yves St Laurent perfume and Thierry Mugler boots: she looked as though she had just stepped out for a day's shopping on Fifth Avenue.

Otto and Ingrid embraced, after a fashion – she squeezed his elbows, which was their only physical contact, and a pretend peck on each cheek was accompanied by an exaggerated smooching sound.

"Thanks for coming, Ingrid," Otto said.

"You look well. Still the blue-eyed boy of the family," Ingrid said, gently pinching his cheek between her fingers. "Well, almost."

Otto frowned: he had brown eyes while both Ingrid and Dieter had Mother's blue eyes.

"Going a bit thin on top, there," Ingrid noted, examining Otto's receding hairline as if it contained lice. "Not sure who you get that from."

"Hello Ingrid," Dieter said, hands clasped behind his back. Ingrid glanced coldly at Dieter and Otto knew what each must have been thinking: when last had they spoken, let alone met each other face to face? He guessed it could have been around twenty-five years ago, after she moved to New York. The vast time difference between Eastern Standard Time and Hong Kong could be blamed, but only partially. Dieter had told him they didn't even exchange cards at Christmas, and then there was that business over Newman.

"Dieter. How are you?" It sounded cold and insincere.

"Good, thank you. How is… er…?"

"We're divorced."

"Oh."

"Where are your bags?" Otto asked, looking behind Ingrid.

"At the hotel."

"Hotel?"

"Mmmmh. The Zum Sperrgebiet near the harbour."

"Aren't you staying at the house with us? I've made up your old bedroom for you."

Ingrid snorted slightly and looked down, shaking her head. "God no, I have no desire to stay here. The hotel is fine."

Otto and Dieter exchanged a furtive glance.

"Would you reconsider, for me?" Otto asked softly. "It would be nice if we were all together at this time. It's only a few days."

"I'd rather stay at the hotel, but thank you. Let's just remember what we're here for – to bury Mum. This is not a family reunion."

Dieter's eyes remained downcast, avoiding contact with Ingrid's as he pretended not to be part of the conversation.

"There is also a lot to sort out," Otto said.

"Like what?" Ingrid said.

"Well," Otto began, half-turning and gesticulating towards the cordoned–off hole in the ground, "this, for one thing."

Ingrid looked across at the tree's splayed roots and paled slightly. Perhaps the gravity of police crime scene tape struck a chord somewhere within her.

"God, it was close to the house," she said. "You guys used to play there, and dig holes." This time she glanced across at Dieter, who looked up and nodded his head.

"It's pretty eerie, isn't it?" Otto said.

"I doubt it will affect us, though. The police will investigate and sort it out," Ingrid said, turning away.

Otto moved towards the door. The air was cooling as the fog bank neared the coastline. "Let's go in and have tea, I'm getting cold."

"You can't be wearing a T-shirt here in this fog," Ingrid said, fingering the flimsy sleeve of Otto's T-shirt.

"It's a lot warmer than Durham."

Ingrid and Dieter hesitated at the door, both waiting for the other to enter. Eventually Ingrid walked ahead.

"I got a call from the local police, from Frans Laubscher. Remember him?" Otto said.

"Oh God!" Ingrid muttered.

"He remembers you, Ingrid," Otto said, filling the stainless steel kettle at the kitchen sink.

"Didn't Frans take you to a school dance?" Dieter blurted out.

"No. Whatever gave you that idea?" Ingrid was indignant.

"He remembers you too, Dieter," Otto added.

"He had quite a crush on you, Ingrid." Dieter seemed to be enjoying this.

"It wasn't me he had a crush on, let's get that straight." Ingrid removed her lavish coat, revealing a designer cream and beige ensemble that just covered her knees. She moved to the white cupboards to search for mugs. "God, I swear this is the same kettle that was here when we lived at home. Look at all this stuff… it's ancient."

"What did Frans want?" Dieter asked, pulling up a kitchen chair at the red melamine-topped table.

"He wants to talk to all of us, tell us what they know and find out what we can remember," Otto said.

"Do we have to?" Ingrid said.

"It's a police investigation so I reckon so," Otto replied.

Dieter breathed in deeply. "Well I'm only here for one week. I have to get back as it's year-end in the business, plus I've got the merger going on."

"Me too. My return is booked for Sunday," Ingrid said as she arranged cups and clinked teaspoons.

"That's too soon, guys. There's a lot to do. We have to sort out the house contents as well as finalise the funeral, let alone deal with the police," Otto said.

"I don't want anything from this house," Ingrid said, glancing around. "It's all so old and… ugh! We may as well junk it all, just get someone in to clear the contents."

"Oh come on, Ingrid, it's not junk!" Otto protested.

"I might take a few things. There's the old grandfather clock, the cuckoo clock…" Dieter said, looking towards the living room.

"You can't have them both," Otto objected.

"You can have the piano. It's a Bechstein, isn't it?"

"Well, I suppose so, but let's take it one step at a time," Otto said.

"I'm just saying that there are some things worth keeping, and certainly some items that I wouldn't mind having," Dieter said with a conciliatory gesture.

"I agree," Otto said.

Ingrid shrugged indifferently and pulled a face as she poured the tea. "You guys take what you like from the house. I'm not interested in anything." Ingrid had a way, not just in her speech but also her body language, of being quite direct, and now she tensed her facial muscles and stiffened her back.

"What about the stuff in your bedroom?" Otto asked.

Ingrid clenched her jaw. "There are no warm memories here that I want to cherish."

Otto and Dieter looked at each other.

"Did we grow up in the same family?" Otto said, somewhat flabbergasted.

"Don't go there," Ingrid said icily. She placed a cup in front of each of them. "You can do your own milk and sugar, if you take any."

They all sat around the table in a silence invaded by the sound of teaspoons on porcelain, and the grandfather clock as it rasped and clicked in preparedness for two loud chimes.

"I have a vague memory of all three of us sitting around this table one night with a candle, pulling hairs out of a hairbrush and frizzling them in the flickering flame while we chatted. Well, I suppose mostly you two chatted, I was quite young I think. Do you remember that?" Otto said with childlike enthusiasm.

"God, Otto, you're fourteen years younger than me and, what, seven years younger than him?" Ingrid said, inclining her head towards Dieter.

"Six," Otto said.

"How do you remember such trivial stuff?" Ingrid furrowed her brow.

"I don't know, but I recall sitting with you two, perhaps because you were so much older than me and you had... included me."

Both Dieter and Ingrid shook their heads.

"What else do you remember?" Ingrid asked.

Otto thought for a moment and then shrugged. "Nothing much."

"When is the funeral going to be?" Dieter asked.

"Mum's body has already been released to a funeral home and they need two to three days to prepare," Otto said.

"We'll have to put a notice in the local paper and contact her friends. Does anyone know who they are?" Dieter said.

Otto nodded and shrugged. "Some. She used to talk about them. But it's such a small place I'm sure everyone knows already."

"Will she be buried next to Dad?" Ingrid asked.

Dieter and Otto exchanged a glance, Dieter raising one eyebrow.

"Dad chose to be cremated," Otto said.

"Did he? Oh." Ingrid sipped her tea.

There was a loud knock on the stained glass front door. The outline of a large figure was visible through the colonial Teutonic–style lead panes. They all looked at each other.

SIX

Dressed in a pale blue, short-sleeved shirt that was strained to breaking point across a substantial belly, the imposing figure of Frans Laubscher filled the entrance hall. Apart from a dark moustache he had lost most of his hair, except for a grey strip above each 'cauliflower ear', a vestige Otto recalled from his years as a prop in the school rugby team.

"Hello! Hello, you guys. Welcome back to Lüderitz," he said in a booming voice, shaking first Otto's and then Dieter's hand with great exuberance. He smelled overpoweringly of cigarette smoke.

Ingrid, sitting alone at the kitchen table, looked on, deadpan. The moment Frans stepped into the kitchen her facial expression blossomed into a broad, insincere smile, and she stood up.

"Ingrid!" Frans said, grinning broadly. "You look amazing!"

"Thank you, Frans. You look... er... well, too," Ingrid managed, her eyes taking in his broad, sloping shoulders, overweight torso and pendulous belly, solid legs and at least size fourteen black shoes.

Otto did not remember Frans' squint being quite so marked, with one eye always at forty-five degrees to the other, constantly flicking back and forth such that one never knew which eye to look at.

"So, you're a policeman," Ingrid said, awkwardly.

Frans nodded and appeared embarrassed. "Ja, thirty–five years now."

"Wasn't your father a policeman too?" Dieter asked.

"No, no, he was a security officer at the diamond company, you know, patrolling the Sperrgebiet."

"The Sperrgebiet?" Otto said.

"Ja, the forbidden diamond fields all around Lüderitz," Frans said. "It's a restricted area controlled by the diamond company. Heavily patrolled."

"Must have been a good job?" Dieter said, gesturing for Frans to enter the kitchen.

"Oh ja, but I could never work for them, not after what happened, no way."

Otto and Dieter looked at each other blankly.

"Come in, Frans; tell us about yourself," Dieter said, scraping a chair across the kitchen floor for Frans to sit on.

Frans wiped his mouth with a meaty hand. "Jees, well, I've been a policeman here in Lüderitz since leaving school, with just one assignment in Windhoek and a year in Swakopmund along the way."

"And you're the chief now?" Otto said with a flourish of his hand.

Frans blushed. "Ja. For the last seven years." He kept glancing across at Ingrid, who managed to avoid his eyes.

"Congratulations, Frans. You've done well," Dieter said without a hint of disingenuousness.

"No, not really. I mean, you guys – you're in Hong Kong, is that right?"

Dieter nodded.

"And Otto in England: a doctor like your pa." Frans nodded

effusively as he met Otto's eyes. "And you live in New York, Ingrid?"

Ingrid nodded begrudgingly.

"It must be fantastic living in New York," Frans said, his deviated eyes dancing, as though he was imaging her world of skyscrapers and city lights.

Ingrid looked up and pulled a face. "It sure beats Lüderitz."

"This is amazing. Here you all are, all the Adermanns together in the house again." Frans was like a puppy dog with his tail wagging uncontrollably.

"I am not an Adermann," Ingrid muttered.

Frans blushed. "Ja, you're married, of course."

"Divorced," Ingrid said with a terse grin.

Frans just looked at her for a moment. "Hey, listen to me, I am so sorry about Mrs Adermann, really, man – my condolences and all that about your ma. It is very sad. She was a wonderful, wonderful lady."

"Thank you, Frans," Dieter said. "Tea?"

"Ja – er, actually no thanks, I just had one at the station." Frans was staring at Ingrid again, clearly making her uncomfortable. "I can't get over how much you remind me of Inez," he said eventually, rubbing his stubbly jowls with a meaty hand and shaking his head.

Otto and Dieter exchanged a puzzled look. Ingrid drew a sharp breath as though she had been jabbed in the ribs, and looked away, out of the kitchen window.

"What can you tell us about this business?" Ingrid said quickly, pointing at the camelthorn tree roots visible through the window.

Frans shook his head, and for the first time his smile faded as his face adopted a sombre tone. "Hey, man, what a shock that was to your ma. Really, I cannot tell you just how much it has shaken this little community as well. You know, Lüderitz is small and everyone pulls together here."

"So, the tree blew down, and then what?" Otto asked, as all of them sat around the table, staring intently at Frans' restless squint.

"Well, it was one helluva storm." He sniffed loudly. "And after the tree blew over the garden boy saw some bones in the bottom of the hole – scared the crap out of him. You know how superstitious they are." Frans chuckled briefly and then became instantly serious again. "Well, the police came, I was called and we found human remains at the bottom of that hole, right up against the rock." Frans was shaking his head.

"Human remains?" Dieter questioned. Ingrid looked stricken, holding onto her mug with both hands, knuckles blanching.

"Well, just bones, you understand, and not too many either. They must have been there a long time."

"How do you know they're human?" Otto asked.

"The skull – you can see that easily." Frans nodded, looking at each one in turn. "Oh ja, definitely."

No-one knew where to look, and for a few seconds nobody maintained eye contact. A body in their own back garden: it was something unimaginable, surreal, beyond immediate comprehension.

"Do you know who it is?" Dieter asked.

Frans shook his head. "No. There are no missing persons who might fit the description, but obviously enquiries are still… as we say… at an early stage."

Ingrid, sitting tight-lipped behind her mug, looked as though she had seen a ghost.

"How long has the body been buried there?" Otto asked.

Frans exhaled. "Difficult to be certain, though we might get a better idea from the pathologists in Windhoek where the bones have been sent, but roughly twenty to thirty years, maybe even more."

"Jesus!" Dieter muttered. "It was definitely there right through our childhood years then."

Frans nodded. "Can you guys not think of something, anything, that might help us?" He looked from one to another around the table, his eyes perhaps lingering on Ingrid's catatonic stare. "Your parents built this house in late 1946 soon after they settled here. Ingrid, you must have been about eleven or twelve then—"

"Twelve," Ingrid said, clearing her throat.

"You might, perhaps even Dieter might, remember something."

Ingrid and Dieter shook their heads, brows furrowed.

"Can you tell if it's a male or female?" Otto asked, unclasping his hands briefly.

"Or how old the person was?" Dieter added. "I mean, could the body not have been there far longer than thirty years? Maybe an old Herero who died and was buried in the sand?"

Frans stroked his moustache thoughtfully as he looked at each of them in turn. "Did your ma not tell you guys?"

Otto glanced at Ingrid, who was staring into her cup. Dieter's eyes were fixed on Frans' face.

"Tell us what?" Otto asked.

"Jesus, man!" Frans shook his head and wiped his face, nervously. "You don't know?"

Ingrid paled further.

"The body is of a young child," Frans reluctantly announced.

33

Otto slumped back in his chair and covered his mouth with one hand.

"A very young child," Frans added.

"Oh God!" Ingrid said quietly, closing her eyes for a second or two.

Nobody breathed around the table.

"It's probably some Herero kid," Dieter suggested flippantly. "They've lived all over these parts for centuries, long before the German settlers ever came here."

Frans fixed Dieter with a look of censure. "Buried wearing leather slippers and holding a teddy bear?"

Otto's heart skipped a beat. Ingrid stood up suddenly, scraping her chair loudly on the floor.

"Excuse me a moment," she said, walking out of the room.

Everyone sat in silence. In the background a toilet flushed and then Ingrid re-emerged, looking uncharacteristically fragile.

"I'm sorry to be so blunt, guys. I thought you knew exactly what was going on," Frans apologised, looking furtively in Ingrid's direction.

"It's not your fault, Frans. It's just… shocking to hear," Ingrid said, speaking for the first time in a while.

Outside the fog had rolled across Lüderitz, reducing visibility and blocking the sun. In the distance a foghorn reverberated intermittently. The atmosphere was thick with the fishy smell of seaweed and kelp.

"I feel really bad," Frans said, ruefully. "You have all been through enough already, what with your ma and everything else."

Otto frowned at Dieter as if to say what's he talking about? "I want you to know, Ingrid, that I keep Inez's grave neat and tidy with fresh flowers every year," Frans added, trying to elicit Ingrid's gaze. "I'm sure you'll want to go and visit."

Ingrid sat frozen. Otto was confused. Dieter's eyes moved, though his face did not flinch.

"Inez?" Otto said.

"I have to go!" Ingrid blurted out, standing suddenly and grabbing her coat in one movement. Her chair fell over backwards, clattering loudly on the tiled floor.

Frans glanced from Otto to Dieter. "There's a fog, Ingrid. Where are you going?"

"To my hotel."

"I'll give you a lift, if you like."

Ingrid pulled her coat tightly around herself and began to walk to the telephone. "It's OK, I'll call a cab."

"Actually, Frans, I need to send an urgent fax to Hong Kong," Dieter said, standing up.

"At the library?" Frans said.

"Unless there's somewhere else."

"Dieter! You promised you wouldn't this time," Otto protested.

"What? I'll be quick. I have to keep in touch, Otto, I'm running a business."

"No problem, Dieter, come with me," Frans said. "Are you sure, Ingrid – the hotel is on the way?"

"Yes." Ingrid was not easily dissuaded. "I'm used to cabs in Manhattan."

Within minutes Otto was left standing in the empty house all alone, staring out at the cloying fog that smothered the small coastal town. It was a truly surreal sight: dense coastal fog colliding with barren, rocky desert terrain. The small, colourful, colonial–styled Bavarian buildings of Lüderitz seemed incidental, immersed in a titanic struggle between the two great forces of nature. Why on earth had his parents chosen this forsaken little town to settle in, Otto wondered? What lured them to build this grand house in 1946 and never leave it again?

SEVEN

The journey from the Adermann house on Bülow Street to the library on Ring Street was short, even for the modest proportions of Lüderitz. A pair of fluffy dice, red with white polka dots, dangled from the rear-view mirror of Frans' rusting yellow Toyota. Even they smelled strongly of cigarette smoke. "It's great having you guys back in town after all these years," Frans said with boyish excitement as he caressed the car along at a walking pace.

Dieter stared out of the grimy window at the enveloping greyness that reached down to touch the rivers of sand flowing into every crevice in the barren little town. "Yeah."

"You know, I retire in a few months."

Dieter's eyes wandered across Frans' profile. Yes, he thought, imminent retirement would fit with Frans' bloated and weathered appearance. He didn't imagine that being a policeman in a small, close community like Lüderitz would be very onerous, but living in this extreme climate could take its toll on a man.

"This will probably be my last case," Frans mused with a little smile.

"Get many dead bodies around here?"

Frans shook his head wistfully. "Not exactly."

Dieter hesitated as he thought back to Frans' remarks about Inez and her grave. "Who was Inez?" he asked.

"Inez?" Frans repeated, frowning deeply.

"Yes, you mentioned her back at the house."

Frans stared at Dieter with a puzzled look in his divergent eyes, for so long that the car began to veer towards the sand-smothered kerb.

"Your sister? Inez?"

Dieter felt a shiver. "I only have one sister: Ingrid."

"Now, yes. Inez died a long time ago; you were very young then. It was tragic, she was such a beautiful woman." Frans shook his head and sighed deeply. "She's buried just outside town."

Dieter felt a pang of sweaty nausea, his bladder dragging in his pelvis as though he was guilty of something. Was he guilty of something, he wondered, thinking about the dream that haunted him? He stared out of the window, stroking his puckered lips with an index finger.

After a few moments of this unexpected silence the car stopped and Dieter became aware of Frans' eyes staring at him.

"We're here, Dieter – the library."

"Oh… er… thanks." Dieter fumbled with the door. "Where is the cemetery?" he asked, turning to face Frans.

"You really didn't know about Inez?"

Dieter raised his eyebrows and shook his head slowly.

"It's not far, along Bay Road heading south. Do you want me to take you there?"

"Maybe later," Dieter said, pushing the protesting door open.

"I admire your ma, Dieter, and Ingrid as well," Frans said.

"Why?"

"Your ma was that sort of woman, kind and thoughtful but strong too, always putting her children first. I mean, that she would protect you from all that pain, just carrying it herself all these years… you know, bearing the burden. Ingrid too."

Dieter contemplated Frans' words as he stood beside the car, smelling the ripeness of the South Atlantic.

"Thank you for the lift, Frans."

EIGHT

Otto willingly let his mind wander back in time as his fingers brushed over objects familiar to his past. Sometimes it was the smell, sometimes the texture, but mostly it was associations that triggered within him waves of nostalgia.

For instance, the lead soldiers that he and Dieter had played with in their sandy garden: he measured the weight of a Napoleonic infantryman in his palm, turning it over softly. They had all been beautifully hand-painted once, in reds, blues and blacks, but their glossy finish was now chipped and worn from hours of imaginative play. These memories were predominantly pleasant: he and Dieter had been good companions as children, despite their age difference, though Otto did recall the instances when Dieter would torment him intellectually with highbrow conversation beyond his comprehension.

"They would never be friends, Otto: the Cossacks are from Russia, and these blue and white soldiers are French – Napoleon's troops," Dieter taunted his younger brother. "Don't you know anything?"

"But they are both fighting against the Turks… together."

"You dig the trenches, Otto, and I will decide which ones are friends with the Cossacks."

Otto smiled, remembering that his only form of retaliation to these mounting frustrations had inevitably been physical, and this would land Dieter in hot water when he reciprocated, because of his sizeable somatic advantage.

Otto turned a Cossack over in his fingers. Both brothers had harboured great admiration for the bravery and endurance of the Cossacks – why, he had no idea, but they were seldom the villains in any of their fantasy battles. The one he held, mounted on a black stallion, had lost the tip of his curved shashka.

His eyes fell upon a handmade sash of diaphanous white ribbon edged in red. On it, in Father's black Gothic handwriting, the words Mein erstes Auto had bled and faded into the adjacent material.

It had been wrapped around Otto's first car, a camel–brown Morris Minor, presented by proud parents to transport him back and forth the seven hundred miles to medical school in Cape Town. Otto swallowed a surge of nostalgia. He had loved that car, rattling along at a top speed of fifty–five miles per hour on straight roads that bisected the arid and hostile landscapes of the Namib, the Richtersveld and the Karoo before finally being welcomed by the sight of Table Mountain, an oasis in the wilderness at the southern tip of Africa. And to have a car as a student in Cape Town in the 1960s – what a prestige that had been. But that Morris had created great discontent in his family too.

"I was never given a car," Ingrid said, eyes downcast, lips pressed together.

"Otto has to get to medical school in Cape Town, Ingrid," Mum replied, "and he has to get between hospitals for his tutorials."

"Yes, of course, Otto is going to be a doctor like Daddy." Ingrid's voice was laced with sarcasm.

"You went to secretarial college in Swakopmund. That's what you wanted."

"It's all about the boys in this house. Always the boys," Ingrid said.

"You didn't need a car, Ingrid, you didn't choose to study far away."

"Oh, so it was my choice, was it?"

"Your father and I have never prevented you from following your dreams."

Ingrid always rolled her eyes, shaking her head in utter disbelief as she sighed deeply.

"Dieter went to fancy Schloss Gracht in Cologne to study business, Otto to medical school in Cape Town and I stayed behind in bloody Lüderitz."

"But you have Frederick," Mum argued, referring to the wealthy businessman that Ingrid had been dating for some time.

Otto remembered that Dad never had the patience to listen to Ingrid's discontent, reminding her always about the hardships he had endured to provide her with a good home, schooling and all the clothes she could possibly dream of. Dad also disapproved strongly of Frederick, regarding him as too old for Ingrid, and of course he had also been married before. They fought terribly, Ingrid and Dad. Mum always said they were too similar: strong-willed, proud. Neither ever liked to apologise.

The foghorn sounded in the murky distance through the brume, snapping Otto back. He pushed the ribbon back on the shelf, as if banishing the dark emotions that it had aroused in his family. His eyes gazed across the dusty boxes of items that safeguarded the remnants of his childhood. Mum, it seemed, had never disposed of anything. He sneezed from the musty odours and shook his head as he chuckled. Then his eyes fell upon a large worn box marked Bell & Howell.

His eyes lit up instantly and he bent down to retrieve the box. Here was something that used to give them hours of pleasure as youngsters: the old family cine projector. He recalled how he used to set it up, threading the film around the toothed sprockets and through the gate, watching the large metal reels turn synchronously as the images flickered onto a white sheet tacked to the living room curtains. It had been utterly magical when he was a child.

Somewhere there would be an old box containing reels of home movies, filmed mainly by Dad who had enjoyed brandishing his black Agfa cine camera whenever family events occurred, like when Otto had been presented with the Morris Minor. Otto smiled and hoped that the films had survived, for they would be an excellent icebreaker when Dieter and Ingrid returned. There were bound to be many happy and amusing moments captured for eternity on grainy black and white celluloid.

NINE

The white taxi stopped outside the Hotel Zum Sperrgebiet, which was almost engulfed in swirling, dense sea fog. Being slightly elevated above the harbour, the views over the water, pier and sailing vessels were pleasant and bestowed upon the little human enclave of Lüderitz a quality far grander than reality. At that moment, though, the thick fog rebalanced the illusion.

Ingrid hesitated, her lower lip furled as she ran her teeth over it. "How far is it to the cemetery?" she asked.

The taxi driver turned his burly frame through forty-five degrees in the front seat, a deep frown etched into his unshaven melon of a face.

"You ever been to the cemetery in a fog, Fräulein?"

Lüderitz residents had a curious tendency to use Germanic expressions as liberally as colloquialisms in their everyday conversations. Many were fluent in a dialect quaintly time-locked in its century-old colonial past.

"Not for a long time," Ingrid said. "Take me there, please."

The driver shrugged and ground the vehicle into gear as he turned to grapple with the steering wheel. The ageing Mercedes wound its way back along Woermann Street in the embrace of the smoking fog, illuminated like phosphorous by the yellow headlights. Then the driver turned into Bay Road, the main route through Lüderitz, entering from the arid and stony south–east before disappearing once again beneath the shifting sands of the Namib Desert just beyond Robert Harbour.

Lüderitz Cemetery was not far out of town, though hidden as it was within the curtains of fog, it was impossible to discern the extent of its geometric format.

"Wait here, I won't be too long," Ingrid said, opening her door.

"It's your money, Fräulein."

Once she was crunching her way along the vapid pathways between rows of granite headstones, Ingrid found her bearings coming back to her quickly. She had walked this way many times before, though not for a very long time indeed. She found the headstone with relative ease, surrounded, as Frans had rightly declared, by colourful wreaths of flowers. Most were plastic, sun–baked and leeched of their colour, but there were also small bundles of fresh flowers tied together with string, thoughtfully placed facing the headstone as if in homage.

Ingrid knelt down and rearranged the flowers, many of them dried by the desiccating desert wind, the wetness of the fog simply too little, too late.

The inscription on the small headstone was facile: Inez, gone too soon, 19.06.1927-11.09.1948.

Ingrid touched the cold granite, damp from the cloying fog, surprised that the headstone seemed smaller to her than she recalled. Compared to those around Inez, with their elaborate designs, polished slabs and plinths, marble vases and ostentatious inscriptions boasting scrolls and flowers, it was clear that little money had been spent on her memorial. On the plot adjacent to Inez's grave a fresh hole had been excavated, the mound of unearthed sand and stony rubble piled high just a few feet away. The depth of the hole surprised Ingrid and she found herself mesmerised by its fathomless permanence.

She did not hear the footsteps on the gravel, nor sense the dark presence behind her as the fog curled around his head and shoulders.

"Why didn't you tell us?"

Ingrid straightened and spun around. She swallowed. It was Dieter. She breathed a little heavily but remained silent. Dieter took a step forward and bent over to study the inscription.

"How did you get here?" Ingrid said tersely.

"Inez," he read. "1948. I was – what – five years old." He turned to face Ingrid whose eyes were open wide, like a startled rabbit's.

"Who told you?" Ingrid said.

"He must have been in love with her," Dieter replied, gesticulating at the fresh flowers and wreaths scattered across the humble white marble chippings on the grave.

Ingrid nodded. "Frans."

"Was he?"

"He adored her, took her to his final school dance, not me, but that was all."

Dieter shook his head, glancing again at the neatly tended grave and its decorations. "Why the big secret?"

It was hard maintaining eye contact with Dieter. They had spoken so little in such a long time that he felt somewhat like a stranger to her, and yet he wasn't. The intensity of this encounter was heavily inflected with the awkwardness of unfamiliarity, like former lovers with intimate carnal knowledge of each other forced into each other's personal space again after too many years apart.

"It is so complicated… you were too young. You were both too young."

"You mean Otto?" Dieter bent down and picked up a bunch of wilting lavender, turning it over in his hand.

"Her favourite colour," Ingrid said, and then her face hardened as déjà vu flashed before her eyes. "I would watch out for scorpions if I was you."

"Scorpions?"

Ingrid nodded subtly. "Black and hairy, with yellow legs. They crawl under the flowers." She paused.

"Are they poisonous?" Dieter asked.

"They're deadly. One sting."

Dieter dropped the flowers and stood up, frowning. "I've never seen those."

"I have," Ingrid said icily.

They stood in silence for a moment, staring at the dropped bunch of flowers.

"You cannot tell Otto about this. I promised," Ingrid said.

Dieter turned to face her squarely, hands on his hips. "Promised who?"

Ingrid sighed and looked down. "Mum."

"Mum's gone, Ingrid."

Ingrid shook her head animatedly. "This will not go away, Dieter; it is far better to forget what you have seen here today and leave Otto out of it. For his sake, trust me."

"Who are you to decide this?" Dieter said, angling his head accusingly.

"Who am I?" Ingrid returned with a sharp tone. "You boys have always lived a charmed life, been in the spotlight, Mum and Dad's favourites, had everything you ever wanted…"

"Oh, knock it off, don't bring that old nugget up again."

"You don't know anything about what is buried with her in that grave," Ingrid hissed, pointing with a dagger–like finger at Inez's headstone. "Believe me, Mum was right – leave it in there and go back to living your comfortable life in Hong Kong when this is over."

Dieter stood stiffly, feet slightly apart and hands on hips as Ingrid began to walk away, swirling the fog around the swishing tails of her fur coat.

"Otto was her brother too – he deserves to know," Dieter said.

Ingrid stopped and turned to face Dieter, raising a finger in the air menacingly. "I will only say it once more, Dieter: if you want what's best for your beloved Otto, then keep your mouth shut." She stared at him. "This is one of the reasons I didn't want to come here again – ever – because you boys always think you know best, that you know everything." She stopped to breathe deeply. "But let me tell you, you don't."

Dieter watched Ingrid disappear into the yawning fog, heard the taxi start up and drive off. He turned to look at the headstone again. Inez – she was twenty–one and he was only five when she died, but he remembered nothing about her at all, had never even heard her name mentioned. Otto would certainly never have remembered her for he was only an infant in 1948.

Why had Mum never mentioned this? And Dad, well Dad had passed away a good ten years back and was never much for talking about family things anyway.

Dieter tapped his chin with a clenched fist. Should he comply with Ingrid's wishes and remain silent? Did Otto not deserve to hear about the sister he had never known? Who was Ingrid protecting?

TEN

That night all three of the Adermann children were independently reminded of the suffocating solitude of Lüderitz, shrouded in its cocoon of fog, trapped between the vast Atlantic Ocean on one side and the expansive Namib Desert on the other: the Koichab Pan of the Great Sand Sea to the north and the forbidden territories of the diamond fields to the south and east. Only the occasional vibration of the foghorn and fuzzy halo of sweeping light from the lighthouse testified to Lüderitz's still-beating heart.

Ingrid sat alone at a table in the lounge bar nursing a generous scotch and ice, staring emptily at flickering images of a travel documentary advertising local tourism on a wall-mounted television.

"The small settlement of Lüderitz was built by diamond prospectors into the only rocky outcrop along the entire inhospitable South West African coastline," said the baritone voiceover. "It is referred to as the Skeleton Coast because of the numerous carcasses of rusting shipwrecks spread along it – over a thousand in total – victims of its legendary sea fogs. The Bushmen of the Namib Desert called it The Land God Made in Anger, and the Portuguese sailors referred to it as The Gates of Hell." The heavy tones of Wagner accompanied panoramic views of sand, sea and desolation.

Ingrid wondered what she was doing in Lüderitz, why she had defied her instinctive reluctance and decided to join her brothers at Mother's funeral. The hotel was average, the food forgettable and Lüderitz more provincial than she recalled. Her uncomfortable encounter with Dieter at the cemetery – not only her first conversation with him in so many years, but also on a prohibited subject cast to the very darkest recesses of even her own mind – had filled her with an immediate desire to return to her sunny Manhattan apartment.

Up on Bülow Street in the old family home Dieter was preoccupied with curled sheets of fax paper, wielding a calculator in one hand and a Mont Blanc pen in the other. He barely even spoke to Otto, who was sitting just yards away from him on the brown velvet sofa looking through the aged contents of a tattered Klipdrift brandy box marked heimfilme. There had been one phone call from Hong Kong, which Otto answered. A man calling himself Jim asked to speak to "my Dieter" and when Otto called him, Jim said, "Thanks darling."

Otto had recoiled slightly from this unexpected familiarity and then spent the next ten minutes trying hard not to eavesdrop on Dieter's conversation – which seemed to be all about business – as he studied the metal cans of film in the box. There were six in total, some beginning to show patches of rust despite Lüderitz's arid climate: less than one inch of rain per year. Must be the fog, Otto thought. Each can had been numbered and dated with black marker pen in Father's handwriting. Two larger cans bore the title of an old film Otto remembered enjoying with the family: One Million BC, part 1 and part 2. He smiled. The old films were just begging to be watched.

There were, of course, also important matters to discuss: the funeral notice and arrangements; disposing of Mother's possessions and the house; not to mention the unpleasant uncertainty hanging over them regarding the unidentified child's body found in the back garden. Otto was desperate to talk to Dieter but never got even the slightest opportunity. Surrendering to his mounting frustration Otto retired to bed, thinking about the memories and mysteries that awaited them on several thousand feet of film.

Morning broke with a vivid blue sky and blinding sunshine, revealing the contained swell of Lüderitz's German colonial architecture – towers, turrets, steep tiled roofs and gables, oriel and bay windows – all perched precariously on parched black rock and aggressively surrounded by sand as far as the eye could see. Ingrid did not appear at the house in the morning and, had it had not been for Frans' visit, Otto wondered whether she would have come at all.

Frans arrived mid-morning, his squint looking less marked than it had the afternoon before, leading Otto, with his GP hat on, to question whether his ocular oddity might be a latent exotropia accentuated by fatigue towards the end of the day.

"The fog has lifted," Frans said, shuffling nervously and appearing ill at ease.

"Yeah, looks nice," Otto said, "but I see a fog bank out there over the sea."

"Ja, but fog out there means settled weather for us here. It's when the south-wester blows the fog away that we have shit weather," Frans explained and then smiled. "That'll be in a few days." He chuckled.

Otto made coffee and they sat around the kitchen table.

"You get sorted with the fax machine?" Frans asked.

"Thanks. Perfect," Dieter replied with an accompanying hand gesture.

"Which local newspaper would be the best for a funeral notice, Frans?" Otto asked.

"Definitely the Lüderitzbuchter. Everyone here reads it."

Otto nodded. "Their offices?"

"Down near Customs House, just before you reach the harbour."

They drank coffee in silence.

"What can we do for you, Frans?" Dieter asked eventually.

Frans cleared his throat but would not make eye contact. He played with the unshaven folds of skin beneath his chin.

"I will need to speak to all of you again, more formally you understand, about the body. The Commissioner in Windhoek has ordered a detailed enquiry, given that it's a child's body and the fact that, to our knowledge, only one family has ever lived on this site."

"Mum and Dad built this house," Otto said.

Dieter shot an admonishing look at Otto as if to say keep your mouth shut.

Frans shrugged. "Ja, well that's why I will need to speak to each of you to see what you can remember."

"Well, nothing – I don't remember anything about a body," Otto said.

Dieter leaned in. "What are you suggesting here, Frans?"

Frans put his mug down and opened his hands. "Look, they want to know how long the body has been down there and who it is. Tests may tell us some things—"

"What sort of tests?" Dieter interrupted.

Frans drew a deep breath. "Apparently there is some new test developed in England... I don't know much about it. Something to do with DMA... I think." He twisted his jowly face.

Otto nodded. "DNA profiling… yeah, I've heard about it. It's very new; not widely available, I don't think."

"What does that mean?" Dieter said, his face furrowed with concern.

"Our DNA is like our fingerprints – unique," Otto explained.

Frans listened, his head unmoving as his eyes flitted between Otto and Dieter, like a predator watching its prey. "Ja, OK, well they want to do DNA tests and… er… we can also do something very simple right here in Lüderitz to give us a pretty good idea of the age of that grave." Frans gesticulated towards the kitchen window with his index finger.

Otto and Dieter glanced at each other apprehensively.

"That was a fairly large camelthorn tree in your garden, its roots covering the body, so we think it grew after the burial," Frans said. "Do you know when it was planted?"

"I don't remember, I was too young I suppose, but I have in mind that we – Mum and Dad – planted that tree after the house was built," Otto said. "Would you agree, Dieter?"

Dieter nodded and shrugged. "Yeah, I think so."

Frans leaned back in his chair, which creaked in protest. "That would fit with the tree being about forty years old. Anyway, we'll cut through it and count the rings and that will tell us exactly how old it is."

"Objective, simple and very clever," Otto said.

"But I do want to speak to Ingrid, though. Being the eldest, she may well remember more." Frans looked around. "Where is she?"

Frans' impromptu visit left Otto feeling unsettled and shaken, as though the spectre of this unexplained body was drawing ever closer, threatening to overshadow Mum's funeral. Otto phoned Ingrid, who sounded hungover and moody. When she heard about Frans' visit she fell silent and arrived at the house a short while later wearing another dazzling fur coat.

ELEVEN

A phlegmatic atmosphere hung over the three of them as they sat at the kitchen table, Dieter and Ingrid barely even making eye contact. Otto seemed to do most of the talking and decision-making, affirmation from the other two coming predominantly in the form of nods and grunts. At times the ticking of the grandfather clock from the living room was deafening amidst uneasy silences.

They agreed the text for a funeral notice to be placed in the Lüderitzbuchter; they finalised an order of service and choice of hymns to take down to the Felsenkirche, the tall, imposing Victorian Gothic church built high upon a black rock, hence its name; and they settled on having a wake after the funeral service at the Goerkehaus, a grand restored palace and former residence of an early manager of the diamond company.

"Mum wanted to be buried," Otto said, staring at papers in his hands.

Dieter and Ingrid sat stiffly at opposite ends of the kitchen table, their faces frozen. Ingrid's arms were folded tightly around her coat, seemingly worn as a shield, while Dieter busied himself eating rye bread and salami.

"The cemetery is apparently not far away... just out along Bay Road," Otto said, failing to elicit eye contact from either of them.

Ingrid's lips were pressed together firmly, and Dieter rhythmically drummed his fingertips beneath his chin as he chewed.

"Are either of you interested?" Otto said in exasperation. "What's the matter with you two today?"

"Yeah, I think I know where the cemetery is," Dieter replied, casting a subtle look in Ingrid's direction. "Any idea why Dad chose to be cremated and not buried in it?"

Ingrid stiffened. Otto shook his head. "As I recall, Mum said his wish was to have his ashes scattered on Shark Island – you know, it juts into the bay." Otto shrugged and pulled a face.

"Perhaps he loved going there. It is a great spot for watching the seals and dolphins."

"What does it matter?" Ingrid snapped irritably. She closed her eyes and rubbed the bridge of her nose. "What else do we still have to do?" she added coldly.

Dieter and Otto shared a glance, and then Otto studied the sheet of paper on the table.

"There's the undertaker to speak to, and pay, we need pallbearers, aside from you and me, that is…" Otto glanced at Dieter and raised his hand.

"Do I not count?" Ingrid asked, looking up with narrowed eyes.

Otto, flustered and apologetic, tried to sound nonchalant.

"Of course you can join us, I just didn't think you… would want to."

Ingrid's eyes wandered over Otto's face for a few moments, leaving him to wonder what she was thinking. "Who is organising the tea afterwards?" she asked.

"Would you like to?" Otto suggested.

"Not particularly."

Otto shrugged. "Then I imagine the church will co-ordinate with the staff at Goerkehaus."

"What are we going to do with this house?" Dieter asked, looking around at the walls adorned with heavily framed paintings: Hamburg's grand and imposing Rathaus, a wintry landscape of Freiberg University, the preserved red brick buildings of Wismar in western Pomerania, and a stag's head mounted on the living room wall. Behind Ingrid in the kitchen, various copper pans hung above an old black cast iron cooker.

"Sell it, surely," Ingrid said. "As soon as possible."

"I don't think we can do anything with it while it's still technically a crime scene," Otto said.

"That's a bit dramatic," Dieter protested. He pushed his chair back and reached for a jar of mustard on the kitchen counter behind him.

"What?" Otto raised his palms. "It is a crime scene until the police close their investigation. In any case, who will want to buy a house with an uprooted tree in the back garden surrounded by police tape?"

Ingrid exhaled noisily, like a whale surfacing for air. "Is there anything else?"

"Yes." Otto fingered one final letter. "The executor of the estate, Willem Krause, wants to meet us all to read Mum's last will and testament."

"Ugh. I don't want anything," Ingrid said, pushing away from the table.

Dieter ignored her outburst. "There's so much still to do. Are we the only benefactors, Otto?"

"I presume so. Perhaps grandchildren? You two got any children tucked away?" Otto asked with a smile on his face.

"Don't be ridiculous," Ingrid said.

"Not very likely, brother," Dieter said, pushing his eyebrows up to emphasise his point.

Ingrid, Otto and Dieter walked into Lüderitz town centre, about half a mile away along Bismarck Road with the imposing Gothic stone architecture of Felsenkirche towering above them on their left. The newspaper offices were situated along Hafen Street, close to the harbour and Ingrid's hotel. A blue sky above provided an artist's canvas for swooping and shrieking white seagulls. Out over the unusually calm blue ocean the distant grey fogbank clung to the water like scum.

"I'm going to nip to the library quickly," Dieter announced, breaking the awkward silence.

Otto felt his annoyance surfacing. "For God's sake, Dieter. We're arranging Mum's funeral!"

Dieter looked at him innocently. "I'll only be a few minutes. I'll see you at the buchter's offices."

Otto shook his head and sighed noisily, looking towards Ingrid for support.

"Don't look at me, Otto, what do you expect from your brother?"

The Lüderitzbuchter was produced out of a small and unassuming building near Woermann House, very close to the harbour. The pungent smell of freshly gutted fish wafted through the air as the concentration of seagulls intensified. At dusk the fishing fleet would return with holds brimful of Atlantic hake and rock lobster caught in the fertile waters fed by the cold Benguela Current, but for now the quayside was relatively deserted.

Behind a plain wooden desk in the office sat a woman in her fifties, greying brown hair tied up in a bun, prominent moles on her cheeks and nose.

"Can I help you?" she asked in a heavily guttural accent.

"We'd like to place this funeral notice in the buchter please," Otto said.

Ingrid hovered slightly behind him, studying the plastic chairs and cheap framed prints hanging off-kilter on the walls with a look of disapproval on her face. The woman took the notice from Otto and glanced at it.

"Oh my, it's for Ute Adermann!" She looked up at Otto with wide, doleful eyes. "You must be her children. I am so sorry about your ma."

Otto smiled and nodded. "Thank you."

"She was so well liked in our little town." The woman paused and frowned to emphasise her point. "So well liked. Your father too, Ernst, what wonderful parents you had. You must all be very sad."

"Thank you." Otto smiled politely. "We are, of course."

"My name is Wilma. I knew your mum really well; we played bridge together every week down at Goerkehaus. What a shock. This whole business in the garden… what a shock! It's bound to be a Herero, mark my words." Wilma sat and shook her head in disbelief, eyes fixed on Otto's face. Then she straightened and glanced at Ingrid. "You must be Ingrid. And you must be…" She thought for a moment, sizing Otto up. "Dieter?"

"I am Otto, but Dieter is here too."

Wilma's face lit up with joy. "Ah, Otto!" she clasped her hands together and looked at him maternally. "Your ma spoke so much about you… so much… I think you must have been her favourite. You were her life, you know."

Wilma seemed oblivious to the discomfort that Otto felt rising within him, heightened by Ingrid stiffening beside him. He nodded in silence, smiling politely.

"I'm sure I was not her favourite."

Wilma tutted. "Oh you were, and just look at you."

Ingrid sighed beside Otto, deepening his embarrassment.

"Is it too late to place Mum's funeral notice in tomorrow's buchter?" Otto asked.

Wilma inhaled deeply and studied the funeral notice again down the length of her nose. "I will make sure this is in tomorrow's edition, don't you worry."

"I appreciate that very much." Otto paused, glancing at Ingrid. "We appreciate it."

"I see the funeral is on the 20th of April?" Wilma raised her eyebrows.

"Yes?"

"Ernst would have been so proud, if you know what I mean." Wilma was shaking her head as she studied Otto and Ingrid. "So proud. He would have thought it an honour befitting the Adermann family."

Otto had no idea what Wilma meant but smiled and nodded, as did Ingrid. They paid for the notice and left amidst further effusive compliments and gushy rhetoric from Wilma.

"What the hell was that all about?" Ingrid asked as they stepped outside, immersed once again in the shriek of gulls and the fishy harbour smell. "Oh, prodigal son…"

"Stop it," Otto said, walking into her purposely. "I have no idea."

There was still no sign of Dieter so on their way home they stopped first at Goerkehaus to discuss the funeral tea, followed by Felsenkirche to hand in the order of service and choice of hymns.

"The wind's changing," Otto remarked, turning his face towards the coastline. "Let's go home and watch the home movies I found. Dieter might be there." He rubbed his hands with childlike glee.

"It'll not bring back happy memories," Ingrid said tersely.

"Why ever not?"

Ingrid looked deeply into his eyes with a steadiness that she had not maintained since her arrival.

"Because there aren't any."

TWELVE

Back in the living room Otto felt as though he was thirteen again, holding the weight and substance of the twelve-inch metal film reel in his hands as he clicked it onto the rectangular spindle. Everything came flooding back: the somewhat vinegary smell of the film stock suffused with stale cigarette smoke; the shiny, smooth texture of the 16mm film emulsion, perforated down each margin; the heavy solidity of the Bell & Howell Filmosound projector with its two reel-arms extended above its head in a gesture of surrender, amid a faint odour of machine oil.

"I don't know why the hell you want to watch these films," Ingrid said, hugging herself defensively as she sat on the brown velvet sofa, staring straight ahead, feet up on the coffee table.

"This first one is marked 1940s," Dieter said, studying the rusty metal film can. "I can vividly remember Dad wandering around with his black and silver box camera wherever he went."

"He loved it, didn't he? He wouldn't go anywhere without it," Otto said.

"Do you remember when he nearly dropped it in the sea filming a seal on that boat trip to Penguin Island?" Dieter said and began to laugh. "That was the only time I ever heard him swear".

Ingrid snorted from the sofa. "He was no saint, you know."

Dieter just stared at Otto and raised his eyebrows in silence, leaving it to Otto to challenge her.

"What do you mean?"

She looked away and shook her head, closing up, pulling her arms even tighter around herself. Otto and Dieter exchanged a that's just Ingrid look as Otto began to thread the film around the sprockets and over the rollers. He swung the hinged lens housing out to open the film gate and carefully laid the film between the aperture and pressure plates.

"You were always the projectionist when we watched films," Dieter remarked. "Can you still remember how to thread it?"

"I loved working with this old projector." Otto chuckled and nodded. "It's all coming back to me. I just hope it still works."

Finally, Otto led the white film leader beneath the lamp housing and threaded it onto the eight-spoke metal take-up reel. He ran his eyes across the film loops, checking that all sprocket guards were shut, that the film was in the channel continuously and that no loops were too big or too small. As he recalled, it could be a fiddly business at times.

"Right, draw the curtains please, we're good to go!" Otto announced with more than an ounce of excitement in his voice.

Dieter pulled the curtains shut and the room was immersed in semi-gloom. Otto twisted the control knob and the projector began to whirr and click rhythmically like a well-oiled toy train as it pulled the film over its rotating guides, rollers and sprockets. The empty take-up reel turned quickly while the front reel loaded with film rotated languidly, in no hurry to reveal its secrets. Otto breathed a sigh of relief when the main lamp burst into life and projected a bright but fuzzy square image onto the white sheet tacked to the curtains.

"Focus, Otto!" Dieter shouted.

"I'm looking, I'm looking," Otto mumbled as he searched for the focus knob beneath the lens.

"That's better, but there's no sound."

"They're silent films, I'm afraid. No soundtrack."

They stared at the flickering images on the screen, black and white moving portraits of yesterday, scratches and marks on the emulsion that constantly appeared and disappeared on the screen in the blink of an eye, like sparks in a log fire.

The little toddler runs across the lawn, bare torso and feet, wearing large frilly bloomers. He holds a small metal bucket in one hand, his face turning constantly to smile at the camera. The journey ends at a small tank of water where a tall girl of perhaps ten holds a hosepipe from which a stream of water flows. The girl is wearing a floral-patterned white dress, her light brown hair tied up in an Alpine ponytail. The toddler holds the bucket out to be filled, and the girl obliges before turning and smiling mischievously at the camera. Suddenly she directs the hose at the toddler.

The smaller child appears to shriek with laughter, turns and runs off rapidly, spilling all the water from the bucket. The camera pans unevenly to follow the toddler, creating a jerky picture on the screen. The toddler stops beside a woman, hugs her white apron worn over a dark full-length dress, and receives a reassuring embrace from the smiling woman, stocky with brown hair tightly tied in a bun on top of her head.

"That's Mum!" Dieter said, pointing to the screen. "Look how young she looks. My God, she must be... what...?"

Otto shrugged, mesmerised by the sight of his mother looking so youthful and full of life, radiant and happy, her future ahead of her, her family still young and dependent on her. It seemed surreal to accept that she was no longer with them.

"Thirtyish," Otto ventured.

The toddler turns, reinvigorated, and runs across the lawn again, back to the water tank where the bucket is obligingly refilled before the hose is again turned onto the little child's naked chest. Apparent shrieks of laughter ensue with constant glances at the camera, seeking affirmation, all in period silence with water splashing everywhere. Then the small child runs energetically back to Mother, little legs pumping like pistons on a miniature steam engine.

The background to this repetitive cycle of action is a modest but well-kept timber-framed house – dark, stout beams separated by white limewashed render, adorned with populated flower boxes beneath the small windows and tiles on the steeply gabled roof. Lace curtains are tied back in each window.

"I presume that's you, Ingrid," Otto said as the tall girl holding the hosepipe appeared on the screen again.

Ingrid sat with her arms folded and legs crossed, staring at the screen, unresponsive.

"And the little guy must be you, Dieter," Otto added.

"I suppose so."

"I like your frilly undershorts, Dieter," Otto said. "Very becoming."

"More than you know," Otto replied.

The image jumps once, twice and suddenly changes to a seaside location, a beach with bathers in striped bodysuits, women additionally wearing small skirts and hats. Most of the men are sporting pencil moustaches and very short hair. The wind is blowing, evidenced by umbrellas straining against the force of the prevailing sea breeze. The image jolts up and down as the cameraman walks towards the water's edge where small waves roll perpetually across the smooth beach sand. Two children in costumes lie side by side on the wet sand that glistens in the sunlight, their feet pointing towards the sea. The girl's swimming cap is pulled tightly over her head, pushing one ear down awkwardly.

Otto laughed. "Oh Ingrid, someone should have helped you with your cap."

A modest wave approaches and breaks over the children's legs, prompting the little child to stand and run up the beach towards dry sand, arms held stiffly in protest. Then in a familiar choreographed cycle, the toddler runs back to the water's edge and resumes his position on the sand next to the older girl. She looks at the toddler with a crooked smile and wipes a wet, sandy hand across his cheek, leaving a smear. The little child prepares to retaliate when suddenly another wave breaks over their legs, sending the toddler into action again, sprinting up the beach.

"Any idea where this is?" Otto asked.

Dieter shook his head. "I don't remember any of this."

"Somewhere on the Baltic coast, I think, perhaps near Wismar. We used to go every year," Ingrid said unexpectedly, without looking away from the screen.

The seaside frolics end and are abruptly replaced with images of uniformed men marching down a city street lined with cheering crowds. The men, who are unarmed but wearing double-breasted military-style shirts and ties, caps, boots and armbands bearing swastikas, march six abreast and at least fifteen to twenty deep. People lining the street smile broadly and children sitting on their shoulders wave swastikas and cheer. Suddenly the picture jumps, followed by a clear white image on the screen.

The projector emitted a jarring sound, like a pneumatic drill.

"Oh shit!" Otto said.

"What's happened?" Dieter asked.

"The film's snapped."

"Can you fix it?"

"It'll need to be spliced but I don't know where the splicer is. I'll just thread it through and tape the broken ends together for now," Otto explained as he examined the damage.

Ingrid sighed. "I'll make tea."

"I fancy a scotch. Want one Otto?" Dieter said, standing up and walking off purposefully to his bedroom.

"Mmmmmh. What you got?"

"Twenty-five-year-old Strathisla."

"Would you like one, Ingrid?" Otto asked.

Ingrid shot a look at Otto. "I don't think I'm included."

"Don't be silly," Otto said.

Having laced the broken film through the projector again Otto taped the jagged edges of film together and wound up the slack on the take-up reel. He ran his eyes over the threaded film carefully.

"Did you see those swastikas?" Otto asked.

"There was a war going on, remember," Ingrid replied from the kitchen. "They were everywhere."

Of course, Otto realised. "Right, we're good to go, take your seats. While you're pouring, Ingrid will have a scotch too, Dieter."

Dieter reclaimed his seat with three tumblers held in a tripod grip, bottle in the other hand. He looked up at Ingrid.

"Scotch, Ingrid?"

"No thanks." She sat back and sipped her cup of tea.

Dieter looked at Otto and bared his teeth slightly. Otto turned the projector on.

The men march right past the camera, chins up, chests pushed out proudly, hands stiffly by their sides. The column seems never-ending. As they pass by, Mother can be seen on the pavement opposite, a little toddler sitting awkwardly on her shoulders, waving a swastika flag and clapping. Beside her stands the tall girl in a white dress, hair tied back in two pigtails with a ribbon on each, looking as though she is dressed for Sunday church.

"Jesus, that must be me, waving a fucking swastika!" Dieter said in horror. "At what looks like a brownshirt parade of all things!"

"Mum looks a bit… chubby," Otto remarked.

A brief silence followed as they studied Mother's swollen profile.

"She looks pregnant, actually," Dieter said.

"Don't be daft, Dieter, I wasn't born until 1948."

"I'm just saying, she does look pregnant. Don't you agree?"

Otto stared at the screen and savoured a mouthful of Strathisla, letting the smooth malty flavours caress his tongue, front, back and sides. Mother did indeed look pregnant, but that could not be. He did not understand.

"Can you remember, Ingrid?" Otto asked.

"No."

Following behind the proud young men is a troop of lithesome girls in white shorts, gym shoes and dark sleeved tops. The crowd cheers with evident enthusiasm and waves flags with renewed vigour. The camera pans wildly to the right and reveals a full-length swastika banner hanging from a lamppost. Further down the road more of these are visible, receding into the distance. The cameraman lingers on this view for several seconds.

Suddenly the film jumps and the image changes to Mother cradling a baby swathed in white. Bobbing about her eagerly is a little girl, smiling and attentive to the infant's occasional cry.

"Who the hell is that?" Otto asked, placing a hand over his lower face and leaning towards the screen.

Dieter stared at the flickering images that reflected cyan hues on his face, casting only a furtive glance towards Ingrid.

A family is assembled in the garden of the timber-framed house, appearing to line up for a photo opportunity. They are formally dressed, several of them older, and a handful of young children run around rolling hoops. In the centre of the group Mother is holding the baby with a broad smile on her face. Someone with grey hair and an extravagant moustache walks around refilling broad-rimmed champagne glasses, joking with guests, his lined face wrinkling at regular intervals as he laughs.

"It's a christening!" Otto blurted.

The tall girl appears, smiling proudly, wearing flat-soled black pumps with short white socks and a wide knee-length pleated skirt and summery blouse. Mother bends over and hands the baby to her carefully, showing her how to support its head and cradle it in her arms.

"That's got to be you, Ingrid," Otto said excitedly. "So who is the baby you're holding? You must remember."

Ingrid stared at the screen, tight-lipped, her cup of tea hanging at a dangerous angle in her grasp. Dieter took a large mouthful of scotch.

The tall girl smiles at the camera and traces her fingertip around the baby's mouth, eliciting a pout and an attempt to suckle it. Then the little girl sidles up to her. She is wearing a summer dress and flat-soled shoes with short socks, just like her sister. She kisses the baby, whose face is almost at the same height as her head, turning frequently to smile at the camera and shade her eyes from the bright sunlight.

"But... isn't that you, Dieter?" Otto said, flabbergasted. "Why are you wearing a dress all of a sudden?"

"Is that me?" Dieter chuckled before turning to face Otto. "You see, even then I knew I looked better in a dress." Dieter laughed, alone.

Suddenly a very unsteady and jerky image of Mother, Father, the tall girl holding the baby and the little girl pressing against Father's legs appears on the screen. They are all smiling effusively as though being encouraged by the cameraman, screwing up their eyes against the harsh sunlight, trying to appear spontaneous. It is an Adermann family portrait in the early 1940s. Two soldiers wearing Wehrmacht helmets with rifles slung over their shoulders are framed in the background by abundant hydrangeas and rose bushes around the quaint timber-framed house, huddled over a cigarette and a match.

"I don't understand what's going on here." Otto rubbed one temple. "Who is that baby?"

"Why are there soldiers in our garden?" Dieter said.

The picture jumps abruptly to Father in a dark three-piece suit posing beside a rounded black Mercedes 170H, tipping his homburg hat to the camera and smiling broadly, revealing his teeth. In one hand he grips a large medical bag. Suddenly the younger girl runs into view, barefoot and wearing a striped dress. She hugs Father's legs. He pats her head fondly but retains his erect pose, glancing down only briefly at the little girl who continues to squeeze and tug at his leg, looking eagerly up at his face but without eliciting a response.

"I have to go!" Ingrid announced, standing up abruptly.

"It's almost finished anyway," Otto protested, glancing at the front reel which was now spinning quickly with less than half an inch of film wound onto its core.

"Then I won't miss anything."

"What's the matter?"

Ingrid sighed. "I've had enough."

"Do you want a taxi?"

Ingrid was already in the kitchen, gathering her coat and handbag. Her teacup rattled in the sink. "I'll walk."

Dieter half-turned, disinterested, to watch Ingrid, who was evidently flustered and determined to leave the house immediately.

Grainy images of the tall girl in a white dress playing tennis on a scruffy court with a bunch of similarly attired girls, smiling and laughing, fill the screen. The tennis racket looks far too big in her hands and appears to unbalance her whenever she swings it at the ball, eliciting a big smile on her face that reveals large adult incisors.

Within a few resolute strides Ingrid had reached the front door.

"Frans is coming around tomorrow to cut the camelthorn. Will we see you then?" Otto asked.

Ingrid breathed deeply and pursed her lips. "I don't know, Otto. Maybe."

With that she was gone.

The girls lob the tennis ball to each other tamely for a while, hitting many balls into the net. Two girls run into each other, bumping heads, causing one to bend over in tears. The picture becomes jerky as the cameraman approaches the crying girl, and then vanishes abruptly as the screen turns incandescent white.

"What's up with Ingrid?" Otto asked, turning the projector off.

"She's tense, isn't she?" Dieter agreed.

Otto frowned and scratched his forehead. "So that was Ingrid, the older girl, and then I thought you were the younger child…"

"More scotch?" Dieter offered.

Otto nodded, deep in thought. "But you… er… were definitely dressed as a girl at the christening, so it couldn't have been you."

Dieter pulled a face and held out the bottle of Strathisla.

Otto pushed his tumbler towards Dieter to be refilled. "That wasn't you, was it Dieter?"

"Which one?"

"The little girl in the dress."

Dieter smiled mischievously and angled his head, apparently weighing something up in his mind. "Perhaps it should have been."

"What do you mean by that?"

Dieter chuckled and fidgeted. He appeared uncomfortable. "Come on, Otto, don't you know?"

"Know what?"

Dieter's eyes held Otto's confidently, his mouth slightly open, hesitating just for a moment, while his legs bounced nervously. "I'm gay."

"What?" Otto thought he'd heard incorrectly.

"Always have been, just never could tell anyone while either Mum or Dad was alive." He paused. "Can you imagine?"

Otto stared at his brother, mouth agape. He wanted to say 'I don't believe it', but deep down he knew that this was not the case. He could see now that the pieces of the jigsaw had always been there but he had simply not fitted them together.

"Why didn't you tell me?"

"It's not that easy, you know."

"Why now, then?" Otto asked, wondering if it had simply been the Strathisla loosening his brother's tongue.

Dieter gesticulated casually at the screen. "It's all going to come out, isn't it?"

"What's going to come out?" Otto asked.

"You know, stuff."

"Does Ingrid know?"

Dieter shrugged and pulled a face. "No idea. Women have a tendency to detect these things, though."

Otto wiped his hand across his face. "I need that scotch now." He gulped at his drink and closed his eyes momentarily. What should he say to his brother? Was it a reason for celebration, for commiseration, for empathy? He eventually settled on, "Jesus, Dieter, are you happy?"

Dieter stared back at Otto and drank from his tumbler. "Sometimes."

Otto finished his drink, welcoming the warm rush. "So who was the baby in the film?" He turned to glance at the kitchen window. It was dark outside and he thought about the yawning, broken hole beneath the fallen camelthorn. "It was early 1940s. Definitely not me. Was it you?"

Dieter poured more scotch. "I honestly don't know." He met Otto's eyes. "Honestly, I don't. But then again… I don't remember anything from that film we just watched." He jerked his thumb towards the screen behind him.

"Why do you think Ingrid left so suddenly? She's been acting strangely ever since she arrived," Otto said.

"She's always been like that."

"No." Otto shook his head. "This is different. She didn't even want to watch the films."

Otto held Dieter's thoughtful gaze, pondering the enigmatic images revealed moments earlier on the screen. The scotch, so avidly swallowed to assuage the shock and disarray, was beginning to slow Otto's brain.

"I don't mean to ignore what you told me just now," Otto said. "I simply don't know what to say."

"You don't have to say anything. I'm OK with it, and I'm just glad you know now."

Dieter watched his brother in silence. He could see Otto shifting uncomfortably under his gaze and he felt for him. It must have been a shock, yet he thought Otto took it remarkably well. He was, after all, a GP and no doubt used to dealing with all manner of awkward situations.

"Let's watch One Million BC!" Dieter suggested with sudden enthusiasm, forcing a smile. He saw Otto's face light up. "I always loved that, campy dinosaurs and cavemen. God, what a laugh!"

Otto chuckled. "You know, as a teenager I had a thing for Carol Landis in her animal skins."

"Come on," Dieter said, "it'll be a great distraction."

"OK." Otto smiled broadly.

Retrieving the enormous 2,000-foot steel reel of film Otto began to mount it onto the spindle.

"Do you remember how we used to watch this on Saturday nights?" Dieter said. He recalled eating sandwiches with cold roast pork and pickles, salami and white asparagus. Father would drink pilsner, the rest of them water. It had been one of the few Hollywood movies they ever saw as youngsters, and they loved it.

"It's coming easier this time," Otto said as he slid the film over the rollers, sprockets and guides. "I think my fingers are remembering."

Dieter poured more scotch for Otto and himself and paused beside his brother, hand on his shoulder. "I'm sorry I never told you, Otto."

Otto looked up from the projector and met Dieter's eyes.

"As your big brother I was afraid I'd disappoint you," Dieter added softly.

"It'll be our secret until you choose to tell Ingrid," Otto said. Otto's little conspiratorial smile and the honour intimated by the clink of their tumblers evoked a deep blush from Dieter. He felt guilty withholding from his brother what he had learned about Inez. Worst of all, he did not even know why he was keeping the secret, and he was doing it for Ingrid who was like a stranger to him these days.

"What's wrong?" Otto said.

Dieter responded with forced nonchalance. "Nothing. Why?"

"You're blushing," Otto said playfully, swaying slightly from the Strathisla.

Dieter felt the heat intensify in his face again.

"Just kidding," Otto said and, to Dieter's relief, turned the projector on.

One Million BC bursts onto the screen in streaky black and white: prehistoric studio swamps, cardboard boulders, scantily clad, clean-shaven cavemen, jerky stop-motion dinosaurs and superimposed close-ups of common lizards. Tumak grunts and grapples his way past sabre-tooth tigers and dinosaurs, to his first kill. Forced to flee from the primitive and aggressive rock people tribe for standing up to the leader, he is chased by a mammoth to a cliff edge where he tumbles into a meandering studio stream.

"I love that part," Dieter yelled, laughing. "So camp." Tumak floats downstream on a log and when he reaches the hospitable and civilised shell people tribe, Loana, wearing only scanty animal skins, rescues him from the river.

Otto whistled approval. "She looks just as good as she did when I was fourteen."

Dieter did not comment. His eyes were not drawn to Loana, but to the chiselled dark features of the man whom she rescued.

Tumak staggers ashore and moves in with Loana's peaceful tribe, eventually saving them from the volcanic eruption that reshapes the prehistoric landscape, followed by Tumak's elevation to leader of the united tribes and his inevitable union with Loana.

Dieter clapped his hands and cheered in mock adulation. Otto switched the projector off, leaving the empty front reel rotating slowly until it finally came to rest. He chuckled in delight.

"It's still a great film," Otto enthused. "That Loana, phwoar! I used to dream about her."

"I'll level with you, Otto," Dieter said, leaning forward on one unsteady elbow, "Victor Mature was more my type, actually."

Dieter sensed a flicker of uncertainty cross Otto's face, as though he was unsure how to respond, what to say.

"You know, I read that Carole Landis committed suicide not many years after making this film," Otto said, looking back at and touching the reel of film.

"Yeah?" Dieter replied.

"She was only in her twenties," Otto said sombrely. "What a waste of a life, an amazing talent… and that pair of legs."

Dieter could not help but think about Inez and the inscription on her grave: Gone too soon. Yes, just like Carole Landis, what a waste. Worse still, he did not know why, and his guilt over keeping this from Otto was mounting, fast reaching that critical point at which he doubted he could contain it any longer.

Just then the phone rang. It was Sabine. She and Otto talked for some time and before long Dieter fell asleep on the sofa in the living room.

THIRTEEN

Frans cut an unattractive figure, especially in profile, Otto observed: a pendulous belly that hung over his belt; bulbous, fleshy arms dangling limply at his side and enormous flat feet to support it all. Despite it being morning, Frans' squint was noticeable and distracting. Otto decided that he would have to reconsider his diagnosis of latent exotropia.

A local Herero man wielding a piercingly noisy chainsaw carved through the camelthorn trunk, like a hot wire through Styrofoam, spraying wood chippings in a projectile arc into and around the gaping hole in the ground. It was windy and the wispy chippings were aerosolised by the stiffening south-wester.

Dieter and Otto watched with apprehensive interest, Dieter with his arms folded and Otto standing with his hands firmly planted on his hips. Neither had shaved and their eyes were cerise, indicative of the blood that surged and throbbed through their hungover heads.

"What's that smell?" Dieter asked, pulling a face as he sniffed the breeze.

The chainsaw had stopped momentarily as the Herero and a supervising tree surgeon planned the next cut.

"I don't know. It smells like…" Otto began.

"Shit?" Frans said, turning to face them.

"Yes."

Frans nodded. "That's what happens when the south-wester blows."

Otto found this counter–intuitively confusing because there was nothing but ocean out there. "But how?" he said.

"It's the smell of guano and seal dung from the islands offshore," Frans explained, pointing out over Lüderitz and beyond the harbour. "Halifax Island, just out there beyond Diaz Point, is laden with guano and a little further south are Wolf and Atlas Bays, home to huge Cape fur seal colonies." His belly wobbled as he chuckled. "Strong today, isn't it?"

"I don't remember ever going to those places," Dieter remarked.

"You can't, they're in the Sperrgebiet," Frans said.

"Is it still so dangerous to enter the Sperrgebiet?" Otto asked.

"Oh God ja," Frans said. "The worst crime in this country is to illegally possess a diamond from the Sperrgebiet. After that comes murder, a distant second."

"Are they still finding many diamonds?" Dieter asked.

"Enough. They find a lot on the sea bed these days – diamond diving – and they control that too."

Otto and Dieter stared at Frans. Otto was trying to imagine this wild west style of wilderness prospecting backed up by the most intense and heavy–handed security imaginable. He remembered that diamond wealth along the Skeleton Coast just south of Lüderitz had been immense at its height

"Nobody enters the Sperrgebiet without clearance and a security escort, and nobody leaves without being X–rayed," Frans said.

"X–rayed?" Dieter said.

Frans patted his ample belly. "To see if you've swallowed diamonds."

"Do they still shoot trespassers?" Dieter asked with a joking smile.

Frans did not smile back. "It has been known."

"Jesus!" Dieter said. "It's not 1885 anymore."

"So what? They run the show here," Frans retorted, raising his eyebrows. "Who's gonna stop them? The government looks the other way – diamonds are big business."

"Awkward for you surely… as a policeman?" Dieter said.

Frans chuckled. "No comment."

The chainsaw started up again and conversation was no longer possible. Wood chippings flew about, hoisted into the air by the breeze, like confetti at a wedding. After a few minutes a two-inch thick disc of camelthorn trunk had been cut. The tree surgeon and Frans placed it on the sandy soil and huddled over it, fingering the wood inquisitively. Dieter and Otto approached, standing over the two men.

"So you count the rings of the tree to determine its age?" Otto said.

"Uh-huh," Frans replied without looking up.

"One ring for every year?"

"Yup."

"Is it accurate?"

The tree surgeon, a man with a grizzled, bearded face and skin aged by the relentless Namibian sun, met Otto's gaze. "It's not bad – not perfect, but not bad. It's called dendrochronology and can date trees back even thousands of years, obviously using tests as well."

Otto could feel his apprehension rising. Soon they would be told exactly how old the camelthorn was, the tree that until now had represented nothing more to him than an extension of his playground as a child. The tree's age would give a reasonable idea of when the child's body was buried in the ground – deduced from the fact that the roots had covered the body. The potential implications of this annular ring count for his family were suddenly intensifying in his mind.

Frans and the bearded man counted in relative silence, pausing occasionally to confer and mumble to each other.

"How old is it?" Dieter asked, chewing nervously on his lower lip.

"It looks like about… forty-two years, thereabouts," Frans said, straightening up with a heave and a groan.

"Thereabouts?" Otto queried.

The bearded man stood up and approached them, holding the eighteen-inch wide disc of wood like a steering wheel in his cracked and grimy hands.

"You see here, some rings are very narrow, typical of reduced growth in a dry year. Of course this is the driest country in southern Africa remember, but even here there will be some climatic variation reflected in the tree's growth. You follow?" He looked up at Dieter and Otto, who nodded in unison. "Now, if a particular growth season is very variable, both wet and very dry, it is possible to get more than one narrow ring forming in one season." He raised his eyebrows. They nodded.

"So you could count two rings for only one year of growth?" Otto said.

"It can happen."

"So how can you be sure of its age then?" Otto asked.

"I can't, not without being able to compare with other samples that grew in the same area and same growth conditions and so on. But there are not exactly many trees in Lüderitz." He chuckled, looking around him across the barren desert landscape, punctuated mainly by black rocky outcrops and occasional green splashes of succulent growth.

"So you've counted forty-two rings?" Otto asked, running his finger across the surface of the roughly severed disc of camelthorn. In his mind he was counting back, imagining where the tree growth would have been when he was of the age to be climbing and playing in the tree with Dieter. Which ring of the tree had his arms and legs rubbed against in juvenile innocence? Which ring of the tree had skinned his knees?

"Forty-three, but I think that there are two insignificant rings that may well constitute one season. It would be from the year 1982 to 1983, just recently, when we had a severe drought in Lüderitz. If you look carefully at these outer rings here…" He pointed and dug his dirty fingernail into the wood pulp near the bark of the disc.

Otto was nodding and calculating in his mind. "So it was probably planted around… 1943?" He looked at Frans and the tree surgeon for confirmation.

Frans made a gesture with his hand. "More or less, give or take a few years either way. As far as I am aware this house was built in—"

"1946," Otto said.

"You say it so confidently, Otto, but you weren't even born then," Dieter mocked.

"But it was built in 1946, that's a fact."

"Ja, it is," Frans acknowledged.

Otto stared at the bearded man who seemed to hold in his hands the key to determining his family's involvement in the buried body. "Could this tree have been planted in or after 1946?"

The tree surgeon turned the wooden disc in his hands, once, twice, contemplating the patterns of rings surrounding the centre. "It is quite possible that there are other years represented further back that could be double growth rings from a single season, yes. We're only talking a year or two either way."

Otto's heart skipped a beat as a sensation of dread washed over him. He felt Frans' eyes studying him as he looked self-consciously at Dieter to judge his reaction.

"Christ, what does this mean?" Dieter said.

Frans stepped forward and slapped Dieter on the shoulder. "Ag, don't worry. This is just one part of the investigation and it doesn't prove anything. It just gives us an idea," he said, shrugging just one shoulder.

Frans thanked the tree surgeon, who left with his African chainsaw operator. The disc of wood now lay beside the fallen tree on a bed of wood chippings, fragments of a happy childhood now shredded and exposed to the world.

"Cuppa tea, Frans?" Otto asked.

"Coffee, please Otto. Black, two sugars."

Otto retreated into the house, lost in his thoughts. Dieter sat on the trunk of the camelthorn beside the gaping hole.

"Jesus, Frans, what does this all mean?" Dieter said, swinging his leg absently.

Frans inhaled. "I'll be honest, I think it means the tree was planted after the body was buried, or the tree was very small when the body was buried."

"Because large tree roots were covering the... er... body?"

83

"Ja, it wouldn't be possible to bury a body beneath the root system without cutting them, you know."

Dieter nodded, rubbing his chin pensively.

"How is Ingrid?" Frans asked.

Dieter guffawed slightly. "You're asking the wrong brother, Frans."

"Oh."

"Do we get poisonous scorpions here in Lüderitz?" Dieter asked, suddenly animated as his eyes met Frans'.

"Oh ja, some of the most poisonous scorpions in southern Africa live here in the desert. They like the dry climate, you know."

Dieter nodded. "What do they look like?"

"Well," Frans formed an imaginary ball with both hands, "the most dangerous scorpions in this area are from the same family, Parabuthus. There is one that's black and hairy with orange-brown legs – sometimes yellow – it's a monster, up to fifteen centimetres long!" Frans' eyes widened.

"And poisonous?"

"Very. Potentially lethal to humans."

Dieter thought back to Ingrid's comments in the cemetery.

"Can you tell which ones are poisonous?"

Frans scratched his stubbly chin. "They say that it depends on the size of the pincers. Big pincers means the scorpion needs them to kill its prey; small pincers suggests very lethal venom so the prey dies quickly."

"And this one?"

"Parabuthus has small pincers. It also hunts in the heat of the day – very unusual, that. He is one dangerous bugger and he likes places where sand and rock are found together." Frans swept his arm around in an arc. "Lüderitz is perfect."

Dieter studied Frans' blubbery jowls as he spoke and observed the sweat rings already visible beneath his armpits, despite the gusty south-wester.

"You know a lot about scorpions," Dieter remarked.

Frans chuckled. "You have to if you want to live around here. Man, I've even found them under my bed. Why do you ask, have you seen one?"

"No," Dieter replied evasively. "Just curious."

Otto emerged through the kitchen door. "Coffee's ready." Dieter rose quickly and placed a hand on Frans' arm as he began to move away. "Can I speak to you more about Inez sometime?"

"Ja sure, anytime."

"Not now, though."

"OK."

"And not here."

Frans frowned. "No problem."

Dieter maintained gentle pressure on Frans' arm for a moment. "Perhaps I can leave with you... after coffee?"

FOURTEEN

After coffee and an informal chat about what Otto and Dieter could remember of their childhoods at the house – which didn't seem to amount to much more than fragmented memories trapped by the usual significant associations with pain, joy and sadness – Dieter asked Frans for a lift to the library.

"Not again, Dieter," Otto sighed. "There's stuff we need to talk about."

"I have obligations to the business."

Otto shook his head. Frans kept his eyes on his feet.

"I'll be as quick as I can," Dieter said.

"Yeah, I've heard that before." Otto sounded frustrated. "I may as well go and see Ingrid."

"Want a lift?" Frans asked.

"No thanks. I'll walk."

"Where do you want to go?" Frans asked as his police car rolled gently downhill under its own momentum towards town.

"Don't mind. Somewhere I can buy you a beer." Dieter glanced at Frans. "Can you have one on duty?"

"I'm the chief – I'm sure I can make an exception. How about the Zum Sperrgebiet?"

"No, not there," Dieter said quickly, afraid of bumping into Ingrid.

"OK. The Bay View then?"

Dieter shrugged. Within a few minutes the car rolled up outside a low building decorated with a tinge of Teutonic colonial fussiness painted vivid blue. It was quiet inside, just one or two tables occupied by tourists on the veranda overlooking the harbour.

"Your usual, Chief?" the African barman asked with a broad smile, revealing flawless teeth.

"Thank you, Samuel. For you, Dieter?"

"Windhoek Export please."

They sat down with tall frosted glasses filled with frothy amber. A lone fishing vessel was chugging into the harbour, listing unhealthily to one side. Frans stared at it with curious eyes as he plunged his eager mouth into the froth. In the background the sound of Wham was as unobtrusive as lift music.

"What's it like in Hong Kong?" Frans asked.

"Busy," Dieter replied. "Full of people, colour, smells. Anything goes. It never rests." He shrugged. "I like it."

Frans studied Dieter's face closely. "Never married?"

Dieter shook his head with a wry grin creasing his cheeks. "What happened to Inez?"

Frans looked down at his meaty hands and traced patterns in the frost on his beer glass.

"I get the feeling you quite liked her?" Dieter added.

Frans leaned back in his rattan chair sheepishly, making it creak. "What has Ingrid told you?"

"Ingrid and I don't really speak."

"Why?"

"It's a long story going back many years. It's not relevant." Frans rubbed his chin with one hand. "Ja, I did like Inez. She was beautiful, just like Ingrid, tall, clever, and she loved rugby. We went to a school dance together in our final year."

Dieter's eyes wandered over Frans' bloated frame, wondering why such an attractive girl would go for a man like him. Perhaps Frans sensed this, for he shifted uncomfortably under Dieter's gaze.

"I wasn't always like this, you know – I was the rugby captain in those days." He paused. "Anyway, there were other people on the scene as well."

"How did she die?" Dieter asked, savouring the superior hoppy malt, a legacy of the German colonialists.

Frans leaned forwards and frowned. "You really don't know about any of this?"

Dieter just met his eyes without replying. It was embarrassing that such a significant aspect of their family history was unknown to both he and Otto. What did it say about his family? What did it imply about him?

Frans exhaled deeply as he prepared himself. "My father worked as a security officer for the diamond company, as you know, patrolling the Sperrgebiet. I used to think it was a great job when I was growing up – the diamond company was wealthy and powerful, and to work for them seemed inevitable in this little town. It was either that or become a fisherman."

They both drank beer simultaneously. In the harbour the listing vessel was mooring at the quayside with the help of a small gang of men.

"Inez met a man after we left school. He was from... er... Keetmanshoop, I think."

"I've heard of that town before."

"Your father used to have a practice there as well, dividing his time between Lüderitz and... er... that one."

"Oh yes." Dieter remembered. "Is that how Inez and this guy met?"

Frans shrugged. "Possibly. Anyway, they seemed to become serious, then they left town for a while, I don't know where they went, and then she came back."

"Without him?"

"I thought so. I was pleased that she was here again – I wasn't married yet you see – but she was not the same person she used to be."

Dieter blinked, trying to take in these extraordinary revelations about a sister he had, until two days ago, not even known existed. "In what way?" he asked.

Frans rubbed repeatedly at the skin below his eye. "She was… sad."

Dieter sensed an anticipatory aura of what was coming.

"As you know, being in the Sperrgebiet without proper authorisation – a permit, and often an escort as well – was strictly prohibited. Still is." Frans inhaled. "I quit smoking but, hell, I could do with a drag now." He drained his beer.

"Another?" Dieter offered, burning with apprehensive curiosity.

Frans held up one hand. "No."

"What happened?"

"My father found your sister's body in an abandoned building in Kolmanskop, a few miles from here."

"The old mining town?"

"Ja. It was in serious decline by the late 1940s and has been a ghost town for at least thirty years. There would have been a lot of empty houses even then, gradually being reclaimed by the desert."

"How did she die?" Dieter said softly, apprehensively.

"Both she and her... boyfriend... had been shot," Frans said.

Dieter's heartbeat pulsated in his ears. Even though he had never known Inez these details of a death in his immediate family shocked him.

"Suicide?"

Frans made a face. "Officially, ja, but it was a bit... messy for my liking. My father found a revolver at the scene but there were no good fingerprints on it."

"What are you saying?"

Frans squirmed uncomfortably, breaking eye contact and staring out at the quayside where the listing vessel was moored, surrounded by people with hands on their hips. As he was about to speak, the barman walked by and collected their empty glasses. "Another one, Chief?"

"No thanks, Samuel." He waited for Samuel to saunter away. "I'm not suggesting anything, but it always bothered me that it was not clear-cut. There was no suicide note and Sperrgebiet security were a law unto themselves in the old days – untouchable, you know. Were they shot because they were wandering around the Sperrgebiet? Was it a cover-up, or was it suicide?"

Dieter could see distant pain in Frans' eyes when he re-established eye contact. How ironic that this man had been so affected by the untimely death of Dieter's sister, mourning her for all these years while he, as a member of her family, had never even known about her existence.

"Could they have walked into the Sperrgebiet wanting to die, inviting it?" Dieter thought, aloud.

Frans raised his eyebrows and briefly unclasped his hands.

"Is that why you didn't become a diamond company employee?"

Frans looked at Dieter with unwavering eyes. "Absolutely. I even viewed my own pa differently after that. It was a terrible time for me."

"What about the people of Lüderitz? It's a small town."

Frans opened his hands, palms up, in a gesture of hopelessness.

"Officially it was suicide. Everyone mourned."

"Who was the man found with her?"

"I can't remember his name."

Dieter placed a clenched fist against his lips as he sank into deep thought. Was it merely shame that had resulted in Inez's identity and existence being banished from the family albums? But what could have driven her to such drastic and desperate measures?

"Your parents never told you any of this?" Frans said, a look of disbelief visible on his face.

Dieter shook his head dolefully. "No." A brief vision of his dream appeared for a moment: the rolled-up carpet, the shadowy faces, the feeling of culpability and that haunting fear of imminent discovery.

Frans glanced at his watch. "I must go, Dieter, I'm expecting a call at one o'clock."

Dieter continued to press his fist against pursed lips. "I'd like to go to Kolmanskop, if that's possible?" he said suddenly.

"Of course. We need permits but I can arrange that. Just tell me when and how many people." Frans stood up with difficulty, squeezing his belly past the chair backs. "Listen, man, I'm really sorry to be the one to tell you such terrible things. Can I give you a lift home?"

Dieter looked up but remained seated. "I'd like to walk, thanks Frans. On your way out perhaps you could ask Samuel to bring me another Export."

"Ja, sure." Frans lingered, his fingers still on the rim of his chair back. "One thing you might all have forgotten as you've lived away from here for so long: Thursday, tomorrow, is fresh vegetable day in the town."

Dieter raised his eyebrows. "Fresh vegetable day?"

"Ja, once a week fresh veg and fruit is trucked in from Swakopmund. It goes quickly, so if you want something…" He shrugged and rapped his fingers on the back of the chair in front of him.

"Jesus, fresh vegetables once a week?"

"The desert hasn't gotten any smaller since you left, Dieter. The closest town with proper links to the outside world is over five hundred miles away."

Dieter considered his empty beer glass in disbelief. "So why do people live here, Frans?"

"You mean apart from the diamonds?"

Dieter pulled a face.

"In my experience," Frans began, looking out of the window at the fishing boat, "people live here either to lose themselves, or to find themselves."

Dieter followed his gaze and both men stared at the increasing activity building around the damaged fishing boat.

"And you, Frans?"

Frans hesitated. "I haven't decided yet."

Dieter felt drained, emotionally exhausted. He was supposed to be here to mourn and bury his mother, but with just days to go his mind could not be further from her funeral at that moment. How could he continue to keep this secret from Otto?

FIFTEEN

The Zum Sperrgebiet was the model of a clean and generically designed chain hotel: deep-pile blue carpeting woven with the hotel crest, square oak reception desk and gleaming chrome and alloy lighting. Barry Manilow softened the airwaves melodiously at the perfect volume.

Otto found Ingrid in the lounge, reading a book through fashionable plus one dioptre readers perched halfway down her nose. She was clearly surprised to see Otto, who slumped uninvited into the empty space beside her on the fleur-de-lys patterned sofa.

"Otto!"

He smiled and stretched his arm out across the back of the sofa. "Morning."

He imagined that in some families he would have leaned forward and kissed her on the cheek, perhaps a little embrace, her hand on his arm briefly, her posture opening up to reassure him that he was welcome. Ingrid carefully marked her place, closed the book and pulled the readers off her nose.

"I've never seen you wearing reading glasses," Otto said.

"We're not getting younger, Otto. It happens to the best of us." Otto nodded and surveyed the room in which they sat: potted green ferns – quite out of place in Lüderitz – and framed landscapes of desert scenery and sculpted sand dunes on the neutral walls.

"It looks nice here."

"It's OK," Ingrid said, making a face. "Definitely not four star, as they claim." She studied Otto for a moment. "So, to what do I owe this honour?"

Otto inhaled. "Well, you didn't come to the house, Frans has been and gone, Dieter's at the library…"

Ingrid tutted and rolled her eyes.

"…So I decided to find you."

"Aaaah," Ingrid said, but it sounded insincere. "Should we order tea, or something stronger?"

Otto glanced at his watch. "Why don't we walk?"

"It's blowing, isn't it?"

"Yeah, but it's not unpleasant. Let's look around the old town again."

Five minutes later they stepped out into Göring Street, Ingrid in a knee-length grey coat with matching fur trim and a charcoal Russian fox-fur hat. As they approached the square colonial monstrosity of Woermann House she unexpectedly hooked her arm around Otto's elbow.

"What's on your mind?" she asked, curling her nose. "God, it smells out here."

The wind was constant with occasional sharp gusts that could be surprisingly strong.

"Frans says it's the smell of guano and seal dung being blown this way on the south-wester."

"Jesus, give me the Central Park pigeons any day."

They crossed to Hafen Street, which flanked the harbour. The lone, listing fishing boat moored forlornly at the quayside caught Otto's eye as he recoiled slightly from the fishy smell of the harbour, effortlessly overwhelming that of the guano.

"I'm sorry your marriage didn't work out," Otto said.

"Which one?" Ingrid retorted with a curl in the corner of her mouth.

"All of them, I suppose," Otto said. "You OK?"

Ingrid laughed cynically, dismissively. "God, yes. I've been through far worse. Growing up in our family prepared me for dealing with rejection in many forms."

"Now that sounds like a confession."

She glanced at him, her eyes unwavering. "I am not the one who should confess."

Otto was pleased just to get Ingrid talking, even though conversation with her often took unexpected twists. The last time he remembered discussing her divorce from Newman she managed to bring up his Morris Minor car, his exorbitant university fees for six years in Cape Town, and Dieter's all-expenses–paid business course in Cologne for four years, including an apartment on Taubenstrasse. She reminded him that even as the eldest child all she got was a secretarial course in Swakopmund for eighteen months and an engagement ring from Frederick. There was never any benefit to pointing out that she had not wanted to go to university and that she had in fact been desperate to marry Frederick, kicking and screaming about having to go as far as Swakopmund to study. She had even forsaken her graduation ceremony to leave by boat from Cape Town on a three week honeymoon cruise bound for her new home in New York.

"And who exactly should confess?" Otto asked.

"You been talking to your brother?" Ingrid asked.

"About what?"

She shrugged. Otto stopped and stared down a finger of land, a peninsula that extended the length of the harbour into the bay. The proximal end was a haven of factory buildings and warehouses, probably fisheries and processing plants, people and forklifts swarming in all directions.

"I think that's Shark Island beyond the harbour."

"Uh-huh," Ingrid said, disinterested.

"That's where Mum scattered Dad's ashes after we left."

"Is that where you're taking me?" Ingrid asked.

"Another time. I want to go somewhere quieter," Otto said, resuming his stride. "It looks very busy around those warehouses."

They turned a corner. Straight ahead would take them into Diaz Street and right past the front of the Bay View Hotel.

"Let's go up here," Otto suggested as they turned sharply into Bismarck Street. "Why did you not attend Dad's funeral?" he asked.

Ingrid adjusted her arm in his. "You know, Otto, I didn't really see eye to eye with Dad. We had our differences, it was no secret; he clearly favoured you boys, that was no secret either…" She paused for effect. Otto ignored the bait. "We just… drifted apart. Living in New York just made it easier."

"That's all?" It always amazed Otto how trivial the causes of lifelong feuds could be, especially in families.

"God, look at this old relic," Ingrid said, stopping to admire the Deutsche Afrika Bank building, now, as the plaque proclaimed, a national museum. "Makes you realise that this dump of a town was once quite prosperous, in its day."

An imposing building of typical German colonial architectural design – chiselled stone blocks to the first floor, supporting a square corner turret and gabled upper structure painted in vibrant white and bottle green to match the tiled roof – it was eye-catching, complete with security bars that had endured the corroding forces of nature for eight decades.

"It upset Mum deeply, you know," Otto said.

Ingrid stiffened and withdrew her arm suddenly. "Mum knew exactly how I felt about Dad, and why. I don't believe she ever expected that I would attend his funeral."

"But something must have happened between you two?"

"Lots of things happened, Otto, but they're in the past now, dead and buried."

"But not forgotten?" Otto said.

She looked at him and narrowed her eyes. "Don't bring them up again."

They resumed walking, now apart with no physical contact, though almost in step with each other.

"Let's go down here, I think I hear waves crashing on the rocks," Otto suggested as they turned into Nachtigall Street, which led them to one of Lüderitz's rugged shorelines.

It was as though they were walking down the western edge of the central spur of a letter W. The blue bay separating them from a rocky headland called False Island – site of Bartholomew Diaz's centuries old beacon at Diaz Point – was spitting white waves under the relentless south-wester.

Otto wanted to press the point and ask Ingrid why she seemed to harbour such animosity towards her family, but decided at the last moment to draw back. If he upset Ingrid she might just leave, something she had done before. He wanted her to stay for Mother's funeral, and there was also that unfinished business at the house.

"Do you want to know what they found with the tree this morning?" Otto asked.

Ingrid looked at him sharply as salty spray from a wave

crashing into the rocks sprinkled over them. "I suppose."

"They cut into the trunk and then counted the rings to establish its age."

"Frans?"

"There was a tree surgeon there as well."

"And?"

Otto glanced at Ingrid's eager face. It was the most interested and animated he had seen her since disturbing her reading at the hotel.

"Forty-two years, give or take a few either way."

"So, that makes it about 19… 43?" Her face lit up. "Well, that's OK, we weren't even in Lüderitz yet."

"It's approximate, Ingrid. There are such things as double annular rings in some years, apparently, so the tree could be younger than that."

They stopped and looked out across the angry waters of the bay, steaming and frothing like a cauldron on the boil.

"What does Frans think?" Ingrid asked.

Otto began to walk slowly with the bay now on his right-hand side, crashing waves sending spray into the air against an arid, rocky backdrop framed by towering sand dunes, creating a surreal scene of contrasts.

"He reckons that it would still fit with the body being buried either before or soon after the tree was planted, because the largest camelthorn roots had grown over the skeleton." Otto tried to engage Ingrid's gaze. "Don't you remember anything, Ingrid? You must have been at least… fourteen or so?"

"Twelve when we arrived in Lüderitz." She drew her shoulders up momentarily. "Ever tried fitting into a new school in a small, godforsaken place like this, as a pubertal adolescent? I remember exactly how old I was."

She walked on, hands now pushed into the pockets of her coat, her furry Russian hat being blown by the swirling breeze that threatened to unseat it.

"You must have missed your friends," Otto sympathised, sensing a crack in the door, the tiniest of opportunities to connect with his sister.

"I didn't like Hamburg – snobby people at my school. But there was no-one here like me." She stopped and looked around, sweeping an arm for effect. "Look at this place, trapped in its colonial past still, nearly a hundred years on, like a living museum."

"I've always wondered – why did Mum and Dad come here?" Otto asked.

"God knows. Dad came first and we followed the next year. It took five weeks to get here by boat and I was seasick all the way." Ingrid turned to Otto and made a face.

Otto, being the youngest and born in Lüderitz, had never felt the schism of being separated from his homeland like the others. He didn't even know the stories about the great migration. They were never openly spoken about.

After a few minutes of walking in silence, enduring the wind and the spray off the churning sea, Otto said, "There's something I really must ask you, Ingrid."

She looked at him, unimpressed. "As long as it's not about Dad or your brother."

A seagull swooped dangerously close and they both instinctively took evasive action.

"Who was that baby in the movies last night?"

"Otto, please."

"Do you know?"

"Did you talk to your brother?"

"Does he know?"

She hesitated. "I don't think he was old enough to remember."

"It couldn't have been me, it was eight to ten years too early."

Silence as Ingrid's eyes stared straight ahead.

"It could've been Dieter, I reckon, but then there would be four children… too many of us."

The wind suddenly gusted and both Otto and Ingrid were temporarily unbalanced.

"Why the big secret? What is going on, for God's sake?"

Otto stopped but Ingrid continued walking on down the rough coastal track, sea battering the rocks to her right and arid, stubborn desert rock heaped up to her left. The image obscurely brought to Otto's mind an iconic scene from the recent film adaptation of The French Lieutenant's Woman.

"Has the baby in the movie got anything to do with the body in the garden, Ingrid?" Otto shouted defiantly into the howling wind, feeling his heart speed up as he spoke, fearing the worst.

She did hear him because she stopped, half-turned and met his eyes assuredly. "No, Otto, nothing at all!"

Otto raised his arms in a gesture of helplessness. "So you do remember something?"

Ingrid began to walk again.

"We're going to watch another reel tonight. I will find out what's going on," Otto said, raising his voice against the wind and the waves to bridge the growing gap between them. "Let's do it together, as a family."

She kept walking.

"Where are you going?" Otto shouted as another arc of spray peppered his face.

Ingrid turned, her face stony, eyes set and unyielding. "I need time to think."

Otto watched as she walked away, almost mechanically, one foot in front of the other. He shook his head. Hard as he tried, it was very difficult to understand Ingrid. What was it? Was she merely stubborn? Was she frightened? Was she traumatised?

Of one thing he was now certain: she knew something.

SIXTEEN

Otto unwound about four feet of film leader from the front steel reel mounted on the projector, and began to methodically thread it around the sprockets and rollers along the film channel, pausing once to drink from a tumbler of scotch.

"She won't come," Dieter said, drawing the curtains.

The last Otto had seen of Ingrid was as she walked away from him, heading nowhere. That was many hours ago.

"She might," Otto muttered.

"She's not interested, Otto; she doesn't want to be here."

Otto closed the film gate and wound the excess leader onto the take-up reel. "Ingrid says you probably don't remember anything from the home movies we watched last night."

Dieter flopped onto the sofa, tumbler in hand. "I don't."

Otto studied his watch. It was eight o'clock. "So you don't know who the baby was in the film?"

"No," Dieter said, straight-faced.

"I think Ingrid knows something," Otto said.

"Why do you say that?"

"I visited her today when you were at the library," Otto said. Dieter looked away awkwardly.

"We spoke about a number of things, including the film," Otto continued.

Dieter sat forward and re-established eye contact with Otto, curiosity etched into his face. "And what did she tell you?"

Otto rubbed his chin and breathed in deeply. "Nothing much, but I sensed that she was constantly measuring up what to tell me, and what not to."

Dieter swallowed a mouthful of scotch and stared at his hands embracing the tumbler, as though deep in thought.

"What are you thinking?" Otto asked.

Dieter seemed to flush slightly. "Nothing."

"How long should we wait?" Otto asked.

"I'm telling you, she won't come. It wouldn't surprise me if she's booked a return flight to New York, the way she flew out of here last night." He paused. "I think she resents us, Otto."

"Why?"

He shrugged, like a petulant teenager. "Because we were given opportunities that we embraced and used to the full."

"Studying abroad?"

Dieter nodded.

"She wanted nothing more than to marry Frederick, despite Dad's advice. No–one made her," Otto said.

"I know, but I still think that's why she resents us. She made her choices and they didn't work out. You and I have both done well."

"That's not our fault."

"I'm not saying it is. But I think that's how she sees it. She reckons we were favoured above her, got special treatment."

Otto drank more scotch. What Dieter said was true; he could recall the numerous occasions when this subject had flared up and caused an argument. His beloved Morris Minor had been just one such point of envious contention.

"Why did she and Dad have such differences?" Otto asked. Dieter shrugged thoughtfully. "It goes back a long way, Otto, but I reckon her marriage to Frederick had a lot to do with it.

You remember how she reacted when I questioned her hasty divorce to marry Newman."

Otto was shaking his head. "There's got to be more to it than that. She's being very... evasive."

Dieter stood up and approached Otto at the projector. "More scotch?"

"Thanks."

Dieter sighed deeply as he poured, appearing to be weighing something up in his mind. He lingered beside Otto.

"Otto, there's something I need to tell you."

Otto studied Dieter's face, sensing the gravity in his voice. An expectant silence hung between the two brothers, neither able to break it, as Dieter seemed to struggle for the right words. Suddenly, there was a loud knock at the front door. Otto's eyes widened.

"Ingrid?"

Dieter exhaled, deflated, and rubbed his eyes as Otto rushed like an eager puppy to open the front door.

"Have you started?" Ingrid asked Otto.

"No, we were waiting for you. Thanks for coming."

Ingrid glided into the living room in a black coat and boots. She regarded Dieter for a moment and then seemed to decide that greeting him was inevitable.

"Hello, Dieter." Her voice could have frozen alcohol.

"Ingrid," Dieter replied. Eye contact between them was perfunctory.

"Anything before we start? Tea, coffee? Have you eaten?" Otto asked.

Ingrid removed her coat as she walked through the doorway into the kitchen and shook out her long, golden hair. "Actually, I'd love a bourbon tonight."

"We have scotch, this isn't New York." Dieter shook his head.

"Don't I know it."

Soon they were all ready in the living room, Otto beside the projector, at the ready.

"Anyone want to say anything before we start?" Otto asked. Brief silence.

"No, Otto, let's just watch the film," Dieter said irritably.

A blurry, square image, heavily lined and scratched, burst forth from the screen as the projector hummed and ticked, pulling twenty-four frames, seven inches, of film through the film gate every second. Otto adjusted the focus.

Two children cartwheel through spreading puddles of murky water in a garden. It appears to be raining, though the film is heavily scratched, jagged lines burning across the image like staccato lightning. The older child, wearing a skirt that clings to her wet skin, is far more proficient than the younger child who keeps veering off course, colliding on several occasions with the older child, legs landing clumsily on the girl's back.

"Is that you, Ingrid?" Otto asked.

No reply.

The younger child is wearing shorts and both children are barefoot, long strands of wet hair plastered against smiling faces. The grass beneath the puddles appears slippery and several times both children lose their footing and fall into the water, to great displays of mirth and amusement. The younger child keeps glancing at the camera, smiling, revealing a missing front tooth.

The scene jumps to one of the children pulling on a black hosepipe in a makeshift game of tug-of-war, repeatedly losing their grip and landing on their buttocks with a great splash in the puddles of water. This becomes repeated so frequently that it eventually appears contrived.

"Where's the baby?" Otto said.

A black car bearing the Mercedes–Benz star on the front grille draws up beside the pavement. A man wearing a homberg steps out with another man and a woman. Everyone is smiling effusively and the woman has bulging, protuberant eyes. They pose beside each other, woman in the centre, smiling self-consciously at the camera.

"That looks like Dad," Dieter said. "Don't know the other two. Uncle, perhaps? Aunt, friends?"

"She looks like she has a thyroid problem," Otto said, analysing her physical appearance.

The scene jumps again. The older girl, wearing a summery skirt, is feeding milk out of a teated glass bottle to a lamb standing eagerly beside her, tugging on the rubber teat. The girl appears to be about thirteen or fourteen; confident and assured on camera. The scene cuts to the younger child stepping into a pair of giant wellington boots that reach up well beyond her knees. Bursting with smiles, the child takes huge, stiff-legged steps to lift the boots off the ground. The scene jags violently to the two children standing side by side as the older girl feeds the lamb. The younger child tries to attract the older one's attention by playfully pulling her hair, but elicits no response.

"God, I hope we never ate that poor thing," Dieter remarked.

"I think we might have," Ingrid replied.

Then the younger child comes around the corner of the timber-framed house, chasing after the lamb but struggling to run in the enormous boots, giving even the spring lamb little difficulty in escaping. Up and down the garden they run repeatedly, until suddenly, in the background, a toddler in a nappy crawls into the frame from behind a flowering hydrangea.

"There it is!" Otto said excitedly. "The baby."

The next shot is of the baby, full-screen, crawling with great concentration towards a bed of flowers. Curiously, the child perambulates with legs fully extended, resembling a dung beetle. As the child reaches the flowerbed one arm crumples and the toddler topples forwards into the flowers, rising somewhat startled a moment later. No tears. Then another view of the baby crawling straight-legged towards the camera at surprisingly high speed, determined to reach out and smudge the camera lens.

"I recall Mum and Dad talking about someone in the family who used to crawl like that, never on hands and knees," Otto said.

Ingrid and Dieter, perhaps self-consciously, shuffled in their seats.

The baby crawls this way and that around the garden, even ascending steps at the front door before descending them backwards, very cautiously, all with legs out straight. In the background the two older children play with the lamb, one minute feeding it, the next chasing it.

"It was me," Dieter said. "I crawled like a spider, Mum used to say."

Otto froze, confused. "So, if that was you, Dieter, then who are the other two? Only one can be Ingrid."

Dieter and Ingrid glanced across at Otto, their faces partially illuminated by the flickering greyscale reflections off the screen, like Nosferatu in a moment of ghoulish deliberation. Their eyes remained locked on each other's for a moment, both Dieter and Ingrid appearing frozen by inertia.

The image on the screen changes dramatically to one of tall, inverted J-shaped concrete fence posts with barbed wire strung between them; barren, muddy ground; guard towers rising at intervals like square rooks on a chessboard; simple, dark wooden barracks with tiny windows; uneven stone paving on which soldiers in Wehrmacht helmets and jackboots patrol the perimeter and watch over the camp from their towers with rifles over their shoulders.

The stark depictions on the screen turned everyone's heads as they stared, transfixed, at the unexpected scenes captured by Father's Agfa camera, presumably held in his own hands.

"What the hell is this?" Otto said.

A work detachment of men clad in baggy striped clothing and linen hats fills a deep trench close to a tall barbed wire fence. Watched over by armed Wehrmacht soldiers the labourers toil with pickaxes and spades, deepening the trench and heaping what appears to be clay soil above their heads on the verge of the trench. Above them another detachment of men, wearing the same clothes and revealing thin arms and skeletal chests, scoop up the chunks of wet clay in bony hands and place them in steel wagons anchored on a makeshift rail track.

"Jesus!" Dieter exclaimed. "This looks like a labour camp." The camera pans unevenly across the detachment of labourers to the land beside the fence where the Wehrmacht soldiers are beating one of the prisoners, kicking and striking him with the butts of their rifles. Some of the soldiers look stern and angry; others appear to laugh as they smoke cigarettes. A rough splice jars the image, which jumps for several seconds.

Otto hastily depressed the loop restore button until the image stabilised.

A large brick building with two wide ramps rising side by side up to the third floor fills the screen. Rail tracks lead to the base of each ramp and on one side three steel wagons, as seen earlier, stand in wait. The camera pans around revealing a narrow gauge railway track and a wooden slatted goods carriage: Deutsche Reichsbahn Kassel 37723G is painted in white on its side. Panning around further the camera stops on a square metal signpost with white lettering painted on a black background: Neuengamme vereinigen Sachsenhausen.

"Jesus, it is a camp," Otto blurted incredulously. "Neuengamme – never heard of it."

"Why the hell was Dad taking this footage though?" Dieter said, staring open-mouthed at the screen. "Was this near Hamburg?"

Ingrid sat with her hands clasped firmly between her knees. Her face, though appearing confused, was a study in concentration.

"How much more is there?" Dieter asked, turning around to look at Otto and the projector.

Otto calculated from the three hundred feet of film remaining on the eight hundred foot capacity feeding reel how much longer the film would run.

"About eight; nine minutes."

The scene changes suddenly to a large, swift-flowing, reed-lined river, a cityscape comprising tall buildings, spires and gabled roofing visible in the background. The water flows quickly past a timber quayside under construction, with dozens of emaciated men wearing striped prison clothing labouring under the unforgiving gaze of armed Wehrmacht soldiers. A sign on a wooden post reveals the river to be Die Elbe. A detachment of labourers to one side are digging a deep trench, several yards wide and deep, using simple hand tools, standing in sucking mud that has soiled their clothing up to their waists, and in some, beyond.

"That must be the Elbe River in Hamburg," Dieter remarked. "Didn't we used to live there?"

"Hamburg?" Otto repeated. Having been born in Lüderitz their former life in Germany was wholly unfamiliar to him.

"Uh–huh," Dieter mumbled, staring at the grainy, scratched images on the screen. "Those people are starving – look at their faces, their necks."

"I didn't know there were camps in Hamburg," Otto said.

"There were camps everywhere, Otto," Dieter replied.

Another rough jump splice and the image is suddenly one of several little kittens climbing in and out of a pair of large, leather shoes on a wooden floor, grabbing at the laces with their claws, watched over lazily by an adult cat in a wicker basket. The boundless energy of the kittens is delightful as they jump on each other, chasing their tails and cavorting tirelessly.

"That was my cat, she was called Flaumschen," Ingrid said, unexpectedly, her face lighting up and softening as she stared at the images.

"What kind of a name is that?" Otto asked.

"She was very fluffy, you see."

The kittens are soon joined by a small brown Dachshund who stands tolerantly amongst them, seemingly reluctant, as though placed there deliberately for the camera.

"Oh God, I'd forgotten the dog… what did we call him again?" Ingrid said. "Kaiser, that was it – the king – because he was treated so royally in the house by Dad. He loved that mutt."

The toddler is back onscreen, seated in front of a large glass bowl, holding a long wooden spoon that seems to dwarf the little child. The toddler's face is smeared with dark smudges, presumably chocolate, emanating from the wooden spoon that is being ineffectually scraped in the bowl to remove every last tempting vestige of cocoa. Even the toddler's white nappy is smeared in chocolate. The child's face concentrates intensely on manoeuvring the cruelly long, flat spoon into its mouth, tongue snaking disobediently about. Suddenly the spoon drops to the floor, eliciting a silent howl of dismay from the toddler. A young girl steps forward, wearing a dress and ribbons in her hair, retrieves the spoon and hands it back to the toddler with a reassuring pat on the head, instantly quelling the tears. The girl looks straight into the camera and smiles. She looks remarkably like Ingrid, with similar facial bones, a pudgy nose and lightly freckled cheeks.

"My God she looks just like you, Ingrid. Is that you?" Otto said.

Ingrid did not look away from the screen.

The scene changes abruptly to the garden, where the older girl is propelling herself on a scooter with bulbous white tyres, one foot on the running board and the other pushing the scooter around in wide circles on the lawn in front of the hydrangeas. The younger girl stands behind her, grasping her waist tightly, and every time the scooter passes close to the camera the younger girl falls off the scooter in a controlled dive, rolling onto the grass. Then she smiles at the camera, revealing her missing two front teeth and hair covered in dried grass, before dashing back to hitch a lift from the older girl again. The theatrical dive is repeated over and over in front of the camera. The image begins to jump and heavy lines scrape across it as the quality deteriorates sharply. Suddenly it ends and the screen reflects clear white light.

Otto switched the projector off and the lights on. A silence beyond the sudden cessation of the rhythmic ticking and mechanical noise of the Bell & Howell projector engulfed all three Adermann children. Outside they could hear the howl of the south–wester as it gusted and swirled around the house, occasionally blasting the windows with a spray of desert sand that sounded like static electricity.

Otto was the first to break the silence. "We cannot go on ignoring what we're seeing in these images." He was perched on the edge of the dining table, swinging one leg absently, watching his pendulous foot in preference to looking at Dieter or Ingrid's averted faces.

"Will someone please tell me what's going on?" Otto said quietly.

SEVENTEEN

"I need a bourbon," Ingrid said, holding out her glass as though she was at the Ritz Carlton in Manhattan. "Scotch, I mean."

Dieter moved thoughtfully through to the kitchen and sat down at the table, his head in his hands, leaving Otto to tend to Ingrid. Otto half-filled her glass and then his own, standing over her.

"Who is the baby?" Otto asked.

Ingrid looked up at him, eyes heavy and apprehensive. "Your brother."

"Dieter?" Otto said, raising his eyebrows.

She nodded and looked away. Otto glanced through the open doorway and saw Dieter sitting in the kitchen, elbows on the table, cupped hands over his nose and mouth, staring straight ahead.

"And the younger girl is... you?" Otto said, softly.

Again Ingrid nodded but would not meet his eyes. "If you hadn't insisted on showing these fucking movies everything could have stayed as it had been."

"It would have come out eventually, Ingrid." Dieter could be heard from the kitchen, muffled, but dissenting.

Otto's head turned from one to the other as he clenched his jaw muscles. He felt as though he was being toyed with, and it irritated him.

"Who is the older girl? Where is she now?" Otto said.

Ingrid looked up and took a gulp of scotch. "I'm sorry, Otto, I made a promise to Mum, many years ago, and as time passed by everything seemed less and less relevant and… well… of no significance to us anymore."

"Mum?" Otto's face twisted in anguish. "She kept this from us?"

Ingrid nodded. "I did warn you, brother. I said, leave things be."

Otto sat down beside her on the couch. Dieter remained in the kitchen.

"I had an older sister – we had an older sister. Her name was Inez. She was born seven years before me, in Hamburg." Ingrid paused, looking down, unable to meet Otto's eyes. "For God's sake, have some scotch, Otto!" she said harshly, as though reprimanding him.

"I don't believe this!" Otto said, barely audibly. "Why the hell am I only finding out about her now?" He took a generous mouthful of the scotch from his tumbler, frowning.

"When we first arrived in Lüderitz in 1946, a year after Dad, I was very lonely at school, hated the local kids, couldn't make friends…" Ingrid stared ahead, her eyes reddening. "Inez was my soul mate, my friend, she understood my pain and my bewilderment. She was eighteen going on nineteen, and I was twelve, hormonal, misunderstood, angry. Dad was so busy establishing his medical practice, not just here in Lüderitz but another one in Keetmanshoop, five hours away in the…" Ingrid gestured aimlessly out of the curtained windows with an outstretched arm.

"Mum was… she tried to understand but I think she was also struggling. Imagine coming from a smart house along

Schöne Aussicht, overlooking the lake, to this." Ingrid looked up and Otto saw that her eyes were moist, revealing the pain that they had held back for so long, silently, invisible to the world beyond her strictly controlled emotional borders.

Ingrid cleared her throat. "Inez was only in school for one year here, but everyone liked her and she made friends easily. She was confident, outgoing, beautiful." She chuckled. "Frans was smitten by her. He took her to a school dance... but Inez could do so much better."

Otto was impatient to get to the point – where was Inez; what became of her? – but he sensed the need to let Ingrid tell her story in her own way, releasing her burden at a pace and tempo that she could manage. Ingrid's composure was melting, her chin quivering slightly and her eyes puffing up and brimming with tears.

"And then suddenly, two years later, just after her twenty-first birthday, she... umm... took her life."

Otto recoiled from this unexpected disclosure; felt the breath escape from his lungs, leaving him gasping. He didn't know where to look, what to say. The disclosure, first that they had a sister whom he had never known about, and then that she had died – tragically – was overwhelming.

"I missed her so – she was my everything here; she helped me to stay sane in those first two years. Yet, I couldn't help her when she needed me, I did nothing to make her happier, to address her own pain and loss." Ingrid covered her mouth with a cupped hand and drew short, gasping breaths.

Otto didn't know what to do. Should he comfort her? This seemed somewhat insincere given their relative lack of familiarity and the fact that he was angry that she had colluded to keep this from him his entire life. He just sat, unmoving, staring ahead, trying to believe that the young girl he had been watching on the screen, so full of life, just minutes before, was no more; snuffed out before her time.

"What happened?" Otto managed eventually.

Ingrid looked up, mascara melting, nose wet, and wiped her face with the back of her hand. "She shot herself."

"Wha…? But…" Otto stumbled. "Why?"

"I don't know, Otto, it was long ago."

"Where?"

"She's buried just out of town in the cemetery. It's not far."

Otto recalled Frans speaking about keeping her grave neat and placing fresh flowers on it.

"I meant where did she die?" Otto said.

Ingrid gulped at her scotch thirstily and waved one hand distractedly in the air. "Here around Lüderitz, somewhere." She sounded tired all of a sudden, all the vitality gone from her body, the spark extinguished.

"Kolmanskop," Dieter said, his voice echoing from the kitchen.

Otto stiffened.

"I've arranged with Frans to visit the place where she was found," Dieter said.

Otto felt his pulse quicken and frowned. "You knew?"

"Only recently. I asked Frans who she was the day he mentioned her grave."

"What!"

"The day he first came here."

"And he told you, just like that?" Otto said sharply.

"He was surprised we didn't know. It seems it was a family secret only because Mum and Dad wanted it to be."

"Why didn't you tell me, Dieter?"

Silence from the kitchen.

"We've got a dead child to identify in our back garden, Mum to bury – we don't need any more secrets between us! Christ, let's just talk to each other!" Otto erupted. "What's wrong with you people?"

Ingrid looked up, perhaps somewhat relieved that Dieter had not divulged their meeting at the cemetery. "Please Otto, this is no easier for us than it is for you."

Otto felt his face throbbing with blood. "For us! Where the hell did that conspiracy come from? You two don't even talk to each other, for God's sake."

Dieter appeared in the doorway. "Calm down, Otto. Frans will take us to where Inez died tomorrow. He has to arrange permits and stuff. I think we will all benefit from going there, letting this all out in the open, and moving forward... constructively." He studied Otto and Ingrid, who listened without protest.

"A permit? Where is this place?" Otto asked.

"Kolmanskop, in the Sperrgebiet," Dieter said, leaning his shoulder against the doorway, arms folded. "Look, we can't question Mum about why this was kept a secret, about who made the decision, but I assume it was to protect us from unnecessary distress." He shrugged and looked over at Ingrid. "It is really unfortunate that you have had to carry this burden alone, all these years, Ingrid."

Appearing somewhat surprised by his compassionate remark, Ingrid looked up at Dieter with a teary, puffy face. She said nothing. Silence was perhaps just what they needed for a moment's private reflection, Otto thought. Then Ingrid stood up.

"I'm going back to the hotel now." She placed her tumbler on the dining table beside the projector and straightened. "I'd very much like to come with you tomorrow. Could you ask Frans to pick me up at the hotel on your way out?"

"Sure," Otto said distractedly.

Ingrid paused beside Otto, ignoring Dieter. "I'm sorry, Otto, you were never meant to find out about this." She looked immensely sad, and tired.

"Why ever not?" Otto said.

Ingrid patted his shoulder gently and walked away.

"Ingrid?" Otto called out more forcefully, turning his head.

The front door closed, signalling Ingrid's defiant departure. Otto and Dieter sat in silence in the living room.

You were never meant to find out. Otto heard Ingrid's apologetic words echoing in his bruised mind, over and over.

"What does she mean by that: I was never meant to find out about this?" Otto asked.

"I honestly don't know, Otto."

"They certainly buried her both literally and metaphorically, didn't they, completely erased from the family memories?" Otto met Dieter's searching eyes. "Why?"

This was not the childhood that he so warmly remembered. Childhoods are naive; childhoods are fond; they are not supposed to be filled with buried sisters and ominous secrets, Otto thought to himself.

Surely, there could be no more. Then his mind briefly returned to the unanswered questions that had been only temporarily cast aside to allow him time to deal with the emotional shock of Inez: who had been buried in the back garden, and what was the significance of those harrowing images of Neuengamme revealed in the home movie?

EIGHTEEN

Bay Road ascended the hill behind Lüderitz, exiting the town in a south-easterly direction and becoming the B4 to Keetmanshoop, over two hundred miles away through the sand of the Namib and the barren black rock of the aptly named Schwarzrand. Frans collected everyone in his yellow Toyota police car at 10am, the vestiges of an overnight fog still clinging to the land in the mid-morning sunshine.

"Is the cemetery out of our way?" Otto asked from the back seat beside Ingrid, who sat with her hands clasped tightly in her lap, lips pressed together and eyes unfathomable.

"We drive right past it along this road," Frans said.

Dieter was wearing a dark burgundy shirt and chinos, Otto a sports jacket and striped tie, while Ingrid was elegantly framed in a demure dark grey – almost black – ensemble, befitting their journey of belated respect for their lost sister.

"It's so small," Otto remarked after they stopped in front of Inez's neat but humble grave. He glanced at Dieter and Ingrid in turn, but they did not respond. Otto bent down and aimlessly rearranged the shrivelled and crumbling bunches of flowers. "I should have brought flowers."

"There'll be fresh ones today with the weekly vegetable delivery," Frans said.

Otto and Ingrid looked up at him in puzzlement. Beside Inez's grave the freshly excavated hole in the arid earth yawned and beckoned ominously.

"Could this be Mum's grave?" Dieter said to no-one in particular.

Otto stared at the new hole, his emotions in turmoil. By rights he, like any grieving child, should have only to deal with the loss and emptiness associated with burying his mother, not the unexpected loss of an unknown sister as well. Yet the reality that he was in Lüderitz to bid his mother farewell seemed furthest from his mind at that moment, as though he had almost forgotten his primary mission in returning to his childhood home.

"I don't believe what I am seeing here," he said, running his fingers across the lettering on the headstone. "And I don't understand why Mum would never have told me... told us." He looked up at Dieter.

Frans shuffled self-consciously on his huge feet. "Do you want me to wait in the car?"

"No, Frans, it's OK," Dieter said. He touched Otto on the shoulder. "I think we should get going."

Otto straightened up. "I'll come back later with flowers."

The journey to Kolmanskop continued in silence, Otto leaning against the side window as he stared out at the endless rolling sand dunes, resembling desiccated ocean swells. Ingrid sat like a nun, knees and arms pressed together tightly, lips closed, eyes devoid of expression.

"Why is this town out here in the middle of nowhere, Frans?" Dieter asked to ease the policeman's evident discomfort.

"Diamonds."

"But why was it abandoned?"

"Ja, it was built in the early 1900s after enormous diamonds were found around here – unimaginable wealth. Back then they said one in five of the world's diamonds came from Lüderitz. After the First World War the diamond market collapsed and of course Germany lost this colony to the British. Within forty years this booming town was dead and abandoned." He looked into the rear view mirror, meeting Otto's eyes. "Now the desert is slowly taking it back."

On the roadside they passed a sign warning in large red lettering that they were entering the Sperrgebiet, and that unauthorised access was forbidden and punishable by the full force of the law.

"So this whole area was out of bounds to everyone?" Dieter said.

"Absolutely, still is." Frans chuckled and readjusted his meaty hands on the steering wheel. "The first X–Ray machine in the southern hemisphere was in Kolmanskop – to make sure nobody swallowed diamonds."

The road was quiet and they did not pass another vehicle. In the distance a small group of brown horses stood and watched them from the crest of a dune.

"Horses – out here?" Otto asked.

"Ja, wild horses. They live out here on the Garub Plains."

"How did they get here?"

Frans shrugged. "Probably the German settlers."

Kolmanskop was six miles out of Lüderitz and within ten minutes they were greeted by its ghostly visage. An extensive area spaciously occupied by double–storey houses and larger buildings in two neat rows along the ridge of sandy rock, all relentlessly and helplessly being reclaimed by the advancing

Namib Desert. The dry, burning heat engulfed them as they disembarked from the air conditioned car.

Diminutive swirls of sand snaked across the landscape, driven by the gentlest of breezes. Sand seemed to be in constant motion out here, perpetually being blown from one location to another, stopping only to collect against immovable obstructions.

"Were these the miners' houses?" Dieter asked, squinting in the bright sunlight.

Frans began to walk towards the first row of imposing and typically Germanic colonial houses. "Ja, miners and a whole community – teachers, nurses, even the architect."

Most buildings were engulfed by sand piled up at an aggressive forty–five degree angle; plaster flaking off the outer walls, window and door frames eroded and disintegrating; corrugated iron roofing rusted and eaten away by desert cancer, exposing crumbling roof timbers beneath.

"And the bigger buildings?" Otto asked, gesturing towards an imposing structure to their right.

"There was a hospital, a school, a theatre, a ballroom…"

"My God, luxury," Dieter said.

"There's even a swimming pool up there," Frans said, squinting into the sun and raising his arm to indicate a square concrete structure just visible on the crest of the rocky ridge.

"How long has it been abandoned?" Ingrid asked, walking with difficulty as her white and black court shoes sank into the sucking sand.

"Since about the late 1940s." Frans was beginning to sweat profusely and puff from the effort of moving his bulk through the heat and the soft sand. "Kolmanskop was like a fuse. It burned very bright… but not for very long."

Otto imagined Inez walking through this sand in 1948, perhaps on a moonless night to escape detection, furtiveness and despair uppermost in her mind. Where would she have chosen to end her life?

They seemed to be heading for the house at the end of the row, its roof collapsed in and the walls in very poor condition. They passed a rusted sign in Gothic Germanic font: Kegelbahn.

Sensing that they were studying it with interest, Frans paused. "German skittle alley – down there, I think." He raised his fleshy arm and pointed.

"Is this the house?" Dieter asked as they neared the ruins, their pace slowing.

"Ja."

They stopped and stared in solemn silence for a moment. Otto found himself imagining their long–lost sister approaching the house in 1948, filled with incurable melancholy and dark intent. A desert wind whistled gently in their ears, stirring up little puffs of sand around their feet. Ingrid, surprisingly, took the first step towards the ruin, her tentative footstep on the wooden veranda eliciting a creaking protest.

"Is it safe?" Otto asked.

Frans shrugged.

The front doorway was the only one to be enjoyed at full height. Every other ground floor doorway was filled with sand, entering through the windows and spilling out of each room like a lava flow, in some rooms reaching halfway up the door frame. The patterns in the swirling sand, as it folded its way around the walls of the house, exuded an abstract beauty that was hard to define.

"Whose house was this?" Ingrid asked, studying each

room in turn with a poignancy that was touching.

"I think my pa said a mine manager's," Frans replied.

Even though the paint was faded and peeling, and plaster had come away exposing brickwork, the bright intentions of the decoration – pinks, blues, striped shades of turquoise, and then white from door height up to the high pressed ceilings above – was still evident.

"It's as though they needed to bring colour into the houses in this drab landscape," Ingrid remarked.

They explored each room and then ascended the wooden staircase, each step smothered in sand, to the precarious, groaning, wooden flooring of the upper floor.

"Who found her?" Otto asked, as they passed the bathroom in which an almost immaculate enamel roll-topped bath languished, half-filled with sand.

Frans cleared his throat and pressed a clenched hand against his mouth. "My pa."

Ingrid's head spun around to face him. "Your father found Inez?" She frowned.

Frans nodded. "In the main bedroom." He pointed into a large room looking out over Kolmanskop through a decadent bay window, now devoid of glass and most of the wooden window frame.

A rusted, sprung metal double bed was the sole occupant of the room, and it looked as though it might disintegrate at any moment. Their feet shuffled on the sandy floorboards as they imagined Inez's final moments; the quiet, forgotten abandonment where she had chosen to depart from this world.

"How come your father found Inez?" Ingrid persisted, almost aggressively.

"I don't know. It was his job to patrol the Sperrgebiet. He was a diamond company security officer."

"And what did he find?" Ingrid asked, like an interrogation.

"Two bodies: Inez, another man, and a revolver."

Otto's ears pricked up. "Another man?"

Dieter and Ingrid glanced at each other.

"Her boyfriend," Frans said solemnly.

Ingrid's eyes narrowed. "Who was holding the revolver?"

Frans smiled nervously, briefly, shuffling his feet. "I don't know, Ingrid, it was a long time ago."

"Hold on – she came here with someone else, and they both killed themselves?" Otto said, slightly agitated.

Frans nodded. Dieter nodded.

"You knew?" Otto said, narrowing his eyes at Dieter, feeling again as if he'd been deliberately kept in the dark, hurt that Dieter somehow knew and had not confided in him.

Dieter shrugged and inhaled. "I only found out yesterday."

"Yesterday?" Otto said loudly. "You've known for a day but I have to find out from Frans?"

Dieter appeared chastened but said nothing, avoiding Otto's accusing eyes. Otto sighed in disappointment and walked to the enormous bay window, turning his back on everyone.

"Do you know what happened here, Frans?" Ingrid asked calmly.

Frans walked over and stood beside Otto at the decaying bay window, surveying the ruins of Kolmanskop as it gradually yielded to its sandy conqueror. "I have seen the files."

"Go on," Ingrid said curtly.

Frans placed one foot on the remnants of the bay windowsill as he gazed through the empty window.

"My pa discovered them the following morning, presumably doing his rounds." He hesitated. "I'm not sure how it came to be that he went into this house."

"Presumably this house was empty then?" Ingrid asked.

"Ja, it was."

"Was anyone living in Kolmanskop in 1948?" Dieter said.

"A few people, not many. It was mostly deserted."

"Did anyone call it in, hear anything; see anything?" Ingrid asked.

Frans shrugged one shoulder. "No."

Otto could feel his heart beating in his chest at this forensic dissection of events that occurred nearly forty years ago; events that until twelve hours back he had not known anything about; events that led to the death of an unknown family member: his sister.

"They were lying in each other's arms over there," Frans indicated the corner of the room beside the double bed, "each with a single gunshot wound."

Dieter winced; Ingrid paled; all Otto could feel was a rushing sound in his ears and weakness in his knees.

"Who was holding the revolver?" Ingrid persisted.

Frans turned to meet her determined gaze. "I think he was."

Silence for a few moments – hot, dry moments. Not even flies inhabited Kolmanskop.

"Who was this man? Boyfriend?" Otto asked.

Frans nodded. "I can't remember his name, I'm sorry. But they were… in love." Frans sounded forlorn admitting this, as though he still cared for Inez, a woman who had chosen someone else above him.

"Two shots… and nobody heard anything," Otto said quietly, almost as though he was talking to himself.

"Did this happen at night?" Dieter asked.

"I don't think anybody can know for sure, but I reckon that was the assumption."

"How did they get here?" Dieter asked.

"Nobody knows." Frans made a face. "They probably walked."

"Was Inez living at home then?" Dieter directed this question at Ingrid, who blushed.

"Yes," she replied, fumbling with her hands.
Dieter looked at her quizzically. "Didn't anybody notice her absence?"

Ingrid's eyes moistened and her gaze faltered. "She was twenty-one; not exactly on a curfew." She wiped each eye with an index finger and sniffed, visibly uncomfortable.

"This is what you were referring to, Frans, when you said that you could never become a diamond company employee?" Dieter said.

Frans paled as he placed a hand over his mouth and stroked his chin a few times, then rubbed his eyebrow, then the back of his neck. He shuffled his mighty feet on the floorboards.

"Ja."

"We're in the Sperrgebiet, right?"

Frans nodded, looking crestfallen.

"Do you think that—"

"That's enough, Dieter!" Otto said.

Otto was surprised by his sudden reaction as emotion and disbelief swelled up within him, forcing him to turn and leave the room, almost slipping on the sandy stairs in his haste. He stood outside in the merciless heat, his back turned to the building, feeling Ingrid, Dieter and Frans' eyes watching him through the bay window.

Ingrid emerged minutes later and she and Otto stood side by side in silent meditation for a few minutes, their hot skins ineffectively caressed by a gentle breeze. The desolate ruins of this once prosperous and thriving town were surreal to behold, as were the revelations about Inez.

"Do you know who the man was with Inez?" Otto asked without looking at her.

"I can't remember, Otto," Ingrid said.

Otto scuffed the gritty sand with his suede Oxfords. Nothing grew in this infertile soil, the only useful fruit it had yielded to its human conquerors being diamonds – heaps of diamonds – and they were all but exhausted now.

"It's so unfair, you know – two days to Mum's funeral and I'm not even thinking about her," Otto said.

Ingrid bent down to empty sand from her court shoes. "God, this fucking place is ruining my wardrobe."

Otto looked at her in disbelief.

"You needn't feel guilty about Mum. Remember, the fact that you never knew about Inez was her doing." Ingrid's voice was laced with something unpleasant: smugness, self-satisfaction; resentment.

"And Dad's." Otto stopped short of saying 'and yours'.

Ingrid rubbed sand off each foot in turn before slipping her feet back into the shoes. "I really hate this place. I wish I'd never left New York."

Her coldness curdled Otto's blood and he didn't know what to say.

NINETEEN

Otto bought dried flowers in Lüderitz later on and Frans drove him back to the cemetery that evening to place them on Inez's grave. He did not linger; the day had been emotional enough. Being at his sister's grave alone this time seemed more significant to Otto, as though he was better able to connect with his personal thoughts about the sister he had never known. He tried not to look into the gaping grave beside hers, forcing his mind away from the arduous matter of Mother's funeral in just a few days' time.

"Don't forget it's fresh fruit and veg day tomorrow," Frans said as he dropped Otto off on Bülow Street.

Nobody, however, had any interest in buying food the next day. Their appetites had been quashed.

"I'm not hungry," Dieter said.

"I'll be gone in two days," Ingrid said.

They sat around the red kitchen table in silence drinking Mother's good coffee without an ounce of pleasure.

"I don't want to watch any more home movies," Ingrid declared suddenly, pushing her chair back and standing. "Let's just do the funeral."

She ordered a taxi and left without saying another word. Nobody protested. Otto phoned Sabine for a lengthy call in hushed and emotional tones, interrupted only by brief and false joviality when the boys came on the line to say hello and then goodnight to their father. Hearing his children's voices seemed to unsettle Otto's composure the most. He suddenly felt very far away from Sabine and the boys. The immediacy of his warm family life contrasted uncomfortably with the emerging truths about his distant childhood, once remembered as comforting and nostalgic, now turning into an apparent conspiracy of cold, secretive falsehoods.

In response to "When are you coming home?" he told Sabine that he was not sure yet. Later, from his bedroom, he heard Dieter calling Hong Kong and speaking to Jim in muted tones. Otto could not tell whether it was business or personal. It was the first day that Dieter had not sent or received a fax.

When Otto awoke the house was empty and he assumed that Dieter was at the library attending to business matters again. It was bright and sunny outside, but visible across the calm and reflective blue ocean was a fog bank that looked as wide as it did ominous. Otto sniffed the air: no smell of guano or seal dung. He smiled.

As he sat down to enjoy a cup of steaming coffee with a slice of buttered toast and gooseberry jam there came a timid knock at the front door. Surprisingly, it was Ingrid.

"I couldn't sleep," she explained, removing a cream fur coat and matching woolly hat to reveal a peach ensemble. "I've been walking... where we did the other day."

She poured coffee and sat opposite Otto, embracing the mug with both hands. Otto ate his toast, considering his sister thoughtfully. Though the aromas of strong coffee and buttered toast were homely and inviting, the atmosphere was not.

"Where is your brother?"

Otto shrugged. "I think he's at the library."

"Christ! Will he actually find the time to attend the funeral tomorrow?" The words were barely cold on her lips before Otto responded to the deep irony in her remark by raising his eyebrows. Ingrid had the decency to squirm. "Anyway, how are you?" she said, looking at him as if to say let's move on.

He swallowed, licking jam off his lips and fingertips. "I can't believe you never told me about Inez."

Ingrid placed her mug on the table but kept her hands wrapped around it. "I was fourteen, Otto – old enough to know, but not old enough to understand." She hesitated. "In this house decisions were made for us. I followed them."

"Is this why you hated Dad?"

Ingrid shrugged in a noncommittal way. "Partly."

"Partly?" Otto repeated, sitting forward.

"Look," Ingrid began, breathing deeply, "you know about Inez, the sister I loved very dearly. The big secret that Mum and Dad imposed on us is out." She unclasped her hands briefly and pulled a face. "Don't expect an epiphany."

"What?"

"The funeral is tomorrow and then we go our separate ways again."

Otto stared at her incredulously. He truly did not understand her. "Aren't you forgetting something?"

Ingrid shrugged and raised her eyebrows.

Otto jabbed his index finger towards the camelthorn roots visible through the kitchen window. "Who is that in our garden?"

Ingrid leaned back ambivalently. "The police will sort that out."

"Yes, and they might arrest one of us."

"You're being overly dramatic."

"It's not natural for bodies to be buried in gardens."

Ingrid paled slightly but quickly regained her composure. "I'm on your side here, Otto. But what can I do?"

"You were at least twelve back then. Surely you remember something?"

Ingrid shook her head.

"You lied about Inez," Otto challenged her.

The blood rose visibly to the surface of Ingrid's face. "Don't you dare! You are in no position to judge me, Otto."

Otto was stunned by her anger as she spat the words at him. "Why, because I was so young?"

Suddenly the front door burst open as Dieter entered wearing tight, shiny yellow jogging shorts and a minute running vest, both of which exposed more than they covered. Rolled up in one hand were a newspaper and a brown folder containing papers.

"Hi all!" he said, slightly out of breath but full of joviality.

"Where've you been?" Otto asked.

"I went to the library; a few faxes…" he raised the folder in the air, "and then a jog along the coast. Have you seen the fog bank out there?"

"You look like one of the Village People," Ingrid sneered, looking at Dieter's running attire.

Dieter walked past the kitchen table and dropped the newspaper onto the corner beside Otto, heading for the fridge. "If the cap fits, sweetie…" Dieter poured a glass of water for himself. "Oh, I told Otto." He gulped at the water. "Haven't told Frans yet. That's a tough one."

Otto was surprised by Ingrid's unruffled look of disinterest. "You knew?"

She rolled her eyes. "Jesus, Otto, didn't everyone? You're supposed to be the observant doctor."

Otto felt he was being ridiculed. "Yeah, but he's my brother." It was reminiscent of his childhood – significantly younger than both Dieter and Ingrid, he was always playing catch–up.

"Mum's funeral notice is in the Lüderitzbuchter," Dieter said, pointing to the paper.

Otto picked it up and began to flick through to the small ads and announcements section. He found the notice and read it aloud. A brief silence ensued.

"It sounds nice, Otto," Ingrid said. "You were right to choose those words. Mum would have liked it."

Otto sighed. "It finally feels as though the funeral is happening. There have been so many distractions. I…"

Otto stopped and stared at the newspaper with his mouth slightly open. A boxed advertisement near the funeral notices had caught his attention.

"What is it?" Dieter asked, rising to refill his glass.

"Jesus," Otto said, frowning as he continued to stare at the newspaper.

"What?" Dieter repeated.

"Listen to this: Saturday 20th April is Adolf Hitler's birthday. Celebrate with us at Kreplinhaus. Drinks reception at 11.30am. Luncheon at 12.30. Guest speaker is Jurgen Göring. Dress formal." Otto's voice tailed off in disbelief towards the end.

Ingrid leaned forward and placed her elbows on the table. "Let me see that," she said, drawing the newspaper closer to her.

Water overflowed from Dieter's filled glass beneath the kitchen tap as he stared over his shoulder at Otto.

"Read that again," Dieter said.

"It's a fucking birthday party for Adolf Hitler! Tomorrow. On the day of Mum's funeral."

"What kind of people celebrate Hitler's birthday?" Dieter said.

"Admirers?" Otto suggested, raising his eyebrows. "But here, in Lüderitz?"

"We all know this used to be a German colony; that's probably why Mum and Dad chose to come here in the first place," Ingrid said.

"Yeah, but nobody celebrates Hitler's birthday – not even back in the Fatherland!" Dieter blurted, resuming his seat. "Do they?"

"Is this a neo–Nazi thing?" Otto said.

His thoughts wandered to the home movie images they had seen on the screen: the brownshirt march, Neuengamme camp, the starving prisoners, the beatings, the Wehrmacht guards, the dingy barracks, the executions. Then he remembered something and pressed a finger to his lips. "Do you remember what that woman at the paper said to us?"

Ingrid's eyes gradually widened. "Something about Mum's funeral on the 20th April."

"Didn't she say Dad would have been proud?" Otto said.

"Proud?" Dieter repeated, pulling a face.

"I'm sure that was the word she used," Otto said.

"Hang on a minute," Dieter said. "What does that mean?"

"Christ, I have no idea. But have you thought about what we've seen on those home movies?"

Dieter looked down at the finely flecked pattern in the red melamine table and picked at it with his fingernails. "Do you know what the Nazis did to homosexuals?"

He didn't have to say like me, Otto knew. In the world dominated by the purist ideologies of Nazism, homosexuals had been exterminated.

"What do we do about the funeral?" Otto asked.

Ingrid made a loud sound of exasperation, like a gasp. "Nothing, we do nothing. The funeral cannot be changed, and in any case, this… thing has nothing to do with us." She raised one hand and gesticulated towards the newspaper in Otto's grasp.

"We could talk to Frans about it," Dieter suggested.

"What the hell for?" Ingrid barked.

They sat in stunned silence for a short while, the grandfather clock ticking dutifully in the background, the dependable sound that Otto would forever associate with being at home.

"There are still two reels of unwatched film," Otto said.

Dieter looked up eagerly and nodded, but Ingrid pushed her chair back and stood up.

"Those films have caused enough misery. I have no desire to be tortured by further images of Inez, or my parents."

"Oh come on, Ingrid," Otto protested. "The secret is out now, where's the harm?"

Ingrid rinsed her mug in the kitchen sink and stood staring out of the window at the camelthorn tree. "Schlafende Hunde soll man nicht wecken," she said without turning.

Otto, never schooled in Germany, looked to Dieter.

"Let sleeping dogs lie," Dieter said with a flicker of his eyebrows.

"It's a bit late for that, isn't it?" Otto said.

After Ingrid's departure Dieter drew the curtains while Otto laced the film leader of reel three through the projector. "This one is marked 1943 onwards," Otto said. "I wonder if I'll make an appearance?"

They stared with nervous anticipation at the screen. In his chest Otto could feel his heart beating faster. For the first time he was not imbued with excitement and expectation; instead he was subdued by apprehension and his fingers trembled as he moved to turn on the projector. He wondered what he might see on the screen, filmed by Father's hand, revealing irrevocably what Father's interests were. Could the next thirty minutes indelibly tarnish the family memories that he had held dear for so many years? How would he feel if what he thought he knew about his past turned out to be so inaccurate, so unsound as to constitute nothing better than a fabrication, leaving him adrift in his adult life without foundation?

Would this change him, or his perception of life and that of his own children growing up around him? His mind flashed to the body of the unidentified young child in the back garden and he steeled himself to an inescapable reality: he had to find out everything he could. There could be no sleeping dogs left undisturbed. Every frame of these home movies needed to be scrutinised, carefully.

"What you waiting for?" Dieter said, drumming his hands on his thighs.

Otto drew breath and switched the projector on.

TWENTY

A streaky panorama reveals the snow-covered rooftops of Hamburg, the predominantly white shades on the screen flecked and lined by dark emulsion scratches. The image jumps a few times and then settles on a group of children at play, throwing snowballs around a life-sized snowman, crudely fashioned with a crooked stick for a nose. The camera pans across to the road showing cars struggling through deep snow, their narrow tyres clogged with great chunks of ice.

The two girls, Ingrid and Inez, are engaged in a pitched battle against three younger children whose dark scarves are spattered with the remnants of shattered snowballs.

"Neighbours?" Dieter said.

Otto shrugged.

A little boy wearing a coat, woolly hat and boots walks confidently into view and joins the girls, determined to be part of the fun. He bends over to gather snow and as he straightens is struck and flattened by a snowball to the chest. He kicks like an inverted beetle and bursts into tears.

The image jumps immediately to a busy port where Mother and three children walk along the dockside across a matrix of rail tracks and past coils of heavy rope and chains. The camera pans from a sign – Hamburger Hafen – to crowds dwarfed beside a large cruise ship moored at the dock. The ship is white with a thick dark stripe stretching from bow to stern, above which several decks of cabins are topped with a single row of lifeboats. The image zooms in on Mother, the two girls and the young boy. Then there is a close–up of the ship's bow with its heavy anchor chain and nameplate – MV Wilhelm Gustloff – followed by the National Socialist Party flag flapping high above the turrets: the swastika.

"I vaguely remember this," Dieter said, stabbing his finger at the screen. "I felt so incredibly small beside this huge ship; it was like a wall, a gigantic building, bigger than I'd ever seen."

"Amazing that you remember that – I mean, you couldn't have been very old," Otto said.

"Yeah, you're right I suppose." Dieter hesitated. "I just recall the sheer enormity of the ship, blocking out the sun."

"What was the Wilhelm Gustloff?"

"It looks like a cruise ship, doesn't it? But presumably the war was on, so…"

The day at the Port of Hamburg continues with sausages and sauerkraut at a waterside restaurant and a shaky lopsided image, presumably taken by one of the girls, of Mother and Father standing close together and smiling broadly.

The projector purred smoothly beside Otto, not quietly, but the sound blended into the background and became an accepted accompaniment to the flickering images flashed up on the screen.

With a smudge of film cement flashing across the screen the image changes abruptly to one of starkness, few trees despite open grassed areas, neatly mown with precise edges. An extensive single storey building, with rows of tall steel windows standing side by side like sentries, fills the screen. There appears to be no activity at all, despite a thread of smoke curling upwards from a slender rooftop chimney. A painted sign at the door reads Walther–Werke. The next scene is filmed inside – gloomy, despite the vertical windows, revealing grim-faced workers clad in stripy pyjamas, operating machinery: lathes, presses, drills. Running the length of the roof space are broad canvas pulleys and belts driving heavily–spoked wheels attached to the machinery.

Armed soldiers walk up and down the rows, mostly with their hands clasped behind their backs, peering at the workers who never make eye contact, baring only their shaven heads and cloth caps. They appear to be making and assembling rifles and pistols. A heavily scratched image of a labourer shaping a piece of wood into a rifle stock seems to capture the camera's attention for some time, as the gaunt prisoner under scrutiny hastily turns a block of harmless wood into a component of destruction.

"An armaments factory?" Otto said, glancing in Dieter's direction.

"Do you think this is part of Neuengamme?" Dieter said absently.

The picture changes to show the inside of a massive warehouse, long roof timbers spanning a floor space punctuated only at its centre by a towering, square brick structure. Packed on pallets around this structure are bricks by the thousand. Pyjama–clad labourers, emaciated and bald, push wheelbarrows loaded with bricks across the vast space.

Then a sudden distant view of men lined up on cobblestones between barracks, barbed wire visible on surrounding fences between inverted J-shaped fence posts, a distant watch tower, soldiers standing around with rifles. The prisoners are once again wearing striped baggy pyjamas, looking unkempt, underfed. One of the Wehrmacht soldiers, wearing a cap, walks up and down in front of the prisoners, gesticulating animatedly, the shine on his jackboots visible through the camera lens. He unholsters a pistol from his belt and walks up to the man on the end of the front row. The soldier points his pistol at the man's head and suddenly the man falls down in a crumpled heap of oversized clothing as a dark stain spreads across the courtyard.

"Jesus!" Dieter said, raising his hands to his face.

Otto felt the sudden urge to urinate, winded, astonished to witness such an event captured on film – a genuine death, an apparent murder. And these were not just any films; these were Father's home movies. Even though the incident had happened over forty years ago, it felt fresh and shockingly real.

"Did we just see what I think we saw?" Otto said.

"He just shot him," Dieter said, a hand drawn up to his mouth.

Otto realised he had witnessed a crime.

The officer walks along the line of prisoners and stops halfway down, points his pistol at a bearded man who grimaces before crumpling forwards to the ground. The camera remains steady, focused, even zooming in slightly. The prisoners on either side of the executed men stand rigid, wide eyes averted fearfully into the distance.

"Jesus Christ, another one," Dieter said, quieter this time.

Otto's heart jumped and his mouth felt dry. This felt so wrong, so utterly wrong. Why was Father filming this? Where was he that he would even see such atrocities being committed? Father was a doctor. This made no sense.

"Where was Dad filming this?" Otto said.

The film jerks to a new scene, four steel doors with handles, the emblem of JA Topf clearly visible, mounted side by side in a brick wall. Men in pyjamas stare at the doors forlornly. They appear exhausted, the light in their sunken eyes extinguished. One opens a door and throws in a few large pieces of chopped wood, revealing a glowing furnace within. Even in black and white the intense heat inside the ovens is evident. Piled high in the corner of the room are pyjamas so dirty that the dark stripes almost blend into each other. Beside them are dozens and dozens of worn boots and shoes.

"I don't like this," Otto said, turning to look at the front reel of film. The reel was at least half-full of film.

Suddenly the picture switches to a garden, flowers, a tree, and a young boy wearing a shirt with anchors on it. Curiously, he is walking backwards in straight lines, looking over his shoulder, evidently immersed in a game that only he understands. Visible in the background is the familiar family home with the older girls – Inez and Ingrid – sitting on the steps eating what appear to be berries.

"Why are you walking backwards?" Otto asked.

Dieter chuckled and shook his head. "God knows. I must have known even then that I wasn't straight."

Otto glanced at his brother. Dieter was becoming increasingly confident and open about his homosexuality, which until a few days ago had been a complete secret to Otto, if not the world, yet now it was the subject of frequent self-deprecatory quips. Otto wondered what it must have been like for his brother, waiting all those years for the right moment to come out and be honest with his family, the opportunity presented by Mum's stroke.

Little Dieter walks past the hydrangeas, his mouth puckered in such a way to suggest he is making sounds, perhaps of a car or an airplane. His arms grip an imaginary object, which he grapples with. Then he turns and walks backwards towards the camera, steadily, without stumbling, glancing behind him only occasionally to check on his path.

Otto began to laugh. "What the hell are you doing?"

Suddenly the family is in a park, mature trees, benches along gravelled paths, a nearby pond with ducks gliding unthreatened across its smooth surface. A wicker basket lies open, disgorged of its contents beside a rug unfurled on the uncut grass. A woman is spread out on her front, head supported on folded arms and turned to one side, sleeping. A little boy approaches her, curiously, studying her as she lies motionless and unresponsive. He sits down on her lower back and looks implacably at the camera, but the woman does not stir.

"That must be Mum sleeping," Otto said.

"Trying to sleep," Dieter said with a wry grin.

The little boy, Dieter, stands up and then almost immediately sits down again, patting Mother on her back, before moving towards her shoulders and peering at her face. He stands up again, walks around her head and then sits down on her shoulders. Still Mother does not stir.

"Do you think Mum and Dad had been at the schnapps?" Dieter asked. "She's comatose."

Otto chuckled. "You're a persistent little shit."

Not satisfied, Dieter stands up and then straddles his mother's back, one foot just reaching the grass on either side, facing her head. He appears to look at the camera for advice, unsure how to elicit a response from his mother. The image jags suddenly to the two girls in a wooden paddle boat, ineffectually splashing their oars in the pond water as their boat turns in circles and drifts away from the shore on a gentle breeze. They are both wearing ribbons in their hair and laughing a great deal.

Otto felt a pang of sadness watching this moment of happiness captured on celluloid for eternity, defying the events that had subsequently shredded this scene of family harmony. He glanced across at the front reel which had about two inches of film left visible beyond the hub.

A row of prisoners in pyjamas are sitting mournfully on a wooden bench set against a white wall, their heads either bowed forward or fixed in a vacant stare. Thin, bony ankles are visible above dishevelled boots, and in some cases dirty, shoeless feet. A doctor, wearing a white coat over a collared shirt and tie, smiles broadly at the camera. His name badge over the left breast pocket reads Dr Alfred Trzebinski. He bends down over a glass flask marked Arsen 1:1,000 and removes the glass stopper, pouring some of the clear fluid into an enamelled water jug. He addresses a small group of men in white coats gathered around him, turning frequently to face the camera. Pouring from the jug into a small glass beaker he holds this up to the light to check the level.

The image jumps to a prisoner drinking from the beaker, his unshaven cheeks gaunt, temples hollowed, eyes sunken and devoid of hope. Then another prisoner, then another, all drink without protest from the beaker, passed down the line and refilled each time.

"Alfred Trzebinski, that name is familiar," Dieter said thoughtfully. "Why?"

Otto's mind raced as he tried to recall the significance of this vaguely familiar name. "What's Arsen?"

Dieter turned around and met Otto's eyes. "Arsenic."

"Jesus." Silence ensued as they watched the harrowing

143

images on the screen: starving men being given arsenic to drink in a clean, clinically perfect environment. "Is this some kind of experiment?" Otto frowned, the morality of his profession under question.

For a second Ingrid's voice echoed in Otto's mind: let sleeping dogs lie. An ominous feeling began to settle around him, on the very day when he should have been remembering his mother and preparing for her funeral.

The earth seems to be on fire, every building is burning, giant flames leaping and swirling skywards in a vortex. Windows glow brightly against the surrounding black of brick walls and night. In the background an explosion flashes and the camera shakes, streaks and puffs of light dance macabrely, illuminating an edgy sky. A view down one broken street reveals cars burning and buildings incandescent with flames pirouetting into the sky.

"Christ, it's an inferno," Otto said in horror.

"The bombing of Hamburg, probably," Dieter said, staring at the screen with disbelieving eyes.

People run down streets between leaping flames, tumbling bricks and glowing roof timbers. Fire engines dispense water helplessly against an onslaught that is too great. A body lies on the pavement, contorted, twisted into an inhuman shape, clothes burnt off the naked body except for the leather shoes. A family sits huddled together in an exposed air raid shelter, their faces frozen in an expression of utter surprise, clothes perfectly intact but the roasted skin of their faces and scalps split open by the heat, exposing the blanched white of skull. More of these images fill the screen, both adults and children, in groups and singly, people taking shelter from the flames but extinguished by the intense heat.

"Jesus, Dieter, this is horrific," Otto said, covering his nose and mouth with both hands.

Dieter was unable to look away from the images on the screen. "Hamburg, I seem to recall, was badly bombed by the Allies." He nodded like a metronome. "It caused a firestorm... absolutely devastating; killed tens of thousands." He hesitated before turning to Otto. "This must be it."

Hamburg burns, bodies lying in silent surrender to the incendiary forces of war, way beyond the survival limits of humans, roasted in their clothing, buildings collapsed in ruin across ash–strewn streets. A swathe of Hamburg is gone. The image jerks and the screen turns white.

The rotating front reel, now mercifully empty of its awful memories, slowed to a stop. Otto couldn't move; his mind was traumatised by what he had seen. "I wasn't expecting that," he said quietly.

Dieter turned to look at him, his head cradled incredulously in his hands.

"Do you remember any of that?" Otto said.

"No, thank God," Dieter said, standing up, "I need a drink. Want one?"

"Is the Pope Catholic?"

Otto switched the projector off and stared at the coils of forty–year–old film wound tightly around the take–up reel. This very film had rolled through Father's movie camera, focused by his own hand on those heinous scenes, capturing events that, unlike the subjects in them, would now live on almost indefinitely in the eyes of those who viewed them.

Dieter returned with two tumblers half–filled with scotch and ice. He rested a hand on Otto's shoulder. "Not your average family home movie, is it?"

"You said something strange to me recently." Otto looked up. "You asked if we celebrated Christmas."

"Did I?"

"Uh–huh, you thought Sabine was Jewish."

"Oh yeah, I remember now."

"What did Ingrid tell you?" Otto said.

Dieter exhaled and shifted his body posture. "I can't remember, honestly Otto. I don't know why I got that notion in my head – something to do with Jews."

Otto frowned, thinking about the scenes they had just watched.

"I was wondering, since we've been watching all this footage of Neuengamme concentration camp, could there be a connection?"

Dieter shrugged. "I don't see how."

Otto's mind was swirling with crazy thoughts. "Obviously Dad and Mum were both German."

"Of course!" Dieter snorted loudly, pulling a face.

Otto paused and drank some of his scotch, his eyes downcast and ponderous. "What was Dad doing in that concentration camp?"

Dieter just looked at him.

"Why did they end up in Lüderitz?" Otto added. "Why don't we still live in Hamburg?" Otto sank once again into the soporific promise of the malt. "Part of me wants to watch that reel again."

"You don't believe your eyes?" Dieter said.

"I'm... astounded... and..." Otto struggled for the appropriate words, forming a contorted clawed shape with his hand.

Dieter took a deep breath and sat down on the corner of the dining table beside Otto. "I'll watch it again with you."

Otto rewound the film and they sat through it once more in complete silence, this time armed with scotch to assuage the abhorrence of the worst scenes.

They looked into the lifeless eyes of starving prisoners, clad in dirty rags, wondering how many of them lived to see the end of the war; watched two men being shot in the head for no apparent reason; they studied Alfred Trzebinski's clean-cut face and sharp clinical eyes, watched as he methodically poisoned innocent men powerless to refuse; they shuddered at the indiscriminate cruelty of war as Hamburg burned like a furnace under the calculated yet indiscriminate retaliation of Allied bombers.

Squeezed in between all of this were fragments of their happy family growing up in evident privilege, blissfully unaware of how fate would tear them apart as time unfolded its dispassionate destiny.

When the film ended for the second time they sat in silence until the phone rang. It was Frans. He had something to tell them, but he wouldn't do it over the phone.

TWENTY-ONE

"You been watching a film?" Frans said, glancing across at the projector and reels of film visible through the door into the living room.

"Just home movies," Otto said, placing three mugs of steaming black coffee down on the kitchen table.

"Where's Ingrid?"

"At the hotel," Otto said.

Frans nodded and tried his coffee, withdrawing abruptly and then blowing over the liquid. He looked uncomfortable, his eyes staring down at his hands and his shoulders constantly on the move.

"Listen, guys, I am sorry about this... what with your ma's funeral tomorrow and all that."

"What's happened?" Dieter asked.

"The Commissioner in Windhoek authorised for a sample to be taken from your ma and sent to England."

Otto felt an immediate pang, a sense of violation, even though he realised that this was unreasonable. Could they do such a thing without the family's permission? He suppressed the immediate urge to protest.

"For DNA analysis?" Otto said.

"Ja." Frans still hadn't made eye contact. "I'm sorry, guys. I just didn't know how to tell you."

"What sort of sample?" Dieter asked.

Frans pulled a face and shrugged. "Blood, I think."

"They'll compare her DNA with that of the body found in the garden, I expect," Otto said, then looked at Frans. "Any idea how long it will take?"

"They said we should have a result by next week."

Otto nodded in acceptance. The deed was done and there was little more to be said. This was a police investigation that had to run its full and proper course.

"Well, thanks for telling us," Dieter said.

"Are you coming to the funeral tomorrow?" Otto asked.

"Of course." Frans looked up for the first time.

Otto bit his lip, deliberating over the controversial notice they had seen in the paper.

"We saw in the Lüderitzbuchter that there is a celebration for Hitler's birthday tomorrow," Otto said.

Frans drew breath slowly and leaned back. "Ja, at Kreplinhaus."

"Why?" Otto asked, pulling a face.

"It happens every year."

"Every year?" Dieter said.

"It won't affect the funeral at all, don't worry," Frans said.

This seemed a small consolation to Otto. "It's abhorrent."

"There are a lot of Germans in this country; many of them were very sympathetic to the Nazi cause." Frans paused. "That has not changed."

"Who is Jurgen Göring?"

Frans raised his eyebrows. "The Görings are famous here. Reichsmarshal Hermann Göring – heard of him?"

Dieter and Otto nodded. Who indeed had not heard of Field Marshall Hermann Göring in the context of the Second World War in Europe?

149

"His father, Heinrich Göring, was one of the early Governor Generals of Deutsch Südwestafrika – er, German South West Africa." Frans fell silent and sipped his coffee cautiously. "Those Governors were responsible for implementing one of the most evil plans ever to come out of Germany."

"The Görings have strong ties to Lüderitz?" Otto said incredulously. He recalled having seen Göring Street in town but had never as a schoolboy made the link.

"Oh ja. They go back a long way here."

"In what way?" Dieter asked.

Frans' squint seemed to express itself suddenly, one eye contemplating Dieter while the other's gaze wandered without commitment about the room. "They created a place of such inhuman depravity… right here in Lüderitz. The worst of it all is that the Governor General's son, Hermann, together with Adolf Hitler and the rest of the Nazi elite, did exactly the same thing in Europe, just thirty years later." Frans measured his words and contorted his hands in tense, clawed balls.

Otto felt a chill run down his spine as he thought back to the images they had watched of Neuengamme concentration camp, captured amongst his family's very own cine film memories, interspersed with family picnics and days at the seaside. He caught Dieter's eyes and perceived in them great perturbation.

"What kind of place?" Dieter said.

Frans sat back and took a sharp, deep breath, glancing from Otto to Dieter. "You guys got some free time?"

They nodded in unison.

"Come with me. I want to show you something you probably don't know about."

Otto felt as though his heart was enlarging within his chest. He was both curious and apprehensive: would this have any bearing on his family history? Did this have something to do with Father? Having been to Kolmanskop and Inez's grave he assumed that the worst was behind him.

The air smelled strongly of kelp and salt, a richly pungent aroma that unmistakeably evoked heady perceptions of fresh fish and deep sea trawlers. The fog bank hugging the Atlantic Ocean was moving ever closer to the shore, looming ominously just beyond reach, threatening at any moment to invade the sanctity of land and obliterate its sovereignty.

Frans drove down to Hafen Street and parked beside Woermann Haus. The fluffy dice hanging from his rear view mirror twirled aimlessly after the car had been parked.

"Have you ever been to Shark Island?" Frans asked them as they began to walk towards the harbour.

"Dad's ashes were scattered on the island, but I don't recall ever going there," Otto said, pushing his hands deep into his chino pockets, warding off not so much cold as fear of impending unpleasant disclosures.

"Were they?" Frans said, raising his eyebrows.

They walked past the trawlers moored at the quayside where toothless fishermen mended nets and tended their vessels, the discordant clang of an occasional hammer echoing across the water. Seagulls swooped and cawed, constantly alert to the promise of fish.

"Is there anything out there?" Dieter asked, pointing towards the end of the Shark Island peninsula that protruded into Lüderitz's harbour like a dagger.

"Not anymore, but I'll tell you what it used to be, because

you won't find this in any books or tourist guides." Frans tapped the side of his nose. "Its history has been well and truly buried."

They walked past warehouses where forklifts moved pallets and crates back and forth. Workers waved to Frans – "Hello Chief," said some; "Gooie dag," said others, all evidently unable to disguise their curiosity as he walked the two strangers through their bustling enterprise to the open expanse beyond. One wrinkled, copper–skinned man with tight curly hair nudged his friend and smiled, revealing massive gaps in his dentition. "I told you not to smoke that dagga, Boesman," he said, and cackled wickedly. "The Chief's come for you."

Beyond the buildings and dockside activity Shark Island opened into a finger of craggy, windswept land fringed on three sides by rocky inlets where the waves crashed on caramel pockets of sand. Littering the sand were scores of dead crimson and purple jellyfish, the giant Namibian sea nettle over thirty inches in diameter, flattened on the sand in decomposing glassy domes, like remnants of a lemming run. Otto's hair whipped around his face and his clothes flapped about his body. When Frans reached the tip of the barren and inhospitable peninsula he stopped and turned to face them, his face silhouetted against the ghostly outline of the approaching fog and ethereal sunlight piercing it.

"Hermann Göring's father is credited as the idea behind this atrocity which his successor, Lothar von Trotha, saw fulfilled." Frans paused as the wind buffeted him "This, my friends, is the site of Germany's first concentration camp for extermination."

Otto thought he must have misheard Frans. "Exterminating what?" he said.

Frans looked at him without blinking. "Humans."

The wind gusted and stung Otto's eyes. A seagull swooped and splattered creamy excrement on the rocks nearby.

"The German settlers were not welcomed by the native tribes here, the Nama and the Herero, and constantly had to battle uprisings by the natives. Well, you can imagine," Frans said.

"It was the same in all colonial countries," Dieter said, resting one foot on a rock.

"Eventually they built the Shark Island concentration camp, right here." He pointed at his large, splayed feet. "In just four years they exterminated thousands of men, women and children. Conditions were apparently appalling." He walked towards the water's edge and gesticulated into the lapping waves. "If you scuba dive in the bay they say you'll find shackles and chains, rusting remnants of the manacles and restraints used on prisoners. But even worse, there are still bones down there amongst the sand and diamonds, Nama and Herero bones, never buried. No–one talks about that."

Frans held their gaze steadfastly, as if measuring the depth of their horror and shock.

"Killed, how?" Dieter said.

"Prisoners were simply worked to death. Many starved, died of disease, and some were just murdered. The camp doctor, a guy called Bofinger, decapitated dozens of prisoners and made the women boil the heads and scrape the flesh off the skulls with sharpened stones to clean them up for shipment back to Germany."

"Here, in Lüderitz?" Otto said in disbelief.

"Right here." Frans nodded.

Otto could feel himself paling. "Jesus Christ!"

"The skulls were sent back to Germany to be studied by

scientists, the same scientists who would later influence and assist Hitler."

"What?" Otto said, appalled.

Frans nodded. "They are still there, sitting in their museums, in glass cases." Frans paused. "Have you heard of Eugen Fischer?"

"Nazi doctor, wasn't he?" Dieter said.

"Ja. He started his work right here in this concentration camp, studying the natives, performing hundreds of autopsies, experimenting on them." He nodded solemnly, pointing to the ground. "Right here."

"No fucking way," Dieter said, mouth agape.

"You heard of Josef Mengele?" Frans asked.

"Of course," Otto said, "the angel of death."

"Did you know that he was one of Fischer's students? Mengele learnt from the best."

Otto swallowed. He had lived in Lüderitz from birth, left when he finished school, yet the place harboured awful secrets he had never heard about. What did this say about his childhood, he wondered? Was it also dissimulated, dressed up in platitudes and smoky half-truths?

"How do you know all of this?" Dieter asked with a look of abhorrence on his face.

Frans sat down on a rough rock. "As Police Chief you have access to lots of information; we call it 'intel'. I've got to know many things about this community. I have seen the Blue Book, a report on the treatment of natives in this country by the Germans, produced in 1918 by the British. They destroyed it a few years later, such was the outcry. In it was written that the lucky ones were shot before they reached Shark Island, that this camp was the first of its kind created with the specific purpose of extermination – a death camp; not for containment. Some of the accounts of violence, rape and torture are… unbelievably inhuman."

"They don't teach this in school, no-one has written about it – it's as though it never happened. But the Hereros know, the Namas and Damaras know: it is their ancestors whose skulls sit in a German university museum, murdered in the name of colonial tyranny."

Otto's brain was bursting, his pulse throbbing relentlessly in his ears even above the buffeting wind. Looking around him at the bleak landscape he wondered why Father had specifically asked for his ashes to be scattered here, on Shark Island. Why the site of a former concentration camp, a place where such atrocities and horrors were not only committed in the name of colonial subjugation, but seemingly exported to a mass market in Europe in 1939? How much did Father know about the island's history? Otto heard Wilma's admiring voice echoing in his head: your father would have been so proud. Proud of what? Proud of whom?

Father's presence in Neuengamme concentration camp could surely only mean that he worked there, or was invited to visit, perhaps in his capacity as a doctor. Was he a colleague of Dr Trzebinski, the man seen poisoning prisoners with arsenic in the films?

Suddenly Otto turned and retched on the rocky soil, and the wind caught his saliva and vomitus and aerosolised it, blowing it back into his face and shirt. Despite the chilly breeze he felt sweaty and wiped at his forehead with the back of one vomit-smeared hand.

Dieter approached to comfort his brother. Their eyes met, both men visibly distressed and confused. Looking back across the waters of Robert Harbour, turned a murky grey by the approaching fog, Lüderitz appeared quite different to Otto now: stark, ornate German colonial buildings imposed upon the hostile and forbidding black rock, just as the Germans themselves had forced their presence upon this land and killed off all resistance.

"You OK, Otto?" Frans asked.

"He'll be fine," Dieter said, turning away from Otto and examining the landscape that was visible from Shark Island. "Jesus, Frans, you sure about all of this?"

"Ja, I'm afraid so."

Otto no longer retched but remained bent over, watching the tendrils of stringy saliva that hung from his chin blowing in the wind. He was overcome with a foreboding sense of dread that they were on the cusp of very unpleasant revelations. Just what might be revealed about each and every one of them, not just Mother and Father but the Adermann children too?

TWENTY-TWO

The fog was gradually enveloping the land, its curling fingers extending across the harbour like a witch's breath, engulfing fishing vessels and dockside warehouses with effortless impunity. Around them the air was ripe with the smells of giant, floating offshore kelp beds, teeming with seals and fish in their own marine playground.

"I'm not sure this is a good idea," Dieter said apprehensively, hanging back at the entrance to the Hotel Zum Sperrgebiet.

Otto, still shaken by Frans' disclosures on Shark Island, pushed through the revolving door. "Let's just call it evening drinks… God knows I need one. We don't have to stay long."

Dieter looked sceptical but did not object as they each ordered a double J&B Rare from the lounge bar. He settled into one of the corner sofas beneath a towering potted ficus while Otto called Ingrid from reception.

"Fancy a drink down in the lounge?" Otto asked casually. The line was quiet for a moment. "OK. I'm just packing my suitcases. I'll be down in five minutes."

Otto frowned and shifted his weight from one leg to the other. "Packing, but the funeral is tomorrow?"

"Exactly. Tomorrow will be busy and I leave on Sunday."

"Ingrid!" Otto said, exasperated. "There's still so much to sort out."

Silence for a moment. "I'm done here."

Otto shook his head and closed his eyes. Ten minutes later Ingrid walked into the lounge looking surprisingly casual: cream pleated slacks, a billowing floral top and open sandals. Otto wondered how many suitcases she had brought with her.

Ingrid stopped abruptly as she noticed Dieter, but made no eye contact with him. "Oh, I see," she said icily.

"What would you like to drink?" Otto asked, rising quickly from his seat.

Ingrid sighed and planted her hands petulantly on her hips.

"We're having scotch," Otto said.

"Yes, so I see." Ingrid folded her arms. "What is this about?"

Otto smiled sheepishly and raised his arms. "Nothing. Come on, it's the funeral tomorrow and we were in the area so I suggested we pop in for a drink. Fog's in, it's Friday night…" He shrugged his shoulders.

Ingrid sat down opposite them, separated by a large light oak table with travel magazines piled neatly just off-centre. "I'll have a gin and tonic."

Dieter and Ingrid sat in silence, staring blankly in different directions while Otto ordered the drink. When he returned he sat on the edge of his seat and looked eagerly from Ingrid to Dieter.

"A toast… to Mum. May she rest in peace," Otto said.

"Mum," Dieter said, raising his glass.

Ingrid nodded and drank, apparently unsure where to fix her eyes.

"I feel really guilty about how little time I've spent thinking about tomorrow's funeral," Otto said, savouring the toasty alkaloids smoothing his tongue and obliterating the bitterness of vomit.

"Don't be," Ingrid said, meeting Otto's eyes. "None of this is of your doing."

The implication could not have been more direct and Otto's mind wandered to that bleak, windswept stretch of Shark Island where he had stood half an hour earlier.

"Frans called by today," Otto said.

Ingrid's eyes betrayed her curiosity. "About what?"

"They have sent a tissue sample from Mum for DNA comparison."

She straightened. "Can they do that?"

"The Police Commissioner in Windhoek ordered it. They want to know if there is a connection to our family, I suppose."

Ingrid's face was stony. "How will they know?" she asked.

"They'll compare Mum's DNA with the bones found in the garden." Otto glanced at a couple who strolled by and sat down in a snug opposite them, speaking German. "Frankly, I'm surprised they haven't taken samples from all of us."

"They don't need to," Ingrid said.

Otto glanced at Dieter, who was listening passively from the perimeter of the conversation.

"Meaning?" Dieter said.

Ingrid flushed and prodded the ice in her drink with a French-manicured fingernail. "Well, we were all children back then, weren't we, so how could we be involved?"

"I still think it will turn out to be a complete stranger," Dieter blurted suddenly, changing position in the armchair.

"Did Frans say anything else?" Ingrid asked, ignoring Dieter.

Otto opened his mouth to speak, frowned and glanced at Dieter. He knew there was no easy way to say this. "Frans took us to Shark Island this afternoon. We've just come from there."

"Why?"

"We asked him about the celebration of Hitler's birthday tomorrow and—"

"What did he say?" Ingrid interrupted.

"He said there are a lot of Nazi sympathisers living along this coastline – Lüderitz, Swakopmund, Windhoek – vestiges of the former German colony."

"I lived here for ten years and never knew anything about this," Dieter said, leaning forward, as if trying to muscle into the dialogue between Otto and Ingrid.

"I suppose it's not surprising – we left here as very young adults, you guys straight out of school. What does one really know about life and the world around you at that age?" Ingrid said without meeting Dieter's searching eyes.

"So, he took us to Shark Island and explained what it used to be back in the days of colonial German South West Africa, early 1900s," Otto continued.

Ingrid and Otto's eyes locked in an expectant, apprehensive stare.

"And?"

Otto drew a deep breath and looked at the whisky swirling amidst the melting ice cubes. "It used to be a concentration camp... a death camp, actually."

The skin around Ingrid's eyes tightened. "You mean like Auschwitz?"

"Not on that scale, they only killed thousands rather than millions here, but in the sense that people were brought to Shark Island with the intention of killing them... yes," Otto said.

Ingrid paled. Her eyes flicked about in her head. "What people?" she said.

"The locals – Hereros, Namas and so forth. They didn't like the Germans being here, taking their land, so the Germans tried to exterminate them. It sounds like genocide," Otto said.

"Jesus Christ."

Otto again thought about Father's wish to have his ashes scattered on the island. Why? Because of its present state: a remote and undisturbed peninsula with views of the surrounding natural beauty? Or because of its past?

"When was it closed?" Ingrid said.

"During the First World War, when the Germans were ejected." Otto paused. "That's when the true horrors of Shark Island were revealed. Frans has seen the reports."

Ingrid breathed in sharply and took a long drink of her gin. "I want to get the hell away from this place, back to New York," she said coldly.

A passing African waiter in a starched white tunic and black trousers, balancing a steel tray in one hand, stopped beside their table.

"Yes," Dieter said, emptying his tumbler in one gulp. "Same again, please."

"You didn't just pop in for a drink, did you?" Ingrid said, slumping back in her chair, almost in surrender.

"Ingrid, we watched another reel of film last night. It showed shocking scenes from inside that concentration camp in Hamburg…" Otto said.

"Neuengamme?"

Otto nodded. "Beatings, executions, medical experimentation. There was also disturbing footage of Hamburg being bombed by the Allies – dead bodies everywhere, destruction." Otto tried to catch Ingrid's eyes. "Do you remember any of that?"

Ingrid sighed. "I really wish you had never found that fucking box of film."

"She has a point," Dieter conceded. "This week would have been much simpler if we had just had the funeral."

"And the body in the garden?" Otto challenged.

The waiter arrived with their drinks. Dieter paid him and nodded. "Keep the change."

"Do you remember Hamburg being bombed?" Otto said to Ingrid, his tone softer.

"I do. It was awful. Terrifying. The noise, the smell, the claustrophobic bomb shelters." She studied her fingernails. "At school they used to talk... you know... tell us about the families who had died in bomb shelters during that firestorm... burnt alive. We were so scared it might happen to us." She glanced instinctively at Dieter but Otto sensed that Dieter was too young to remember. "I had nightmares for years afterwards," she added.

"Did you see the firestorm?"

Ingrid shrugged. "We were nowhere near that, thank God. Thousands died in it." She shook her head. "Thousands."

Dieter clasped his hands and began to wring his fingers. "I also have nightmares – dreams, really. I've been having the same one for years, always the same. It's about something being carried out of the house in a rolled-up carpet." He looked at Otto and Ingrid, who were both staring at him. "Do either of you have these, because I don't understand them?"

Otto and Ingrid shook their heads. Dieter seemed lost in his thoughts, his brow creased.

"I see a rolled-up carpet, which I think is that green one from my bedroom, being carried out of the house by a few people. I can never identify who they are – is it Mum, is it Dad?

– and I can never work out why I'm there – am I watching or am I taking part? There is something rolled up in the carpet and I… I fear that it is a body, though I've never seen it in the dream." He paused, deep in thought. "Whose body it might be, I have no idea."

Ingrid's face was drawn, her eyes staring glassily at Dieter as though she was watching a ghostly apparition.

"I don't know where the carpet and body end up – sometimes I see a skip against the wall, but none of it makes sense."

"Why have you never spoken about this before?" Otto asked.

"I feel so terribly guilty, as though I have done something wrong, waiting to be caught, anticipating that tap on the shoulder, or that phone call – expecting the inevitable repercussions."

Otto's stomach felt hollow just listening to Dieter, a gnawing emptiness that matched the yawning abyss of uncertainty deepening in his own mind.

"Since they found the body in the garden I've been wondering if there is more to my dream than I realise." Dieter looked at Otto. "I've never told anyone. How could I? It sounds in part like a guilty confession, like I know of some dreadful, incriminating deed in my past."

A sombre silence descended on the trio, united only by the clink of ice in their drinks and the sound of Supertramp in the background: Breakfast in America. The German couple opposite them burst into spontaneous but politely muted laughter as they shared a bottle of champagne.

"I have to know what's going on, I have to find the explanation for this dream and put it to rest. I can't go on living with this nagging guilt." Dieter looked at them intently.

"I've decided to cancel my flight back on Sunday, despite the merger going on. I'm going to stay until we know the truth. Today's visit to Shark Island has made me change my mind."

Otto could not suppress a small satisfied smile, and glanced at Ingrid. How he hoped she would change her mind and not leave straight after the funeral. He sensed an opportunity for them to put the past to rest and address their disharmony.

"What are you looking at me for?" Ingrid said gruffly. "Don't expect me to hang around."

"Frans said it'll only take a few days," Otto pleaded. "In any case, there is still another reel of film to watch."

"Oh God!" Ingrid said, rolling her eyes. "Not tonight."

"I agree," Dieter said, his face becoming animated. "Let's get mortared tonight."

"That's not what I had in mind," Ingrid said dismissively.

"How about dinner then, at that seafood restaurant overlooking the harbour?" Otto suggested.

Ingrid shot an icy glare at Otto as she drank from her highball glass. "And talk about what, Otto?"

Otto felt disappointment. He had thought he was breaking through Ingrid's barriers, that she was softening; not necessarily warming to her brothers, but at least becoming slightly more receptive. But the wall was up again, like a roller shutter deployed at the touch of a button.

"Mum?" Ingrid challenged. "Dad? Shark Island? Concentration camps?" She stood up with her drink in hand. "Christ, how can anyone even think of us as a family?"

"Family is only what we make of it," Otto said.

Ingrid looked at Otto, her face hard, her lips pressed together, her eyes unyielding. "Well no–one has made much of ours in the past fifty years."

"How can you say that?" Otto said with a pained look on his face.

"Because I know, Otto."

"Didn't you feel any sense of relief, of liberation from your burden when the truth came out about Inez?" Otto asked.

"Truth?" Ingrid smirked, shaking her head, almost mockingly.

"Can't you see the change in Dieter since he came out about his... you know... holding it back all these years out of respect for Mum and Dad?"

Ingrid almost laughed. "You must have been about the only person who didn't know, Otto, come on."

Otto was stung by this remark. He sensed his cheeks glowing.

"Knowing what I do now about Shark Island, about this community and possibly about Dad, I thank God that I never came out earlier," Dieter said, upending his tumbler again.

Ingrid manoeuvred her way between the table and sofas, holding on to her drink. "I don't want to watch any more of those home movies. I'll see you at Felsenkirche at 10am tomorrow." She paused and turned, casting a perfunctory glance at Dieter. "Thanks for the drink."

When she had gone Dieter emptied his tumbler and sat back in his soft armchair. "Ingrid is such a bitch."

"Dieter!" Otto admonished.

Dieter looked up in astonishment, lifting his hands in mock innocence. "What? She is. She doesn't give a shit about any of us."

"I think she's frightened."

"Of what?"

"That's what we need to find out. Come."

TWENTY-THREE

The telephone was ringing as Dieter and Otto entered the house, shrouded in an ethereal gloaming light that permeated the suffocating fog.

Dieter answered. "It's for you." He held the receiver out. "Sabine."

Otto knew from Sabine's first stressed sentence that something had happened. He sat on the armrest of the sofa and cupped an elbow in one hand.

"Where have you been?" she asked. "I've been calling all afternoon."

"What's wrong, honey?"

"It's Max, he broke his arm."

"What!" Otto stood up sharply, almost pulling the telephone off the little half-moon table.

"He had a fall during football – greenstick fracture of his distal radius." The helpful part of Sabine's medical background was that she didn't waffle.

"Is he OK?" Otto asked, frowning.

"What's happened?" Dieter whispered beside him, wearing a concerned look.

Otto shook his head and gesticulated aimlessly.

"He's asleep now. We were at A&E for several hours… you know what it's like. They gave him some morphine," a little waver was audible in her voice, "and he tried ever so hard to be brave."

Otto could hear Sabine's voice cracking. "You did great, honey, thank you. I'm sure he'll be just fine. Has he got a plaster on?"

Otto, trying to sound more nonchalant than he felt, heard Sabine sniff away some tears, melting his heart, the guilt of his absence from the warm nucleus of his family suddenly strikingly evident to him. He should have been there to support Sabine, to comfort Max and ease their collective burden.

"Yeah. It's one of those new fibreglass ones, in red and white, so he's quite proud of it." Sabine chuckled slightly but it made her sound even more upset.

Otto smiled – the colours of Max's favourite football team – but his guilt was growing. "I'm sorry I'm not there, love. I feel... awful."

"It's not your fault." Pause. "When is the funeral?"

"Tomorrow." Otto didn't know how to tell her that he was not planning to return immediately afterwards, that there was still unfinished business to tend to. "How is little Karl?"

"He's very concerned about his brother. I had to take him to Nell's, couldn't have him at A&E with me, you know."

They spoke more and Otto's guilt receded as Sabine's composure returned. The crisis was subsiding and there were no serious casualties. But the inevitable question he had dreaded eventually resurfaced.

"When can I tell the boys you'll be home? They miss you," Sabine said.

Otto felt a huge lump forming in his throat. "I want to come home after the funeral, but there are still some loose ends that need sorting. Just a few more days, OK?"

Otto was shaken after the call, walking around the lounge in deep thought. He began to feel that he was neglecting his family back in Durham, his priority. Then he thought of his mother's funeral and how little time he had spent thinking about her, grieving for her, and his guilt intensified further. He felt immensely disconsolate.

Dieter emerged from the kitchen eating a slice of rye bread and cheese. "Everything alright?"

Otto sighed. "Max broke his arm today."

"Oh man," Dieter said.

"He's fine, in plaster, but…"

"You feel you should be there?" Dieter said.

Otto nodded dejectedly.

"You can't be burying Mum and holding Sabine's hand simultaneously, Otto." Dieter laid a comforting hand on his brother's shoulder. "Let's just get tomorrow out of the way."

Otto knew he was right.

"Do you want to watch that last reel of film?" Dieter suggested with a mouthful of bread.

"You know, I don't. I'm not up to it right now. Can we do it tomorrow? I'm going to shower."

Otto felt suddenly exhausted, emotionally frayed from the day's disclosures. He needed sleep before the rigours of seeing his mother's coffin draped in white lilies, trucked in specially all the way from Swakopmund.

When Otto emerged fifteen minutes later from a hot shower he heard Dieter speaking on the phone, he presumed to Jim. The conversation became lively, Dieter raised his voice, and though Otto tried not to listen he was unable to suppress voyeuristic curiosity about his brother's domestic circumstances. This was, he could not forget, no ordinary lovers' tiff, and he was still coming to terms with his and Dieter's new sense of normality. Dieter ended the call and stormed through, catching Otto with the bath towel around his waist.

"You know what the worst thing about being gay is?" Dieter barked.

Otto raised his eyebrows.

"Men can be so fucking insensitive," Dieter said.

"Jim?" Otto ventured apprehensively.

Dieter nodded. "Sometimes I wonder whether he loves me, or my money."

Otto did not know how to respond, feeling unprepared and uncomfortable. What should he say to his brother: words of comfort, solidarity, enquiry? He had never had such a conversation with Dieter before and he was at a loss as to where and how to initiate it.

Otto rubbed his eyes. "I'm tired. Let's get some sleep and I'll see you for breakfast. Seven o'clock?"

Dieter scuffed the wooden floor with his shoes. "Goodnight. I… er… might go to the library early… some business to attend to."

"Dieter!" Otto chided. "It's the funeral tomorrow."

"It's urgent," Dieter said defensively before skulking off.

The grandfather clock in the lounge rasped to a precarious climax and struck nine times. How often had Mother not heard that familiar sound, Otto thought to himself? He realised that the clock represented constancy in his childhood memories: it had always been there, and unlike so many other facets of his former family life, it was still there. It had no doubt been there for Inez. It was there when Father was alive. It was there for

Mother after Father died. How odd that something as inanimate and uncaring as a clock should form one of his most reassuring and dependable childhood reminiscences.

Here he was sitting on the end of his old bed, alone, Ingrid segregated from them down at her hotel, and Dieter distanced from him by a gulf of unfamiliar waters. Had he expected that Mother's funeral might lubricate acquaintance between his siblings; soften the scarred edges of old wounds? Were they any closer than when they had arrived, or had the unwelcome intrusions of buried secrets simply driven them even further apart?

His mind turned to his children in Durham, growing up and forming their own memories. What would they recall fondly and reassuringly when they looked back one day? What would Max remember from this traumatic episode, shouldered entirely in his father's absence? How would it shape his childhood recollections?

The clock continued to tick as the chimes dissipated into the night, reverting to its quietly rhythmic state, a sound he would forever associate with the solitude of darkness in his childhood dreams. If only the clock could talk, he thought, what might it reveal about their early years, about Inez?

Had it seen more than the lens of Father's cine camera?

TWENTY-FOUR

Otto awoke to an empty house, again. On the morning of his mother's funeral he felt incredibly alone, abandoned, the protective layers of parental security stripped off him and his naked vulnerability laid bare with not even a brother or a sister to reach out and touch.

Breakfast comprised two cups of strong coffee. He had no appetite. By 9.30am he was shaved and dressed in the black suit he had brought all the way from Durham, reserved these days for sombre and formal occasions. At 9.40am Dieter crashed through the front door, dropping a sheaf of papers on the half-moon telephone table.

"Shit. Sorry Otto."

Otto's eyes were fixed on the herringbone mahogany flooring. "Of all days, why today Dieter?"

Dieter stopped, turning with his hands open in papal clemency. "I said I was sorry. You will thank me later, though."

Otto looked up at him angrily.

"I found something interesting in the library archives this morning," Dieter said.

Otto clenched his jaws and took a deep breath.

"Very interesting," Dieter said.

"We're going to be late! What are you on about?" Otto could no longer contain his annoyance.

"I'll have to tell you later. I've only got ten minutes to dress." Otto glanced at his watch. "Five!"

Felsenkirche was only two hundred yards down the hill from Bülow Street, the vertically stretched Gothic architecture on its pedestal of black rock, known as Diamantberg, towering above the little town of Lüderitz and visible for miles around. Ingrid was waiting at the arched stone entrance with her arms folded tightly across a magnificent knee–length black silk dress, white pearls around her neck and patent leather designer heels on her feet.

"Everyone's inside," she snapped. "The coffin is already in as well."

Otto and Dieter looked contrite but said nothing, straightening their jackets and adjusting ties.

"Jesus, you haven't even shaved!" she said, shaking her head at the sight of Dieter's stubbly face.

The melancholy tones of the organ being prodded and goaded by unpractised fingers wheezed from within. The interior of Felsenkirche was remarkably bland in contrast to the exterior colonial German stonework and steeply gabled Bavarian roof. Whitewashed rendered walls met a plain tiled floor covered sparsely with dark wooden pews. The most striking features were the enormous ornate stained glass windows donated by Kaiser Wilhelm II, set in vast stone Gothic arches. Vibrant regal hues of red, blue, green and yellow glowed in the sunlight around the crest of the emperor: Gestiftet 1912.

Resting peacefully on a chrome trolley in the nave, several yards back from the altar, was a light oak coffin draped in white lilies. Otto slowed and felt as though he'd been winded. This was finally it. This was goodbye. He knew in that instant that he would never forget the antediluvian smell of the Felsenkirche, tempered only slightly by the scent of the flowers and the odours of the mourners.

The congregation turned almost as one to stare at the trio of Adermann children as they walked conspicuously up the aisle to the front row. Wilma caught Otto's eye and smiled sympathetically. Frans' imposing bulk, squeezed into an ill-fitting suit, loomed in the right of Otto's vision. Other than the two of them there was not another familiar face in the church.

Otto found himself staring at the coffin most of the time, trying to will back memories of tenderness and warmth at the hands of his beloved mother, now preparing for her final journey in the box just yards away from him. He would never speak to her again, never hold her, never be held by her. Dieter appeared upset when they sang the final hymn, Abide With Me, and this surprised Otto as he fought to maintain his own composure. Ingrid never made eye contact with either of them.

Where is death's sting? Where, grave, thy victory?
I triumph still, if Thou abide with me.

Considering the distractions of the past few days Otto was not prepared for the sudden release of emotion as he watched Mother being wheeled down the aisle towards the waiting hearse by the undertakers. He and Dieter consoled each other, a brief reminder of the bond they had shared all those years ago. The congregation began to file out, many detouring past the front row to offer condolences.

Wilma, wearing a hairnet hat over her bun, kissed each of them on the cheek but lingered awkwardly in front of Otto. "My deepest condolences, Otto. Just remember, your mother thought the world of you and was so proud of how you've turned out." Why was it that Wilma insisted on embarrassing him in front of his siblings, Otto wondered?

Frans shook their hands in turn, holding them firmly in both of his, his face tortured by something indefinable. He seemed genuinely moved by the funeral service, his large frame appearing broken. "I will miss seeing your ma around town. She always had a smile and a wave for me," he said.

Everyone else was unfamiliar, mostly older men and women – lots of grey hair, balding heads, spectacles and walking aids. An extremely old man, walking slowly with the support of a younger woman and a Zimmer frame, stopped in front of the children. His face was lined and his cheeks sunken, yellowed eyes teary and veined in deep sockets. A persistent tremor racked his frail body.

"I knew your father," he said in a squeaky voice, nodding excessively.

Otto smiled back at him.

"I worked with him in Keetmanshoop."

Otto was interested. "Are you a doctor?"

"Was sagen Sie?" he said, leaning closer.

"Are you a doctor?" Otto repeated, louder.

The old man stared at Otto quizzically. "Was?"

"Ihre Hörrohr, Vater," his young daughter said to him loudly, prodding him, her mouth pressed against his hairy ears.

"I'm sorry, he is ninety and very deaf," she said to Otto.

The man rummaged in his coat pocket and produced a battered old brass Maelzel ear trumpet which he proceeded, after much fumbling, to insert into one ear.

"Are you a doctor?" Otto said again.

The man pulled a face, then suddenly nodded, his face brightening. "Ja, ja. I worked with your father in Keetmanshoop."

Otto took a deep breath and smiled.

"He was a good man, your father. I knew your mother too. We all respected them, admired your father for what he did." The ear trumpet shook in the old man's ear from the trembling grasp of his bony fingers.

"I didn't know he had a partner," Otto said.

"Was?" The old man said, screwing up his slack face.

Otto leaned towards the ear trumpet. "Thank you," he shouted.

The old man nodded eagerly. "I also remember your sister Inez. You know, I took her all the way to Otjiwarongo for your father when she was ill."

Otto glanced at Ingrid, who was busy speaking to another woman, and then at Dieter, who frowned. Otjiwarongo was nearly six hundred miles north of Lüderitz, the gateway to Etosha in northern Namibia.

"Otjiwarongo?" Otto repeated.

"Was sagen Sie?"

"Why Otjiwarongo?" Otto shouted.

"Ja. Otjiwarongo. Your father knew some German people there. They looked after her."

Otto struggled inwardly with the relevance of this difficult conversation. It was Mother's funeral and here he was trying to understand an old man's rambling recollections about Inez. He could not suppress a rising sense of irritation and he wanted to end the conversation, return his attention to Mother, but an enigmatic curiosity prevented him from doing so.

"It took me two days there and two days back."

The daughter smiled inanely at Otto, patiently waiting until her father was done.

"How long was she there – Inez, I mean? How long was Inez in Otjiwarongo?" Otto said loudly and deliberately.

"Was sagt er?" the old man said, half-turning to his daughter who spoke loudly and directly into his ear trumpet.

"Ah," the old man said, his face lighting up. He adjusted his position within the Zimmer frame. "Almost a full year."

Otto's mind was swirling. "What was wrong with her?"

"Was?"

"What… was… wrong… with… Inez?"

"Was sagt er?" The old man turned his veined and almost translucent face, resembling a pink gooseberry, towards his daughter. When she had repeated the question for him his eyes slackened and looked down, his entire body appearing to deflate a little. "I don't remember. She was very sad."

Why would Father send Inez so far away, Otto wondered? Surely not for reasons of psychological inadequacy. Had Mother known? Would she have endorsed such a decision? Instinctively Otto glanced behind him, through the arched entrance into the bright light outside, looking for Mother's coffin in the hearse. Why, even now as he was trying to bid her farewell and remember her fondly, were revelations continuing to emerge that questioned her complicity in distorting his childhood memories?

"Her boyfriend was from Keetmanshoop," the old man suddenly volunteered, causing Otto to snap his head around to face him intently once again.

"You knew him?" Otto asked.

"Was?"

"Did you know him?" Otto shouted. "The boyfriend?"

The old man's daughter recoiled slightly at Otto's sharp tone.

"Ja, ja, his family were from Keetmanshoop. Ja, I remember him. Nice boy."

The old man's daughter was beginning to smile awkwardly, trying to urge her father to move along, to allow the funeral to proceed according to its preordained ritual. The old man smiled and began to shuffle away under her guiding arm.

"What was his name?" Otto called out.

"Was?" The old man looked at his daughter. She tapped him on the shoulder and pointed at Otto.

"What was her boyfriend's name?" Otto repeated.

"Was sagen Sie?"

Dieter nudged Otto and leaned closer, whispering. "I know his name, don't worry the old guy."

Otto frowned at Dieter. "How do you know?"

"I told you I found out some things at the library. I'll show you later," Dieter said.

"Was?" the old man said again, grimacing such that his top denture flopped down slightly in his patulous mouth. His daughter spoke into his ear trumpet.

"Ah. His family name was Solomon, and his name was… ach… Ich habe vergessen…" He shook his head. "Solomon. Ja." He looked very pleased with himself, smiling as his daughter ushered him away.

"Nice to meet you, sir," Otto said, waving to him as he moved away, inch by inch. He caught the daughter's eyes. "Did you drive all the way from Keetmanshoop just for the funeral?"

She shrugged, slightly awkwardly. "Well, yes, but Father never misses the birthday celebrations."

Otto was suddenly reminded. "Oh."

"Jurgen Göring is speaking today, will we see you there later?"

Otto stared at her, aware that Dieter was too. "No."

She smiled thinly and moved away slowly with the old man.

Otto glanced at Dieter. "What the hell was that about?"

"The name's right. Neil Solomon."

"What did you find this morning?"

Ingrid began to move out of the pew. "Come you two, the cortege is leaving for the cemetery."

"I'll tell you later. Better still if I show you," Dieter said.

TWENTY-FIVE

It was a pitifully small gathering around Mother's grave and Otto considered that many of the mourners might have slipped off to Hitler's birthday celebrations at Kreplinhaus, eager to hear the provocations of Jurgen Göring. He wondered how few people might attend the tea they were putting on at Goerkehaus.

The three of them stood almost on top of Inez's grave, Otto separating Ingrid from Dieter. As the priest droned on at the head of Mother's grave, Otto studied the faces of those gathered in sombre abeyance. Frans stood opposite them, appearing to stare intently at Inez's headstone. Wilma was there, clinging to a man with silver hair and a pencil moustache, but the old man and his daughter were not in attendance, no doubt rubbing shoulders with their old friends at Kreplinhaus.

"Ashes to ashes, dust to dust," the priest chanted, casting a handful of sandy Lüderitz dirt onto the coffin.

Otto's wandering mind was drawn back momentarily by these words and he watched intently as his mother's coffin descended slowly into the quiet, rocky hole. He felt Dieter resting his head against his shoulder and was surprised to feel his brother's body shaking with grief. Glancing at Ingrid he could see her stony eyes staring past the priest, towards the east, the sand dunes and open desert.

He wanted to be upset, knew he should be inconsolable as the youngest, favourite son, but he was not. He wasn't sure how he felt. His mind was fizzing with irreconcilable thoughts: about Inez, about Keetmanshoop, about Otjiwarongo, about Neil Solomon. What role did these things play in his sister's death? What role did his mother play? How many secrets was she taking into the ground with her? He sighed and tried to catch Ingrid's eye. He failed. She was too far away.

After everyone had left and the fog was beginning its advance on the coastline once again, its tendrils snaking across the sandy soil, Ingrid, Dieter and Otto stood in silence staring at the two graves, side by side: Inez and Mother.

"Father should be here as well," Otto said, thoughtfully.

"You'd have thought he'd want to be buried next to Mum," Dieter said.

"And his daughter," Otto added.

"Why Shark Island?"

Otto knelt down and arranged some of the flowers on Mother's grave, taking a bunch of fresh lilies and moving it to Inez's grave. He moved some of the dead flowers out of the way.

"Watch out for scorpions," Dieter said.

Otto looked up. "Scorpions?"

"They like to shelter under the flowers. Apparently they're deadly around here."

Otto stood up. "Who told you that?"

Dieter nodded towards Ingrid. "She did."

Otto glared at Ingrid.

"It's true," she conceded.

"Poisonous?"

"Very."

"Frans told me the same thing," Dieter said.

"Frans?" Otto was confused, feeling as though he had missed something, been excluded from furtive discussions.

"Can we go now? I don't want to be in the fog wearing this – it's Armani silk," Ingrid said, turning and moving away.

The intensifying fog was beginning to bleed the colour out of their waiting taxi.

"Did you hear what that old man had to say about Inez?" Otto said to Ingrid as they walked.

"Old man?"

"The guy with the Zimmer frame and ear trumpet, I was shouting at him in the church. You must have seen him," Otto said.

"What did he say?"

"He said he drove Inez to Otjiwarongo for Dad when she was ill," Otto said.

"Ill?"

"She spent a year there… with friends of Dad's." Otto pulled a face.

Ingrid frowned. "I knew she went away, that's all."

Otto studied her face, evaluating her answer. "What was wrong with her?"

Ingrid paused beside the taxi. She looked across at Mother's fresh grave and gesticulated. "They're both resting now and it's finally all over. Please just leave it."

Otto was exasperated. "Jesus, Ingrid, what's finally over?"

Ingrid's eyes glowed defiantly as she opened the door of the taxi. "Not today, Otto. Just… leave it."

"Leave what?" Otto was angry suddenly and felt heat rising in his face.

He looked across at Dieter, who shrugged and turned away.

"I'm going to walk."

"I think I'll join you," Otto said, slamming the taxi door he had just opened.

The taxi pulled off with the sultry figure of Ingrid visible in the back seat, staring straight ahead, arms folded.

"I told you, she's a bitch," Dieter said.

Otto was angry. It was his mother's funeral and yet he was unable to mourn. He felt robbed of his duty as a son, of his right and indeed every human's need to grieve the loss of his mother. They walked in silence. Otto turned to look upon the mound that marked his mother's resting place but it was no longer visible, consumed by the grey fog.

A pair of hazy lights emerged out of the ethereal mist and drew closer. It was Frans' yellow Toyota police car. The car inched up to them, its wheels crunching on the gravel. Frans opened the window and his fleshy forearm came into view.

"You guys want a lift?" he asked.

"Thanks Frans, I think we'll walk," Dieter replied, scuffing the sand–smothered road with his shoe.

"Where's Ingrid?" Frans said, squinting past them into the deepening fog.

Otto sighed. He was embarrassed by his family's behaviour. Why could they not be like any other normal family?

"She left in a taxi," Otto said.

"Did something happen?" Frans asked, one hand on the steering wheel and the other elbow resting in the open window.

"I… er… I honestly don't know," Otto said, shaking his head. "Anyway, it doesn't matter, she's leaving tomorrow," he added and then instantly regretted it.

He sensed Frans studying them both through narrowed eyes, scraping his fingers across his stubbly chin, and for the first time Otto felt as though he was being scrutinised by a policeman who was investigating a dead body. The gravity of the unsolved crime weighed heavily upon him suddenly. Then

Otto wondered why Frans had come back. An uncomfortable thought made him shudder: was Frans watching them?

"She's leaving?" Frans said, scratching his ear nonchalantly.

"So she says."

Frans looked away and paused. "Are you going to Goerkehaus?"

"Are you?" Dieter said.

"No, I have to get back to the station, but I'll drop you off. It's not safe to walk in the fog. Drivers can't see you."

As he and Dieter climbed into Frans' police car Otto was filled with dread and a feeling of inexplicable guilt. Mother was buried and now all that remained was the serious unfinished business of the body, in which he was, by association, implicated. Suddenly he was wary of Frans, for he represented the law in Lüderitz.

TWENTY-SIX

Ingrid had not expected to see Frans at her hotel. She had bypassed Goerkehaus, deciding to forego the funeral wake, and was sitting in the hotel lounge listening to Cyndi Lauper singing Girls Just Want To Have Fun over a cup of steaming Darjeeling when he walked in. She stopped, teacup suspended in mid-air, as Frans approached with his languid lope.

"Hi Ingrid."

"Frans." She tried to hide her surprise.

He sat down, easing his bulky frame into a rattan chair with as much delicacy as he could muster. "You OK?"

She pulled a face and sipped her tea. "We've just buried Mother."

"Ja, I still remember when we buried Pa, it's... unsettling."

They looked at each other in silence for a moment. Ingrid wondered what he wanted.

"You didn't go to the tea at Goerkehaus?" Frans said.

Ingrid shrugged. "It seemed that most people were probably at Kreplinhaus for the fucking Führer's birthday party. Any case, I'd had enough for one day."

Frans could not disguise his surprise at hearing Ingrid swear. "I dropped Otto and Dieter off at Goerkehaus," he said.

So, Frans probably knew that she and the boys had parted awkwardly, Ingrid thought, staring at his squint, wondering which eye to concentrate on when he spoke.

"Can I ask you something, Ingrid?" Frans said with an intake of breath, leaning forward and clasping his hands between his meaty knees.

Ingrid's heart leapt into her throat and she put her teacup and saucer down on the table for fear of it rattling in her grasp.

"Do you remember Inez's funeral?"

Ingrid was not expecting this. "God, that's cruel." She felt her eyes moisten.

Frans sat back. "I know you were very close to her – she was your big sister." He paused, appearing to drift off for a moment. "I had an older brother who died. I know what it's like."

Ingrid looked down at her hands, willing herself to remain calm and unflustered. Inside though, her heart was pounding like a thoroughbred at the final furlong.

"What do you want to know?" she said without looking up.

"Can you remember her funeral?"

Ingrid bit her lip. "Yes."

"It must have been very traumatic for you. How old were you, thirteen?"

"Fourteen," Ingrid replied coldly.

Frans folded his arms over his protruding belly and angled his head. "Do you not remember anything about this body in the garden?"

Ingrid studied Frans' face, nervous to blink, suddenly aware that he was watching every reaction, every instinctive response; suddenly conscious that she was talking to a policeman, alert to the reality that she was being tested. Ingrid knew she had to be extremely careful about every word she let slip from her mouth.

She shrugged, looking away. "Fourteen is still a child."
Silence for a moment. Cyndi Lauper was finished. German

tourists milled in the foyer, talking and laughing loudly. Ingrid picked up odd words: Kolmanskop; Kreplinhaus; Felsenkirche; Jürgen Göring.

"You're leaving tomorrow?" Frans said.

Shit, Ingrid thought, the boys must have told him. She didn't want to appear flustered or defensive, and smiled nonchalantly. "I've got to get back. The funeral's over."

"What about the house, the furniture, personal belongings?" Frans said, pressing the ends of his fingers together in front of his chin.

"The boys will sort that out. I'm not interested in anything."

"Would you mind coming with me?" Frans said. "It won't take long."

"Erm…" Ingrid hesitated, caught completely off guard.

"I wouldn't ordinarily do this on a day such as this, but if you're leaving I won't have another chance, you understand," he explained.

"What's this about?"

"I want to show you something down at the police station."

Ingrid felt light-headed and she tried to swallow, but her mouth was too dry.

"Don't worry," Frans said with a chuckle. "It's OK."

Ingrid knew she could not refuse, as much as she was deeply reluctant and apprehensive about what he might be about to show her. Why did he specifically want her to come along? Why not Dieter and Otto? Why not all of them? Or had they already been shown whatever it was he wanted her to see?

She smiled nervously, trying to appear nonplussed. "Sure. Whatever."

Lüderitz Police Station was close to the Adermann house on Bülow Street, just across from Bismarck Road on the way out of Lüderitz. It was an old German colonial building decorated in white with beige coloured frames around the sash windows. Sand was piled up against the walls that faced the Namib Desert, and also formed an eccentric mound around the base of the flagpole.

"Hello Chief." A uniformed African officer greeted Frans as they entered.

"Sergeant," Frans returned, walking through to his office situated behind glass–panelled walls.

His office was like a goldfish bowl in the centre of the building and it made Ingrid feel very exposed and vulnerable to scrutiny. On the bland government–issue desk was a photograph of Frans' obese family, framed in rustic quiver tree wood.

"Are you going to fingerprint me or something?" Ingrid blurted out nervously.

"Do I need to?" Frans replied, unnervingly confident on his own turf. He closed the glass panel door and walked over to a steel filing cabinet. "Sit down, please Ingrid."

Ingrid's heart was racing. She felt out of control, cursing her presence in Lüderitz. She blamed Otto for persuading her to leave the comfort and security of her Manhattan apartment in the first instance, without which she would never have ended up sitting in the centre of Lüderitz Police Station, frightened out of her wits. Frans pulled the top drawer open along its squeaking rollers and then stopped, turning to face her.

"This might be difficult for you; take a deep breath."

"You're frightening me, Frans," Ingrid said, her voice wavering. She pressed her knees together tightly, squeezing her clasped hands.

"It's OK." He smiled. "After we gathered the remains of the child's body we sent the skull to a forensic laboratory in Johannesburg. Have you heard of forensic artists and forensic anthropologists?"

Ingrid's ears were rushing as adrenaline-fuelled blood pumped through them. "No."

"What they do is to reconstruct facial features in three dimensions using clay, for example, to substitute for each layer of tissue: muscle, fat, skin. You understand?"

"Uh-huh." Ingrid dug her fingers into each other in her lap.

"It's not perfect but can be remarkably close." He drew breath and plunged both hands deep into the open drawer. "I'm going to show you a reconstruction of the child's skull. See if it rings any bells."

Ingrid covered her mouth with one hand, her eyes flinching as though she were in pain. She was trying ever so hard to exude calm indifference, fully aware that she was subject to prying scrutiny in Frans' transparent office. But her nerves were making this impossible. When the little reconstructed skull was lifted from the drawer, revealing a bald head and smooth face sculpted in grey clay, she gasped at the unnerving resemblance to an infant child she had not seen for four decades.

"You OK?" Frans said, pausing in mid-air with the clay head.

"I've never done anything like this before," Ingrid said, her lungs hungry for air. "How do you expect me to be?"

Frans slowly placed the reconstructed child's head on the desk in front of Ingrid. A round metal support protruded from below the head onto a wooden base. She shrank back from it, even though she couldn't take her eyes off it.

"Is the real skull… inside?" Ingrid asked, hesitantly.

Frans nodded. "Sometimes we use a plaster cast, but in this case it is, yes."

The thought of that child's skull sitting right in front of her, albeit smothered and disguised by clay, made the hairs on Ingrid's neck rise. This very same skull had lain undiscovered in their garden for nearly forty years.

The reconstructed features were fine: a small nose, flat brows, full infantile cheeks and a defined chin. In place of eyes two indentations in the clay simulated pupils.

"Jesus." Ingrid suddenly looked away, burying her face in both hands.

"The ears are usually a guess; don't pay attention to them. Sometimes the nose as well, though to a lesser extent. But I'm sure you'll agree, it is certainly not a Herero child, nor a Damara, or any ethnic African. This is a European child."

When Ingrid looked back at the reconstruction she was aware of Frans' eyes on hers, his belly hanging over his belt, one shirt button undone near the navel revealing pale hairy skin. Her eyes wanted to look anywhere but at the child's head. A sudden rap on the glass door made Ingrid jump.

Frans dismissed the uniformed officer. "Come back later, Eric, I'm busy, OK?"

"Why are you doing this to me?" Ingrid asked in a tiny voice.

"You said you remembered Inez's funeral?" Frans said, inclining his head.

"So?" Ingrid's voice was barely audible.

"You are the oldest of the three children and therefore most likely to remember something. Evidence suggests that the body was buried around the same time as Inez's funeral, maybe a few years earlier: 1946, '47 or '48. Dieter was probably too young, being only... what... four or five, and Otto just an infant."

Ingrid's frightened eyes met Frans' confident gaze. She felt on trial, her bladder weakening, her knees trembling, and she cursed her mother, only recently buried, and her father. Damn him. Damn them both. It was their fault that she was sitting in Frans' office at that moment.

"Do you recognise this face, Ingrid?" Frans said calmly. "Look carefully."

Ingrid forced herself to study the reconstructed head again. The artist had set the thin lips slightly apart, breathing a sense of life into the little child's inanimate clay face. She shuddered.

"Why do you think I should know this boy?" Ingrid said. Frans rubbed his chin without a flicker of expression. "You think it's a boy?"

Ingrid felt lightheaded. Jesus, what had she said? She was not handling this well. "Didn't you say it was a boy?"

Frans shook his head slowly. "I didn't say that."

"Is it a boy?" Ingrid's desperate eyes sought Frans' face.

"We don't know, yet. What do you think?"

Ingrid stood up and turned away. "Why are you asking me these things, making out I've done something? Christ, Frans, we've just buried my mother!"

"So, you've never seen this face before? You don't recognise this child?" Frans asked directly, pointing to the head.

Ingrid didn't know what to say. She was trapped and alone. She feared that saying the wrong thing might implicate her. Equally though, saying nothing could be misconstrued. For some inexplicable reason she suddenly wished her brothers were there with her, or at least Otto. She felt desperately forsaken, singled out and under interrogation, in a police station.

"This is a shocking thing to see," Ingrid said, pointing behind her back towards the desk without looking. "You could have warned me."

Frans leaned his frame against the edge of his desk. "It's a necessary part of the investigation, Ingrid; just a formality. We have to figure out what happened."

Ingrid felt nauseous. "Can I go now please?" She sensed Frans' eyes upon her, examining, probing, as though she was transparent.

"I would like to ask you, nicely, not to leave tomorrow. This child's identity has to be established and your family are the only people to have lived on that site."

"Meaning?" Ingrid retorted tersely.

Frans shrugged his rounded shoulders and maintained his silence as his disconnected eyes flicked across Ingrid's face. Her heart beat faster and faster. She had not seen this coming, this noose tightening around her neck.

"You already have Mother's DNA?" Ingrid said.

Frans shrugged. "That may not be enough."

"Am I under arrest, or suspicion?"

"Ingrid, I can't force you to stay, but the Commissioner in Windhoek might." His face softened and he smiled. "Please just hang around a little longer: you, Otto and Dieter. Let's not get the brass in Windhoek involved, eh?"

When Ingrid reached her hotel room, she shut the door in sudden relief and sat down in a daze on the edge of her quilted king size bed. Then she burst into tears almost immediately, covering her face with both hands, trying to smother the tears, hoping to force them back inside. Her body shook as her lungs longed for air, and she felt as though consolation was as unattainable as immortality. She could not remember when last she had cried. Not for Father. Not for Mother. It had been a long time ago. God, how it hurt.

TWENTY-SEVEN

The tea at Goerkehaus was poorly attended, and after idle chatter with a few of Mother's and in some cases Father's friends, all wholly unfamiliar to him, Otto found himself standing alone with Dieter in the large, echoing room. Devoid of any decorations to soften the starkness of light yellow walls and well-trodden parquet flooring, it was fittingly bland and funereal.

"This is not what I imagined it would be like, you know," Otto reflected over his third cup of tea.

"In what way?" Dieter said.

Mother was buried. They had met and shaken hands with many strangers who had come to pay their last respects. It suddenly felt very deflating, final, yet almost insignificant.

"I'm not sure," Otto admitted. "For one thing I thought we'd all be together today."

Dieter scoffed.

"What did you find this morning?" Otto asked, angling his body towards Dieter surreptitiously.

Dieter glanced at his wristwatch, his eyes suddenly animated. "The library's still open. Let's go and I'll show you."

Lüderitz Library was small and unassuming, a provincial library in every sense, right down to the middle-aged bespectacled woman bent over the reception desk. She smiled warmly at Dieter, revealing nicotine–stained teeth.

"Grüss dich, Dieter."

"Hallo Eva." Dieter nodded and gesticulated to Otto. "Das ist mein Bruder."

"Angenehm," Eva said, glancing perfunctorily at Otto.

Otto smiled and greeted her, catching sight of the large fax machine just to Eva's left and imagining the hours Dieter had spent on it right beside her. Noticing Eva's wide eyes returning swiftly to Dieter, Otto wondered if she fancied him – after all, he was a handsome man of about the right age for her. It made him feel peculiar realising what an absurd notion this was, though Eva was probably quite unaware of it, as indeed he had been until a few days ago.

Dieter moved towards the back of the quiet room, past low shelves stacked with books and a few empty reading tables with desk lamps centred on each one. Otto followed dutifully. The library was empty and the mousy smell of old paper was strong.

"I was amazed to find they have back issues of the Lüderitzbuchter archived on film," Dieter said, sitting down in front of a Canon microfiche reader.

He opened a drawer beside his left leg and flicked through the sections until he reached 1948. Pulling this out he opened the plastic binder and leafed through A4-sized sheets, each revealing multiple rows of small images.

"Here it is," he said, extracting one and inserting it into the scanning tray of the microfiche reader.

With the lamp switched on, a grainy and marked image of each page of the Lüderitzbuchter was projected onto the display screen. Dieter moved the tray around until he found what he was looking for.

Local doctor's daughter found shot in Kolmanskop

Yesterday the bodies of a young man and woman were found in an abandoned house in Kolmanskop. They had both been shot in what local police chief Andre Strydom called apparent suicide. Though no note was found police have said they do not suspect foul play.

Willem Laubscher, security officer at the diamond company responsible for patrolling the Sperrgebiet, made the discovery. He also found a revolver, from which two rounds had been fired, beside the bodies.

The woman, Inez Adermann (21) is the eldest daughter of local doctor Ernst Adermann, and had only lived in Lüderitz for two years since emigrating from Germany.

The man has been identified as Neil Solomon (23) from Keetmanshoop. His father, Jacob Solomon, is a prominent member of the South West African Transport Company and has been credited with developing rail links between Windhoek and the southern towns of Keetmanshoop and Oranjemund, as well as into the Union of South Africa. This is a project that his late father, Isaac Solomon, was involved with under German colonial rule in the early 1900s. Isaac Solomon was honoured for his services to Deutsche–Südwestafrika by Governor Lothar von Trotha.

Neil Solomon was buried in the Keetmanshoop cemetery yesterday and Inez Adermann's funeral will take place in Lüderitz on Saturday 15th September.

The shootings have shocked residents of Lüderitz, who are unaccustomed to such tragic events in their quiet community. Willem Laubscher said it was not unknown for lovers to meet up in the abandoned houses in Kolmanskop, though he admitted that in this particular case this was mere speculation.

Police are not investigating.

Dieter looked up at Otto, who was reading over his shoulder.

"Jesus," Otto whispered.

"The old man was right: Inez's boyfriend was from Keetmanshoop. Sounds like he came from an influential family."

"Neil Solomon," Otto mused. "I wonder how Dad felt about this?"

"What do you mean?"

"Well, Dad had a surgery in Keetmanshoop. They must surely have met through his association with the town. After all," Otto shrugged, "it's isolated, over two hundred miles away in the desert."

Dieter and Otto locked eyes. "You thinking what I'm thinking?" Dieter said.

"Do the Solomons still live there?"

Dieter nodded, glancing back at the dimly illuminated screen. "Would you want to go there?"

Otto thought about this. Did he want to know more about his dead sister: about what happened to her and possibly why; about the reasons why Mother and Ingrid had conspired to keep not only her death but indeed her life secret, long after Father passed away?

"Absolutely," Otto said.

Strangely, it felt to Otto as though this journey might represent an opportunity for some closure after the tumultuous events of the day. Burying Mother had left him very unsettled, struggling with more questions than answers, and it was not an enviable position to be in.

"How would we get there?" Otto said.

"I'll speak to Frans," Dieter said.

"And Ingrid?"

Dieter shrugged indifferently. "She leaves tomorrow anyway."

The sounds of papers being shuffled and keys jangling echoed across the room. Eva was closing up. Otto looked up at the wall clock: 5pm.

"Let's go home and watch the last reel of film."

TWENTY-EIGHT

For the first time that he could recall Otto was apprehensive as he lifted the heavy steel reel laden with hundreds of feet of film onto the spindle. Lacing the film leader through the projector, over sprockets and around rollers, filled him not with the customary anticipation and excitement, but with anxiety. What further dark secrets might await them, captured in moments of apparent innocence and wholesome intentions, etched frame by frame onto celluloid for the unsuspecting eyes of subsequent generations to scrutinise and question?

He checked the sprockets, the loop of film preceding and following the film gate, repeatedly, stalling the inevitable moment of truth.

"Are you ready yet?" Dieter called back over his shoulder from a sofa in the darkened room.

Otto drew breath slowly. No, he was not, he thought to himself. Closing his eyes momentarily he tried to reassure himself: surely there could not be any more shocking surprises.

He switched the projector on. The screen lit up as the Bell & Howell's mechanical purr filled the silence, effortlessly transforming twenty-four individual images every second into fluid movement on the screen.

Grainy, lined black and white images of Lüderitz town fill the screen from left to right, the view panning from the rocky and desolate Diaz Point with its beacon, right around to the unspoilt kelp–strewn Agate Beach north of the town. The image dwells on the small fishing harbour in which half a dozen wooden vessels gently pitch and roll on the swell. A rough splice flashes and the screen fills with Felsenkirche and its imposing tall Victorian Gothic steeple. In the background the uninviting emptiness of rolling sand dunes appear stark and uninhabitable.

"Dad taking in his new home," Dieter mused.

"I wonder if we were here yet?"

The image of a rusting shipwreck partially submerged in the consuming sands of a beach appears. Most of the keel and lower hull is covered with sand and the rest has been devoured by the elements. Reaching up like a clawed hand, frozen in rigor mortis, or perhaps resembling a Blue Whale's skeleton, remnants of arched bulkheads and hull beams create a vague impression of the past solid grandeur of the vessel. The camera passes in between the rusting steel girders that tower above the viewfinder. In the background the steeple of Felsenkirche can be seen.

Another messy splice smears the screen and then a new wreck comes into view, far less corroded and more intact than the first one. It lies stricken on a narrow beach nestling at the foot of an immense ellipse of barren rock forming a bay, like a gigantic crab's pincer. The camera zooms in to the bow, revealing the word Otavi in rusted white letters. The hull is clearly breached, its keel broken, yet it looks as though it has not been long on the sand.

"I remember the Otavi!" Dieter said. "We saw it on a boat trip up the coast."

"I've never seen it."

"It was amazing. It didn't look like that when I saw it,

though, it was far more rusted and falling apart."

"Why did we never go there?" Otto asked.

"It's in the Sperrgebiet – I'm pretty sure."

The diamond company controlled almost everything that surrounded Lüderitz, Otto reflected. "What was the name of that bay again?" he asked.

He could see Dieter scratching his head. "Spencer Bay," he said, raising an index finger in triumph.

"I wonder if the wreck's still there? I'd love to see it," Otto said, with a slight surge of boyish enthusiasm.

"We should ask Frans."

The image changes abruptly to a barren piece of rocky land forming a slope. It looks like any other undeveloped area of Lüderitz: black rock smothered by invading sand. A small huddle of people stand together on the rocks. The camera zooms in on their faces. Mother, windswept and unsmiling, failing to keep her curly hair out of her eyes. A tall, slender young woman in a skirt, short socks and black shoes; pretty, smiling face with sharp features. Beside her an unhappy-looking adolescent girl with pouting lips and arms folded stares away into the distance, one leg pointing to the side, while a small boy, barefoot and dirty, holds onto Mother's leg and sways around it as if testing its strength.

"Christ," Dieter exclaimed, "that's us here in Lüderitz. I would guess that must be Mum, Inez, Ingrid and me." He sounded quite excited, sitting forward in his seat, gesticulating at the screen as he picked out each family member.

Otto's heart jumped – it was a strange thing seeing images of the family from so many years back, captured in pure naive innocence, a moment never to be repeated but preserved in time forever. Who could have known on that windy day when

Father filmed the family that Inez would not endure in its bosom for very long? What was it that had ripped this cohesive family image apart, consigning it to wilful deception, buried secrets and years of accumulated resentment?

The next image shows the little boy clamouring over brickwork and into foundation trenches, smiling into the camera lens at every opportunity when he is not checking his footing on the hazardous building site. In the background African labourers with bared torsos swing pickaxes above their heads and smash them into the unforgiving rocky ground, others mix cement and water in great volcanic heaps, while a solitary European man, smoking a pipe beneath a straw fedora, lays bricks amidst a cloud of white smoke.

"Hey, I bet they're building our house!" Otto said, studying the shaky images carefully, looking for something that he might recognise as familiar and be able to place in the finished home in which they now sat.

"Must be about 1946, I guess. Isn't that when the house was built?" Dieter said.

"Uh–huh."

The panoramic view from the house, over Felsenkirche's steeply gabled Teutonic roof, reveals the entire little port town of Lüderitz, the contained harbour with moored fishing vessels and the finger of Shark Island protruding into the bay.

"Dad sure chose a great spot for the house," Dieter said.

The unfinished walls of the house are now near roof height, the unpainted concrete shell clearly identifiable as their future home. The camera pans from one side of the new house to the other, revealing the early stages of construction work on the brick wall that will surround the property, and the rocky garden that is devoid of any plant life.

"Do you see that?" Otto said, feeling a shiver run down his spine.

"What?"

Otto felt slightly queasy. "There is no camelthorn tree."

Otto's eyes were drawn to the relatively flat patch of sandy soil near what appeared to be the incomplete kitchen window, still just a raw square space in the wall. He wondered if the soil beneath the builder's feet had been violated yet and transformed into a grave.

Father stands, smiling demurely, beside a gleaming plaque bearing his name in Gothic script: Dr Ernst Adermann. The shaky image reveals a doorway and the facade of a typical German colonial building in Lüderitz. He lifts his homberg and enters the building, large black doctor's bag in hand. Suddenly the little boy, wearing a striped short–sleeved shirt, runs into view and disappears through the darkened doorway behind Father. The image begins to jump, blurring the picture on the screen beyond recognition.

Otto leapt into action and depressed the loop restorer. The jarring noise in the projector subsided and the steady picture returned.

Mother smiles thinly at the camera. She looks tired, and when the camera angle changes the reason becomes clear. She is pregnant.

"That must be you, Otto," Dieter chuckled, gesticulating at the screen excitedly.

Otto smiled – his first appearance in the family home movies. There was Mum, young, full of life and bearing another child, her life ahead of her. It reminded him painfully of the inexorable bond between a mother and child: had it not been for her, captured forever in those few seconds of film, her immortality preserved in celluloid for eternity, he would not have life. He would not have the capacity to question what she had done, what decisions she had made while raising her family – the consequences of which they were now unravelling, slowly, painfully.

Her chapter in the book of their family had ended that morning when they watched her sink down into the rocky soil of Lüderitz, not dissimilar to that she was standing on in the film. Yet for a few moments longer she lived on in black and white in their living room, fresh, youthful and energetic.

"Strange thought, isn't it?" Otto said, tapping his lip with a finger.

The scene jags to a celebration in their house, revealing the living room, the kitchen, the entrance hall with gleaming herringbone flooring. Heavily framed paintings of German scenes adorn the walls: Hamburg; Freiburg; Pomerania. Men are dressed in suits and narrow ties, wearing hombergs and trilbies, and women glide about in long dresses with brooches and gloves, smiling and chatting in small groups, drinking tea and eating cakes.

Mother appears, smiling and holding a baby swaddled in long white baptism robes in her arms. All the women hover like bees and lovingly touch the baby's cheeks repeatedly.

"Lüderitz welcomes Otto Adermann," Dieter said in a mock announcer's voice.

Otto smiled involuntarily. There he was, a bouncing baby boy of not very many months old, in his mother's arms. The trickery of film made it seem as though it was yesterday.

Suddenly Father is holding the baby, smiling proudly, homberg still firmly on his head, a thin and manicured moustache across his upper lip. Then another jump change to the family gathered in the living room in front of the window, the image unsteady and angled. Father and Mother stand in the centre holding the baby; the pouty face of a smartly dressed adolescent girl beside Father, tolerating the attention but not smiling; and the little boy in shorts, a jacket and tie, hanging onto his mother's leg.

"It's weird, but I think they were filmed standing exactly where the screen is now," Dieter remarked, pointing to the sheet suspended in front of the living room curtains.

Otto nodded. But for the passage of four decades the whole family could just as well have been standing there at that very minute.

"Where is Inez?" Otto asked.

"Haven't seen her yet."

"This is obviously 1948, it's the year she died," Otto said, painfully aware that his entrance into this world had almost simultaneously marked Inez's departure, as though in accordance with a divine plan to maintain equilibrium. Yet he had been utterly unaware of this until last week.

Baby Otto's face fills the screen. His eyes dart about and then settle in fascination on the camera, staring straight ahead. He has a small upturned nose above a long philtrum, and grasping hands that plunge in and out of his yawning mouth.

Otto stared at himself, captured on film thirty-seven years ago. He tried to imagine what those undeveloped eyes might have seen, what his immature brain might have been thinking.

The screen fills with a sports field resembling a dustbowl, flat and grassless, across which twenty-two children swarm after a football. Netless goalposts, like leafless trees, stand guard on each end of the forlorn scene. The camera pans up and down the field, trying to keep up with the haphazard action around the ball. One team of boys wears white and the other striped jerseys. The image zooms in on a boy kicking the ball only for it to rebound straight back at him. He hesitates, then dribbles the ball left of his opponent and, as an opposition player stumbles over his own feet leaving the goalposts unprotected, the boy kicks a goal to the delight of his teammates and supporters around the field.

"Did you see that, Otto?" Dieter said, turning around in his seat. "Left foot, edge of the penalty box. I used to have it."

"That was you?" Otto said.

"Uh–huh. Top goal scorer in my senior year."

The camera zooms in on the spectators. Mother stands at the halfway line cradling an infant. Beside her, looking away, is a solitary, gangly adolescent girl with her arms folded.

"Mum with me, Ingrid next to her, and you on the field, Dieter. No Inez," Otto observed.

"No Inez," Dieter said.

A messy splice is followed by an image of the harbour, a group of adults and children embarking a small seagoing vessel. Mother is there, Ingrid with her hair in a ponytail, Dieter wearing a sports cap, and a toddler waddling beside them with a broad gait, holding Ingrid's hand. The next scene is of the bay, light reflecting sharply off the water and dancing in the camera lens while seagulls, oystercatchers and flamingos swoop around the boat. The camera leans over the boat revealing seals playing in the water, following the boat like dolphins. An island comes into view, its rocky shoreline smothered in penguins. Several people on the boat pull out cameras and take snaps of the undisturbed fauna teeming in its thousands.

"I think it was on this trip that Dad nearly lost the camera overboard," Dieter reminisced.

The boat turns away from the island, exposing on the port bow the panoramic view of Lüderitz town across the bay. The tip of Shark Island comes into view and beyond this, on a desolate stretch of rocky shoreline, an abandoned whaling station. A rusted white sign is visible on the beach as the camera zooms in: Sturmvogel Bucht.

Mother sits on the wooden bench seat keeping Otto within her range as he waddles around unsteadily on the deck, occasionally thrown to his knees by the sudden movement of the small vessel. Ingrid sits on the opposite side beside Dieter, looking around with apparent disinterest, while Dieter is delighted by the occasional spray of seawater as it aerosolises off the bow, trying to catch it in his hands. Otto swaggers over to Ingrid and lurches forward, falling onto the wooden slatted deck. She bends forward and picks him up, placing him on her lap.

"I look about two years old there," Otto said as he watched his infantile image on screen.

"I remember this trip," Dieter said. "Well, parts of it anyway."

The boat sails around a peninsula of boulders that yields to a bay guarded by a steep rock face. On the narrow beach lies the wreck of the Otavi, battered and broken by the waves, the corrosive salt and the south-wester, reducing its once proud structure to fragmented scrap.

"Spencer Bay!" Dieter said, pointing at the screen. "This must have been the boat trip I remembered."

A jagged splice introduces an image of a mountainous sand dune with a family on its crest, standing around a wicker basket on a picnic blanket. Mother looks older, lines on her face and grey streaks in her fringe. Ingrid is present, sitting beside a man with a receding hairline and silver temples. They each hold a wine goblet; she rests her head against his neck. A tall Dieter and a younger Otto are sliding down the steep face of the rippled dune on square boards, kicking up arcs of sand amidst broad smiles.

"Could that be Frederick?" Otto said.

"Maybe," Dieter mumbled. "I guess so."

The camera focuses mainly on Dieter and Otto as well as the panoramic views of rolling sand dunes that stretch eastwards as far as the eye can see. To the west, over the little town of Lüderitz nestled against the black rock below the picnickers, lies the sparkling Atlantic Ocean.

"I'd say Ingrid is about to get married and leave Lüderitz. How much is left?" Dieter asked.

Otto glanced at the rapidly turning front reel, which had only an inch of film left to project. "About three minutes."

Dieter met Otto's eyes and shrugged, a look of disappointment across his face. "There's nothing much on this reel. Nice memories, that's all."

"Thank God for that," Otto replied.

The image jumps to a four-prop Vickers Viscount rushing down the runway and becoming airborne, silver aluminium underbelly with white livery on top, BOAC visible on the fuselage. The camera pans around the airport terminal to a table beside a window where Mother is sitting next to Dieter and smoking a cigarette. Otto, looking playful, walks up to the camera and takes it. The image jerks all over the place and then Father can be seen walking over to the table and sitting next to Mother. He is wearing his homberg, his hair grey and his face strained in sincerity. Dieter waves at the camera and holds up his ticket with a proud smile. Lufthansa.

"1959," Dieter said, lifting his feet up onto the coffee table. "I was off to Cologne to study."

"Where is this?"

"Windhoek, probably."

"Oh yeah, I remember the long drive."

Dieter is now hugging Mother, who is tearful and repeatedly wipes her eyes; then he embraces Otto for several moments, slapping him on the back a few times. They all wave to him as he disappears through departure gate one.

Otto felt a lump of nostalgia form in his throat. He had missed his brother immensely after he left home to study in Germany, and they had never really spent any meaningful time together again after that. Long distance phone calls and occasional gatherings simply did not fill the void that separation created. Watching that watershed moment unfolding in real time cemented for Otto the inevitability of their subsequent estrangement.

"Where's Ingrid?" Otto said, confused.

"She must have been in New York already. She moved there after she married Frederick, remember."

"That's right – '58, wasn't it?"

"'56, I think," Dieter said.

Otto felt a sudden stab of empathy for Ingrid. There was not a frame of film footage from her wedding. Father had filmed Dieter playing football, Otto and Dieter playing on the sand dunes, Dieter leaving for university. But Ingrid had simply disappeared from the family movies, just as Inez had. Father's own brand of censorship, perhaps, he wondered.

A splodgy splice introduces a view of the Adermann house with a significant camelthorn tree growing in the back garden. Otto emerges from the kitchen door, running his hands through his side-parted hair, and walks briskly past the camelthorn. He looks excited as he descends the twenty-three steps to the sandy roadway below the house. The camera zooms in, creating an aerial view of Otto and a shiny Morris Minor 1000 draped in a white sash ribbon. Mother is waiting for him beside the car, they hug and Otto walks around the Morris, running his hand over the curvaceous wheel arches, admiring the metal emblem mounted on the bonnet. Eventually he climbs into the car. The image pans back to the house, the empty garden, and the lonesome camelthorn tree. The screen burns incandescent white.

"Twenty years ago that was, when I left for Cape Town and medical school," Otto said, shaking his head in disbelief. He turned the projector off. "The sight of that camelthorn made me feel sick. It's like going back in a time machine, isn't it? You want to shout out – hey, there's a body under that fucking tree."

Dieter sat with his cheek pressed against one hand. "That last film doesn't tell us anything useful, Otto, does it? Nothing we didn't already know."

"No."

Dieter stood up and stretched. "Tomorrow I'll call Frans and ask about Keetmanshoop. You in?"

"Definitely," Otto said.

Otto wanted very badly to call Sabine and hear her voice. It had been a strange day, unsettling and unfulfilling in equal measure, as though he had developed a yearning, a need that had to be met before he could say goodbye to Mother and move on with his life once again.

No child could expect the day they buried their mother to be easy, Otto thought, but under these circumstances he had not felt that the funeral had received due attention or any emotional sacrifice from him. There was unfinished business hanging in the way, impeding proper mourning, with so many disturbing questions about his childhood still unanswered.

But when he picked up the receiver to phone his home he realised how late it was in Durham. The boys would be in bed and so, most likely, would Sabine.

Yet again, replacing the receiver, he felt very alone.

TWENTY-NINE

On the Sunday morning Frans offered to drive Otto and Dieter to Keetmanshoop once he had been to church with his family. Otto recalled that the Lutheran congregation of Lüderitz was both fervent and close. It was generally considered more desirable to be in church and fall asleep than not to attend at all.

"Frans is a great guy, isn't he?" Dieter said as he and Otto sat drinking coffee and eating toast in the kitchen.

Otto nodded, mindful that Frans was also so much more: the local police chief, the man charged with determining the identity of and circumstances surrounding the child's body in their back garden, and the man who after agreeing to drive them to Keetmanshoop had said to Otto, "No problem. There is just one thing you two can do for me in return."

"I'd better call Ingrid and tell her," Otto said while chewing his toast and strawberry jam.

"You think she cares?" Dieter said.

"I feel I should, after yesterday."

But Ingrid was not at the hotel. Otto let the receiver drop down slightly from his face in disappointed acceptance.

"What?" Dieter asked.

"She's not there."

"I told you."

Frans arrived at 10am, dressed in his Sunday best: a black suit and tie worn with a pressed white shirt. Under all this reverent clothing he was perspiring like a farm animal.

"It's a four hour drive so we should get going," Frans said. "You should bring water." He loosened his tie and folded his enormous jacket into the cluttered boot.

"This is really good of you, Frans," Dieter said as they settled into his Toyota.

"Ag, it's no problem. I still have a crime to solve and any possible clues unearthed in Keetmanshoop could help me too," he said matter-of-factly.

"A crime?" Dieter said.

"Ja," Frans said, as though it was self-evident. "A body buried where it shouldn't be is against the law."

Otto was deep in thought as they drove out of Lüderitz on the B4, past the cemetery, reminding him of all the death that surrounded him. Inez and Mother buried side-by-side in the cemetery; Father's ashes scattered on Shark Island – for reasons not yet clear – and the body buried right in their back garden almost forty years ago, beneath the camelthorn and the patter of their young feet.

"Where is Ingrid?" Frans asked, turning to Dieter in the passenger seat and meeting Otto's eyes in the rear view mirror.

"She's leaving today," Dieter said.

Frans sighed and adjusted his grip on the steering wheel, staring at the road. "I asked her not to leave Lüderitz yet," he said tersely.

Otto gazed out through the grimy windows, seeing nothing on either side of the road but sand, dunes and occasional protrusions of black rock. Perilous incursions of sand across the road surface restricted their speed of travel.

"What is it with you guys and Ingrid?" Frans asked.

Otto hesitated, hoping Dieter might answer. He didn't.

"You know, living so far apart in the world is not easy," Otto said lamely. "We haven't been together under the same roof for twenty... thirty years."

"But you two seem OK?"

Otto found Dieter's eyes staring at him in the mirror and grimaced.

"Ingrid seems to feel that we got more than our fair share from Mum and Dad, more than she did. Since then we have done well while her marriages have all failed," Dieter said, pulling a face.

"She's been married a few times?" Frans asked, his eyes searching for Otto's in the rear view mirror.

"Yeah, about three times. Divorced the last one six months ago apparently," Otto said.

Frans shook his head, adjusting his bulky frame behind the fulcrum of the steering wheel. "Something's bothering her."

"I gather she was very close to Inez," Otto ventured, feeling strange mentioning his lost sister so casually in conversation, a name he had not even known less than a week ago; a life he still did not understand.

"Ja." Frans nodded. "Very."

"I think maybe Inez's death affected her more than she lets on," Otto said.

Frans met Otto's eyes in the mirror. "Ja." Then he turned to Dieter, nudging him on the shoulder. "And you and Ingrid don't speak?"

Dieter looked at him. "No."

"Why not?"

Dieter shrugged. "She doesn't like me."

Otto cringed and covered his eyes with one hand. Discussing their petty family dynamics with Frans made them seem so trivial and baseless. Despite the biting, divisive reality of family feuds, trying to explain them to strangers inevitably gave the impression of such puerility.

"And I'm not sure I like her much either," Dieter added.

"But she's your sister," Frans said incredulously, taking his eyes off the road to peer at Dieter.

"It doesn't feel like it."

God, Otto thought, Mother must be turning in her freshly dug grave. He looked out of the window. They were driving through a cutting, surrounded by strata of burnt rock layered upon each other like brown and black sponge cake. Soon it was just sand again. Sand. More sand. Occasionally pirouettes of sand danced whimsically across the road under the spell of a swirling desert breeze.

"Did you know the Solomons?" Otto said suddenly.

Frans looked up into the mirror. "I've heard of them, vaguely. Keetmanshoop is on the Trans–Namib Railway and the father did a lot of work on the rail networks. But I didn't know them."

"It's a long way to Keetmanshoop," Dieter remarked. "Do you know how Inez met this guy?"

Frans shrugged and pulled a face. "Your pa had a surgery there, didn't he?"

Dieter nodded.

"Maybe it was through that?"

"Why did Father have a surgery way out there?" Otto said. "I never understood that, nor as a child did I appreciate the distance. I just remember him being away from home a lot."

Frans scratched his head. "These little communities out here in the desert are very isolated. Even a place like Lüderitz with only twelve thousand people is isolated. The smaller towns really depend on bigger ones for support."

One long sandy stretch through the Tsaukeib Plain was so flat and straight that Otto nodded off several times in the back seat. Monotonous, never-ending desert as far as the eye could see. The road ahead shimmered under the glassy reflection of a heat mirage and Otto understood how people dying of thirst could mistake them for oases in the desert.

"What would we do if we broke down out here?" Dieter asked.

"I've got a radio," Frans said, tapping a bulky contraption covered with knobs and dials in the dashboard.

"And if we didn't have a police radio?"

Frans chuckled, his great belly heaving behind the steering wheel. "Pray!"

Ausweiche provided some visual pleasure as they drove through a canyon between dramatic, arid, rocky outcrops on both sides. The rock appeared to have been charred by the unrelenting sun, parched of every scrap of goodness. Past the little town of Aus they entered a landscape punctuated at intervals by low rocky outcrops with flat tops, like hills that had been sanded down to a smooth surface. Otto was mesmerised by their unearthly beauty.

"This is what I imagine it looks like on Mars," Otto said, face pressed against the cool glass of the window. "How does anyone live out here?"

With every mile that they travelled eastwards the terrain seemed to comprise more rock than sand. Otto awoke at one point, disorientated and struggling with a dry, leathery mouth.

"These are the famous quiver tree forests," Frans said, pointing out of the window.

Enormous quiver trees – reminiscent of cinnamon-coloured broccoli with stunted growths of mustard–coloured succulent leaves sprouting forth – dotted the landscape amidst chocolate brown boulders and dry tufts of bleached grass.

"A forest of a different kind," Dieter remarked.

"In desert terms, this is almost a jungle." Frans chuckled. "They're actually aloes. We locals call them kokerboom."

"Why quiver tree?" Otto asked, captivated by the unusual appearance of these giants of the desert.

"The San hollow out the branches to make quivers for their arrows," Frans replied.

Keetmanshoop was eventually revealed as a contained, flat and featureless little town. German colonial architectural influence was abundant and the settlement was poignantly bisected by Kaiser Street. They drove straight to the police station.

"What do you guys want to drink?" Frans asked as he opened his door, which protested at the accumulated dust.

"Anything cold," Dieter said.

Frans heaved his sweat–stained bulk into the flat–roofed brown building and returned ten minutes later with three cans held in one hand by a formidable grasp.

"Here you go," he said, settling himself into the seat. "The sergeant says the last of the Solomons moved away many years ago. He thinks they all congregated in Windhoek."

Otto felt enormously deflated by this news, especially after that exhausting drive through the most desolate countryside he had ever experienced. Why had they not simply phoned?

He knew the answer: he had wanted to see the place for himself.

"We'll start at the cemetery." Frans seemed upbeat as he cracked open his can of Fanta.

They drove to the edge of town to a very derelict–looking rendered wall, once painted white, now losing chunks of plaster as it struggled to support a pair of dilapidated iron gates. Behind this disrespectful boundary, granite headstones languished in gravelly rows in the desert sunshine. Immersed once again in the heat they crunched their way methodically between the grey monoliths looking for Neil Solomon. They found Dr Carl Hahn, pastor and missionary, Schmidt, Stern, Ahrens, many dating back to the 19th century, but no Solomons. Aloes, cacti and succulents, randomly scattered throughout the desiccated graveyard, looked on in silence.

"He was third generation," Frans muttered, turning around to survey the headstones. "There must be a few Solomons here, somewhere." He planted his hands on his hips.

"There's another section through there." Dieter gesticulated.

When they reached the smaller walled cemetery attached to the main area by an arched gateway, they stopped. The headstones had a different appearance: taller and more ostentatious. Dieter read aloud. "Horwitz, Marks, Kaye, Rosenstein."

"This is the Jewish cemetery," Otto said, noticing the Hebrew lettering and the Star of David on the headstones. He turned back, thinking it had to be a mistake.

"Solomon," Dieter called out.

Otto froze. "What did you say?"

All three men stood still, their eyes meeting uncertainly.

"I see a few Solomons," Dieter repeated, much softer this time.

A memory of Dieter asking him if Sabine was Jewish fluttered into Otto's mind and he covered his nose and mouth with cupped hands.

"Jesus!" Otto said.

Frans stood his ground awkwardly. Then, as if sensing their bewilderment and shock, he turned on his heel and began to walk the rows. "Let's find him."

It did not take long as the Jewish cemetery was relatively small. They gathered in front of Neil Solomon's imposing black granite memorial erected by his grieving family to commemorate his premature death. Its contrast to Inez's humble headstone back in Lüderitz could not have been more absolute.

"Neil Solomon," Otto read aloud. "23.11.1925–11.9.1948. MHSRIP." He felt cold suddenly, despite the hot, dry, windless air. "I don't understand the Hebrew bit."

"Jesus Christ!" Dieter said, staring in disbelief at the memorial. "He was Jewish."

"I hadn't realised there were Jewish communities living here," Otto reflected, quietly.

"Why?" Frans said. "Because it used to be a German colony: Deutsche–Südwestafrika?"

"Yeah, I guess so."

"It is still very German," Dieter commented.

Frans just looked at them, hands clasped in front of his pendulous belly.

"Dad would not have approved of this," Otto said, walking slowly around the memorial stone, examining it from every angle. "That's for sure." The craftsmanship was exquisite, carved finials and scrolls, elaborate sand–blasted lettering and patterns adorning the polished surface. He stopped and met Dieter's eyes across the lavish memorial in silence.

"I think you mean he would have been fucking furious," Dieter said softly.

Frans cleared his throat. "It certainly makes their suicide more understandable."

"Doesn't it fucking just?" Dieter blurted.

"Star–crossed lovers," Otto said.

Frans just looked at him.

"Romeo and Juliet?" Otto tried to explain. "Forbidden love?"

"Oh ja, now I'm with you."

Dieter sat down on the edge of an adjacent headstone, swinging one leg absently. "So, Inez falls in love with Neil, father finds out he's Jewish, goes ballistic, they run away, have to come back home, are not permitted to be together and…"

"No," Otto said. "That old guy at the funeral said he drove Inez to Otjiwarongo because she was unwell."

"What old guy?" Frans asked, frowning.

"Some old chap, deaf as a post, was there with his daughter. He said he was Dad's partner here in Keetmanshoop."

Frans nodded. "Otjiwarongo, that's a long way from Lüderitz."

"Ingrid says she doesn't remember any of this," Otto continued. "I don't understand why Otjiwarongo, nor what was wrong with Inez."

Frans shuffled his feet on the dusty gravel beneath their feet. "Otjiwarongo has a large German population. Perhaps your pa knew some people up there?"

"Yeah, but why send her there?"

"To get her away from Neil Solomon?" Dieter suggested with a little hand gesture towards his headstone.

"I think we should go and talk to this old partner of your pa's," Frans said.

Otto pulled a face and shook his head. "He's very old and painfully deaf, Frans, and he was awfully vague on detail. I spoke to him and to his daughter quite a bit at the funeral yesterday. It was difficult."

"They didn't go to the cemetery?" Frans said.

"No, they went to Goerkehaus."

"Ah."

Dieter lifted his head. "Did Dad used to attend those Hitler bashes?" He directed his gaze first at Otto, who dreaded the answer, and then at Frans.

Frans squirmed and nodded. "Ja, to my knowledge he did."

Otto felt a chill and looked away sharply. "The things we never knew about our parents." Then he gazed back to the memorial stone, to the name Neil Solomon, to the residua of Father's rigid and intolerant beliefs. He glanced at Dieter, whose head was supported in one hand, eyes staring ahead, and imagined what might have happened if Father had known about Dieter's homosexuality. He felt a sudden pang of sympathy for his brother, who most likely sensed this, and had been forced to live a painful lie for all these years.

"Do you think Ingrid knew about this?" Otto said, inclining his head towards the headstone.

Frans and Dieter gazed at him.

"In my opinion," Frans began carefully, "Ingrid knows more than she is admitting."

"But why?" Otto said, trying to understand what could have motivated Ingrid to be complicit in the deception about Inez.

"That's what I need to find out," Frans said, wagging his index finger in the air before tapping it against the side of his nose. "And I have to tell you guys that I believe it will be connected to the body in the garden."

Otto felt winded. Dieter paled visibly.

"You think our parents had something to do with the body?" Dieter said.

Frans studied them both without a flicker of reaction. "That is one possibility." His unsteady eyes flitted from Otto to Dieter, like a hawk hunting a field mouse.

The silence grew uncomfortable, with not even the sound of a distant bird or the buzz of an insect to break it. The air was still, hot, and accusing. Otto did not know what to think. He was frightened to think too much. The memories from his childhood were failing him, leaving him feeling exposed and lost. What more might he discover? What might Frans, the upholder of the law, discover?

"Careful Otto, there is a scorpion near your foot," Frans said, raising one arm.

Otto froze and looked down at the hot gravel beneath his feet. "Where?"

"Beside the plastic wreath. Just walk towards me."

Frans beckoned with outstretched arms for Otto to approach. Once safely away Otto turned and scrutinised the wreath, its flowers bleached by the merciless sun. Adopting its customary C-shaped posture, with tail and deadly sting poised above its body to strike, a large dark brown scorpion with yellowy-orange legs sheltered on the marble chippings in the shadow cast by the wreath.

"Parabuthus villosus," Frans said. "Very poisonous."

"God, it's huge," Dieter remarked.

"Ja. Give them a wide berth," Frans advised. He looked up at the sky, squinting towards the sun. "Let's go and find the old man," he said, making a move towards the gates. "I want to talk to him before we leave."

The old man lived in the centre of Keetmanshoop near the Rhenish Missionary Church, an impressive Gothic construction of local brown stone erected by the German colonials. The police said his name was Klaus Abert. Once they had all settled in his parlour, smelling overpoweringly of oiled wood and unwashed linen, Otto realised that Klaus' hearing was far worse than he remembered. Even with the Maelzel ear trumpet jammed into his hairy ear, Klaus screwed up his wrinkly face and stared blankly whenever anyone spoke to him.

"We have come to ask you about Inez Adermann," Frans said.

"Was sagst du?"

In piecemeal fashion Klaus told them that he had been Ernst Adermann's partner, and that he had driven Ernst's eldest daughter to Otjiwarongo because she was unwell and needed the invigorating climate of the Waterberg plateau to convalesce.

"It took me two days to reach Otjiwarongo and two days to get back again," he said with a grin, as if it had happened yesterday.

Otto and Dieter glanced at each other. Klaus was simply repeating what he had told Otto in the Felsenkirche the day before.

"What was wrong with Inez?" Frans asked.

"Wer?" Klaus yelled, leaning towards Frans with his ear trumpet aloft.

"Inez Adermann," Frans repeated slowly and loudly. "What was wrong with her?"

Klaus' eyes met Otto's and then Dieter's with a look of puzzlement. "Ja, I took her to Otjiwarongo for Ernst. He said not to tell anyone."

Otto straightened. What a strange thing to say. What a peculiar request to make. "Not to tell anyone?" Otto repeated. "I wonder why?"

"Who did you take her to?" Frans yelled.

Klaus looked at him through watery eyes for a moment before replying. "Otjiwarongo!"

Frans sighed and turned to Otto. "This is pointless."

"Like I said," Otto replied, "I'm not sure if he just can't understand us or if he's forgotten."

Frans drew breath and licked his lips, turning back to Klaus, leaning towards the ear trumpet. "Why did Ernst ask you not to tell anyone?"

"Was?"

"Why did Dr Adermann ask you not to tell anyone about taking Inez to Otjiwarongo?" he repeated slowly.

Klaus pondered this for a moment, his smooth tongue snaking restlessly around his edentulous mouth. "Dr Adermann was my partner. Ja." His eyes flicked from Frans to Otto to Dieter, seeking affirmation.

In the background a ticking clock chimed politely four times. Frans appeared frustrated, tapping his shoes on the floor and staring at the floorboards.

"Did you ever see Inez again?" Otto asked.

"Was?" Klaus turned to face Otto, his lined face drawn in around a purplish nose.

"Did you ever see Inez again?" Otto repeated very slowly.

A sad realisation seemed to pervade Klaus' eyes as he gently shook his head. "Nein."

"Did Neil Solomon go to Otjiwarongo?" Otto yelled.

"Solomon... ja... was?"

"Did he go to Otjiwarongo?"

Klaus suddenly shook his head animatedly, releasing the trumpet from its purchase in his ear. "Ah – nein, nein. Solomon was eine Jüden." He continued to shake his head vehemently. "I only took Inez to Otjiwarongo."

Otto sank back in his threadbare seat and met Dieter's searching eyes. It seemed clear to Otto that Father had separated Inez and Neil Solomon. The illness, of which Ingrid apparently knew nothing, was probably a ruse. What plagued Otto, having just buried Mother the day before, was whether she knew about this? Was she in agreement with sending her daughter away to Otjiwarongo? And why had Ingrid so willingly conspired with both of them to withhold all of this from her brothers?

The long drive back to Lüderitz was filled with silences, thoughtful, disturbing silences. Of one thing Otto was certain: there was more to Father than he remembered as a child. There was more to his entire childhood than he recalled. There were quite evidently chunks that he had never known about, but then being the youngest by some margin, this in itself was not entirely unreasonable.

Were there discrepancies, however, in the bits that he could remember, or that he thought he remembered? How could he be sure after so many years? What a dreadful development, he considered, to be questioning every cherished childhood memory that he had held on to over the years.

THIRTY

On Monday morning Frans fetched Dieter and Otto and drove them to the police station. They did not know what it was for, and both sat quietly in his glass office while he organised coffee for each of them. Policemen busying themselves at desks cast furtive glances in their direction. Dieter could not suppress little flashbacks to his recurring dream; that feeling of guilt, that one day the police would catch up with him and tap him on the shoulder. He felt as though every examining stare was looking through Frans' transparent office walls into his darkest secrets, deciphering his inexplicable guilt, preparing to expose him. It seemed to him that everyone in that police station knew about his dream, that his dark secret was finally out. The day he had long dreaded was finally upon him.

"I keep thinking about that dream," he whispered to Otto. "What dream?"

"You know, the one I told you about – the rolled–up carpet and the body inside."

Otto's eyes widened as he stared at Dieter. "Christ, you don't think you actually saw something, do you?"

"I just have no idea anymore," Dieter said. His palms felt sweaty, and he rubbed them on his trousers. Suddenly the door burst open, startling him, as though he had been doing something illicit.

"Here you go, three black coffees." Frans set them down on his desk.

"What do you need from us, Frans?" Otto asked.

Dieter swallowed, imagining fingerprints, perhaps a blood sample for that DNA analysis, lie detector testing. Frans moved to the steel filing cabinet and slid open the top drawer.

"I want you to have a look at this," he said, removing the child's reconstructed clay head and placing it on the desk between them.

Otto frowned and Dieter shuffled in his seat.

"This is a forensically reconstructed likeness built around the child's skull that was found in your garden," Frans explained.

Dieter did not like the word 'your', implying their culpability. The first image that came to mind as he looked upon the clay head was of the rolled-up green carpet. Did some neglected childhood memory circuit in his brain make a connection between the two?

"How accurate are these reconstructions?" Otto asked.

Frans pulled a face. "Not bad. We used a specialist in Johannesburg." He leaned forward and turned the head slightly. "Do you recognise this face?" He paused. "Have you ever seen it before?"

Dieter noted the fine nose and long upper lip, and the chillingly small size of the head. It reminded him of the face from the home movies they had watched on Saturday night. But then, he considered, he was no expert on babies and they did all look somewhat alike to him.

"How old do you think this child was?" Otto asked, studying the face with curiosity.

Frans pouted his lips. "Around one year, give or take a few months either way. That's what the forensic people have told us."

"Jesus," Dieter said; "just an infant."

Dieter and Otto examined the head carefully for a few surreal moments, staring at something from 1948 that had, chillingly, almost been brought back to life, its lips slightly parted, as if to breathe. This was the face of the child they had played on top of, Dieter reflected.

"I was only tiny myself," Otto said. "You should have asked Ingrid."

"I have," Frans said.

Dieter's heart skipped a beat. "You've shown this to her?"

Frans nodded in a noncommittal way.

"What did she say?" Otto asked.

Dieter could feel his heart quickening. He felt sweaty. He could picture the rolled-up carpet, shadowy figures moving about with it at shoulder height, going nowhere distinct. Could it have been this child concealed inside?

"Not much," Frans said, reaching for his coffee. As he sipped he kept his eyes on Dieter and Otto's faces.

"I've never seen this child before. It's definitely not Herero though," Dieter said.

"No," Frans agreed.

"Boy or girl?" Otto asked, angling his head as he studied the sculpted face.

"We don't know yet."

"The DNA test will tell you," Otto said.

"On Saturday we watched the last of the family home movies, filmed here in Lüderitz. There was a small child in them," Dieter said, gesticulating towards Otto, "but you could clearly see it was Otto."

Dieter could not drink the coffee. It was weak and bitter.

"What now?" Otto said, half-turning away from the head.

"Well, we should get the DNA results back in a day or two. I'll let you know." Frans smiled. "Depending on what they reveal we'll know… er… what to do next."

Dieter stood up, followed by Otto. He wanted to get out, to stop thinking about his dream.

"Thanks again for yesterday, Frans," Dieter said.

"My pleasure. It was very revealing, I thought," Frans said. "Do you want a lift up the hill?"

Otto shook his head with a wan smile. "It's OK, thanks, we'll walk."

"Jesus, that was creepy," Dieter said once they were out of the police station.

The seaweed smell of the fog permeating Lüderitz was strong that morning, and it seemed to transmit the sounds of the harbour very clearly, as though it was solid.

"Why didn't he tell us before now that he'd shown it to Ingrid?" Otto asked.

Dieter stared at Otto, unblinking. "You think he's playing us?"

Otto was silent for a moment. "Frans?"

"Biggest mistake anyone can make is underestimating a copper," Dieter said. "Don't be fooled by his squint."

Otto pondered this sobering thought. He did not know what Ingrid knew. He did not even know what Dieter knew. And what was that dream of Dieter's all about?

"I wonder how Ingrid reacted to that head?" Otto said.

"Frans didn't say much about her, did he?" Dieter said.

"She was about fourteen then. Surely she'd remember something?"

"Well, she's given Frans the slip now," Dieter sniped.

They walked past Felsenkirche, its steeple just visible through the asphyxiating grip of the fog. It should have made Otto think of Mother, but it didn't. Barely two days since her funeral and he was thinking about the reconstructed clay head, about Dieter's dream, and wondering where Ingrid was. It was as if the funeral had not even taken place.

"We need to go through all Mum and Dad's old things at home, see if we can find anything," Otto said. "I can't stand this nagging question hanging over us."

"That's got a rather seedy feel about it, though, hasn't it?"

"What do you mean?" Otto said.

"You know, going through your parents' things, searching for clues, for something out of the ordinary. Like we don't trust them."

Otto breathed hard as they climbed the steep hill up to Bülow Street. Dieter's words reverberated in his mind, cutting, making him bleed at the unpleasant prospect. Father had been gone ten years already, but he could not imagine questioning his mother's character in the way that he was now, had she still been alive. It made him feel disrespectful.

"Children inherently trust their parents, don't they?" Otto said eventually. "Implicitly." A vision of Max and Karl burst into his mind. He could not entertain the possibility that they would not trust him for the rest of his life. But the rest of his life was not as long as the rest of their lives.

"When was that unreserved trust first shaken for you?" Dieter asked, searching Otto's eyes.

Otto was taken aback. "I don't know what you mean."

"You do," Dieter chided him. "You know, parents tell you about Father Christmas and the tooth fairy, and going to heaven and all that shit."

"Uh–huh."

"Well, when was the first time you realised that they didn't always tell you the truth?"

Otto was stunned by this question. They walked in silence for a few moments, the sound of their footsteps on the road clipping the eerie stillness.

"You mean before Inez?" Otto said, rubbing his temples.

"You know when things changed for me?" Dieter said. "When I realised I could not tell them I was gay. I knew I dared not confide in my own mum and dad about who I really was. They made me choose to live an invented life because it suited their ideology."

"That's not a lie," Otto objected.

"Oh, it is. I didn't mind the little things, tooth fairy and so forth." Dieter rubbed his chin thoughtfully. "When I left for Cologne they told me my best friend was going away and couldn't come to Windhoek to say goodbye."

"Marko?"

Dieter nodded. "They lied. Father had threatened him that if he came anywhere near me again he would speak to the church priest."

"Why?"

Dieter looked at Otto quizzically. "Don't you remember Marko?"

Otto tried to remember. "Not well… he was always nice to me…"

"He was very effeminate," Dieter said. "You were too young to notice, I guess. Marko and I were very close friends at school." He paused, an old wound visible behind his eyes. "Anyway, Marko wrote to me, eventually, and explained about Dad and the airport. I never saw him again."

Otto realised this must have hurt Dieter deeply.

"Have you always believed them?" Dieter said, creasing his brow.

Otto looked into Dieter's incredulous eyes and nodded.

"Even after finding out about Inez?" Dieter said.

Otto closed his eyes. He had never envisaged having such a conversation with Dieter, questioning the moral character of his parents, challenging the very fabric of his lifelong memories and his cherished emotional bond to them.

"Until... until I found out about Inez," Otto heard himself whisper. "This last week has just been a nightmare... beyond belief. Where will it end?"

The awful realisation about the deceit over Inez had been a turning point in Otto's heart and his mind. With his words still fresh on the moist foggy air Otto felt a greater hurt in this declaration to Dieter than he had at Mother's funeral.

"With the truth," Dieter said. "I know what it's like to live with lies, and I know how emancipating it is to reveal the truth."

"Maybe Ingrid was right," Otto said quietly.

"About what?"

Otto looked into Dieter's eyes, trying to measure in them the depth of his own despair. "Let sleeping dogs lie."

THIRTY-ONE

Searching through Mother and Father's personal belongings was a task laden with emotional time bombs, exploding at irregular intervals when least expected. They began in the bedroom, in heavy walnut wardrobes filled with the musty smells of old clothing.

"Mum kept all of Dad's clothes," Otto remarked as he fingered the heavy fabric of Father's favourite Thor Steinar jackets.

"Creepy," Dieter said, opening the drawers of their bedside cabinets.

Rows of Father's fine leather shoes were neatly ordered beneath the jackets, suits and pressed trousers. For the first time in his life Otto found himself staring at them, wondering what sort of man had worn them. They were no longer simply Father's shoes: he now knew that they had carried a man who had very likely inflicted considerable suffering on his family.

"There's nothing in Dad's bedside cabinet except a Lutheran Bible and a pair of reading glasses," Dieter said, surveying the room through narrowed eyes. "What's in that polished wooden box?"

Otto glanced across to the domed object of Dieter's interest. "I think it's Mum's sewing machine," he said.

In the corner, behind a pair of well-worn black Speziell

Angefertigt shoes, Otto uncovered an old Birkenstock Orthopädie shoebox. He levered it out of the wardrobe.

"Something here," he said, lifting the lid off a wave of napthalene.

The contents comprised yellowed papers and a few monochrome photographs. Otto made himself comfortable on the threadbare rug and began sifting through them.

"Birth certificates: Dad born 1899 in Baden–Baden, Mum in Wüppertal in 1904. Baptism, marriage certificate: 17 February 1926. Christ, Mum was only twenty–two when she married Dad."

"That was normal back then," Dieter said.

"So she was… how old then when Inez was born?" Otto said, counting on his fingers.

"Inez died in 1948 aged twenty–one, so she was born a year after they married," Dieter said quickly.

"You've always had a good head for maths," Otto said.

"That's why I'm in business." Forced smile from Dieter. "What else is there?"

"Oh, look at this – a cabin aboard the Warwick Castle in 1946: you, Mum, Ingrid and Inez."

Dieter walked over to examine the frayed and yellowed cards bearing the Union Castle Line logo.

"Passage from London to Cape Town, via St Helena," he said, pursing his lips and tapping the tickets against his hand thoughtfully, running his eyes over their handwritten names on the sturdy cards. He turned a ticket over: Union Castle Mail Steamship Company; Second Class; Berth 242A; 27 July 1946.

"How old were you?" Otto asked.

"About four, I think."

"It must have been quite an experience," Otto said

thoughtfully. "Travelling from Hamburg to England, by train was it?"

"Not sure."

"Then several weeks at sea to Cape Town."

"The only thing I recall is being seasick into this smelly steel toilet. Otherwise I have no memory of any of it."

"How did you get from Cape Town to Lüderitz?" Otto asked.

"I have no idea."

"You remember nothing?"

Dieter pulled a face and shook his head. Otto continued pulling documents from the box. Tattered and yellowed smallpox vaccination certificates for all four children, including Inez, were folded into neat squares.

"Look here," Otto said, holding Inez's certificate out for Dieter.

Otto examined a few sepia photographs of their old house in Hamburg, recognisable to him now from the home movies they had seen: timber frame, gabled roof, window boxes and abundant hydrangeas.

"What's in the envelopes?" Dieter asked, leaning closer.

Otto opened each of the two envelopes in turn. "My letter of acceptance at medical school in Cape Town and, presumably, yours for ISMT in Cologne – it's in German."

Dieter took the letter and read it in silence.

"Letters of good standing from the local school for the three of us, a newspaper clipping about Ingrid marrying Frederick, Dad's funeral notice in the Lüderitzbuchter, an obituary for him – Dr Ernst Adermann, 1899–1975 – and a few photos of this house being built..." Otto looked up in disappointment. "That's it."

He and Dieter shared the moment of deflation, Dieter massaging his forehead rhythmically with several fingers.

"Let's read Dad's obituary," Dieter suggested.

Otto unfolded the neatly cut newsprint.

Dr Ernst Adermann, respected family doctor in Lüderitz since 1946, died from heart failure in his home on Sunday 5th January 1976. He was seventy-six years old and is survived by his wife, Ute, and three children, Ingrid, Dieter and Otto. Born in Baden–Baden in November 1899, he studied medicine in Karlsruhe and practised in Hamburg until emigrating to Lüderitz with his family in 1946. His passion as a caring and sympathetic family doctor earned him great respect amongst local families and soon he had opened a second practice in Keetmanshoop, sharing his time between the two. Dr Adermann was a devout Christian and faithful member of the Felsenkirche congregation. His sense of public spirit was limitless and earned him many friends and admirers throughout the German community in South West Africa. His youngest son Otto has followed in his footsteps and works as a family doctor in England. Dieter is a successful businessman in Hong Kong. The funeral service for Dr Adermann will be held on Friday 10th January at 2pm in Felsenkirche.

Otto stared at the news cutting in his hands, noticing his fine, almost imperceptible tremor. "They didn't even mention where Ingrid ended up."

"She didn't attend the funeral," Dieter said.

"That's gotta hurt, though," Otto said, tapping the news cutting.

"You think she even knows about it?" Dieter said.

Otto entertained an uneasy thought. "Do you think Mum wrote the obituary?"

Suddenly Dieter's face lit up, as if overcome by an epiphany. "You know what's missing?" he said, raising his eyebrows.

"What?"

"There is not a single thing in that box of keepsakes about Inez's death or her funeral. Nothing," Dieter said.

Otto flicked through the papers and photographs again, eyes narrowed in concentration. "We have her ticket for the Warwick Castle, her smallpox vaccination certificate... and that's it." He looked up and met Dieter's eyes. "They were not happy with her," Otto proffered, shaking his head.

"Or with Neil Solomon I bet."

"It's as though she was erased from the family, never to be mentioned again," Otto said. "Even Ingrid didn't speak of her." Dieter glanced absently at his watch and then, his eyes widening, stood up suddenly. "Jesus, is that the time? I have to get to the library for a fax."

"Oh come on, Dieter, not now."

"Business doesn't stop because I'm feeling sentimental, Otto." He paused, as if checking his irritation. "I won't be long."

"I've heard that one before," Otto muttered under his breath.

In a flash Otto was alone, surrounded by ageing mementos of a broken family. He packed them back into the shoebox and moved to the next room, his bedroom. Mum had meticulously stored every toy of his in cardboard boxes, even labelling them for easy identification. He found his old cowboy suit with black hat, sheriff's badge and gunslinger's holster. A metal earth grader with adjustable scoop and rotating tracks, somewhat perished, that brought back memories of scraping the gritty sand beneath the camelthorn tree. The scoop was still crusted with residues of soil, the same soil that extended down a few feet to surround the decaying corpse of a young child.

Otto recoiled from touching the soil and replaced the grader in its box. He found a linen bag filled with chipped marbles and, fondling the milky marbles – always his favourite – recalled how he and Dieter would spend hours on their knees in the dirt trying to outplay the other. He usually lost – Dieter was simply too good.

Soon he ventured into Dieter's bedroom and found more toys that he remembered playing with, including a fishing rod. His mind filled with sunny images of him and Dieter dangling their legs off the pier in Robert Harbour, the water dancing like glitter beneath a mirror ball. Otto could not recall Father ever fishing with them. He was always at work. Otto pushed the fishing rod away.

Dieter had loved woodwork and Otto discovered several of his carved pieces carefully wrapped in old newspaper and stowed in a box. Some were rather good, he thought: birds, an airplane, a cluster of heads – presumably the three children.

Otto found nothing of importance and moved through to Ingrid's old bedroom. Her wardrobe was packed with dresses and slacks, many of which appeared to have been hand-sewn, probably by Mother. Wide collars, no collars, flared and tight-fitting trouser legs, revealing the changeable fashions through Ingrid's years at home. Several cardboard boxes were stuffed full of dolls, their ageing porcelain glaze cracked and peeling, the cotton clothing grey and lifeless. Some of these must have been very precious to her, he thought, yet all had been cast aside, unwanted.

A small box at the back of her wardrobe caught Otto's eye. He pulled it closer. Eugen Ising Film Splicer was printed on the stiff card.

"Here you are!" Otto said to himself, as if addressing an errant child.

He opened the box to reveal a die cast metal 16mm film splicer and a half–empty bottle of Agfacol film cement. He recalled the hours he had spent splicing film ends together, enjoying the sensation of celluloid in his hands and joining strips of magical imagery together to produce a homogenous product. He opened the bottle to savour the acetic smell of the cement once again, and smiled as memories flooded back.

There was something else in the box, beneath a card shelf. Lifting this up, as if revealing a false bottom, he found seven coils of tightly wound film. Offcuts, he initially thought, discarded strips scooped up off the editing room floor. But why conceal them in what appeared to be such a clandestine way, beneath a cardboard shelf?

Otto unrolled one and held it up to the light that streamed in through the window, straining his eyes to examine each frame. It was difficult to make out the images clearly, though they appeared to show men in military uniform. Otto frowned.

The phone rang.

"Otto."

"Oh, hi Frans," Otto replied. He wondered if Frans was calling with results of the DNA analysis, and felt his mouth drying.

"I just had a call from Ingrid," Frans said.

This surprised Otto, who had not spoken to her let alone said goodbye to her properly after the funeral, three days ago.

"She's in Windhoek," Frans said. It sounded as if he might be chewing something as he spoke.

Otto moved the receiver around to his other ear. By now she should have been back in New York. "I don't understand," he said, trying to suppress rising annoyance that she would choose to call Frans but not her brothers.

"She wanted to know if I had the DNA results," Frans explained.

"Did she miss her flight or something?"

"No. She decided to delay her return."

Otto hesitated. "But why not stay in Lüderitz?"

He could hear Frans exhaling. "I'm just pleased she hasn't left the country yet."

Otto rubbed his eyes in exasperation. Most of the time he felt no closer to understanding Ingrid; this was how it had been for many years. "Where is she staying?" he asked.

"The Furstenhof."

A silence, somewhat embarrassing for Otto as his family divisions were further laid bare, occupied their conversation like an unwanted intruder.

"She hasn't called you, obviously," Frans said.

"No." Was Frans tracking her as a suspect, Otto suddenly wondered? In that case, why let her leave Lüderitz? "Thanks Frans," Otto said. "No more news?"

"A few more days I reckon."

Otto returned to the box of hidden film strips feeling chastened. What was Ingrid's game, he wondered? Absently he collected the coils of film, the splicer and cement and returned to the dining table. The grandfather clock took a deep, rasping breath and began to chime.

Retrieving an empty film reel from the box of home movies he set to work splicing the film fragments together: lining the strips up in the splicer, perforations over the sprocket guide, cutting the ends neatly with the hinged guillotines, roughening them with the abrasive tool to create purchase for the layer of film cement, and joining them together. How many minutes should he allow for the cement to set? He could not remember. He had no idea what he was joining together – what it would reveal, or why it was hidden in the back of a cupboard in Ingrid's unused bedroom.

THIRTY-TWO

Sporadic flashes of light crash on to the screen. Nine...
eight...seven... six...

Otto hugged himself, feeling the reassuring embrace of his own arm around his chest, the other hand clasping his chin. The once-soothing whirr of the Bell & Howell motor, the rhythmic soft staccato of the film being clawed through the gate – none of it was exciting him as it always had. It was as though a deep visceral apprehension had been roused within him, and he feared that he was about to witness images that would forever, and indelibly, alter his family memories.

He glanced at the unhurriedly rotating front reel of film, not with the usual sense of anticipation, waiting for the thousands of frames to be illuminated in rapid succession, transformed magically into a moving picture on the screen, but with trepidation, fearing the imminent unmasking of dark secrets long hidden from his world.

Four... three... two...

A crisply focused scene of uniformed men gathered around a table bursts onto the screen. Scratches and a few rolling lines are the only blemishes to tarnish the impeccable, professionally procured image. The men are wearing black Schutzstaffel

241

uniforms trimmed in silver with pips and sig–runes on their lapels, sitting with their arms resting on a polished wooden table in a large, well–lit room. The camera pans around the table, revealing the faces of at least a dozen officers, smiling, chatting, casually relaxed though conscious of the camera that captures their every move. Furtive glances into the lens, tugs on the earlobe, fingers rubbing noses, hands clasped together protectively on the table.

The image zooms in to the face of a middle–aged man with greying temples and an affable smile sitting at the head of the oval table. He nods and forms small hand gestures as those beside him speak. The printed sign in front of him on the table reads Standartenführer Max Pauly.

The next man onscreen has short black hair, neatly slicked and combed back from a beakish face. His eyes dart about restlessly, his hands clasped together. His sign reads Hauptsturmführer Kurt Heissmayer.

More faces occupy the screen, stern yet disarming, dark eyes coupled with broad smiles, manicured hands and neatly combed hair: Hauptsturmführer Bruno Kitt; Hauptsturmführer Alfred Trzebinski…

Otto felt a chill as he read that name. It was both familiar and sinister and yet he did not know why. Where had he seen it before?

Rottenführer Adolf Speck; Unterscharführer Wilhelm Bahr; they laugh, politely it appears; they nod and glance about the table at each other in a show of unity for the camera. A waiter wearing a white starched tunic and bearing a silver platter hands a glass of champagne to each officer. The camera zooms in on an officer in a black SS tunic and insignia. Dark eyebrows brood over steady eyes. The sign on the table in front of him reads Hauptsturmführer Ernst Adermann.

Otto felt a knot of nausea twist his stomach around and threaten to eject his lunch into his lap. He stared into the unmistakeable face of his father, seated at a table with fellow SS officers drinking champagne, toasting a success. Otto wiped at his mouth, dry as a desert rock behind parched lips, and stared in disbelief at what was being projected onto the screen.

The officers gathered around the table all stand up and turn to face the central figure, Standartenführer Max Pauly, who remains seated. They raise their glasses in a gesture of mutual commitment captured for eternity on celluloid in teasing silence. Pauly nods humbly and allows his subordinate officers to drink to his health before lifting his glass to his own lips.

Otto watched his father drink, eyes upon his senior officer in the centre. The look on Father's face was unmistakeably one of pride, admiration and reverence. How could this be? Surely it was not true? For a moment Otto's gaze faltered and he stared down at his feet in shame, but then quickly looked up to the screen again for fear of missing something vital.

The film jerks through a splodge of film cement to an outdoor scene as the group of officers in SS tunics, flared trousers and caps bearing the SS–Totenkopf, walk beneath trees swimming in manicured lawns. They stop beside a brick building crammed with elongated rectangular metal windows, like rows of predatory teeth, and gesticulate at a sign: Walther–Werke. Max Pauly leads the group as they stride into the building; Ernst Adermann follows immediately behind Alfred Trzebinski. Inside labourers wearing ragged striped uniforms work at various machine stations tooling the components of rifles and pistols. Their heads, close–shaven and often bearing scabs and blemishes, bow down to avoid eye contact as the party of high profile officers files by inquisitively.

Ernst Adermann stops beside one labourer and points to the part he is making. The startled labourer stares back through wide eyes and holds out the angular piece of metal. Adermann grabs the man's hand roughly and turns it over to reveal missing index and middle fingers. A slight commotion ensues as a foreman appears and remonstrates with the worker, cuffing him across the face. Adermann saunters away indifferently to rejoin the group, slapping his black gloves across his left forearm absently. Behind him the worker is led away from his work station, prodded in the back by a Wehrmacht soldier's rifle.

A pulse of bitter vomit surged to the back of Otto's throat. He managed to swallow it. What had his father just done – with such callous dispassion? Otto could not reconcile in his mind that the action he had just witnessed was perpetrated by his own loving father.

A further smudge of film cement is the prelude to the next scene outside yet another nondescript brick building, this time signposted Carl Jastram Motorenfabrik – U–Boot. The entourage of uniformed officers makes their photo call beside this sign and then dutifully moves into the building behind Max Pauly. Labourers in pyjamas, thin and gaunt, unshaven and dirty, work without a flicker of emotion at lathes, presses and drills. The officers, many of whom walk with their hands clasped behind their backs, nod to each other in approbation at what they see.

A labourer, emaciated and sweaty, slumps forward at his work station, his arm narrowly missing the spinning drill bit. Nearby workers watch in terror, their hands maintaining a perpetual activity, afraid even to slow down. Alfred Trzebinski approaches the labourer, his hands still clasped firmly behind his back, rocking on the heels of his jackboots. He bends over stiffly at the waist, casting a sneering look over the ailing worker as one might inspect a stricken farm animal. He makes eye contact with the attending Wehrmacht soldier and shakes his head, making a quick gesture with his index finger beneath his chin. Instantly the incapacitated labourer is dragged away from his post without a flicker of protest.

Otto swallowed and glanced at the reel of film. How much more was there? This was far worse than he could ever have imagined, and he felt as though he was committing a crime merely by watching the incriminating images.

The next splice heralds a clinically utilitarian room furnished with glass cabinets and an examination couch. Alfred Trzebinski is wearing a white laboratory coat over his SS tunic. Beside him stands a tall, gaunt man with very closely cropped hair that more keenly resembles that seen on prison labourers. The prominent tag on his white coat reads Obersturmbannführer Ludwig–Werner Haase. Haase is addressing Trzebinski and two others, one of whom is Ernst Adermann, whilst holding in his hand a conical glass flagon etched with the letters ARSEN and containing a colourless liquid. He removes the glass stopper and inserts a pipette into the flagon, siphoning out a measured quantity which he checks by holding the pipette up to the light of the window. Trzebinski and Adermann watch Haase intently as he adds the ARSEN to a jug of water, using the pipette to stir the mixture a few times. Replacing the stopper in the flagon he moves to a blackboard and begins to write numbers and formulae on the board. Adermann and Trzebinski nod, huddled behind Haase as they watch his every move. Then Haase walks across the room and produces a canister which he places into the neck of another jug, returning briefly to jab his finger at the blackboard once more. He turns to study the faces of the men gathered around him, says something, and then Ernst Adermann pours the liquid in the jug containing ARSEN through the canister into the second jug.

The next scene shows a row of prisoners wearing pyjamas, some with matching linen caps on their shaven heads. All men are painfully thin with sunken cheeks and eyes, sitting in resigned acceptance with their hands in their laps. A metal cup is passed from prisoner to prisoner and refilled each time from the jug. Adermann, Trzebinski and Haase watch with smug satisfaction as all the men consume the ARSEN. Haase turns to the others and shrugs his shoulders, upon which a Wehrmacht soldier shepherds all the inmates away and locks them in a small room.

Otto could feel the perspiration building up beneath his armpits and on his upper lip. He felt dirty, voyeuristic, watching something seedy and criminal, implicating and tarnishing the memories of his father and his family, and by inference even him. He thought of Max and Karl at home in Durham, blissfully unaware of their grandfather's nefarious actions, and was immediately deeply ashamed.

He had seen images similar to this before when he and Dieter had watched Father's personal films several nights earlier. In this footage, however, Father's presence was unequivocal, his collusion beyond dispute. He was not the cameraman, he was the perpetrator amongst ignominious company. How did Father manage to keep this from all of them and take his sinister past with him to his grave?

The camera pans across the grubby yet cherubic faces of twenty young children seated around a table tearing chunks off round sourdough loaves. They wear roughly woven linen shirts and shorts, most of them barefooted. Many smile, though reservedly, chewing their food hungrily. The man with slicked-back hair and a beakish nose walks around the table, like a headmaster with his hands clasped behind his back. Some of the children, no older than six, watch him warily.

The scene abruptly changes to reveal a young boy with black hair parted down one side lying on an examination couch, his right arm exposed to a nurse who preps his skin with a wet swab. He suddenly turns away and shuts his eyes tightly, creasing up his entire face around a button nose as a fearsome glass syringe is produced and plunged into his arm, its contents injected. Relief floods back into the boy's face as he realises it is over, only to evaporate again as his shirt is unceremoniously hitched up under his chin to reveal his ribs. Prepping his chest with the wet swab causes him to withdraw as a look of sheer horror paralyses his face. He begins to writhe but several strong hands descend to restrain him. This time the beak-nosed man, identifiable by his badge as Hauptsturmführer Kurt Heissmayer, steps forward with a syringe and inserts the needle between the boy's ribs near his nipple before deftly discharging the contents.

The boy's face erupts, his mouth open wide in a silent howl that exposes his uvula and tonsils at the back of his mouth. The film cuts to another boy being injected in similar fashion, once again by Heissmayer. On this occasion Ernst Adermann is visible in the frame, holding the boy down by his arms as his chest is violated.

Otto's eyes stung from dryness as he stared in abhorrence at the images that flickered on the screen, unable to blink. His father, holding down young boys to enable them to be cruelly assaulted in the name of medical science, the same father who raised him as a boy and tousled his hair lovingly. It was unbearable to contemplate the mechanisms behind what he was seeing. How could this be the same man he had known as Father?

Heissmayer stands in front of a chart headed with the word Tuberkulose as he addresses a small audience of SS tunic–clad officers in a wood–panelled room. Smiling, he taps on photographs of young children displayed on an easel; frightened young faces staring back innocently at the seated audience. Heissmayer draws his hand up the opposite arm and across his chest towards his armpit, lifting his arm to allow him to prod this space as he speaks.

A bubbly cement join yields to the body of a young boy with torso laid bare, lying on a linen–covered table with a Schimmelbusch mask held on his face by an anaesthetist. The boy's arm is splayed at ninety degrees to his chest exposing his hollow armpit, which a nurse in a surgical gown is prepping with a dripping swab, leaving a smudge on the skin. A gowned surgeon hidden behind a face mask steps forward and incises the skin, probing its darkening interior with gloved fingers and steel forceps as blood pulses out from within, staining the white linen drapes. He extracts numerous lumps of tissue that resemble tonsils. These he drops into clear liquid in a glass jar before suturing the skin back together.

The next scene shows a line of twenty children, naked to their waists, standing against a white wall with one arm raised above and resting on their heads. The camera pans slowly down the line from one to the next, showing clearly the jagged scar in each child's right armpit. The children stare back impassively, some younger ones grinning stupidly. At the end of the line the camera lens fills with the images of Heissmayer, Adermann and another man, all wearing white coats and standing with their arms folded across their chests. They smile proudly and puff on stubby cigars.

A grubby splodge of cement precedes a dark scene, heavily scratched. Shadows dominate with occasional dimly lit brick arches visible in contrast. A row of clothes hooks are mounted along one wall, a row of steel lockers down another. A bad splice, more lines smearing the image, then twenty small bodies dangling lifelessly from the hooks, like discarded football shirts, stiff fingers barely protruding from the sleeves, little feet pointing to the ground, the shadows concealing most of the ghastly naked truth.

The screen went white, the front reel had stopped turning but the take-up reel, heavy with film, rotated futilely, rhythmically slapping a trailing edge of film against the table with every completed revolution. Otto just made it to the bathroom and retched into the toilet bowl. His eyes watered, his lungs ached to scream out in useless protest at the terrible images he had witnessed.

But he knew it was too late for protest. It was done. His fate and that of his family had been sealed in those moments of madness over forty years previously.

Why, Father? Why? Another surge of vomit silenced Otto's attempt at a scream.

THIRTY-THREE

Otto was staring into the hole beside the fallen camelthorn when Dieter emerged through the kitchen door, hands pushed into his chino pockets, whistling a Spandau Ballet tune.

"What are you doing out here?" Dieter asked, continuing to whistle.

Otto did not move a muscle; arms folded tightly, glassy eyes peering into another world. "Where the hell have you been?"

Dieter recoiled visibly and stopped whistling. "At the library... working."

Otto unfolded his arms and tapped his wristwatch. "For three hours?"

"What are you, head boy?"

"Fuck off!" Otto said.

Dieter opened the palms of both hands in a gesture of surrender. "Jeez, what's eating you?"

"Christ, Dieter. We're supposed to be here for Mum's funeral, sorting her stuff. You're never around."

Dieter frowned and approached Otto slowly. "What's going on?"

Otto's chest heaved, though his eyes remained fixed on the crumbling recesses of the makeshift grave. "I found some films." Otto paused, looking up.

"What films?"

"Let's walk," Otto said, turning away.

They ambled in silence down Bülow Street, into Bismarck Street and onwards to town, heading for Robert Harbour. The sun was melting into the horizon, casting casual tangents of pink and orange across the unblemished blue. Hugging the coastline, like scum at the edge of a pond, a fine mist of sea-spray softened the frontier where ocean met desert.

"What's going on?" Dieter said, stroking his bushy moustache.

Otto looked up into the burnt orange sky. "I came here to bury Mum, to be reunited with you and Ingrid, to… I don't know… remember old times." The thud of their footfall broke the interlude. "I didn't expect to find out about Inez – the sister kept secret from us, to discover that it was a young child buried in our garden, to contemplate that it might be connected to us, to find out that Inez committed suicide over bad blood with Dad about her Jewish boyfriend, to find out that Dad had his ashes scattered on the site of a former concentration camp here in Lüderitz—"

"Yeah, the ashes thing is very disconcerting, isn't it?" Dieter interjected, meeting Otto's eyes.

"Especially when you know why," Otto replied coldly.

They crossed Hafen Street and walked across the silent docks beside abandoned and locked warehouses. Fishing trawlers rolled gently on the harbour swell, straining their sturdy rope moorings with ghostly creaking noises; forklift trucks stood silent, their operators relaxing in the taverns of Lüderitz.

"Do you know why?" Dieter said, raising his eyebrows.

Otto nodded solemnly. "I found several films coiled up and hidden in a box in Ingrid's bedroom."

"Hidden?"

"That's what it looked like."

"And?"

"I spliced them together."

"You've watched them?" Dieter said. Otto wasn't sure if it was curiosity or censure he heard in his brother's voice.

Otto nodded as they passed the warehouses and began to pick their way across the rocky terrain. The wind buffeted their faces and flicked their hair about with abandon on the exposed peninsula. They stopped and Otto surveyed the open, poniard–shaped land that constituted Shark Island with disdain. He tightened his jaw muscles.

"Well?" Dieter prompted.

"Dad was a Nazi."

"What?"

"He was a Hauptsturmführer – I saw him in his SS uniform, mingling with other SS people."

"What's a Hauptsturmführer?"

"It's a military rank."

"Jesus!" Dieter exclaimed.

"They did medical experiments on prisoners... on children... Christ, it's awful to watch." Otto thought he might sob, clutching at his face with one hand.

Dieter stared at him open–mouthed. "Are you sure it's him?"

"I think I'd recognise my own father," Otto said tersely. He turned away from Dieter, his eyes flitting from one sharp rock to another across the inhospitable terrain, a former site of mass murder at the hands of the German colonialists just eighty years back. "What kind of sick monster wants to be laid to rest on a site like this, where innocent people were murdered in their thousands?" Otto said.

He sat down abruptly, paralysed by a yawning ache that was hollowing him out in the middle. He couldn't breathe. Dieter sat down beside him and rested his arms on his knees. Their eyes met.

"The kind of person who does not want to be buried next to his daughter," Dieter said, "or even in the same cemetery."

Otto stared into Dieter's eyes. He could see the personal anguish masked behind Dieter's brazen exterior and regretted his earlier outbursts.

"All because she had a Jewish boyfriend?" Otto said, his intonation rising towards the end.

A dismissive expression crossed Dieter's face momentarily. "Possibly."

Otto lowered his gaze to the coarse soil between his feet. "They killed young children, Dieter, Dad and his SS cronies. I saw it."

The colour drained from Dieter's face. "It's in the film?"

Otto nodded and hung his head in shame between his knees, aware of a slimy exudate that dripped from his nose to the sandy soil in slavery strings. Trying to think of something good, he pictured Sabine, Max and Karl, but then immediately felt guilt over Max's broken arm, and then shame at the thought of them discovering their grandfather's true identity.

"You thinking about the body in the garden?" Dieter asked.

Sniffing loudly, Otto looked up. "How can one not?"

Dieter stared at him, deadpan. "Surely not?" He shook his head as if banishing any such thought.

"I'll tell you what I keep wondering: how much of all this did Mum know?" Otto said.

Dieter held up the flattened palm of one hand, as if directing traffic. "Stop, Otto, don't do this to yourself." He shook his head, swallowing. "We've just buried Mum for God's sake."

Both brothers breathed heavily, their stunned eyes looking around the island, as if searching for the ghost of Ernst Adermann who had returned to haunt them.

"I've got to see this film," Dieter said, staring out to sea.

"We must call Ingrid too," Otto said.

Dieter nodded. "I suppose. Should we tell Frans?"

Otto stared at his brother, his eyes taking in every detail on his face: the moustache that he used to associate with Tom Selleck but which now made him think more of the Village People; the misshapen nose that he had inherited from Dad; the chipped tooth from the steps down to Bülow Street; the scar on his chin. Until that moment Otto had not considered Frans in the context of Father's Nazi bombshell. "I don't know."

"Let me see the film first. We can decide who we tell afterwards."

"Ingrid needs to see it too before we—" Otto began.

"Well she has to get her uptight arse back here then, double quick," Dieter replied. "When is Frans expecting the DNA results?"

"The next day or two," Otto said. He felt his throat drying out. "Christ, a week ago I would never have believed that body had anything to do with our family."

"You think it has?"

"I don't know what to think. But I keep saying to myself: why was Ingrid in such a hurry to leave town?"

THIRTY-FOUR

Otto never got to call Ingrid at her hotel in Windhoek on their return. Upon opening the front door to escape the deepening gloom of nightfall he heard the phone ringing and dashed to reach it. It was Sabine.

"When are you coming home, Otto?" she asked plaintively.

Otto felt a lump rising in his throat. He wished she was in front of him – he needed to feel the warmth and reassurance of her embrace, to rest his weary chin on her shoulder and smell her hair. He was in desperate need of some constancy. Almost everything he had regarded as immutable in his childhood was disintegrating around his feet. It was like standing on quicksand.

"I so badly need to see you," he said, sitting down on the brown velvet sofa and rubbing his temples with the fingers of his free hand.

"What's happened?" she asked.

Where should he begin? "Tell me something nice," Otto said.

"Honey, what is it?"

"How are the boys?" Otto asked.

"They're just fine. Max is managing so well with his cast, you wouldn't think he had hurt his arm at all, and Karl is great. They miss you."

Otto hesitated. "Sabine?" He struggled to find the words. "What do you think the boys will one day think of me being away these past weeks?"

"I don't know what you mean."

Otto shifted position on the sofa, wrestling with something in his mind, like a troublesome pebble in a shoe. "It worries me that Max will always remember my absence during the trauma of his broken arm. What will he and Karl think of me – think of us – when they look back, many years from now?"

Silence. "I don't understand."

"You know, what we recall of events in our childhoods is not always the way it actually was. What will Max think of me for not being there? What will both boys remember about us? Will they one day see the things we did in a different light?"

"OK, you're worrying me now. What's going on?" Sabine said, sympathetically but firmly.

Otto could not utter the words. It felt as though he was breaking a family confidence, flinging the front door open for the world to see the Adermann secrets.

"I found some old films, Sabine, hidden away, as if they were not meant to be seen." He hesitated. Silence: just her breathing and the distant sound of the boys' laughter in the background. "It seems Dad was a Nazi."

"What?" Sabine said loudly. "Never!"

"I know. Unbelievable."

"But he was always so nice to me," Sabine said.

Otto closed his eyes. "You're a German, Sabine."

"Yeah, but…" She fumbled.

"I never saw it coming; no suspicions. Like a lightning strike on a clear day," Otto said softly. He could feel his heart beating behind his ribs.

"You think that's why he left Germany in 1945 and settled in Lüderitz?" Sabine asked, and then, quietly, "Oh my God."

"It's quite possible," Otto replied, eyes closed, the pieces falling into place.

"Was he a war criminal?" Sabine said in a forcible whisper.

Otto pressed his fingertips into his temples. The word criminal reverberated in his mind with an image of the skeletal remains of a young boy in their back garden. "Uh... the film doesn't make it look good." He sighed.

"How did he get away?" she asked.

Otto shook his head almost imperceptibly. "I have no idea. He came out here at least a year ahead of the family, that's all I know."

"Oh my God, Otto. Are you alright?"

Otto shrugged like a petulant child, as though Sabine could see him. He felt his eyes filling and glanced about self-consciously in search of Dieter.

"What about Dieter, and Ingrid?" she asked.

"Ingrid's in Windhoek. She left after the funeral."

"Why?"

Otto shrugged again but did not reply. "I wish you were here. The recollections of my childhood are falling apart, Sabine. Nothing is what I thought it was." He swallowed to regain his voice. "It's a nightmare."

He reflected on the changes that had been thrust upon him in one week: Inez, Dieter, Father and Ingrid complicit in deceit – and how much more – and then there was Mother...

"Come home, love. You've buried your mum. Just leave now and come back home to us... to normality," Sabine suggested with warmth and sincerity in her voice.

This sounded so appealing to Otto that it hurt. "I can't Sabine, not yet. We're waiting for the official outcome of the body in the garden." He swallowed as he prepared to continue. "Imagine if it turns out our family are involved in that."

Sabine hesitated for just a second. "Do you want us to fly out to Lüderitz to join you?"

"No!" Otto said quickly. "This is no place for the boys. I just want to get everything wrapped up and come home." He reflected unexpectedly on Ingrid's words. "I think Ingrid was right."

"About what?"

"She said this was not her home anymore."

"Oh Otto," Sabine said softly, before adding more sharply, "do you think she knows what's going on?"

Otto exhaled loudly. "I'm sure she knows more than she's letting on." He dabbed at his eyes, feeling his composure failing. "Please tell the boys I really love them and I have missed them every day I've been away from home."

"Oh, darling, they know that."

"Please tell them anyway... for me. I want them to know they grew up with a loving and caring dad, even when I was away from them."

"Oh Otto..."

"They must never have doubts about the sort of father that I was."

Otto was emotionally exhausted when, just minutes later, the unwelcome knock came at the front door, as he was beginning to imagine immersing himself in a large scotch. Dieter answered the door.

"Oh hi Frans," he heard Dieter say.

Otto's heart sank. Not now. He wiped his eyes roughly and cleared his nose.

"Dieter," was Frans' throaty reply. "Is Otto here?"

"Uh–huh. He's in the living room. Come in."

Otto stood up and stretched a smile across his face, feeling like an amateur actor in a local production. He thrust out his hand awkwardly to shake Frans' meaty paw. Frans obliged with a frown.

"You OK?" Frans said.

"I've been talking to Sabine… my wife."

"Ah." Frans nodded and stood squarely on his large feet. His squint was noticeable and Otto struggled to find a comfortable point on his face to gaze at.

The silence lengthened, filled only with the ticking of the clock. Frans' eyes took in the projector and reel of film on the take–up arm.

"You guys been watching movies again?"

Otto twisted his body through forty–five degrees to look at the Bell & Howell. "Yeah. Just home movies."

"Good?" Frans said, raising his eyebrows.

Otto exchanged a furtive glance with Dieter. Then they replied simultaneously.

"Yeah," Otto said.

"A few surprises," Dieter volunteered.

"Ja?" Frans prompted.

"Well, Inez, for one," Dieter said. "But you knew about her."

Frans simply nodded his head, causing the folds in his neck to quiver.

"Nothing about a body in the garden," Otto said, feeling foolish as soon as the words were cold on his lips.

An uncomfortable silence enveloped them. Otto tried to catch Dieter's eye discreetly.

"How well did you know our parents, Frans?" Dieter said.

Otto froze, shocked by Dieter's brazen question. Frans twisted his shoulders and pushed his hands into his baggy trouser pockets.

"Not that well, I suppose." He paused. "How well do any of us really know our parents?"

"What do you mean?" Dieter said.

"Well, what did my pa really do when he worked for the diamond company security team? Did he ever shoot people in the Sperrgebiet?" Frans pulled his hands from his pockets and opened them in a questioning gesture.

"I see what you mean," Dieter said softly, looking down at the herringbone floor.

"But your pa, Dr Adermann, was a respected man here in Lüderitz, a man of principles and honour," Frans said.

They glanced at each other awkwardly for a moment. Otto felt his heart beating under his shirt. He took no pleasure in Frans' compliment, for he doubted its veracity.

"I believe he was a good doctor," Frans added quickly, studying first Otto then Dieter. "He was my family's doctor until he died. He was always kind to my boys."

An image of the small bodies hanging in the basement stabbed its way into Otto's mind. Why should a film of such an abhorrent scene be found in his father's house?

"Did you find out something about him in the films?" Frans asked, gesticulating lazily towards the projector.

Otto felt blood rushing through his ears and realised that he could never bluff his way through a lie detector test.

"Nothing that helps your investigation into the body," Dieter said with a measured detachment that impressed Otto.

"No?" Frans said with a bemused look on his face, then

clapped his hands together. "Well I do have some news to share with you."

Otto wiped his sweaty palms on his shirt. "Do you want to sit down, Frans?"

Frans nodded. "Ja. I think we should sit down for this."

Otto remembered being summoned to the headmaster's office at school for taking the cap off little Jan Smalberger's fountain pen and putting it back in his blazer pocket as a joke. That sense of foreboding, of guilty apprehension, came flooding back to him.

"Is it the DNA results?" Dieter asked.

"No, it's something quite unexpected."

THIRTY-FIVE

Frans declined a coffee and made himself comfortable in Father's ornately carved walnut armchair, the cracked leather groaning beneath his weight. He rested his elbows on his corpulent rugby thighs and clasped his hands together tightly as his crooked gaze flicked from Otto to Dieter thoughtfully.

"I had a few beers with Willem Krause last night," Frans said.

"Willem Krause?" Otto questioned.

"He's an old friend, a local attorney. He's the executor of your ma's estate."

"Oh shit! We're meant to be meeting him today, aren't we?" Dieter said.

"Tomorrow, I think," Otto replied, then narrowed his eyes momentarily and shook his head. "Jesus, I can't remember."

"Ja, he said he hadn't read the will to you yet." Frans looked down at his hands briefly. "Anyway, this is somewhat unusual, but Lüderitz is a small place, as you guys well know. People talk." Frans looked up at Otto and Dieter, both of whom stared back at him like puppets, waiting for him to pull their strings. "Willem asked me if I had identified the body in the garden yet." Frans felt uncomfortable about what he knew, biting his lip and wringing his hands.

"You haven't yet, have you?" Dieter said.

"No, no," Frans said quickly. "But Willem was very interested."

"Why would he be interested?" Dieter asked.

Frans shrugged, inclining his head self-consciously, then rubbed his unshaven chin with one hand. "We were just chatting, you understand, but I sensed that something in the will worries him."

He saw Otto glance at Dieter. Both brothers sat on the edges of their seats, hands clasped together over their knees.

"You are a German family, ja?" Frans said.

Otto and Dieter nodded.

"That's what we thought too." He paused. "There's something in the will about a Jewish person." Frans stopped and held his hands up in surrender. "All I know is that Willem is worried about it, in the light of the body found in the garden. He simply wanted to know how the investigation is going."

Otto frowned. "What does that mean?"

"I don't know, guys. You'll find out I'm sure when he reads the will."

Frans could see that Otto and Dieter were perplexed and edgy, Otto appearing particularly pale and clammy as he fidgeted with his hands. Frans wished that Ingrid had been there as well.

"I couldn't help but think immediately about our trip to Keetmanshoop," Frans said.

"Christ! Neil Solomon," Dieter blurted out, covering his mouth with a cupped hand.

"I don't know if it has anything to do with him, but..." Frans began.

"How many other Jewish people are connected to our family?" Otto finished.

Frans nodded as a brief silence ensued, all three men sitting with hands clasped together, staring ahead into an uncertain void.

"Why are you telling us this?" Dieter asked.

Frans scratched at the bridge of his nose. "I think we should get Ingrid back here, in case there are issues relating to the will."

"Issues?" Otto said.

"In any case," Frans continued, "I should have the DNA results back pretty soon. It would be best if she was here." He scratched self-consciously at his eyebrow. "It's just my gut instinct as a policeman."

Otto stood up and paced around the room. Frans leaned back in the armchair and placed the fleshy tips of his outstretched fingers together.

"So, you think there is a Jewish link with the body from the garden?" Otto asked, stopping to study Frans intently.

"I'm not thinking anything," Frans said with a dismissive shrug. "I'll wait for the evidence. Willem is concerned by something he's seen in the will, that's all... and I don't know what that is."

"Someone Jewish?" Dieter said, pensively.

"Ingrid doesn't have any children, I'm pretty sure of that," Otto said.

"You think she might have had a Jewish husband along the way?" Dieter said.

"I've never thought of it before," Otto said. "Maybe. But she never had children."

"What about you guys?" Frans said.

Dieter and Otto glanced at each other quickly.

"No!" Dieter said boldly. "I have no children."

"And you, Otto?" Frans asked.

"I have two, and Sabine is first generation German."

"What about Inez?" Dieter interjected. They all stared at him.

"Inez?" Otto said.

Dieter gestured with his arms. "Why not?"

Otto sat down again, and Frans could see that he had paled even further. He felt empathy for Otto, the youngest and potentially most vulnerable, having to deal with not only the loss of his mother but all of this additional unexpected baggage as well. Bad enough to discover after your mother has died that you had a sister whose existence was kept from you.

"Inez and Neil Solomon..." Otto said quietly, staring at the floor.

Frans slapped his thighs with the palms of his hands. "Look you guys, we're speculating here, which isn't doing any good." He stood up. "Let's get Ingrid back, see what Willem reveals tomorrow when he reads the will, and wait for the test results from England."

"If they did have a child... where is it?" Dieter said, gesturing with both hands.

"Jesus," Otto said, glancing towards the kitchen window. "You don't think...?"

THIRTY-SIX

Dieter had every reason to dream that night. Not only because of Frans' visit, delivering an inexplicable bombshell from which neither he nor Otto had recovered by the time they said their muted goodnights to each other in the darkened hallway, but also because they had sat down and watched – with infinite loathing – the hidden film which Otto had found, sequestered in a remote corner of Ingrid's wardrobe.

Dieter could not believe that he was watching footage disclosing images of Father associating with fellow Nazis who had become despised the world over for their cruelty. Dieter was certain that some of those present with father had swung from the gallows for their heinous crimes after the war. What was Father doing in the company of these odious men? Dieter felt as if he was observing a pantomime with everyone dressed in costume. But this was no pantomime. The moments captured for eternity on film were chillingly revealing and brutally authentic. They were also uncomfortably close and personal.

In a perverse way he shared Otto's earlier ponderous sentiments in the profound, stunned minutes that followed the film screening.

"Even though we have just buried her, in a peculiar way I feel a greater sense of antipathy and resentment towards Mum," Otto said after the film ended, pausing and tapping a finger against his lips. "Despite the fact that she was not the Nazi up there on the screen."

"Because you think she knew about it?" Dieter questioned.

"Probably. I mean, she must have known, surely she couldn't have not known, and yet she chose to collaborate and to perpetuate the fabrication, long after his death." Otto's face appeared twisted in pain. "Lying to all of us."

Dieter stared at the white sheet tacked to the curtains. "What do you remember about Dad?"

"That's just what I said to Sabine: what will the boys remember about me, about us one day?"

Dieter pulled a face.

"How can we be sure that what we recall from our childhoods, patchy and corrupted by so many factors, in any way accurately reflects what actually happened, the life that we really lived? Do you ever fully understand – as a child – what the hell is going on around you?"

"I don't remember a lot about Dad. He didn't beat me, he didn't neglect me, but I don't remember him loving me much either. Yeah, he paid for my studies in Cologne and I never went without – as Ingrid always reminds us – but…"

"You're trying to interpret your memories of Dad, formed when you were a child, from the perspective of an adult who now knows he was a Nazi during the war," Otto said.

"I don't follow."

"You can't reconcile your childhood memories of Dad, formed in an entirely different context and framework of personal reference, with the way you see and understand the world today," Otto explained, using his hands to mould air.

"Why not?"

"Because then you were a child who didn't even know what

a Nazi was, and Dad was simply Dad; now it appears he was a Nazi who experimented on prisoners and possibly colluded in murdering children. The brain cannot resolve both versions, Dieter," Otto said.

"Why not, if I can remember it?"

"Because they're vastly different things, adult memory and childhood memory. Even if you knew Dad was a Nazi when you were a boy your viewpoint would have been formed using a different perspective to the one you inhabit now," Otto said. Dieter pulled a face.

"We're trapped with adult awareness and the incongruity of childhood glimpses," Otto said ruefully.

They sat in silence for a moment.

"What about all the people here in Lüderitz? Did they know about Dad's past when he arrived in 1945? Did they shelter him from the authorities?" Otto said, gesturing with his arm. "Was everyone in on this?"

Dieter raised his eyebrows. "Frans?"

"Christ, I mean where did the Nazi criminals flee to after the war? Places without extradition treaties, Venezuela, Brazil, places sympathetic to the Nazi cause... like remote, former German colonies?" Otto continued.

Dieter looked down and picked at the cuticles of his fingernails. "They would have been very disappointed in me," he said softly. He felt Otto's sympathetic gaze on him. "If I had told Mum and Dad I was gay, I just don't see how the man we saw up there on that screen," he pointed to the sheet, "or the mother who protectively guarded his past, could have accepted me as their son." He shook his head dispiritedly. "No way."

"Don't think that, Dieter."

"It's true though, isn't it? They would have excluded me

like they did Inez." Dieter sat back and placed his hands behind his head.

Otto sat quietly and began to thread the film back onto the front reel to rewind it. "I don't understand why Dad didn't simply destroy this film," he said. "Why the hell keep it, hidden in a splicer box?"

Dieter gazed around the room, hands still firmly clasped behind his head. He looked at the paintings of Hamburg and Freiburg and Wismar, the old Gustav Becker grandfather clock, the Bechstein piano with its brass candelabras, the mahogany Biedermeier secretaire chest, and the pair of hinged walnut Gründerzeit side tables. Then he turned to Otto. "Pride?"

Otto stared back at him as the projector hummed and the reels spun at high speed, rewinding the film. "Christ, Dieter, that's chilling."

The dream came quickly to Dieter that night. The rolled-up carpet leaving the house, being carried by familiar yet obscured faces. That feeling of guilt, of panic, of wrongdoing, of imminent and inevitable discovery and punishment was as strong as ever. It made him sweat, as always, and he would awaken covered in a sheen of perspiration. This time he recognised Frans amongst the faces bearing the carpet, his huge lumbering frame unmistakeable. He tried to determine how large the object concealed within the carpet was. Could it be a person, an adult, a child? Was there indeed anything hidden in the carpet?

This time there was no skip, there was in its stead a fallen tree with roots radiating in every direction, like the snakes on Medusa's head. In the background stood a man in a black uniform wearing a shiny cap glistening with silver insignia. Father.

Dieter awoke and sat up abruptly. He was wet with perspiration, and he was angry. Why had Frans crept into this dream, contaminating and corrupting it? He was clearly not a participant yet his presence and significance in Dieter's mind had inserted itself into this dream.

Dieter rubbed his temples in the dark and began to wonder whether anything he recalled in this dream could be regarded as reliable. He no longer trusted his memory.

Turning on the light, he saw that it was 3am. He wanted suddenly to hear Jim's voice. He had been away from Hong Kong, and those he loved, for far too long now.

THIRTY-SEVEN

Otto called Ingrid in the morning. The sky outside was grey but there was no fog, and only a light offshore breeze that brought with it the smell of guano and seal dung. Ingrid sounded very surprised to hear Otto's voice.

"Otto?"

"Hi, Ingrid."

"What's happened?" she said immediately.

"Can we not speak unless something has happened?"

He heard her sigh.

"I thought you'd gone back to New York," Otto said. He was sitting in the living room on the velvet sofa, cup of strong black coffee in hand. Dieter was still asleep.

"I wanted to, believe me."

"Frans would like you back in Lüderitz, Ingrid."

"Ugh. OK, what's happened? DNA results back?" Ingrid said with evident disinclination.

"Not yet. That's still to come."

"Brilliant."

Otto drank coffee and caught a glimpse of the full reel of film that contained the grim reality of their poisoned ancestry. "It's not easy to tell you over the phone. There are two things, actually. One is to do with the will—"

"I told you I want nothing."

"There's something in it about a Jewish person," Otto said.

"What?"

"I don't know any more than that." Otto crossed his legs and rested the coffee cup gingerly on the armrest.

Silence.

"Do you have any children from any of your marriages, Ingrid?" Otto asked.

Ingrid snorted. "Hell no."

"You have no children by anyone?"

"I've told you, Otto. No. What is this about?"

Otto felt his pulse quicken, and an uneasiness brewing in his stomach. "Where can a Jewish person have come from in our family?"

"Jesus," he heard Ingrid whisper.

"I know."

"Has the will already been read?" Ingrid asked aggressively.

"No."

"How do you know this then?"

"It's… complicated. Everyone's a bit twitchy about the body in the garden, I think," Otto said.

"Don't discuss this with anyone, Otto; keep it to yourself," Ingrid said quickly.

Otto frowned. "Frans already knows."

"Oh God. How?" Ingrid said.

"As I said, it's complicated."

All Otto could hear was Ingrid breathing heavily on the line.

"What's the other thing?" Ingrid asked.

Otto bit his lip and looked across at the incriminating reel of film once again. "I found some old film hidden in the house that reveals Dad's secret past… in Germany."

A fertile silence took root yet again.

"Don't tell me, he was a Nazi?" Ingrid said, coldness discernible in her voice.

Otto felt a shroud of icy air descend over him as he watched the fine hairs on his arms rising. "How did you know?"

Silence.

"Ingrid?" Otto prompted.

Ingrid exhaled. "I didn't know but it suddenly... makes sense," she said softly.

"Please come back to Lüderitz, sis. I think Frans wants you back in town, and... there's something you just have to see."

"What is it?"

"I cannot possibly describe it over the phone," Otto said.

Another long silence.

"Now, I know you're not interested, but the reading of Mum's will takes place tomorrow at 2pm; Willem Krause's offices." Otto studied his hands, turning them over.

"OK," Ingrid said, sighing in resignation.

Otto smiled with a miniscule rush of surprise and satisfaction.

"Have you told Frans about Dad yet?" Ingrid said with sudden urgency.

"Not yet."

"Well don't. Wait for me."

THIRTY-EIGHT

Willem Krause, Attorney at Law, Divorce and Conveyancing, had his premises in the Krabbenhöft und Lampe Building. The plaque proclaiming it a National Monument cited its construction in 1910, and Otto noted with a bitter irony that the original Krabbenhöft und Lampe business had been started in Keetmanshoop. What a poignant place in which to wrap up Mother and Father's affairs, he thought to himself.

"My God, it's really close," Dieter uttered in surprise as they came upon the building barely two hundred yards from their house.

The imposing three-storey structure, the top floor of which was incorporated into a double-tier Bavarian gabled roof, was on the corner of Berg and Bismarck Streets, right around the corner from Bülow Street. Shielding his eyes from the searing sunshine, Otto glanced around and back up to their house situated slightly further up the hill.

"One can see how the discovery of the body in the garden didn't escape Mr Krause's attention," he said.

The interior of the law firm's office was air conditioned, smelling vividly of the sturdy kudu leather armchairs and waxed original oak floor. Draped over one of the chairs was a sable and cream mink coat that protectively enveloped Ingrid. She smelled overpoweringly of rose petals and appeared immersed in thought.

"Ah!" Otto said, moving towards her with arms outstretched.

She sat with her legs crossed in a crushed silk dress that glowed like sunset, but didn't get up, barely moving a muscle in greeting. "Otto."

Otto bent over awkwardly and managed to plant a light kiss on one cold cheek before surrendering and straightening. "You just disappeared after the funeral... we thought you'd returned to New York," he said.

Ingrid glanced briefly at Dieter without a flicker of acknowledgement. "Yes, well... I'm here now. You can tell Frans to call off the search party."

"I don't think it was like that, Ingrid," Otto said, suppressing irritation with difficulty. Why was Ingrid always so bristly, he wondered?

An oiled wooden door opened and a haggard man in a dark pinstripe suit appeared. He smiled perfunctorily, revealing angular teeth stained yellow by nicotine. "Mr Adermann, Dr Adermann, Mrs... er... Forsyt," he said, and gestured with his arm for them to follow him.

"Forsythe," Ingrid said as she gathered her coat.

"My apologies, madam," the gaunt man said. "I am Willem Krause, executor of your mother's estate. Please come in."

He was leathery and drawn like a palm date, prune-textured skin ineffectively hidden by a short grey beard. Behind large gold-framed spectacles his yellowed eyes darted about actively. There were only three padded seats arranged in front of his excessive leather-inset desk, behind which he retreated, settling into a plush leather armchair beneath a gold-framed oil painting of Felsenkirche.

"First of all, may I offer my condolences on the passing of your mother, Ute Adermann? We have known each other, and indeed been friends, for over thirty years. I knew your father well too and I was also the executor of his estate." Krause spoke slowly and deliberately, in measured legal tones, not a word or an intonation out of place. A noticeable Teutonic inflection dominated his vowels. "They were fine people, Ernst and Ute, I need not tell you – well liked and well respected in our community."

Otto shifted in his padded chair. He studied Krause's deep-set eyes, the eyes of a principled and conservative man; the same eyes that would have looked upon Father while they recorded Father's last will and testament, God knows how many years ago. What had made Krause decide to confide in Frans over a beer, Otto wondered?

"Would any of you care for a smoke?" Krause asked, lifting an ornate wooden box off his desk. "Or a brandy; whisky perhaps?"

They all shook their heads.

"Well, I hope you don't mind if I smoke?" Krause said without inhibition as he lifted a cigar from the box and clipped the ends. "I find it focuses my mind."

Ingrid exhaled audibly. Clouds of aromatic blue smoke soon encircled Krause, who seemed lost in his own world as he puffed, his puckered cheeks moving in and out like a blacksmith's bellows.

"When did you first meet my mother and father?" Otto asked.

Krause continued to puff, raising a solitary finger in the air to signal that he had heard. He eventually pulled the cigar from his mouth and inspected it with satisfaction.

"It was around 1950, a long time ago." He smiled thinly as smoke curled out of his mouth.

"So you didn't know our sister Inez, then?" Otto added.

"I never heard your mother or your father speak of her."

"Did you know about her?" Otto pressed.

Krause's eyes reacted and flicked from Otto, to Dieter, to Ingrid. "We'll come to all that."

Ingrid crossed her legs and folded her arms across her chest. Otto glanced at her and tried to elicit eye contact, but he could see the hardness set in her face.

"Now in many ways it is not a complicated will," Krause said, resting one elbow on the desk with cigar aloft while the other hand opened a folder on his desk. His head was bowed as he studied the contents. He looked up and gestured at the three of them. "You are the only three surviving children of Ernst and Ute Adermann." He looked at them. "Correct?"

They nodded. Dieter cleared his throat.

"You did bring your passports with you, didn't you?" Krause added, closing the folder on his desk almost as an afterthought.

Otto reached into his jacket pocket and produced his passport. "Yes."

Dieter did the same. Ingrid sat with her arms folded for what seemed an eternity to Otto, before she reneged and produced her passport. Krause leaned forward and collected them from the front of his desk before pressing an intercom.

"Miss Meyer, please come in."

A young blonde woman with her hair tied up and secured by an ornately carved wooden hairpin entered and took the passports.

"Two copies of each please, my dear," Krause said with a smile. "Right, where was I?" he continued, opening the folder again as smoke enveloped him. "Ah yes, it is a relatively simple will insofar as you, the three direct descendants, are concerned. In summary the estate of Ute Adermann is to be divided equally between all three surviving children." He paused to puff on the cigar as he turned a page. "Everything was bequeathed to your mother upon your father's death in 1975 on condition, something called a fideicommissum, that the only benefactors of the estate on your mother's death would be Ingrid née Adermann, Dieter Adermann and Otto Adermann."

Krause paused and looked up, as if to check that they were still present. "The estate includes the house on Bülow Street, the premises from which your father practised in Keetmanshoop, and cash assets totalling approximately four hundred thousand rands. As none of you currently resides in Lüderitz it might be best to sell the properties to release their equity." He looked up at them. "But that is up to you. Any questions?"

Dieter cleared his throat. "What happened to Father's practice here in Lüderitz?"

"He sold that when he retired, about six years before his death," Krause said.

"But he kept the one in Keetmanshoop?" Dieter said.

"Yes," Krause replied with apparent disinterest. Then all of a sudden he spoke again. "I believe his partner in Keetmanshoop, Dr Abert, continued to work for several more years."

Krause looked down at the folder and puffed on the cigar, appearing to savour every moment of it. "There are a few specific items that have been bequeathed to individuals." He paused. "The Walther 30-06 and Anschütz hunting rifles are left to the oldest son, Dieter; the Bell & Howell projector and equipment to Otto, along with all the oil paintings. The Bechstein piano and Biedermeier secretaire chest go to Ingrid."

"I don't want them," Ingrid interrupted. "You can have them, Otto."

Krause looked both bemused and irritated as he made a casual hand gesture. "These are trivial matters to sort out afterwards."

A gentle knock on the door was followed by Miss Meyer entering and returning the passports and several sheets of photocopied paper. Krause studied the photocopies as Dieter retrieved and distributed the passports.

Krause pointed at Otto with the cigar. "Otto?"

"Yes."

"Now, you are the only one with children, is that correct?"

Otto glanced first at Dieter and then at Ingrid, both of whom nodded. "Yes."

"Your mother has them down as Karl and Max... both Adermanns?"

"That is correct."

"They must have been born subsequent to your father's death as he did not list them in his will," Krause muttered, as though talking to himself.

"Yes," Otto said, "the oldest is only nine."

"And their mother, your wife, is Sabine... née Goethe." He fixed his eyes on Otto. "Yes?"

"Yes," Otto said.

"German?"

Otto felt an uneasiness that was difficult to place, but confirmed the information.

Krause nodded. "OK. But neither you, Ingrid, nor you, Dieter, have any children by any relationship whatsoever?" He studied their faces in turn. "According to the details in the will."

"No," Dieter said.

Ingrid slowly shook her head. "Why do you ask?"

Krause leaned forward and placed both elbows on the desk, locking his fingers together carefully so that the cigar remained uppermost in his left hand. "This is where we find something unusual." He puffed on his cigar, releasing a cloud of smoke. "When your father left his entire estate to your mother he did so on explicit condition that the only benefactors upon your mother's death should be his surviving children," he gestured towards them, "namely you three."

The cigar plugged his mouth again, his eyes thoughtful. Otto wasn't sure whether they were expected to say anything. Did Krause know that Frans had spoken to them? Had he wanted Frans to reveal his concerns?

"Did Mum agree to this condition in her will?" Ingrid asked. "I mean, Dad's been dead almost ten years."

"That is a fair point," Krause acknowledged, pointing the cigar casually towards Ingrid. "Fideicommissum is a very old and popular legal institution in Roman law. It was commonly employed to keep property in families. By invoking this principle your father clearly intended to keep his assets strictly in the family."

"Did Mum know this?" Ingrid asked.

"She would have had to consent to the fideicommissum and conditions when she accepted his inheritance in 1975," Krause said.

"What conditions?" Dieter asked, sitting forward.

"Well…" Krause scratched his eyebrow on the left side as he lowered his head to study the papers. "Basically the testator explicitly forbids inheritance to be paid to any surviving family member, or descendants, with any Jewish ancestry."

Otto felt Krause's eyes studying each of them in turn. He now understood why Krause had quizzed him about Sabine and he felt as if they were on trial, himself and his family being scrutinised for acceptability, just as Father and his Nazi colleagues had done in Neuengamme. History was repeating itself. How excruciatingly ironic, Otto thought.

"I don't see how this affects us," Otto said, sweeping his arm to include Dieter and Ingrid.

Ingrid squirmed in her seat, pulling at her dress with fingers hungry to be active.

"Your father was a very specific man; he must have had someone in mind," Krause said, with not a flicker of emotion on his face.

"Did he never tell you?" Otto asked. "You were his friend for nearly thirty years."

Krause blinked a few times. "No, he didn't."

"Is such a thing even legal?" Ingrid blurted. "It's obscene."

"Well it's not what we term contra bonus mores – in other words, contrary to public policy – and it's not illegal or criminal, so yes... it has to be legally upheld."

Ingrid hugged herself even tighter, her chest rising and falling with each deep breath, staring at her feet. The room descended into silence, broken only by the self-conscious creak of leather as Otto moved in his chair. Then came a light tapping on the door.

"Come!" Krause said, startling Otto.

Miss Meyer entered with a tray, cups and a white porcelain pot emitting the delightful aroma of Arabica. She placed this on Krause's desk subserviently.

"Thank you, my dear," Krause said.

She left wordlessly.

"Who makes the final decision on eligibility to inherit?" Dieter asked.

"I do," Krause said, "but if that is challenged, the courts of course."

Otto leaned forward, propelled by a sudden notion. "Look, it's obviously not any of us, so was Father perhaps protecting himself – his estate – against claims from a possible love child?"

Ingrid shot an intrigued look across at Otto, her fidgeting fingers suddenly motionless in anticipation.

"Love child?" Krause repeated, frowning.

"An illegitimate child, somewhere out there, born of a Jewish mother perhaps?"

Krause almost spat out his cigar. "Your father? Never! He was a dignified and honourable man and would certainly not have consorted with any Jews." He paused. "Those were his beliefs, a man of his generation."

An uncomfortable silence embraced the room. Otto met Ingrid's searching stare.

"But if no Jewish person is identified, and we know of no such person, then there is no contention of the will, surely?" Ingrid said, looking at Otto but turning to face Krause right at the end.

Krause opened and then clasped his hands again. "Yes, of course you are right. The only thing troubling me is the matter of the child's body… yet to be identified."

"If they identify it," Ingrid said.

"Yes," Krause conceded. "If they identify it."

Otto suddenly felt hollow inside. How this body in the ground had crept into every aspect of their lives in the past week: Mother's funeral, Mother's will, Father's past and now the spectre of unknown relatives with ancestry evidently abhorrent to him.

"How can the body possibly influence the execution of Mother's will?" Dieter asked in cautious tones.

Krause made a small hand gesture. "In all probability, not at all. But, if there has been a crime…" he paused for effect, "the law must be satisfied that no parties have been unfairly or criminally advantaged." He plugged his mouth with the cigar once more, eyes confident and small. "I doubt it will come to that."

"Is that it?" Ingrid asked. She looked pasty suddenly.

Krause closed the folder on his desk. "More or less. As I said, it is essentially not a complicated will." He looked at Ingrid, then Otto, then Dieter.

Otto rapped his fingertips on the armrest of his chair, wondering how long they would have to wait for the investigation surrounding the body to be concluded.

"Any questions?" Krause asked, rising behind his desk.

"No," Otto and Dieter said simultaneously as they stood.

Krause looked at Ingrid.

"What is there to say?" she said, rubbing her forehead.

"Good. Then I will begin instructions. Shall I proceed to have the properties valued and place them on the market… or auction?"

"Market," Dieter and Otto replied together.

"Auction," Ingrid said emphatically. "We all have lives to get back to." She sounded resentful.

Krause smiled thinly. "Let me know when you have a decision." His eyes settled on the refreshments. "Would anyone like coffee?"

"No thank you," Ingrid said quickly, rising from her seat.

Otto and Dieter shared a bemused look and they moved en masse towards the door. Otto paused with his hand on the ceramic doorknob and turned to Krause.

"So, my mother knew about this... condition?" Otto asked.

Krause was standing with both hands in his trouser pockets, cigar clenched between his teeth. He returned Otto's intense gaze for several moments before plucking the cigar out of his mouth.

"As I said, she would have had to accept the fideicommissum when she inherited from your father. I cannot of course be certain that she was aware of every sub–clause and proviso, or that she read them carefully, but..." Krause raised his index finger in the air, "she could not alter any of them."

Otto stopped. "She couldn't?"

"No."

He became aware of Ingrid and Dieter's increasing interest in the conversation as they hovered closer, like iron fragments drawn to a magnet.

Krause stepped forward two paces. "But your mother and father were always very close, and I think it very likely they would have wanted the same thing."

Ingrid inhaled sharply, straightening. "You cannot possibly know that." Her tone was bristling, accusatory.

Krause seemed to retreat slightly. "No, I suppose not."

THIRTY-NINE

They stood in the blazing sunshine outside Krabbenhöft und Lampe in a momentary daze. Advancing ominously over the navy-blue ocean was a solid wall of fog; grey, impenetrable and unrelenting. The wind before it heralded the approaching Atlantic odours of kelp and salt.

"What the hell did you make of that?" Dieter said, pushing his hands deep into his trouser pockets.

Otto met his brother's eyes but remained silent. His mind was still spinning from the rush of revelations over the recent days, as though a sluice-gate restraining the Adermann family history had been opened, releasing a tidal wave of surprises and anguish.

"We need a taxi," Ingrid said.

"Don't be silly, the house is just there," Otto said, indicating with an outstretched arm. "Five minutes on foot."

"Do you think Dad might have had an illegitimate child?" Dieter said.

"I don't know. He certainly did spend a lot of time away from home," Otto replied.

They began to walk up Bismarck Street, gently helped by the onshore breeze bringing the coastal fog ever nearer. Ingrid pulled her fur coat around her neck.

"What about Inez?" Dieter said.

"Yes, Inez," Otto reflected. "Her boyfriend was Jewish…"

"How do you know that?" Ingrid said sharply, her eyes dark and narrowed.

"He's buried in the Jewish cemetery," Otto said, waiting for Ingrid to make eye contact.

She walked on, tight-lipped.

"Dieter uncovered an old newspaper article about Inez's death in the Lüderitzbuchter. We found her boyfriend's name – Neil Solomon – and traced him back to Keetmanshoop," Otto explained.

"You went to his grave?" Ingrid said incredulously, looking up momentarily at Otto.

"Frans took us."

Ingrid looked flabbergasted.

"But… if Inez had a child, then where is it?" Dieter said, making a face.

Ingrid stopped walking and turned. Behind them the fog was beginning to blur the demarcations of Robert Harbour, engulfing the fishing fleet moored at the quayside. She opened her mouth to speak, and then seemed to change her mind.

"Is that perhaps why Dad sent Inez to Otjiwarongo?" Otto said. "The old guy, Dr Abert, he couldn't remember, or possibly didn't know why he took her there for Dad." He turned towards his sister. "Ingrid?"

She seemed startled to be singled out and looked up, eyes wide. "What?"

They turned into Bülow Street, the imposing footprint of their family home looming above them a short distance away – threatening, as ever, to slide down the angled black rock upon which it was built.

"You must know what happened to Inez?" Otto said.

Ingrid forced a contemptuous laugh. "Why me?"

"You were old enough to remember."

"Perhaps I didn't know."

"Perhaps you just don't want to tell us," Dieter said.

Ingrid shot a look that could freeze lava at Dieter. "I warned you to shut it," she hissed.

Otto observed the icy exchange with curiosity. "What's going on?" he asked.

"Nothing," Ingrid said quickly.

"If you know something you need to come clean, Ingrid. There's no more time for pissing about. Frans will know who the body is in a day or two and there's this will thing hanging over us as well," Otto said, studying his sister's face closely.

"What would you like me to tell you, Otto?" Ingrid challenged him, looking straight through him.

Otto hesitated. "Let's simply have the truth so we can get back to our lives and put this behind us."

Ingrid laughed coarsely, like a witch tending her cauldron.

"The truth," she said sarcastically, mocking Otto.

They stopped at the foot of the long flight of steps up to the house. Otto scuffed the sandy road with his shoe. "Just tell us what you know," he said.

Ingrid looked away, left and right, hands on hips. She bit her lip.

"Please," Dieter said softly.

Ingrid looked at him, and Otto thought he could discern something in her eyes: sadness, regret, perhaps even fear.

"You don't know what you're asking," she said, her eyes beginning to fill with moisture.

"Will it implicate you?" Otto asked.

Ingrid breathed in deeply and shrugged. She had that look about her that Otto had seen many times before: she didn't want to be there.

"We are a family, Ingrid. We will deal with this as a family," Dieter said.

Ingrid looked at Dieter, her estranged brother of many years who was now reaching out to her. She sniffed and wiped her nose. "You guys have no idea."

"We too have seen things that defy comprehension, Ingrid," Otto said. "We have seen Inez's boyfriend's grave in the Jewish cemetery and we know how Dad despised Jews; we have seen images of Dad dressed in a Nazi uniform, consorting with people who were in all probability tried and executed after the war." He stared into her eyes, frightened eyes yearning for escape. "We need to talk about what you remember, about what happened."

Otto was beginning to think that Ingrid was relenting, finally softening to their familial embrace.

"I should never have come back," she said, shaking her head. "I knew it would be a mistake."

Dieter sighed and began to climb the steps. Otto was losing patience and trying very hard to contain his mounting irritation and frustration with Ingrid's lack of co-operation.

"Why don't you watch the film we found, and then make up your own mind?" Otto suggested, turning his back on her and following Dieter up the stairs.

FORTY

Ingrid watched the flickering images on the screen. She recognised Father's sharp features beneath his SS cap, remembered being up close to his neck when he had held her as a little girl, the neck that was now partially covered by a black and silver SS tunic lapel adorned with the sig–rune and insignia. The bold and proudly worn Nazi symbols diminished both his credibility and his pre–eminence as a father in her eyes.

She pressed clammy palms together as she read the names of his comrades in arms – Trzebinski, Pauly, Heissmayer – names familiar to her in a chilling and yet indeterminate way. Why did she recognise them? Glancing to her right, she saw their ghostly images reflecting off the faces of Otto and Dieter, whose eyes were glued to the screen, engrossed yet simultaneously horrified, but seemingly unable to look away.

Ingrid felt nauseous. She could not halt the tide of disclosure revealed on the screen; she could not deny its authenticity nor claim ignorance of the evident facts. A tightness was enveloping her, restricting her breath, accentuating her growing unease. History was catching up with her. It was catching up with all of them. As she stared at images of Father helping to administer arsenic to prisoners she began to doubt that her waning resolve to keep their past at bay could endure much longer.

Seeing Father turn the prison labourer over to the guards because he was missing several fingers was a chilling reminder of his brutal capabilities. She had observed that icy disaffection at first hand, witnessed its calculated destruction as it tore into her beloved sister. Instinctively she covered her mouth with one hand, biting down on a knuckle.

She recalled searching Father's eyes for signs of humanity, acceptance and forgiveness, hoping to be able to convince him of tolerance and persuade him towards absolution for her sister's sake. But she never found what she so desperately hoped to evoke in him, and consequently she never saw Inez again.

Father's unyielding face, his poised, self-assured eyes, so confident of his own moral righteousness, shone out of the screen images and impaled Ingrid in her heart. Seeing Father inhabiting a world that she had never known, never imagined, participating in medical crimes so heinous that most of those onscreen beside him were hanged soon after the war ended, left Ingrid gasping for air, realising that the father she had struggled to know and failed to love was in reality an unlovable beast. History had finally judged him.

Otto and Dieter never once took their eyes off the screen. Ingrid felt a sudden inexplicable pang of empathy for them, caught up in Father's conspiratorial web of congenital evil when they were still so young and impressionable, oblivious to the extent and depravity of his fervour. What a shock this must have been to them.

By the time the images of young boys and girls being probed and painfully injected by sadistic hands glared at her from the screen, Ingrid's eyes were swimming with tears, blurring the monochrome images of unimagined savagery that glimmered before her. Droplets soaked into her silk dress, forming craters of deepening anger.

Twenty lifeless souls, still dressed in threadbare and ill-fitting coats and trousers, suspended barefoot like puppets by their murderers in the shadowy retreats of yesterday's oblivion. But it had surfaced to haunt them yet again.

Ingrid rose suddenly and rushed to the bathroom, retching her anger and shame into the toilet. She was not of such stock, not capable of such heinous acts and to demonstrate this she had tried to put distance between herself and her parents, those who had been accomplices to unimaginable injustices.

So why had she colluded? She cried out and vomited more, trying to expel the demons from her soul.

FORTY-ONE

The phone rang and Dieter answered it in a few strides. He was expecting it to be Jim, and could not hide his disappointment.

"Oh, hello Frans."

"Dieter?" Frans sounded unsure.

"What can I do for you?"

"How did it go with Willem Krause today?" Frans asked.

Dieter made a face. "OK, I guess; nothing earth–shattering. Mum's estate is left to the three of us."

"OK, that's good then," Frans said. "Listen…"

"What is it?"

"I've had a call from our forensic division to say that the scientists in England are having difficulty with the quality of the DNA in those bones. They were in the ground a long time, you see."

"Meaning?" Dieter asked, cradling the phone against his shoulder.

He could hear Frans sucking air through his teeth. "Well, at best it's going to take longer."

"How much longer?"

"I don't know. Days, weeks."

"I've got to get back to Hong Kong, Frans. I've got a business to run," Dieter said.

"I know, I know. We can't expect you all to hang around here – I mean, we may not get any answers."

Dieter switched the phone from one ear to the other. "Really?"

"I guess it's possible."

"What do you want me to do?" Dieter asked.

"Just tell Otto and Ingrid. Is she there?"

"Yes." Dieter nodded.

"I'll need to speak to her again. Maybe tomorrow. Tell her, please."

"OK, Frans."

FORTY-TWO

It was evening, the setting sun ingested by a shroud of fog that threatened to consume the very fabric of Lüderitz. Ingrid said that she had to get out of the house, unable to be surrounded any longer by the symbols of a family past that she abhorred. They walked three abreast, Otto separating Ingrid and Dieter, down Nachtigall and Diaz Streets to reach the rocky and menacing esplanade beside the bay. Visibility was less than ten yards and the waves breaking onto the shoreline could be heard but not seen.

Otto spoke first. "Did you know about any of that?"

He glanced at Ingrid, her eyes still puffy and pink, staring ahead emptily, raw from what they had been watching.

"I suspected that Dad had a military connection, even wondered years later about whether he was in the SS because he was always so secretive about his past at home." She pushed her hands into her mink coat pockets, shuddering slightly. "But I never dreamt…"

"It's fucking humiliating," Dieter said. "Our father, a bloody Nazi criminal. We'll all be shamed and ostracised."

"Not around here," Ingrid retorted with a snort.

"I guess now we know why they chose to settle here," Otto said.

"The far end of the bloody world," Dieter added.

The fog curled around them, its tentacles at certain times appearing to separate them, at other times encircling and embracing them as one.

"Did you ever see anything?" Otto asked, feeling his skin crawl at the very implications of his question as he glanced at Ingrid.

Ingrid turned to him briefly. "In Hamburg, no. There were Wehrmacht soldiers at the house from time to time, but then we were at war, so…" She shrugged, appearing to reminisce. "Sometimes a fancy staff car would call for Dad and take him off, but…" she frowned, "we never saw him in uniform, had no reason to suspect he was anything other than a doctor."

"What made you think he might have been a Nazi then?" Otto asked, remembering her response when he had called her in Windhoek.

Ingrid met Otto's eyes, and in her gaze he could see deep, brooding resentment.

"His manner, his behaviour: he was so strict, so formal, so unyielding. Not an ounce of compassion in his bones. He destroyed Inez. He… killed her."

"Because of Neil Solomon?" Dieter said, concentrating on his footfall over the rugged pathway.

"Obviously!" Ingrid said. "I tried to talk to him, I begged him, but he wouldn't listen."

"And Mum?" Otto asked.

"What about her?" Ingrid said.

"What did she do?"

Ingrid glared at Otto as though it was he who was to blame. "Not enough," she said.

The sea breeze had calmed, the waves were less angry – it was as though the fog had induced serenity over the land. Otto wanted to ask about the body in the garden but felt it would be a reach too far. Not yet, he thought, it's going too well. Don't push it.

"We were wondering if we should tell Frans," Otto said.

"About Dad?" A look of horror was evident on Ingrid's face. Otto nodded.

"No," Ingrid said quickly. "Not yet. What did he call about?"

"He said they were having difficulties with... you explain, Otto," Dieter said.

"They're struggling to extract sufficient intact DNA from the old bones for the analysis," Otto said.

"Meaning?" Ingrid stopped and turned to face Otto, her eyes locked on his.

"It may take more time... or it may not even be possible," Otto said.

She stared at him, her eyes darting about his face, her breathing deep and rhythmic. "Well I'm not hanging around this fucking dump indefinitely, if that's what he's suggesting."

"They just want to get to the bottom of this, Ingrid. If you know what happened, tell us, tell Frans, and then we can all go home," Dieter said in tempered tones.

Her eyes flicked to Dieter and narrowed, lingering on him for longer than Otto could ever remember her looking at their brother.

"Do they teach you about traumatised childhoods at medical school?" Ingrid said.

"Come on Ingrid, you were only a child at the time, no-one will ever blame you for what happened. Just talk about it. Tell us the truth we are so desperate to hear," Otto said.

"The truth?" Ingrid said with a dismissive smirk, looking away.

"Yes. Who are you protecting?" Otto asked.

Ingrid's resolute gaze faltered and she looked down at the stony pathway, turning a pebble over with the point of her shoe.

Otto studied her profile, sensing within her a titanic struggle – perhaps the fearful little girl nervous about repercussions, grappling with the bitter and resentful adult she had grown up to become.

She looked up and drew breath. "I am as appalled and sickened by what I saw on that film as you guys are." Her eyes filled again momentarily. "Dad and I had our differences over the years, yes, some of which I can never forgive him for. But Jesus, I never realised what a monster he was. It's… indescribable." She bit her lip and dabbed at her eyes, the gathering fog softening her tightly clenched jaws. "And he got away with it as well – escaped justice." She faced Otto again, determination in her eyes. "Well, not this time."

She drew a deep breath and shuddered slightly. "Let's invite Frans over. Show him the film first, and then I'll tell you what I can remember."

Otto could not believe his ears. He wanted to smile and thank her but fought against this inappropriate effusiveness in the midst of her evident emotional turmoil, feeling within himself as well a sudden quickening of his heartbeat.

"You won't regret it, Ingrid," Dieter said, trying to sound encouraging.

"Don't bet on it," she said without looking at him.

Otto was on the verge of stepping forward to embrace his sister when she spoke again.

"But tonight I want to be left alone to think," she said, and for the second time that week abandoned Otto on the esplanade as she sauntered off into the mouth of the fog, pulling her coat up around her neck.

FORTY-THREE

Ingrid struggled with her thoughts as they sat and watched the grainy, lined footage of Father in his SS uniform, strolling regally around Neuengamme in the company of notorious Nazi figures – Trzebinski, Pauly, Heissmayer. Ingrid imagined momentarily that she could detect a smirk on Father's face as he stood, hands on hips, basking in the contagion of his notorious collaborators.

Frans sat to her right, his jowly face cupped in meaty hands as he watched with piscine eyes staring widely at the flickering images. The muscles of his jaw worked tirelessly beneath his fleshy fingers. Dieter sat on the floor, knees drawn up to his chin, and Otto hid behind the projector, his eyes downcast, seemingly unable to look at his Nazi father for a third time.

Frans had welcomed Ingrid back to Lüderitz effusively when he arrived. "You have made the right decision to come back, Ingrid. Thank you."

"Did I have a choice?" Ingrid said.

"I want to get this investigation wrapped up and begin handing over to my successor. I'm retiring, you know?"

"Are you now?" Ingrid said derisively.

"Ja. Anyway, Willem Krause needs to execute the will and in the absence of those test results from England you are the key to helping us sort out this mess."

Ingrid stared into his eyes as they darted about disobediently. She could not believe that the runt of the Laubscher litter had become the Chief of Police, and that she was now answerable to him.

"Watch the film that Otto found first. Then we'll talk," Ingrid said.

The images were distracting her. Every time she began to prepare her intended words to Frans, another breathtaking image of sadistic cruelty would flicker onto the screen, Father's face always to be seen somewhere in frame. She wanted to shout at Father, she wanted to strike out at him, for being the man he was, for destroying his family, and for putting all of them through this hell so many years later.

Ingrid had almost forgotten Father. She never thought of him and had certainly not shed a tear for him from her Manhattan apartment when he died. But now his sharp, youthful face was thrusting its way back into her consciousness, evoking memories that she had worked so hard to forget.

Damn you, she wanted to say out loud. Damn you to eternity.

She looked at her naked left ring finger. Three times she had worn a wedding ring on it. Three times she had removed them. Ingrid recalled the furore when Frederick had placed the first ring onto that finger. First there had been the tragedy surrounding Inez, and then Frederick had proposed: it was on that day when Father had refused his blessing that she realised she could never look him in the eye again.

Then she glanced past Frans' intensely concentrating face, his jaws still clenching as though he was chewing, and studied

Dieter and Otto's forlorn faces. Being the oldest, she still felt duty–bound. She had to see this through, whatever the cost. If circumstances had unfolded differently she may have been able to get away with maintaining her silence, but they were well past that point now. All that she could do was try to minimise the damage.

FORTY-FOUR

19 September 1948

Mother sat rocking the infant in her lap, its eyes heavy and losing the struggle against gravity. Mother was wearing a full-length black dress and laced shoes. In a wicker and steel-framed Frankonia stroller beside her, another infant slept beneath a pale blue blanket.

Father sat cross-legged on the sofa, holding his ornately carved nicotine-stained Meerschaum pipe in his mouth. He stared at Mother through the fragrantly spiced smoky haze, his eyes resolute, his dark suit immaculate.

Ingrid walked sombrely into the room in a knee-length pale green dress, hands clasped together in front of her waist, a beret perched at a jaunty angle on her head.

"May I please go into Inez's bedroom?" Ingrid asked.

"The door should be locked," Father said sharply, looking accusingly at Mother.

"Yes, Ernst." Mother rocked the infant with greater enthusiasm as it began to stir in her lap, its fingers opening and then closing again as if grasping at something invisible.

Father turned to Ingrid. "Please, Inga, your sister is gone. I will clear her room before I—"

"I will clear her room while you are away," Mother interrupted.

Father clasped the pipe between his teeth again as he contemplated Mother with a disdainful look. "Do not keep things, Ute," he warned her.

"There are some special things in Inez's room that are mine," Ingrid protested, gently stamping her flat-soled black pump on the floor.

Father sat forward. "Enough! We will not mention Inez's name in this house again, understand?"

Ingrid's chin wobbled as she looked to Mother.

"Ssshhh, Ernst, you will wake the child."

"Don't ssshh me, that is not even my child."

Mother looked at him with large doleful eyes, resignation in her body posture as she rocked the infant. "Well who is to care for her child now, Ernst?"

Father stood up and walked away from Mother. In the far corner of the room Dieter sat on the floor in khaki shorts and a loose flannel shirt held up by braces. He was setting up rows of lead soldiers and watching as his coiled metal Slinky magically wormed its way along into his troops, knocking them over.

"The child must go for adoption," Father said, back still turned to Mother.

Mother's eyes widened as her cheeks sank inwards. "Ernst?"

He turned around, pipe in hand. "I will not have that… that Jewish child in my house." He gesticulated towards the sleeping infant in her lap.

"This is Inez's son," Mother pleaded.

"Yes, Papa, please… can't we keep him?" Ingrid pleaded, moving to her mother's side.

"That's enough!" Father said, waving his pipe at Ingrid

threateningly. "This does not involve you, Inga. Please, leave us, and take Dieter with you."

"What have I done?" came the plaintive voice of little Dieter.

"Please, Papa," Ingrid pleaded.

"Out!" Father pointed to the door with an outstretched arm, holding the smouldering pipe aloft.

Ingrid and Dieter left dutifully without a further whimper of protest. The infant in Mother's lap began to stir and Mother made to unfasten her blouse and expose her breast.

"For God's sake, Ute, not for the Jewish child," Father said.

"What will you have me do?" Mother said, looking up at him, the infant now crying and reaching for her breast.

"That is for Otto," Father said, pointing at her bosom. "This Jewish child must go."

"It is all we have left of Inez."

Father's head spun back to confront Mother. "We have nothing left of her. She is gone, do you understand? Dead."

Mother's eyes stared at him, hurt and loss crumpling the edges of her composure. "You would abandon your own grandchild?" she asked softly, "He looks so like Otto."

Father slumped back down on the sofa and crossed his legs. "He is a Jew, Ute, he is not my grandchild." He contemplated Mother and the infant for a few moments. "We gassed children like that in Germany, remember? How do you expect me to raise one now as my own? I will be a laughing stock."

Mother's gaze faltered and she looked down at the screwed–up little infant's face she was denying as she buttoned up her blouse.

"I will not do it, Ute. The child must go."

Otto now began to stir in the pram, soon bawling lustily.

"Look what you've done," Mother chastised Father.

Father stood up.

"Please just pick Otto up for me and see if he'll settle. He hasn't slept long enough," Mother said.

"I'm going to pack." Father walked to the door and then paused. "I am very serious, Ute: when I return from Etosha in two months' time I want that child gone." He brandished the pipe menacingly at the infant in Mother's lap, as if he was holding a pistol.

Mother sat in stunned silence, a solitary tear clinging desperately to each lower eyelid, gently bouncing one crying infant on her knee as a beetroot-faced Otto bawled from his pram. Ingrid entered the room cautiously.

"Oh, Inga, please pick Otto up," Mother said.

"Where's Father going?" Ingrid said as she cuddled Otto against her shoulder, gently patting his back.

Mother sighed. "He's off on a hunting trip to Etosha with some of his Otjiwarongo friends."

"How long will he be gone?" Ingrid asked.

"Quite a long while."

Ingrid walked around in a contained circle, rocking Otto, whose crying had abated. "Can we clear Inez's room together then please?" Ingrid's eyes filled with tears. "There are things I want to keep."

Mother smiled sadly and swallowed. "Of course, Inga. Just don't tell your father. It'll be our secret."

Ingrid tried to smile, but her eyes were drawn to the cherubic face of her dead sister's child. "What are we going to do with Johan?"

Mother's face crumpled together as her chin quivered. "I don't know, Ingrid. I just don't know."

Dieter sat dutifully in the rocky sand, scuffing his black shoes back and forth. He was wearing a double-breasted jacket over his braces, seemingly dressed for Sunday school. He drew patterns in the dust with a finger. Close by Otto and Johan crawled about, inspecting flowers and wreaths and turning over everything they encountered.

Mother, in her black dress, knelt beside the mournful mound of barren Lüderitz soil piled on top of Inez's fresh grave. Ingrid stood behind her, hand on Mother's shoulder. They both cried, tears rolling down Ingrid's cheeks and dripping onto the parched earth.

"I miss her so much, Mum," Ingrid sobbed and sniffed, wiping at her wet face with the other hand. "Why did this happen?"

"Put that down, Otto," Mother said, turning her head to see what the two crawling infants were up to.

Ingrid walked over and removed the plastic wreath from Otto's resolute grasp.

"I am so sorry, Inez my dear," Mother said, speaking to the mound of earth as though her daughter could hear her. "We've come to say goodbye. Little Johan is leaving us." Her shoulders shuddered and she looked down, pinching the bridge of her nose as she winced, trying stoically to suppress her sobs. "I cannot do anything, I'm so sorry. It'll be for the best, I'm sure."

Mother placed the palm of her hand on the soil tenderly. "Say goodbye to your mama, Johan." She began to sob openly, wailing in embarrassment, trying to hide her miserable face from Ingrid.

Johan suddenly let out a piercing cry, more like a scream, and did not relent. The tear-streaked faces of Ingrid and Mother turned sharply towards him. In his lap lay a bunch of flowers. His face was turning red, like a poached tomato, as his lungs squeezed chilling cries from his gaping, wet mouth.

"It's OK, baby," Ingrid said and bent to lift him.

He cried even more, his eyes staring around fearfully, his mouth dripping saliva.

"What happened?" Mother said.

"I don't know."

"Put him in the pram. There's a bottle of milk there."

Mother turned back to the grave, rubbing her temples, gently rocking herself back and forth.

"What's wrong, Mama?" Dieter said, coming up to his mother and pressing himself against her side.

"I'm very sad, my boy. But I'll be alright," Mother said and forced a smile for Dieter, rubbing his nose playfully.

Ingrid laid Johan down in the pram and rocked him gently, plugging his mouth with the bottle of milk. He cried and cried.

"It's as if he knows," Ingrid said, turning to glance at the grave and Mother's hunched profile.

Soon Johan calmed and fell silent. Ingrid knelt down beside Mother and stared at the mound of earth. So emphatic. So final.

"Every morning when I first wake up, I forget that she's gone. My heart does not ache straight away. Then suddenly…

I remember," Ingrid said, her eyes filling with tears. "Every day, it's the same."

"Look, Mama, a giant spider!" Dieter said excitedly. He was pointing at something, his face a blend of fascination and horror.

Ingrid glanced across to where Dieter stood and went to investigate. What she saw chilled her blood. "Oh my God, Mum. It's a scorpion!"

Scurrying away on hideous yellow–orange legs towards an adjacent headstone was a black scorpion, its long body covered with fine hairs. Behind it lay bunches of fresh flowers from Inez's grave. Ingrid screamed and covered her mouth with one hand. Then she pulled Dieter out of harm's way.

"Oh my!" Mother said, now standing, her deadpan face apparently mesmerised by the size of the scorpion. "Oh my…"

"Is it a spider?" Dieter said.

Otto came crawling along to the flowers, reaching out.

"No!" Ingrid shouted, grabbing him by the arm and lifting him away.

He cried out in protest and perhaps some pain as he dangled in Ingrid's grasp. In a flash of simultaneous deduction, Mother and Ingrid both turned to the silent pram. Mother began to wail as she rushed towards it. When she reached the pram the haunting sound of visceral suffering that she was emitting suddenly intensified.

"No, no, nooo…" Mother screamed as she lifted the blue and floppy body of Johan out of the pram. "Oh God, noooo…"

Ingrid, feeling weak at the knees, stared in shock, still holding Dieter's hand. She lifted Otto up to her shoulder as both he and Dieter began to cry, frightened by what they did not understand.

"We need Father," Ingrid said, staring at Mother for affirmation.

But Mother flopped back hard onto the mound of fresh earth on Inez's grave, shaking her head, Johan's lifeless body in her embrace. She sobbed, her tears wetting the infant's purple face and glassy eyes. It was as though Ingrid was afraid to go near Mother and the dead child. She kept her distance, holding Otto as she knelt beside Dieter, comforting them both as they all stared at Mother, howling in heart-wrenching salvos. It was too shocking for Ingrid to comprehend, as though her mind was shutting down in self-defence. Dieter pawed at her shoulder, rivulets of snot running down his upper lip.

"What's happened?" Dieter asked, looking at Ingrid with naive innocence.

Ingrid did not know how to respond, and she pulled Dieter closer to her as he pushed his thumb into his mouth. Rising up from the shore was a wall of leaden fog, obliterating both horizon and sky, approaching fast, soon to swallow Lüderitz and all its misery.

"This is all your father's fault," Ingrid said softly, and kissed Otto on the head. Inside, she felt cold. Her tears had dried up. Her eyes burned from staring at Mother's broken body holding Johan.

FORTY-FIVE

Frans stared at Ingrid, his divergent eyes worse than ever in the semi-gloom of the darkened living room. Otto and Dieter had gathered around them, Dieter still sitting on the floor, hugging his knees as he might have done as a boy while listening to a story being read to him.

"Had your pa already left for the Etosha hunting trip?" Frans asked.

Ingrid sniffed away tears and licked her dry lips. "No. He was home."

Frans frowned almost imperceptibly. "So, what did he do?"

Ingrid shrugged. "Nothing. Johan was already dead."

"From the scorpion sting?" Dieter asked.

Ingrid nodded.

"Jesus," Dieter mumbled.

"If it was a black and yellow scorpion," Frans said, turning to Dieter, "as I've told you, they are very poisonous, especially if you are a small child."

Otto felt his heart pounding in his chest. The thought that he had been crawling about in juvenile ignorance beside Johan, perhaps inches away from the lethal sting that had claimed his young nephew, horrified him. How cruel and arbitrary the fates could be.

"And then what happened?" Frans asked.

Ingrid took a deep breath. "Father panicked. Nobody in Lüderitz knew that Inez had an illegitimate child – let alone with a Jewish man – and Dad was deeply concerned about his reputation, his honour and esteem." Ingrid's voice betrayed a bitter tone.

"Did she have the baby in Otjiwarongo?" Otto asked.

"I think so." Ingrid nodded, looking briefly at Otto. "He and Mum went to his study and locked the door for a few hours. They told me to put Dieter and Otto to bed. When they came out it was already dark."

Ingrid bit her lip. Otto felt nauseous, both from knowing what was coming and seeing Ingrid in such an atypically emotional state. He had never seen her like this before, stripped of her layers of armour.

"Dad went out and dug in the back garden for hours." Ingrid stared ahead blankly for a few moments, though whether trying to recall or banish images from her mind Otto was not certain. "I was so exhausted, but I couldn't go to sleep. Little Johan was wrapped up in a sheet or something in Dad's study, like a doll." Ingrid covered her eyes momentarily, drawing a few shuddering breaths.

"Did you see all of this?" Frans asked.

Ingrid nodded, her pink eyes refusing to engage with anyone in the room. "I remember it like it was yesterday. I watched first from Dieter's bedroom upstairs, while I put him to sleep."

"You saw your father dig a hole in the back garden – where we found the body a few weeks ago?" Frans asked.

"Yes."

Frans wiped his stubbly chin with one hand and frowned. "Man," was all he said, blinking furiously as if to straighten his eyes.

"It must have been after midnight before the hole was deep enough." Pause. "They carried him out – Mum was crying and Dad told her to be quiet, and all I did was watch from the landing on the stairs."

Otto studied Ingrid's tortured face, tears streaked through her perfectly applied make-up like bicycle tracks. He had never seen his sister like this. She was always in control, aloof, confrontational. It was unsettling to see her struggling with such bitter memories, and he felt a sudden surge of empathy for her, feeling that he had probably misunderstood her motivations all these years.

"I've had a dream for many years," Dieter said, quietly at first, clearing his throat into a balled fist. "It's always the same, and it takes place at the back of our house."

Frans turned around to fix one of his eyes on Dieter.

"I see people carrying a rolled-up carpet – a green one – out of the house."

"Your bedroom carpet was green," Ingrid said.

"I know, it makes no sense. In the dream I know there is something in the carpet, something that is wrong, very wrong, something that could get me into trouble, but I don't know what it is. For some reason, I think it is a body."

"Can you see who is carrying the carpet?" Frans asked.

"Never. The faces are always in shadows. There are a few people – two, maybe three. It leaves me with a hollow fear that one day it will be discovered and I will be in trouble."

They all sat in silence.

"Do you see the carpet being buried?" Frans asked.

Dieter shook his head. "No. I never see a hole and I usually wake up then, so I don't know where the carpet goes."

Ingrid stared at Dieter with a deep frown etched into her forehead. "You couldn't have seen that. You were… what… five? You were asleep."

Dieter shrugged. "I know. Maybe I heard it later, you talking about it…" He shook his head. "I have no idea. Until today, I have never understood the dream, but now…"

Frans turned back to Ingrid. "What happened the next day?"

"Father left for his hunting trip and told us never to speak of Inez or the baby again." Ingrid pulled a face.

"Christ, Ingrid. You've shouldered this all your life?" Otto said. "You should have told us, it would have eased your burden."

"I promised Mum. Then it just became a…" She trailed off, unable to find the words.

"And your ma?" Frans asked.

"She would never say anything against Dad. That's how she was. Love and obey," she said sarcastically.

After a while Frans stood up slowly, as though his back was hurting. He arched his body and pressed his balled fists into his lower back. It seemed that he wanted to say something, but he took his time before speaking.

"I am really sorry for you guys. This is a terrible thing to discover, especially so soon after your ma's funeral. Terrible."

"It was Dad's fault," Ingrid said coldly.

"Eh?" Frans turned.

"It was all because of Dad. He drove Inez to suicide, he wouldn't have her child in the house, he buried the body in the garden, he swore us all to secrecy to protect and preserve his honour." Ingrid was seething. "When I saw that film of him prancing around in his fucking SS uniform…" She shook her head slowly.

Otto stepped forward and embraced Ingrid. She hesitated and then he felt her head against his shoulder and her arms around him. Dieter joined them, placing one arm around Ingrid and one around Otto. They stood in silence for a while; Otto could not remember how long. There was nothing to say. Otto heard Frans let himself out the front door.

FORTY-SIX

That evening Otto, Ingrid and Dieter went down to the seafood restaurant on Robert Harbour and sat around the same table, sharing two bottles of pinotage. No-one seemed hungry, Otto certainly wasn't, but he sensed that there was a shared need for togetherness to mourn for all the lost years and wounding secrets.

They spoke little about the events that Ingrid had recalled, her chilling words still fresh and raw. Amidst numerous silences they pushed grilled hake, buttered lobster tail and creamed potato around their plates.

Otto was disorientated, his mind spinning. He could not think about the mother he had come all this way to bury; he could not even turn his mind to his wife and children whom he so badly missed.

"I am sorry, Ingrid, for never understanding what you have been through," Dieter said.

She shrugged. "How could you have known?"

"I don't know how you did it," Otto said.

Though he said this, he felt that he knew the answer. Ingrid had withdrawn from the family, retreated to her own iceberg, a cold and unfriendly place from which she seldom ventured. She had never encouraged relationships with the family, keeping everyone at a safe distance. This way, he thought, she had avoided constant reminders of those terrible events she witnessed as a young girl, forced into a subservient pact of collusion that she had honoured until now.

"I want to go back home, now. I am tired," she said, clinking her fork down and pushing her plate of uneaten hake away. "I will never visit Lüderitz again."

She looked exhausted, Otto thought, emotionally eviscerated. Her eyes were still puffy and her eyelids layered, as though she had suddenly aged. Dieter picked up his starched napkin and wiped his mouth.

"I want to get home too," Dieter said suddenly, eyes on Ingrid.

Ingrid looked up at him, her expression certainly receptive, even if not warm. "Is there someone?"

Dieter nodded and carefully placed his napkin on the table.

"Yes, my business partner, Jim."

"It's a good thing Mum and Dad didn't live to find out," Ingrid said somewhat derisively.

"Don't I know it. Why do you think I waited?"

Otto smiled as he watched Ingrid and Dieter over the glow of his wine glass. It had been a very long time since he'd seen any convivial exchange between his brother and sister.

"I suppose Willem Krause will now be quite happy to execute the will," Ingrid said. "And I mean what I said – I don't want the piano or anything from that house. I don't much care what you do with any of it."

"And your share of the money?" Otto said.

Ingrid made a face. "I have money."

"We all have money," Otto said. "It's your entitlement as one of their children."

Ingrid winced, as though she had been stabbed beneath the table. It was subtle, but Otto noticed. Her chest rose and fell for a few moments as she looked at him. What was she thinking, he wondered?

"Well, I guess this is it then," Ingrid said.

"Why?" Dieter asked.

"I'm leaving tomorrow, back to Windhoek and I'll catch the next flight I can to JFK."

Otto held back a polite protest. There seemed no point now. This funeral gathering had gone on for much longer than anticipated, and had exposed more than he could ever have imagined in his worst nightmare. It was time to go home, he to Sabine, Max and Karl; Dieter to Jim; and Ingrid to... he realised then how little he knew about her life in New York.

"Shall we meet up at Christmas somewhere?" Otto said.

Ingrid pushed her chair back to stand up. "Let's walk before we run, Otto." She rubbed her eyes. "I need sleep, I am finished."

Though brief and somewhat unconsummated, Otto felt good about the fact that they had managed to go out and dine together as family. Their childhood memories would never be the same again, but at least they all knew the truth about their parents, as revealing and unpalatable as it was.

FORTY-SEVEN

19 September 1948

Mother stared in horror at the bloated cerise face in the pram. Beside her Ingrid screamed hysterically.

"What's wrong with him? What's happened?"

Mother pulled the tiny, limp body out of the pram in her strong arms and laid it down on the gravel beside Inez's grave. Kneeling down in the sandy dirt she bent over the moribund infant and began to blow into his nose and mouth. Then she pushed rhythmically on his chest with several fingers in concentrated silence, her face drawn, as first one and then several tears rolled down her rounded cheeks and soaked into the arid soil.

"Mum, what are you doing?" Ingrid asked, clutching a wide-eyed Dieter against her leg.

"Put the pram in the car and get both boys in," Mother said as she bent down to inflate the infant's chest once again.

"Is he alright?"

"Just do it, Ingrid, quickly! There is no time to waste," Mother said sharply.

Ingrid seated the two boys in the back seat. They were both crying and their round faces suffused with a rush of blood.

"Why is Mummy crying?" Dieter asked in between cries.

Ingrid stifled a sob as she tried desperately to reconcile in her young mind what had happened: the sight of that black and yellow scorpion scurrying away burned into her mind.

"We need to get home," Ingrid said as she loaded the pram into the dusty old black Mercedes 130H, imported to Lüderitz long before the war even began.

Mother was still hunched over the tiny, stricken body, its arms spreadeagled on the infertile desert surface.

"Can you drive the car?" Mother asked without interrupting her attempts at resuscitation.

Ingrid paled. "I'm only fourteen, Mum."

"Can you do this then?" Mother asked, making brief eye contact with her.

Ingrid cried and sniffled. "I don't know what you're doing."

Mother bent over to breathe into the infant's lungs before fixing Ingrid with a steely stare, her eyes cold and unsympathetic.

"For God's sake, Inga, don't snivel, you are going to have to grow up quickly in the next five minutes."

"Mum?" Ingrid felt her knees weaken. She was frightened, overwhelmed and felt very alone, the world around her suddenly large and confusing. Urine trickled down her leg.

"Get behind the wheel, I'll tell you what to do," Mother said sternly.

Once in the car Mother held the flaccid child in her lap, hunched over it, continuing to compress the chest and breathe into its lungs. Her face was becoming flushed and perspiration dotted her forehead. Dieter's crying intensified in the warm, claustrophobic cabin of the car.

"Start the car," Mother said, pointing at the keys in the ignition.

Ingrid's hands were shaking and she was startled as the engine burst into life, vibrating the car.

"Push the clutch in with your left foot." Mother paused to breathe into the child's lungs. "Gear into first."

The car began to roll backwards.

"I'm scared, Mum, I've never done this before," Ingrid snivelled.

"Listen to me. I need you to grow up right now! It's only you and me that can do this, understand?" Mother's tone was unyielding. "There is no-one else."

"We're going backwards!" Ingrid wailed, holding the steering wheel helplessly.

Dieter bawled in the backseat, his little fists held aloft in ignorant protest.

"Put your foot on the accelerator and let the clutch out slowly," Mother yelled as she pressed on the child's chest.

The car bounced, jerked violently and stalled, almost propelling the infant off Mother's lap. She yelled at Ingrid, who was crying in unison with Dieter. The car started again and Ingrid tried desperately to get it moving, but with the same failed result. Mother screamed – a cry of frustration and anguish. Her chest was heaving and she looked exhausted. Ingrid watched as she put her ear next to the child's mouth and then pressed a finger into his blue-black mottled neck. It no longer resembled a little infant boy. Ingrid averted her eyes from its spoiled skin.

Mother leaned back in the seat and let out a moan, an indescribable visceral sound of torment. She closed her eyes, squeezing a large tear out of each, and rested her hands on his chest.

"What is it, Mum?" Ingrid asked apprehensively, almost in a whisper, feeling her heart pounding in her chest.

Mother wiped one eye. "I'll drive, you come and sit here and hold him."

"But I don't know how to…"

"You don't need to anymore."

Mother drove slowly and in silence, both boys in the back crying lustily, Ingrid sobbing almost hysterically with the dead infant in her lap, unsure where to put her hands, astonished by its floppiness, the little dry mouth hanging open. How could such a thing happen so quickly? A few times she swallowed bile.

Back at home on Bülow Street Mother wrapped the infant in a towel and placed it in Father's study, locking the door. She put on her apron and moved through the house with a steely purpose, silently, wiping her eyes occasionally but not uttering a sound. Ingrid kept the boys busy, leaving Mother undisturbed in the kitchen, slicing vegetables, boiling meat, buttering bread and setting the table. She fed the children, though neither she nor Ingrid ate very much, and then instructed Ingrid to put the boys to bed.

When Ingrid returned to the living room she found Mother sitting in darkness, her face buried in her hands, a glass of brandy beside her. Ingrid hesitated, feeling that she was intruding upon something beyond her comprehension, something not meant for her to witness.

"Come, sit," Mother said, sniffing away tears and patting the seat beside her.

Ingrid sat and straightened her skirt. Mother took a deep breath and took hold of her hand.

"Your father cannot find out about this." She paused, looking into Ingrid's eyes. "Do you understand?"

Ingrid nodded, though her childlike comprehensions were being extended to the limit.

"You and I will have to do this together, Inga, in it for as long as you live." Mother took both of Ingrid's hands and held them firmly between her calloused, dry fingers.

"I'm scared Mum. What will happen?"

"That is up to us, dear. Your father is away for a long time. He doesn't need to know about this."

"But how?"

Mother bit her lip and looked upwards, as if searching for divine inspiration. "I have already lost one child this week. I'm damned if I'm going to lose another."

Ingrid started to cry again, reminded of losing her big sister Inez, the one person in the world who understood, the friend to whom she could always turn.

"We should bury him in the garden, that way he will always be close to us. Think of it that way," Mother said softly, looking into Ingrid's eyes again.

"But Mama—"

"Hush, Inga. Listen to me. Just like you, I do not wish to forget Inez forever. But your father's wishes will have to be respected in this house. That does not stop you and me from having our own secrets." Mother patted her hand and tried to smile.

Ingrid sniffed and swallowed. "What do we do?"

"We bury him next to the new camelthorn tree – the ground is freshly dug there – and we pretend nothing ever happened."

"But when Dad comes home—"

"You and Dieter and Otto will be here, just like before."

Ingrid stared at her mother in horror and bewilderment. "But—"

"If we act normally your father will never suspect – or know – anything otherwise," Mother said, smiling tautly.

Ingrid blinked a few times, her sobbing now reduced to the occasional shudder. "Are you sure, Mum?"

Mother reached for her brandy and took a generous mouthful. She swallowed and appeared to struggle for breath.

"You need to promise me, Inga, that you can keep this a secret – from your father, from the boys, from everyone. No-one will benefit from knowing about this tragedy."

Ingrid stared fearfully at her mother and nodded.

"Tell me you promise," Mother insisted.

"I promise, Mum," Ingrid said, nodding effusively.

"Forever?"

"Forever."

"Good girl. Here, drink this to seal our word." Mother passed the goblet of brandy to her.

Ingrid drank a little and coughed so dramatically that she thought she might choke. Her throat burned worse than the time she had accidentally bitten a chilli. Mother smiled at her and squeezed her hand.

"Now, we have work to do."

The two of them spent most of the night digging a hole beside the camelthorn. Ingrid was so terrified of being caught, of being seen, that she nearly vomited several times. In the morning she awoke to find Mother asleep in the living room, still wearing the same black dress from the previous day, torn and soiled with dust, just like a peasant. Beside her was an empty bottle of brandy.

FORTY-EIGHT

The knock on the front door was so loud it startled Otto as he was carefully removing the oil painting of Freiburg University, his favourite, from the wall. He was somewhat surprised to make out Frans' burly figure looming in the entrance vestibule.

"Hi Otto." Frans looked ill at ease.

Otto frowned. "What is it?"

"We have a problem. Is Dieter here?" Frans said.

"Uh–huh."

"Ingrid?"

Otto shook his head. "She'll be at the airport now, flies back to Windhoek…" He glanced at his wristwatch.

"Shit!" Frans said, glancing around furtively as if someone was stalking him. "Can I use your phone?"

Otto ushered him in and pointed to the telephone in the hallway. Frans dialled immediately, pawing at his face constantly. "Hello, airport security please, this is an emergency."

Otto frowned. His genteel and tranquil morning spent sorting through Mother's belongings had been brought crashing down around his ears.

"Ja, hello, this is Chief Laubscher here. Listen, has the flight to Windhoek left yet?" Frans nibbled on the inside of his lip as he listened. "Good. There is a passenger I want you to hold for me, please."

Otto's heart skipped a beat. What on earth was going on? Dieter emerged from the passage, alerted by the stern tones of Frans' voice.

"What's going on?" Dieter asked.

Otto shrugged.

"Well, in that case you will have to take her off the plane. Her name is Ingrid…" Frans looked at Dieter and pulled a face.

"What's her surname?"

Dieter shrugged and deferred to Otto.

"Forsythe," Otto said.

"Forsythe. Ingrid Forsythe. I am on my way. Please keep her in the departure lounge. What?" He narrowed his eyes as he listened. "No, no cuffs. Just hold her there."

Frans replaced the receiver and wiped his mouth with a spade-like hand. His excitable eyes flicked from Otto to Dieter.

"What's going on?" Dieter repeated.

"Ingrid lied to us. We need to speak to her again," Frans said with a resigned sigh.

"Lied to us… about what?" Otto said.

"Let's go, I'll tell you on the way." Frans was already heading down the long flight of concrete steps to his car on the sandy roadway below.

Within minutes they were driving out of Lüderitz, heading south-east on the Kolmanskop road. Frans drove aggressively, revving the protesting Toyota engine mercilessly, the fluffy dice swaying pendulously beneath the smudged mirror. On the road ahead tiny swirls of sand pirouetted across the shimmering tarmac.

"They had a breakthrough with the DNA tests and faxed the results through this morning," Frans said.

Otto and Dieter made apprehensive eye contact in the rear view mirror.

"What Ingrid told us is simply not possible," Frans said. Otto felt winded. Why would Ingrid lie? He had seen her face, listened to her emotional confession and felt her relief as she had revealed her childhood recollections of that traumatic episode. It had all sounded perfectly plausible to him.

"But why would she lie?" Otto said.

"That's what I need to ask her," Frans said.

They passed the cemetery, a place that now held so many tragic memories for Otto. Some distance later they passed the turning to Kolmanskop, and then not long after that, Lüderitz Airport.

Situated on a flat plateau of rock and sand the airport was as remote and isolated as any place could be, evoking in Otto the impression of a base on the moon. A small collection of low buildings connected by tarred roads swept clean of sand; sand that waited impatiently at the verges for the next opportunity to drift across and cover everything again.

The runway resembled a strip of black paint rolled down a camel brown meadow. Keeping it clear of sand must be a thankless task, Otto thought to himself. Frans pulled up sharply right outside the terminal building, his car at an overtly illegal angle, and alighted from the vehicle with surprising agility for a man of his size.

The terminal was small and poignantly provincial, a single atrium that served both departures and arrivals. On one side a few car hire desks; on the opposite side a vending machine for drinks; and in the centre a few rows of moulded plastic seats, empty but for one person.

Ingrid sat, with two security guards standing behind her, her face set like a thunderstorm about to unleash bolts of murderous lightning. Frans nodded to the security guards, who retreated slightly.

"What the fuck are you playing at?" Ingrid shouted at him.

In the background the drone of an aircraft gathering speed could be heard, and through the wall of windows Otto saw a Beechcraft twin-prop accelerate noisily down the runway and lift off into the melting heat of a mirage.

"That was my flight to Windhoek!" Ingrid said, jerking a thumb towards the windows. "There probably isn't another one for a week in this fucking dump."

Frans sat down opposite her in the plastic seats. Otto and Dieter hovered, unsure where to sit. Otto felt betrayed as he studied Ingrid's stony face, conned by her apparently phony act the previous day. But she would not make eye contact. Dieter eventually sat next to Frans, and Otto beside Ingrid.

"I'm sorry Ingrid, but I had no choice," Frans said. He was perspiring and his eyes appeared totally disconnected from each other.

Ingrid was wearing a mint green dress with black trim, black high-heeled shoes, and pearls around her neck. She folded her arms defiantly, but said nothing.

"We got the DNA results back, Ingrid," Frans said.

Ingrid swallowed and shifted in her seat, refusing to meet Frans' eyes. "You said they were unlikely to get a result," she said accusingly.

"Well," Frans shrugged, "they did." He maintained his steady gaze in the face of Ingrid's mounting discomfort.

"So you pulled me off my flight just to tell me that?" Ingrid said, truculent to the end.

Otto thought back to their meal the previous night: the sense of togetherness that he had not felt for so many years; the promise of closer ties in the future and even a degree of fledgling reconciliation between Ingrid and Dieter. What had happened to that? It had all appeared to evaporate. Was it merely a fabrication, like so much of his childhood?

"You lied to me, Ingrid." Frans glanced at Otto and Dieter. "You lied to all of us."

Ingrid rubbed her temples.

"The DNA test shows beyond doubt that the body in that grave was not Inez's child," Frans said, with surprising sympathy in his voice.

Otto felt lightheaded. What was Frans saying? If the child buried in the garden was not Inez's, then…

"So did the DNA not match with Mum?" Dieter asked.

Frans did not reply, appearing to direct the question to Ingrid with an enquiring rise of his eyebrows.

"You did not test Inez's DNA," Ingrid said, a flicker of tension visible beneath her eyes.

"We don't need to, we know who it is now. You also know who the child was, Ingrid," Frans said.

Ingrid shifted her weight in the plastic seat. Otto swallowed ineffectively against dry resistance in his tightening throat. Dieter appeared sweaty, wringing his hands together.

"Oh for Christ's sake, Ingrid," Dieter blurted. "Tell us who it is."

Ingrid stared at them, and then her gaze faltered and she looked down at the polished floor. "He was your brother," she said softly.

"What?!" Otto said.

Frans unclasped his hands briefly. "I don't pretend to know the technical details, but the scientists say that the body is a certain match with your ma's DNA."

"Meaning?" Dieter said, staring wide-eyed at Frans.

"He was your ma's son."

Otto felt a spasm across his chest, and an aching hunger for breath. "But…" he said, staring for a moment at the grey flooring. "There were always only three of us, after Inez died…"

"Oh my God," Dieter said, straightening. "Jesus, oh fuck." He bit his knuckle. "It's…" He glanced at Otto, who met his eyes and then suddenly felt his senses overwhelmed by a warm, prickly invasion.

Ingrid lowered her head.

"Is it true, Ingrid?" Otto asked apprehensively, sitting forward to gain a better look at her face. Otto realised that he was pleading with her, begging her to refute his darkest suspicions. Ingrid remained tight-lipped.

"It wasn't Johan that died in the cemetery, was it Ingrid?" Frans said.

Ingrid was breathing heavily and avoiding eye contact with everyone. Otto wanted to stand up but feared his legs would not carry him. His fingers dug into each other between his knees.

"It was Otto who was stung by the scorpion," Frans said.

Ingrid stood up suddenly and walked around, placing one hand over her mouth. The two security guards flinched.

"This was never… ever meant to come out." She turned and met Otto's pained stare as her eyes filled instantly with tears.

"Ingrid?" Otto pleaded, angling his head, hoping she would deny it.

"Jesus, I am so sorry, Otto," Ingrid said, her face tortured by a grimace – begging forgiveness.

"Oh my God." Otto stood up, but his knees buckled and he sat down heavily.

Dieter moved forward and sat beside Otto, who was breathing laboriously, his fingers trembling around his mouth.

"This changes nothing, Otto – you have been our brother all these years, and you were always Mum and Dad's favourite son… we all know that," Ingrid said, her voice remarkably composed though tears streamed down her face.

Otto wiped his nose with the back of his hand and bit his lip. He didn't know what to do, what to say. He didn't even know how he felt. How should he feel: he was dead? He wasn't Otto. He was Inez's son. Breathing became difficult; he felt as though he might suffocate. He was panicking. He needed to calm down, he knew that, but he couldn't.

Frans walked over to the vending machine, and after slamming a few coins into it returned with a can of Coke which he handed to Otto.

"We couldn't tell Dad… he wanted nothing to do with Inez's son. He wanted him – you – adopted. He thought Mum had taken you for adoption while he was away," Ingrid said, eyes fixed on Otto.

"Only you and Mum knew?" Dieter said, looking at Ingrid with searching eyes. "Dad never suspected?"

Ingrid shook her head. "I would never have told you. Even though it hurt me deeply to see how Dad treated you with such favour over me, and I knew you weren't even his child." A slight edge to Ingrid's voice escaped at the end. She didn't say it, but Otto knew what she meant: he was a Jew.

"But why didn't you tell us yesterday?" Frans asked.

Ingrid sat down, two seats away from Otto, her chest heaving. "I was protecting Otto. When you said there was a chance they might not be able to get a DNA result… I had to make a choice."

They all stared intently at her. "A choice?" Dieter said.

"I could tell the truth and our lives would never be the same again, or I could take a gamble – cement the lie and put it to bed forever by implying it was Inez's son in the back garden."

"But why?" Otto said.

"Isn't it obvious, Otto?" Ingrid said, turning to him and reaching out to take his hand in hers. "The will."

Otto was stunned. He had never even thought about that. Being Inez's half–Jewish son, according to the terms of the will, he was no longer eligible to receive any of his mother's estate.

"You knew about that as well?" Dieter asked, angling his head menacingly.

"No," Ingrid said, "not until the will was read. But Dad would have believed that Inez's child was still alive, you see, adopted and living somewhere in this country." She stared into Otto's eyes. "Don't you get it? That's why he inserted that clause."

Otto slumped into his seat. Dieter stood up and walked to the vending machine, leaning against it.

"What a fucking mess," Dieter said quietly.

Frans sat back and rubbed his face thoughtfully. "Did Otto die from a scorpion sting, pretty much as you told us yesterday?" he asked.

Ingrid looked at him quickly. "Everything happened exactly as I told you, except that it was Otto and not Johan that was stung. And Dad had already left for Etosha, so Mum and I had to do everything." Her eyes filled suddenly. "Have you any idea what it's like burying your own baby brother when you're just fourteen?"

Otto was in emotional turmoil, but he perceived Ingrid's fragility and moved closer, placing an arm around her shoulders.

"Will Willem Krause find out about this?" Dieter asked.

They all looked at Frans who sat in ponderous silence, studying his sausage-like fingers as they writhed in his lap like bloodworms.

"You know, I retire next month," Frans said quietly, not looking up.

They stared at him. Otto's mouth felt like blotting paper. In some ways he was no different, but in other respects his entire universe had just been shifted, and that of his family back in Durham. This revelation, he realised, would inexorably affect the next generation.

"When I close this case," Frans stood up slowly, groaning with the effort, "no-one will look into it again."

Ingrid's eyes were hidden behind her manicured hands and painted fingernails. Dieter leaned in deep thought against the humming vending machine. Otto felt hollow, empty, like a nomad. He was numb.

"Come, I'll give you guys a lift into town," Frans said, jangling the keys in his pocket.

Frans drove away gently, Dieter in the front with him, Otto staring out of one rear window and Ingrid out of the other. The police radio crackled.

"Chief, call in please, Chief. This is Eric."

Frans swiftly pressed a button and silenced the radio. Otto's mind had turned to Sabine, Max and Karl. What should he tell them? Suddenly he was afraid of revealing the truth. Surely Sabine would not mind? Could she? It was her father Otto worried about. Heinrich Goethe was a proud German who had evidently approved of his only daughter's marriage to Otto. In a miniscule moment of levity, Otto wondered if he would have approved even more had he known about Father's Nazi connections. And then, with less jocularity, Otto considered how he might react to the revelation that his son-in-law was in fact a Jew. Otto looked ahead to see the Lüderitz cemetery signpost approaching.

"Can we please turn in here, Frans? I would like a moment," Otto said, clearing his thickened throat.

"Good idea, Otto," Dieter said.

Frans tactfully sat in the car while all three children walked to the graves of their sister and mother. For Otto, standing at the foot of Inez's grave, staring at her name and dates of birth and death etched into the stone, this distinction between sister and mother was now, and forever would remain, blurry and indistinct. He had only learned about Inez a week ago and now he had discovered that she was his mother. It did not feel real. He never knew her, didn't even have a clear idea of what she had looked like when she brought him into this world.

Beside her was the fresh mound of rocky soil piled on Mother's grave, his grandmother in reality, but in every other sense of the word his mother. Dieter placed an arm on Otto's shoulder and squeezed twice.

"I am so sorry, Otto," Ingrid said, tears once again dripping soundlessly down her cheeks.

Otto drew breath slowly to suppress a shudder of deep-seated emotion. "It wasn't your fault."

Dieter nudged Otto and drew his attention to the mound of earth on Mother's grave. "Look!" he said.

On top of Mother's grave, crawling out of a bunch of shrivelled lavender, was a hairy black scorpion with yellow legs. It stopped, tail poised in the air, ready to strike. Otto held his breath. Ingrid emitted sucking sobs as Otto drew her closer with his left arm.

"You know, Otto," Dieter said. "If it hadn't been for the scorpion, you wouldn't be here with us today."

Otto acknowledged this to be a sobering analysis of the tragedy and nodded, unable to take his eyes off the fearsome creature.

"Surely, even our family is better than no family at all," Dieter said.

Otto felt himself surrendering to the immense emotion churning within him.

"What are you going to do?" Dieter asked.

Otto shrugged and sniffed away tears. He didn't know how to respond. What should he do?

"Take my advice, Otto, and keep this to yourself. Let it be our secret," Ingrid said in a calm and measured voice.

EPILOGUE

Frans retired two weeks after closing the case of the child's body discovered at the Adermann House on Bülow Street. As most people in Lüderitz had long forgotten or never even known Inez, Otto assumed it must have been simple to pass the child off as having been hers. After all, life went on – no-one was affected and the Adermanns were gone. It did, however, leave Otto feeling somewhat hollow, because officially he was dead; he did not exist; he was merely an imposter.

But as a direct consequence of this benign outcome Ingrid, Dieter and Otto each inherited their equal share of the Adermann estate.

Otto took a languid mouthful of Aberlour and savoured it on his tongue.

"What are you drinking for?" Sabine asked, sitting down beside Otto on the rattan snug in their orangery, placing her hand on his.

"I'm thinking about Dieter," Otto said.

He felt Sabine squeeze his hand and push her fingers between his. He gently tightened his grip on her hand, savouring the delicate floral scent of her presence.

"It was nice that Ingrid joined you at his funeral," she said, "and good to meet Bernie as well. They seem very happy."

"I've never seen her happier," Otto said.

Much to Otto's surprise, eleven months after Mother's funeral Ingrid married Bernie Kaminsky, a wealthy Jewish tycoon on Manhattan's upper east side. Otto was disappointed not to have been invited to the nuptials, though he acknowledged that it was probably a low–key affair, given that it was not Bernie's first marriage and most certainly not Ingrid's either. Otto hoped that she had found a sense of inner peace, at last.

Looking up at the oak beam lattice, he smiled wryly.

"What is it?" Sabine said.

"I'm sorry Dieter never met Bernie. I think he would have liked him."

"Isn't it odd that you three never met up again after your mum's funeral?" Sabine said.

Otto nodded and savoured more Aberlour. It was indeed odd, and also disappointing. An opportunity lost, he felt. They had at least begun to exchange birthday and Christmas cards anew after Mother's funeral, kept in annual contact and even spoke on the phone occasionally. But he and Ingrid had not met up again until one week ago, at Dieter's funeral in Hong Kong in November 1994. Dieter had wasted away, along with most of his friends, from the new plague: AIDS.

But despite his regret over their failure to reconnect as siblings, Otto was massively relieved that Father's past as a Nazi criminal at Neuengamme never became public knowledge, and did not live to haunt the remaining members of the family. Ernst Adermann's ignominious background had successfully died with him and was blown to oblivion by the offshore winds on Shark Island, never to be heard of again.

Otto's most difficult decision was whether or not to tell Sabine, her parents and his children the truth about who he really was, or what had happened in the sequestered little community of Lüderitz in the year that he was born. At first this gnawing deceit festered within him like an ulcer, because he feared the unanticipated consequences of an inconvenient truth. But with time the normality of his family's unchanged existence soothed his conscience and he grew comfortable with the lie.

"I was thinking... after Dieter's funeral," Sabine said, straightening with a look of sudden intensity on her face, withdrawing her hand and clasping them together in her lap.

"About what?" Otto said.

"Did they never identify the body in the garden?"

Otto did not think he hesitated for long, burying his face in his whisky glass before meeting her sincere grey eyes as confidently as he could, shaking his head nonchalantly.

"No, they didn't."

Inez Ellenberger died of gunshot wounds with her boyfriend on 27 December 1934 at the age of 25. Her father, Edmond, a French attorney, had forbidden Inez's relationship with the man because he was a Jew.

My grandmother, Eileen, was Inez's older sister and she wrote this tribute in the funeral notice.

A broken string in memory's harp
Is softly touched today.

AUTHOR'S NOTES

Deutsch Südwestafrika (German South West Africa)

Deutsch Südwestafrika was a German colony from 1884 to 1915. In 1885 a convention was held in Europe to divide Africa amongst European nations at the behest of Bismarck. Borders were negotiated with the Portuguese in Angola and the British in South Africa. By 1888 the Nama and Herero peoples of South West Africa began to resist the continuing confiscation of their lands and cattle by the German colonialists.

Adolf Lüderitz was the first magistrate of the colony, having been the tobacco merchant who first bought land along the barren coastline in 1882. His successor until 1890, Heinrich Göring, was Nazi Reichsmarshal Hermann Göring's father. In 1915, during the First World War, troops from the British colony of South Africa occupied South West Africa and drove the Germans out. In 1920 a League of Nations mandate handed powers of administration to South Africa.

The legacy of Nazism has persisted in South West Africa into the new independent nation of Namibia, established in 1990. Reports in the media still proclaim the presence of strong pro–Nazi groups in Namibia, many in Swakopmund, where it is rumoured that some Nazi fugitives have been hiding since 1945. Disruptive behaviour at public meetings, leaflet distribution, protests and racial hate crimes are continuing evidence of right–wing Nazi extremist presence in Namibia to this day.

The Portuguese sailor Bartolomeu Diaz first discovered Lüderitz Bay in 1487 and erected a cross on the peninsula immediately south of the bay. Lüderitz town began as a trading post supporting whaling, guano harvesting and fishing. In 1882 Adolf Lüderitz purchased the coastal land, which was named Lüderitzbucht in his honour when he died on an expedition to the Orange River a few years later.

Before the Shark Island concentration camp was established it was reported that Lüderitz had only five buildings. As a result of the military presence associated with the camp and the importance of the port during military operations in southern Südwestafrika, the town flourished and grew rapidly.

In 1909 diamonds were discovered and the resulting rush propelled Lüderitz to unimagined wealth. Kolmanskop was built south-east of Lüderitz as a diamond mining town within the Sperrgebiet or forbidden zone, a vast area with restricted access and tight security that completely surrounded Lüderitz. Stories abound about the lawless and trigger-happy security patrols who ensured that trespassers did not ever return to the Sperrgebiet.

By the late 1940s the diamond rush was over and Kolmanskop became a ghost town soon thereafter. Diamonds are still mined in both the desert and on the ocean bed, still under strict control, though the Sperrgebiet can now be visited with permits and escorts.

Today Lüderitz is a thriving little town of 12,500 inhabitants in a precariously isolated location. Trapped in a century-old colonial time warp, it is packed with grand buildings whose charming and incongruous architectural style date back to the early days of German colonial optimism. With diamonds gone, tourism, fishing, nature conservation and rail network links are Lüderitz's hopes for the future.

Shark Island Extermination Camp

Impatient for a solution to the tribal uprisings against German colonial inhabitants in Deutsch Südwestafrika, Kaiser Wilhelm II appointed Lothar von Trotha as governor of the colony. Von Trotha pursued an aggressive and brutal campaign against the Herero and Nama peoples, shooting them, driving them into the desert and poisoning their water holes. Tens of thousands were killed.

In 1904 the Shark Island Concentration Camp was established on the rocky peninsula of land jutting into Lüderitz Bay. It is now acknowledged as the world's first Vernichtungslager: extermination camp. In just four years around three thousand men, women and children died in the camp, more than eighty per cent of the inmates.

Conditions were appalling, food scarce, beatings frequent and medical care non-existent. Racial experimentation was performed on prisoners by the notorious Dr Bofinger. Bodies were decapitated and women forced to boil the heads of their own people before scraping off the flesh with shards of glass. These skulls were transported back to Germany by the crate for examination at elite universities.

Many surviving photographs taken by German military personnel, showing appalling conditions, tortured victims, physical abuse and soldiers loading skulls into wooden crates, were turned into postcards and sent back to friends and families in Germany.

As recently as 2011 the University of Freiburg identified fourteen skulls in their anatomical collection as those from Hereros and Namas killed in the Shark Island Concentration Camp between 1904 and 1908. At a ceremony in September 2011 twenty skulls were repatriated to a Namibian delegation at the University Hospital Charité in Berlin, and returned to Namibian soil the following month.

Lüderitz thrived during the time of the Shark Island concentration camp, growing from a small settlement into a bustling coastal town. Eugen Fischer, notorious Nazi doctor, spent time at Shark Island and examined skulls. He wrote a book, The Principles of Human Heredity and Race Hygiene, which massively impressed Adolf Hitler. When Hitler came to power he appointed Fischer as chancellor of the university in Berlin where he established the Kaiser Wilhelm Institute for Anthropology, Human Heredity and Eugenics.

Josef Mengele, responsible for appalling medical experimentation crimes in Auschwitz, and Hendrik Verwoerd, South African Prime Minister who fully implemented apartheid, were both students of Eugen Fischer.

Neuengamme Concentration Camp, Hamburg

Neuengamme was established within the districts of Hamburg by the SS as a sub-camp of Sachsenhausen concentration camp in 1938. It functioned predominantly as a labour camp to service the needs of the German war machine initially, but also carried out exterminations.

Aside from the main camp, based in the village of Neuengamme, there were a further eighty sub-camps that fell under Neuengamme concentration camp, including four in the Channel Islands.

Neuengamme was in operation until 1945, when it was liberated and occupied by the British Army. During this time more than half of the estimated 105,000 prisoners perished. Inadequate food, shelter and medical care resulted in outbreaks of pneumonia, tuberculosis and typhus, some of which killed thousands. Prussic acid was used to gas prisoners and lethal injections were also widely employed. Allied air raids were extremely hazardous to prisoners, who were not allowed to use air raid shelters during bombings and were also given the dangerous task of clearing the streets of rubble and unexploded munitions in major cities like Hamburg and Bremen after bombings.

In the beginning most prisoners were German dissidents, but by the end of the war Soviets, Polish, French and Dutch nationals accounted for eighty per cent of those interned. Prisoners were used to construct a canal between the rivers Elbe and Dove, and to dig out clay for the onsite brickworks. Several factories using thousands of prison labourers were established in the camp, notably Walther–Werke, which made weapons and small arms; Carl–Jastram Motorenfabrik, which manufactured parts for U–Boats; and Deutsche Mess–Apparate, which produced fuses for grenades.

Though Neuengamme initially used the Hamburg municipal crematoria for disposing of its dead, the camp built its own crematorium in 1942 and thereafter more systematically killed prisoners unable to work. In addition it is believed that about two thousand Gestapo prisoners were brought to Neuengamme specifically to be killed by lethal injection.

Nazi doctors also performed medical experimentation on prisoners in the camp. The Institute for Maritime and Tropical

Diseases used prisoners to test methods of countering lice-borne typhus. Dr Ludwig–Werner Haase tested the effectiveness of filters for removing massive doses of arsenic from water administered to prisoners.

Amongst the most notorious and abhorrent of the medical crimes committed at Neuengamme were the tuberculosis experiments on Jewish children performed by SS physician Dr Kurt Heissmayer, which he undertook as original research in order to obtain a professorship. Twenty children were injected with live tuberculosis bacilli into their blood and lungs. Every child later had the lymph nodes surgically removed from their armpits and were photographed holding one arm above their heads to reveal the scar. All of these photographs survived the war.

Upon the collapse of the Western Front and with the British Army approaching, orders were received to murder the children. Since its abandonment due to bombing damage, Bullenhuser Damm School had been used by Neuengamme to house prisoners. The children were taken to this school by three guards, a driver and SS physician Dr Alfred Trzebinski, who was Kurt Heissmayer's supervisor at Neuengamme.

Trzebinski sedated the children with morphine and they were then hanged from pegs on the wall in the basement. Of those involved in the killings, Neuengamme Camp Commandant Max Pauly, the three guards and Dr Alfred Trzebinski were all found guilty at Nuremberg and hanged in 1946.

The death register at Neuengamme indicates that more than 55,000 prisoners died in the concentration camp.

ACKNOWLEDGEMENTS

I would like to thank Susanne Annheuser for her invaluable help with the German dialogue, and also Christopher Wakling at Curtis Brown Creative – for helping me to make the most out of this novel.

My grateful thanks for the invaluable advice on inheritance law of fifty years ago in South West Africa goes to Barry Cloete and Jonathan Latham: any errors of interpretation are mine alone.

QUENTIN SMITH

The

SECRET
ANATOMY
of
CANDLES

Justice is temporary…